Praise for Anna Nicholas's Mallorca travel series

'Terrific!'   Lucia van der Post, contributor, FT *How to Spend It*

'As intelligent as it is entertaining. From simple escapism to a much more complicated story about the difficulties of balancing life in two places...'   Leah Hyslop, *The Telegraph*

'Anna Nicholas is one of those lucky swine who has dared to live the dream and write about it.'   Harry Ritchie, *The Daily Mail*

'Witty, evocative and heart-warming. Another Mallorcan pearl from Anna Nicholas.'   Peter Kerr, author of *Snowball Oranges*

'A beautifully written and highly entertaining account of the upside of downshifting.'   Henry Sutton, *The Daily Mirror*

'A hugely entertaining and witty account of how to juggle life and work between two countries, keep fit and stay sane!'   Colonel John Blashford-Snell, CBE, British explorer & author

'An enjoyable read for anyone wanting to live their dream.'   Lynne Franks, OBE, broadcaster & author

'If you thought that glitz and glamour don't mix with rural country living you must read this book.'   *Bella* magazine

'This is Anna's comic and observation̶̶ ̶ ̶ ̶ ̶ its very best.'   ̶ ̶'s *Inns* magazine

'Endearing, fur̶̶ ̶ ̶ ̶ ̶ ̶ld one wish for?'   *Travel* magazine

Anna Nicholas is the most prolific British author writing about Mallorca today. Her successful series of six travel books explores the history, culture and delights of the golden isle. An inveterate traveller and experienced freelance journalist, she is on the Telegraph's travel team, and has contributed travel features to FT *How to Spend It* and many other British national newspapers. Anna regularly participates in humanitarian aid expeditions overseas and runs an international marathon annually for her favourite causes.

The Devil's Horn is her first novel.

Twitter/Instagram @majorcanpearls

Also by Anna Nicholas

Mallorca travel series
A Lizard in my Luggage
Cat on a Hot Tiled Roof
Goats from a Small Island
Donkeys on my Doorstep
A Bull on the Beach
A Chorus of Cockerels

Memoir
Strictly Off the Record with Norris McWhirter

THE DEVIL'S HORN

AN ISABEL FLORES MALLORCAN MYSTERY

ANNA NICHOLAS

burrobooks

LONDON

Burro Books,
2, Woodberry Grove
London N12 0DR
www.burrobooks.co.uk

Published by Burro Books Ltd 2019

ISBN: 978-1-9996618-4-7
Ebook ISBN: 978-1-9996618-5-4

Printed and bound by CPI Group (UK) Ltd, Croydon, CR0 4YY

For Karen Chandler

Loyal reader turned enduring friend

PROLOGUE

Pollença Beach, Mallorca. Monday 20, August, 2pm

With a fleeting glance back at her mother, Miranda began running across the hot sand, pursued by a relentless and savage sun. On her back the small but heavy rucksack bobbed up and down, the plastic straps chafing her bare shoulders. Now and then she faltered, pushing the damp hair from her face and regulating her breath as she skipped on, dizzy with the heat and excitement.

Oblivious to the swell of humanity around her, Miranda nimbly skirted sunloungers and lively ball games, her gaze fixed on the glinting, jittery waves ahead. Some distance from the shoreline she looked about her and stopped abruptly to discard a red plastic bucket and spade. Moments later she arrived at the water's edge, where burning golden sand gave way to cool, dark silt. With relief, she bent down to splash herself, enjoying the sensation of soothing water between her toes but it was short-lived. Seconds later, a sudden shiver took hold of her as she became aware of being observed, of a silent and patient presence close by.

Beside her, caught in a halo of sunlight, stood a woman with long fair hair, an enigmatic smile playing on her lips. Miranda squinted upwards, aware that she was being addressed, but the din of laughter, lisping waves and her own urgent heartbeat drowned out all sound.

As if in slow motion, she felt a cool and decisive hand firmly clamp one of hers, drawing her urgently away from the beach, its owner leading her with fast steps in the direction of the promenade. Miranda struggled to keep up, her mind muddled, her breath laboured. A blue car flashed its headlights, almost indiscernible in the harsh daylight, but the woman strode purposefully towards it, her hand tightening on that of the little blonde girl at her side. A moment later the vehicle pulled away.

Smiling and turning from the counter, Mrs Walters slipped the restaurant receipt into her purse and snapped it shut. Yawning happily, she stepped onto the shady terrace, her eyes lazily searching for her daughter, whom she'd left playing contentedly just outside. She called her name as she slowly descended the steps of Café del Mar and began exploring the beach. Miranda was nowhere to be seen. Within minutes, a primaeval fear and panic gripped her. She zigzagged hurriedly across the hot sand, her increasingly anguished cries of *Miranda, Miranda* merging with the desperate screeching of swooping gulls. But it was all too late: Miranda had gone.

ONE

Just above the craggy ridge of the Tramuntanas that encircled the valley like a benign and dozing lizard, a tentative sun emerged. With effort it hoisted itself onto the most precipitous peaks, casting its gentle gaze across the orchards of oranges and lemons before its attention wandered to a diminutive yellow car that was climbing up the helter-skelter of mountain roads at some speed.

By the time Isabel Flores Montserrat had delivered the last raucous chord of 'Big Yellow Taxi' to an appreciative breeze, the sun was hanging high in the sky like a skittish balloon and blinding her vision of the road ahead. She leant forward and flipped down the sun visor before resuming her position, left elbow resting on the open window while her right hand lazily manoeuvred the steering wheel. Her damp ebony hair was already forming into dancing ringlets as she flicked some rogue strands away from her face and narrowed her eyes against the harsh sky. Dropping a gear to cope with a particularly tight bend, she was surprised to discover evidence of human life in the form of a pensioner pedalling laboriously ahead of her. At this early hour it could only be old Bartomeu. She broke into a grin and, with a perfunctory toot of the horn, slowed down until she was level with the bike.

'Want a lift?'

The veteran fixed his watery grey eyes on her and gave a hoarse cackle. '*Gràcies*, Bel, but I value my life.'

Isabel laughed and, offering a friendly wave, revved the little tiger of an engine and shot past him. Tapping her fingers on the wheel, she addressed the juddering car. 'Now, Pequeñito, when we get to the village I want you to keep your eyes peeled for a parking space.'

The little Fiat panted as Isabel began the steep climb into Sant Martí and shuddered as she accelerated along one of the narrow cobbled streets. To Isabel's dissatisfaction she observed that most of the on-street parking had already been snaffled by holidaymakers, all no doubt still slumbering in their beds. These vehicles were magnets for petty thieves because most sported a rental car sticker on the windscreen, a telltale sign that they were hired and did not belong to local residents. As a former policewoman, this exasperated Isabel, because as sure as *huevos* were *huevos*, a few would be burgled by one of the foreign gangs that drove from Palma to the rural zones in search of rich pickings during the summer season. She slowed down as she reached the quiet square, turning left along Calle Feliu and finally right into the tiny car park of the town hall. A visitor space, shaded by a tall plane tree, winked from the far end. She darted into the slot and killed the engine, patting the dashboard affectionately.

'See you, Pequeñito.'

It was only as she made her way to the village square that she noticed Pau, a local police officer and the village's perennial guardian, striding towards her. He was wagging a finger and pointing at Pequeñito.

'Bel, you can't park there. That space is reserved for the tourism minister. He's visiting the mayor today.'

Isabel threw out her arms dramatically. 'I don't see his name written on it! If it wasn't for the tourists, I wouldn't need to park here at all.'

'That's as may be, but I still need that space.'

'Come on, Pau, shouldn't you be pestering the minister for a new car park in Sant Martí? If he wants more tourists, he should cough up.'

The young man pulled off his dark blue police cap and mopped his brow.

'It's getting hot. Been swimming, as usual?'

She nodded. 'I'm going for a coffee. Want to join me?'

He puffed out his cheeks and slowly replaced his cap. 'Thanks, but I've got to hang around for the minister's arrival.'

'Too bad. Well, I guess I'd better move the car.'

She uttered a little sigh of defeat as she began a half-hearted search for her car key. He touched her arm.

'Forget it. I'll find another place for the guy's chauffeur. You're right, who do these politicians think they are? It's about time we got funding here for a new car park.'

Isabel dazzled him with a smile. '*Gràcies,* Pau. You're an angel.'

As she sauntered off in the direction of Bar Castell, a shadowy tangerine sun tiptoeing behind her, she wondered to herself why all life's little problems couldn't be so easily resolved.

*

A high-pitched screech ripped through the muggy morning air in Plaça de Sant Martí, prompting Isabel to bob up from her wicker chair on the terrace of Bar Castell. Abandoning her newspaper, she peered up into the fierce blue sky, puzzled to see not a squawking gull but a gracious booted eagle drifting on the breeze. Her momentary reverie was rudely interrupted by a loud and insistent voice from the *plaça* below.

'Hey, Bel! Are you sleeping up there?'

Isabel blinked and scanned the cobbled square two floors below until her eyes rested on a young woman joggling a wailing child in her arms. She was happy to see that it was her friend Marga and young daughter.

She grinned down at them. 'Was that Sofia shrieking?'

The woman shrugged. 'Who else but your mischievous god-daughter? She fell in the fountain. Can we join you?'

Isabel threw back her mane of dark curls and beckoned to them. '*Venga!*'

She gathered up her newspaper, the *Diario de Mallorca*, and was about to fold it in two when she caught sight of the regional president winking at her from the front page. She tapped him on the nose with a bitten fingernail and stared him square between the eyes. 'Don't flirt with me, *señor presidente*. Right now you should have better things to do than cutting the ribbon of some fancy new gallery.' She threw him into her bag along with the day's habitual felons that squirmed between the news pages – corrupt politicians, fraudulent building contractors, drug dealers, pickpockets and abusive husbands. Rafael, the bar's owner, observed her as he stood polishing a glass at the counter. Sensing his eyes resting on her she looked up and offered him a smile. Isabel had been coming to Bar Castell as far back as she could remember, but Rafael seemed ageless. She sometimes pondered whether he'd discovered some miraculous potion that prolonged the fountain of youth or had long before cut a deal with the devil. Either way, his wild pewter locks remained stubbornly abundant and he maintained the sort of bearing that a man of half his age might envy. Not that she knew his age, of course.

He called over to her. 'Not like you to hang around. Are you sure young Pep can hold the fort?'

Isabel gave a yawn. 'There's no harm in cutting him some slack – besides, he always complains that I'm breathing down his neck in the office.'

As Marga and the frowning Sofia entered the bar, having puffed up several flights of steep steps, Rafael turned to Isabel. 'Poor Pep.

I feel for the lad. I wouldn't want to work for a woman. You treat us all like slaves.'

She slid him a smile. 'True. So where are our coffees?'

The two women exchanged kisses and Isabel plucked the little girl from Marga's arms, but she wriggled from the embrace and somewhat haughtily tottered off with the rubber legs of an old tippler to join Rafael at the bar.

Isabel's eyes trailed after her. 'Some loyal god-daughter you are!'

Marga sighed. 'I'm afraid she'd sell her soul for Rafael's chocolate milk.'

Hastily she pulled open her voluminous straw bag and shook out a tiny pair of wet shorts, socks and a tee shirt which she spread along one of the broad tiled windowsills of the bar, directly under the sun's glare. 'Luckily I had a spare set of her clothes with me.'

Rafael lifted the infant onto the counter. 'Fancied an early dip, eh?'

He tousled Sofia's hair and taking a small bottle of Cola Cao chocolate milk from the fridge, prised the cap off and placed it in her hands.

'*Pajita!*' she demanded.

Rafael pulled a blue paper straw from a terracotta pot and stuck it in the mouth of the bottle. She shook her head.

'*Roja y blanca*, Rafa!'

Patiently he replaced it with a candy-stripe one and laughed when Sofia nodded in approval.

Marga followed her friend onto the narrow terrace, flopping down on a seat shaded by a giant cream parasol. A few minutes passed and Rafael shuffled over with two small cups of steaming coffee, returning with a fresh snail-shaped *ensaïmada* pastry for Marga. The women, as Spanish coffee rituals dictate, vigorously shook their miniature sugar packets before releasing the crystals into their cups.

'So, how are things working out with my little brother?' asked Marga, tearing a piece from the fluffy pastry and popping it into her mouth.

'Pep? Oh, he's coming on fine. Although...'

Isabel took a sip of her strong *cortado* and savoured the taste for a moment, the kick of the caffeine, the sweetness of the sugar and the smoothness of the steamed milk. Rafael knew how to make a good coffee, which was why she favoured his understated bar with its modest upstairs terrace more than Café Jordi on the other side of the square. It wasn't that she didn't like Jordi, the loquacious, card-playing owner – he was, after all, a close confidante of her rascally but loveable Uncle Idò – but he used cheap coffee beans and served his *cortados* in bijoux glasses rather than cups, with too much foamy milk on top, making them appear more like small, inferior cappuccinos.

Isabel observed her old school friend across the table. Their lives had followed very different paths since their sun-wrapped childhood when, inseparable, they had studied side by side on the same rickety bench in the village primary school. They'd even etched their names together on the wood in small, faltering strokes using a prized penknife belonging to Isabel's elder brother Eduardo, which she had secreted into her school satchel early one morning.

There were lazy summer days as sticky as melted toffee when she and Marga would roll *canicas*, the small almond-eyed marbles, or race their scooters around the *plaça* under the benevolent gaze of the town hall's aged clock. Sometimes they let off stink bombs or firecrackers in the back pews of the church, outraging the senior plump matrons in their black lace *mantillas* who genuflected with creaky knees at the altar. Once Isabel and Marga had released a bucket of frogs in the vestry and even swigged half a bottle of holy wine stashed away in the back of an armoire containing Padre

Agustí's liturgical garments. They were rarely rumbled and on principle never owned up to their villainy in confession, although they dutifully made the sign of the cross before bed.

When the olive season beckoned, the two girls would join family and friends in a convoy of clapped-out vehicles that wheezed and spluttered all the way up the winding mountain roads to the *olivars*, the olive groves, high above the village. They would toil for hours under a sadistic late summer sun, plucking the green fruit from the trees until their fingers were as puffy and red as jalapeño peppers. And when the sun melted into liquid gold, blinding the craggy face of L'Ofre, one of the jewels of the Tramuntana mountain range, they would gather up their pungent booty, load it into the vans and return to the village where they were rewarded with a few *pesetas* and a glass of *limón granizado*, home-made lemonade with crushed ice, in Bar Castell.

Despite having moved away from the island to Castilla-La Mancha on the mainland as a teenager, Isabel and her family would return to the Mallorcan hills every summer as surely as the blossoming oleander in June. And then the long holiday would stretch out before her like a delicious and never-ending piece of bubblegum until the beginning of autumn. Now, both in their early thirties, she and Marga remained close friends.

Isabel's thoughts suddenly flitted back to Pep, Marga's younger brother, whom she'd recently hired to help run her holiday rentals agency.

'You know, I think Pep's found it hard working for a woman.'

Marga grunted and threw a meaty, tanned arm in the air. '*Claro*! Of course. He's a macho like them all.'

Isabel briefly considered Pep's machismo tendencies. 'I've known worse. Mind you, Furó's not so sure of him. I think it's that Italian aftershave he wears.'

'Your little ferret's got a good nose. Pep smothers himself in that stuff – and what about his clothes?'

Isabel nodded. It was true. Pep wore all kinds of exotic brands from America, Italy and France, but he was only twenty-four, an age when image was important. She didn't recognise most of the designer labels and couldn't fathom why anyone sane would pay astronomical sums to sport goods with advertising slogans. Then again, she was one to talk. Had she not recklessly paid €800 to Bernat the mechanic the previous year when she fell hopelessly in lust with a vintage Fiat 500 bequeathed to him by an elderly Italian resident? How she adored that irrepressible canary yellow *bambino*, with its temperamental engine and wobbly gear stick. Just thinking of her beloved Pequeñito made her want to jump back into the front seat and tear off up into the mountains.

'How's work?' Marga asked.

'Busy. A lot of holidaymakers are arriving this month.'

'Well, I hope Pep rises to the challenge. Otherwise he'll have to go back to tiling.'

Isabel gave a wry smile. 'He'll be fine. It's just that I'm not used to having someone else in the office. How's the salon? You said business was slow.'

Marga shrugged. 'It's suddenly got very busy with all the tourists. Imagine five hairdryers blasting away in this heat. We might as well be running a sauna.'

She sat back in her chair and examined her old friend. 'You're looking fit. Still swimming at Repic beach every morning?'

Isabel wiped a bead of sweat from her forehead and glanced up at the sky, defiantly outstaring the sun.

'You bet. It's the best place to think.' She recalled the empty beach and soft violet waves that she had savoured only a few hours earlier. The tang of salt still played teasingly on her lips as she replayed the moment when a graceful heron swooped low over the sea, emitting a screech as it went in search of prey. Draining her glass, Isabel stood up and slung her pannier over her shoulder. At the counter she took the giggling Sofia in her arms and whizzed her around while Marga gathered up the tiny damp clothes and headed for the door, grumbling when she heard nine chimes from the village clock. Isabel followed, passing a crumpled five-euro note to Rafael.

'Keep the change,' she said breezily.

'You owe me a euro,' he called after her, before shoving the note into the pocket of his apron. 'Women!' he grumbled.

Once on the street, Isabel sauntered along the west side of the sun-dappled *plaça*. She passed Café Jordi on her left, with its yawning patio strewn with cream canvas easy chairs and wrought-iron tables, and walked through the huddle of silvery plane trees towards the stone fountain in front of the town hall. She stepped up on to the marble podium, took a long draught of water and then wiped her mouth with her hand.

For a village of just six hundred residents, the square seemed rather too broad and the neo-Gothic church of Sant Antoní overpoweringly ornate with its fussy baroque interior and imposing *campanar*, the strait-laced bell tower. The *ajuntament*, the town hall, which faced her, was a different story. Constructed from reassuringly robust grey limestone, it had a cosy feel despite its grand arched entrance and its antiquity. Those of an imaginative disposition claimed that the building was haunted by Antonio Ribes, a wealthy nobleman who, mortally infected by the terrible plague that killed countless Mallorcans during the seventeenth century, had apparently thrown himself off the rafters onto the cobbles below. Josep, the town hall's ghoulish caretaker, would habitually hold forth in Café Jordi of an evening, recounting how in the dead of night he'd witnessed the naked spectre floating through the mayoral office covered in boils as big and black as plums and howling in agony. By the time the old scoundrel had vacuumed up a carafe of robust *vino tinto* and his fifth tot of Fundador, his favourite brandy, the story had taken on epic proportions.

A cluster of locals were chatting with Padre Agustí outside the church. The priest stood patiently with hands clasped loosely against his sombre black cassock, his white downy head tilted away from the slivers of sunlight splitting the trees. One of the massive arched doors of the town hall creaked open and Llorenç Bestard, otherwise known as the *batle*, the town's mayor, came scuttling out like an overzealous spider, a plump one at that. He stopped in his tracks when he spied Isabel, his mouth forming a perky smile. 'Hey, *guapa*! Just the woman I wanted to see.'

She stepped forward to kiss him on both cheeks.

'Look, if it's about my using the VIP parking space…'

He gave a guffaw. 'Ah, yes, Pau told me about that. Fancy tricking the poor boy so naughtily! As if we need a car park in Sant Martí. We've got enough tourists as it is.'

'In Fornalutx village they now have three car parks.'

'Bully for them!'

Isabel folded her arms. 'But there's never anywhere to park during the summer months.'

'A small price to pay for local tourism. Besides, I'm sure I can squeeze your little Fiat into my VIP area from time to time.'

His eyes flitted stealthily from the opening of her white shirt to her navy linen skirt and lean tanned legs.

'That's very good of you, Llorenç. So, what did you want to see me about?'

'It's not so urgent. Some British tourists want to report a theft of a purse. Naturally, they don't speak any Spanish – or Mallorquí, for that matter.'

Isabel frowned. 'Did it happen here in Sant Martí?'

He whisked a hand through the air impatiently. 'Of course not! It was stolen from them in Soller market. The local police need to file a crime report but there's no one in the office today who can speak any English. They asked, as usual, if you could help.'

She nodded, having got used to often being called upon to assist with such tasks. 'Did they actually see the thief?'

He shook his head vigorously. 'No, but it's bound to be a foreigner. The market's full of them these days – Ecuadorians, Peruvians, Eastern Europeans, Moroccans...'

'God forbid that it should prove to be a Mallorcan,' Isabel replied with a straight face.

The mayor puffed out his chest. 'Are you mocking me, Bel?'

She supressed a grin. 'How about I pop by at noon?'

'Excellent. I'll have seen off the minister by then. That way we can have it all sorted before lunchtime. Perhaps you can join me for a bite?'

Isabel hesitated long enough for Llorenç to fix her with imploring eyes. 'You should know that Can Busquets is serving fresh *gambas rojas* today. Just how you like them, grilled with a little olive oil, parsley and garlic.'

Isabel pricked up her ears. Llorenç had correctly identified her Achilles heel. She simply didn't have it in her to refuse a plate of succulent and sweet red prawns lured from the querulous waters north of Port Soller.

'Lunch it is,' she beamed and with a wave headed off towards Calle Pastor, a cobbled lane accessed by a slender alley to the side of the church. Padre Agustí called out to her in a frail voice but not wanting further distraction she responded with a cheerful *'Uep!'* –a popular Mallorcan greeting of no substance – and walked purposefully ahead.

TWO

Despite the early hour, the sun simmered on the horizon, casting a ruby glow on the tips of the Tramuntanas. Emerging from the alleyway, Isabel stood and surveyed her street. It was a peaceful oasis away from the hubbub of village life, lined with shady plane trees and terraced houses crafted from roughly hewn, amber stones. The front garden of Ca'n Moix, the house of the cat, stood out from the rest with its stubby palm trees and profusion of terracotta pots overflowing with wild flowers and herbs. Bougainvillea spilled over a stone wall that separated the house from its neighbour on the right, owned by Doctor Ramis, and the rich perfume of jasmine filled every crevice. As Isabel lifted the latch on the gate she turned momentarily to admire the towering peak of Puig Mayor, star of the serrated mountain range that formed a vast and rocky corona around the valley.

The arched porch lay ahead of her, partially masked by a bushy almond tree and climbing ivy that had already gobbled up most of the stone façade of the house in its ambitious quest to reach the upper windows. The front door gaped open, allowing frenetic music to spill out into the sunshine. Isabel shook her head and exhaled deeply before striding into the cool *entrada*, the hallway, and casting off her sandals. The room was saturated with golden light that poured in from two elegant French windows directly facing the front door. Beyond their panes a patio gave onto a garden and orchard bursting with orange, lemon and olive trees where a cockerel and his harem of skittish hens played hide and seek in the long grasses. To the right of the hallway sat a traditional limestone hearth and on the far side of the room a marble staircase led to the upper two floors. On the first of these Isabel had established her offices and on the higher level, her private living space.

The rustic kitchen with its walk-in pantry looked directly out onto a patio of smooth grey and white pebbles, each one having been lovingly laid by hand to form a series of ever-concentric circles. A wrought-iron table and four wicker chairs flaunting brightly coloured Moroccan cushions had been placed at its centre under the protective embrace of a cream canvas parasol. It was here late in the evening that Isabel was accustomed to sitting by candlelight with a crime thriller and a glass of robust red wine, examining the stars above and listening to the rhythmic hum of the cicadas. The nights she most relished were those when the rare kiss of a mountain breeze, pungent with rosemary and thyme, rattled the shutters and sent the candlelight into a wild and Bacchic dance.

Now, as she plodded up the cool marble steps to the office, she was aware of busy and, to her ears, discordant music. She walked into the room and discovered Pep sitting with his back to her, legs outstretched on his desk while his head bobbed to a heavy persistent beat. From the sofa an inquisitive Furó eyed him warily and with an evident touch of disdain. Isabel grabbed the nearest file and gently coshed him over the head with it. He leapt from his seat, an aggrieved expression on his face.

'What was that for?'

Isabel studied the tanned and muscle-toned youth before her. She took in the designer jeans, pristine white tee shirt and doe eyes as large and black as olives. She marvelled at his twin forests of dark, curling eyelashes – thick and long enough to sweep the floor. Isabel wondered whether Pep could hear the beating hearts of the village girls as he strode through the *plaça* each day, flexing his muscles and flashing those whiter than white teeth. But there was of course only one girl for him – or so he claimed – the mercurial Angélica, the mayor's only daughter.

She turned to him. 'If you want to run a disco, live in Ibiza.'

He killed the music on his mobile phone. 'Come on! It's not that loud. Look, even Furó likes it.'

At the sound of his name, the ferret looked up, his whiskers twitching enquiringly. Isabel softened and strode over to him, bending down to stroke his russet fur. She felt guilty for not having taken him along for her habitual early swim, but he'd been sleeping so soundly she hadn't wanted to waken him. 'You don't like this noise, do you, Furó?'

On cue the ferret gave a low growl.

'Creep!' Pep hissed across at him.

'So,' Isabel continued brightly, 'tell me about your weekend.'

'What weekend? Angélica was furious. Those new clients, Mr and Mrs Fox, were sailing here from the mainland on their fancy yacht and because of a choppy crossing didn't arrive in Port Soller until eleven at night. Their boat's called *Monique La Magnifique*, whoever she is.'

'Maybe Monique is Mrs Fox.'

'No, I found out her name is Sarah.'

'So what time did they get to the rental property?'

'Midnight. That was the end of my evening.'

'Dedication, Pep – that's what work is all about.'

He rolled his eyes. 'You tell that to Angélica. Anyway, I stayed in the stifling car until they came and…'

'Why didn't you wait inside?'

'You think I'm going to sit in a haunted house in the middle of nowhere?'

Isabel eyed him in some exasperation. '*Venga, hombre*! You don't believe all that nonsense?'

'Listen, my brother helped restore that *finca* and he told me about strange goings-on. One time he heard a child singing upstairs but there was no one there and another—'

Isabel cut him short. 'I've heard it all before. Ca'n Mayol has a sad and troubled history but every old house around here has a tale to tell. The problem with this village is that everyone is ghost crazy. Anyway, did they like the house?'

He nodded. 'I think so. Sarah Fox was nice enough but he was quite grumpy. I think she's French by the sound of her accent but I don't know about him. Apparently, he's a writer and wants complete peace during their stay.'

Isabel absentmindedly cast an eye over an open file on Pep's desk and shrugged.

'Suits us, but as they've booked the house for a month Uncle Idò and the girls will still need to pop by once a week to clean the pool and change linen.'

'And what about our cocaine-sniffing lawyer and his family renting Ca'n Julia in Fornalutx?'

'Mr Jay? He and his wife fly back to England later this evening. Will you pick up the keys from them?'

She nodded. 'I need to have a few words with him alone.'

Pep cast an anxious glance in her direction. 'You're not going to accuse him of being a druggie, are you? Even if he is, it's none of our business. He's just a client.'

'I'm perfectly aware of that, *gràcies*.'

Isabel crossed the room to her own office that overlooked the rear garden and dumped her pannier on the desk. Reaching inside, she pulled out a crumpled white towel and damp red polka-dot bikini, which she flung over the back of her antiquated swivel chair. She noticed that stray husks of sunflower seeds lay scattered about her papers. Pep called after her: 'I bet lots of tourists take cocaine.'

Using her left hand, Isabel coaxed the stripy monochrome shells off the edge of her desk and into a wicker wastepaper basket. She wondered how many sunflower seeds she munched a day. Two hundred, maybe? From the open window she looked down into the garden and whistled to two of her hens stalking about the corral.

'*Buenos días*, Mrs Buncle, *buenos días*, Cleopatra!'

They blinked at the sound of her voice and cocked their tawny heads in her direction. She breezed past Pep, who stood frowning by the door.

'Why do your hens have such ridiculous names?'

'If you bothered to read, you might find them not so odd.'

She walked back into the main office and turned to him.

'Now, about Mr Jay. It's not just his cocaine habit that concerns me. I'm sure he's also having an affair. Of course that's his business, but it can only add to complications in his life.'

'How have you leapt to that conclusion?' Pep exclaimed.

'Last week while I was watering the plants there I overheard him talking on his mobile in hushed tones to someone called Francesca.'

'It was probably his mother. Mine's always driving me mad ringing for this and that...'

'Don't be absurd. Besides, he reeked of guilt.'

Pep shook his head. 'Sorry, are we running a detective agency here?'

'You're very lippy for a subordinate. I shall have to tell Marga to keep you in line.'

Pep fiddled with a pen on his desk. 'You know your problem? You still think you're a cop.'

'Inspector, if you please.'

'You see! You miss it. All the excitement, the drug crime and murders.'

'You have a fertile imagination, Pep. Police work is mostly routine.'

'Maybe, but you have to admit that you loved all the action stuff as a cop on the mainland. When you came to Mallorca it must have seemed so boring.'

'Not at all, life was never dull when I served with the Policía Nacional in Palma.'

Pep sighed. 'The problem is that nothing ever happens here. What we need is a good grisly murder.'

Isabel offered him a pert smile. 'Be careful what you wish for.' She hesitated.'Actually, I prefer my life now. I have my own business, good money and total freedom. What more could a woman want?'

But of course Pep's words had riled her. It had been two years since she had relinquished her position as a detective inspector with the National Police in Palma and taken over the small, ailing rentals agency run by her widowed mother, Florentina. In that short time she had turned it into a flourishing business with luxurious properties as far away as Pollença to the north and Santa María and Binissalem inland. She had named it Hogar Dulce Hogar – Home Sweet Home – and in the space of six months had ditched long-term local lettings for the far more profitable holiday rental market.

There were, of course, other agencies in the valley run mostly by outsiders, but that never bothered Isabel. She had more work than she needed and a waiting list of foreign residents clamouring for her services. The agency now employed six cleaners, as well as her mother's elder brother, Uncle Idò, a glorified jack of all trades, and Pep, who handled bookings and client liaison with her. Isabel also used the local *gestor*, the bookkeeper in the village, to afford some measure of legality to the business. Tax and social security contributions had to be paid – not, of course, at the expense of *dinero negro*, black money, but a token demonstration of financial transparency was always wise. Was she in denial? Did she ever pine for her erstwhile days as a detective in Madrid and Barcelona and more recently in Palma?

There were times when Isabel followed a crime story in the media and felt an itch once again to be a part of a high-profile investigation, but the moment would pass. Her last police case had been a little too close to home and had sapped all her strength, and nearly destroyed her family into the bargain. She couldn't imagine being back in the force, governed once more by petty rules and swamped by bureaucracy. Her meteoric rise up the ranks to the position of detective inspector before her thirtieth birthday had been well deserved – after all, she'd solved enough cases – but her methods had been considered eccentric and unorthodox by her superiors, while her peers had viewed her with suspicion and even a little fear. Some nicknamed her *la bruja*, the witch, for her uncanny ability to lay bare the culprits in seemingly unfathomable cases, while other less successful colleagues put her triumphs down to luck. Isabel shook off her detractors and continued to rely on her wits and a gut instinct that rarely betrayed her.

She had told herself that it had been the right time to give up the badge. After all, she still had good chums in the local police force that served under the town councils across the island, and she counted her old boss in Palma, Chief Inspector Tolo Cabot, a close friend. Some former colleagues implied that there was more to their relationship, but that was the nature of office banter. People were always looking for romance where it didn't exist.

What's more, she'd had more than enough of relationships for the time being. Her former beau, Fernando, a pampered lawyer, had, within a few months of their courtship, grown tired of her eccentricities and she of his hollow, glitzy lifestyle. Whatever had she seen in him? It was true that the ticking of her biological clock had been growing louder, but she reasoned that there was still plenty of time to think about having children and besides, she had several in her life already – the two young sons of her older brother, Eduardo, who often visited from Toledo, and Sofia, her god-daughter. Isabel's relationship with Fernando came to a resounding halt when her neighbour, Dr Ramis, gifted her Furó, a creature he considered to be little more than vermin. Either he or the ferret had to go. Naturally, she chose Furó.

Aside from the police, Isabel was on first-name terms with local officers of the Guardia Civil, the green uniformed military force that had jurisdiction of the rural communities of Mallorca. They often popped by her office for a coffee, usually as a pretext to seek her opinion on a local crime matter. She wasn't so keen on one of the Guardia's leading lights, the autocratic and ambitious Capitán Álvaro Gómez, but that was another story.

Isabel scooped up Furó just as the phone rang. Pep scrambled for the receiver.

'Home Sweet Home, how can I help you?'

Isabel smiled to herself. She admired his fledgling attempts at speaking English. As a teenager she had been forced to endure private lessons and her father, an ambitious *jefe superior* for the National Police in Castilla-La Mancha, was himself a polyglot. At home the family would enjoy linguistic gymnastics, swinging between the Mallorquí dialect of Catalan – her mother's native tongue – and the more widely spoken Castilian Spanish that her father had spoken. Mealtimes were always a challenge, as her father switched between English, German and French to keep Isabel and her brother, Eduardo, on their toes.

Moments later, Pep waltzed triumphantly into Isabel's office. 'I've just taken a booking for the whole of September. How about that?'

'*Enhorabuena*! I might even pay you this week.'

Isabel deposited Furó in his basket and plonked herself down at her desk. 'Time for a Chupa.'

Pep recoiled in mock horror. 'Urgh. Those things will rot your teeth.'

'I know, so avert your gaze and go and do some work.'

She slowly unravelled the waxed paper of a garish red lollipop, one of an assortment that sat in a colourful heap in a terracotta bowl on her desk, and popped it into her mouth. Pep stood in the doorway shaking his head in disapproval before sloping off to answer a call.

*

Isabel parked Pequeñito on a dark side street in the port and looked about her. It was still dusk and a stubborn moon continued to hover on the horizon, spilling pallid light onto the waves. After a fretful few hours trying to sleep in the pulsating summer heat, she had finally jumped out of bed and with Furó at her heels, driven to the harbour. There wasn't a soul in sight as she made her way along the silent esplanade and down to the beach. Before her, on the dark fathomless water, yachts and fishing boats creaked and whined in the teasing breeze as they strained on their moorings. With a smile Isabel caught a glimpse of a sporty looking vessel bearing the name *Monique La Magnifique*. Mr and Mrs Fox, the new arrivals, evidently had a bob or two.

Removing her espadrilles, she sighed with pleasure as her hot feet were caressed by tiny rippling waves that rushed to greet her on the shoreline. Furó splashed along at the water's edge, seemingly unperturbed at being taken for a stroll at so early an hour. Having made her way to the farthest end of Repic beach, Isabel whiled away the time sitting on her favourite rock that offered a perfect vantage point out to sea. But she suddenly bristled when a poorly lit vessel came into view, nosing urgently through the waves towards the harbour. By its laboured movement she surmised that it was an old trawler, but what was it doing out at sea at this ungodly hour? Curiosity got the better of her, and with a wolf whistle to Furó, she headed at a brisk pace back along the beach.

By the time she reached the harbour, the deep rumble of the boat's engine could be heard as it backed slowly into a berth at the quay. Isabel replaced her shoes and, attaching a lead to Furó's collar, slipped silently past the phalanx of bobbing yachts and stepped into the shadowy doorway of a nearby bar. After some minutes the motor died and she became aware of raised and angry voices. Furó gave a low growl and strained on the leash as Isabel coaxed him back behind her legs. Moments later a young woman appeared on the quayside, remonstrating loudly with two men. Straining to hear the conversation, Isabel frowned when she discerned the word 'police' uttered. She retreated further into the shadows as the woman headed along the esplanade, her slight frame forming a dancing silhouette in the smudgy darkness. Angrily one of the men sped after her, swinging her round and shaking her hard. Isabel felt her heart race and was debating whether to intervene when the girl began sobbing and with head lowered, dejectedly followed him to a white van a stone's throw from Isabel's hideout. She held her breath as the two began arguing again.

'Listen, Felip, I want nothing to do with it – just take me home and don't contact me ever again.'

He rounded on her. 'You make me sick, you know that? You're involved whether you like it or not. Now shut up and get in.'

Pulling the door open, he brusquely ushered her into the front passenger seat while he waited for his companion to catch them up. The smaller, swarthier man soon appeared, lugging two dry tube bags behind him. Once he'd loaded them into the boot, he jumped into the back of the van and the vehicle screeched away, but not before a visibly shocked Isabel caught sight of the occupants by the fleeting light of a street lamp.

THREE

After her night's adventure Isabel had returned home, slept for a few hours and set off early morning to run a few errands. So it wasn't until eleven o'clock that she arrived back at Ca'n Moix, a pannier of lemons and aubergines hooked over one arm and on the other, a large bag of washed and ironed linen that she'd collected from one of her cleaners. Furó pattered a few paces behind her on the staircase, making small snuffling sounds as he investigated every nook and cranny with renewed vigour. Entering her office, she dropped both loads onto the seat of her beloved Chesterfield sofa, bequeathed to her by an elderly British resident of Sant Martí. It was nutmeg in hue and so old that tufts of white stuffing were beginning to peek out from the cushions like rabbits' tails, but she loved it all the same.

Furó jumped into his basket and instantly fell asleep, which didn't surprise Isabel given his earlier exertions in the port and the fact that he habitually dozed for large periods of the day. She sat down heavily in front of her computer, yawned and checked through her e-mails. There was nothing very urgent. Moments later the door to the main office banged open and Pep appeared before her looking slightly dishevelled, his forehead glistening with perspiration.

'Is that really for me?' she purred as he placed a *cortado* on her desk.

He frowned. 'What happened to you?'

'I had a broken night. You don't look so great yourself.'

Pep flopped onto her sofa, casting a wary glance in Furó's direction.

Isabel winked at him. 'Don't worry, he's already had breakfast. So what's up?'

'I hate August. It's just too hot.'

'Don't be such a baby.'

Pep flapped his tee shirt in a futile effort to cool down. 'Even in here with the air conditioning I'm sweltering.'

'You're lucky we have an air conditioning unit up here, although Uncle Idò says it's a complete waste of money.'

'Idò would. He doesn't have to work here.'

She took a sip of her coffee and pulled a face. 'No sugar?'

Reluctantly, he pulled a small packet from his pocket and tossed it onto her desk.

'So what kept you up last night?'

Isabel slowly stirred her coffee. 'A strange thing happened. I couldn't sleep with the heat...'

'See, you don't like it either.'

She ignored him. 'So I got up and took Furó for a walk in the port.'

'What time was this?'

'About three o'clock.'

'You're nuts.'

'Anyway, before long I noticed a trawler sailing into the port.'

'That's odd. No fisherman's out on the water at that hour.'

'Precisely. That's why I went to investigate.'

Pep stifled a groan. 'Go on.'

'I hid in the doorway of El Campesino with Furó and waited until two young men and a woman disembarked. They were having a serious altercation.'

Pep sat forward, spellbound. 'So what happened?'

'I saw them loading two heavy bags into a white van.'

'What do you think was in them?'

'Sadly, my psychic powers weren't working. Body parts, perhaps?' She gave him a mischievous wink.

Pep shuddered. 'Don't joke, Bel. Then what?'

'They all got into the van and drove off.'

'And that's it?'

'Not quite,' replied Isabel. 'As the car passed by, I caught a glimpse of them. I recognised them all.'

Pep could hardly contain his excitement. 'Well, who were they?'

'Aina Ripoll, the daughter of the baker in Morells village, and those two rascally young fishermen brothers, Felip and Francesc Torrens.'

'You're kidding? What were they doing out in a boat at that time of night?'

Isabel massaged her chin thoughtfully. 'I've no idea, Pep, but I intend to find out.'

'Is that wise?'

'Probably not,' she replied.

He paused. 'Well, unlike you, I had a thoroughly uneventful evening.'

'How so?'

'Miraculously, both rental couples arrived on time and so I settled them happily into their *fincas* and went for dinner with Angélica.'

'Nice bunch?'

'Swedish. Very friendly. And how was your lunch with our esteemed mayor yesterday, since you never made it back to the office?'

Isabel grinned. 'You should be more respectful about Llorenç. After all, he is your future father-in-law.'

Pep winced. 'That sort of joke makes me nervous.'

'As it happened he introduced me to an English couple who thought they'd been robbed. It turned out that the wife had accidentally dropped her purse in the market and that a gallant Moroccan stallholder handed it in to Soller town hall.'

'So, a happy ending?'

'*Exacto*. That's why Llorenç and I decided to celebrate with half a bottle of Viña Sol and a gigantic plate of *gambas rojas* at Can Busquets.'

'It's all right for some.'

She raised an eyebrow. 'Actually, we were discussing weighty matters such as the lack of car parking in Sant Martí and preparations for the Nit de Foc fiesta in Soller.'

'The Night of Fire? I wish I wasn't on the organising committee. No one ever listens to me, let alone Llorenç, and he was the one who roped me in.'

'Just remember that he might be your father-in-law one day, so tread carefully.'

'I wish you'd stop reminding me.'

Isabel gave a sigh. 'I can't believe that the fiesta's come round so soon. You know it's just two weeks away? And now Llorenç has got it into his head to hold our own village celebration the night before.'

Pep laughed. 'Well, count me out. I need all my strength before running the gauntlet with those crazy devils in Soller. Last year one sprinkled red hot embers on my sock and nearly set it alight.'

Isabel could hardly contain her mirth. 'You were wearing socks in August? I thought you were supposed to be hip, Pep. Anyway, Llorenç has been busy ordering trays of *coca* and *sobrassada* sausage for our own village affair, so you have a duty to be there to gobble it all up.'

'*Coca* again? I mean, I like it, but it's not much different from pizza, is it? And at home we eat *sobrassada* most days. Can't we break with tradition for once and have something else?'

'Don't be silly, we're in Sant Martí. What on earth do you expect?'

'They have canapés at events in Palma,' replied Pep wistfully. 'We don't have to serve up *sobrassada* every year.'

'But it's the very heart and soul of Mallorca. Imagine the skill involved in curing and blending the pork with paprika and spices.'

'I try not to.'

'Banning it would be like ordering the Italians not to eat pasta or Greeks, moussaka or the British, eggs and bacon.'

'I didn't say to ban it, just to try something different one year.'

Isabel raised her arms dramatically. 'Or the Bulgarians, shopska salad...'

She paused, marvelling to herself at how the Bulgarians had butted so unexpectedly into her culinary rant. Sitting back in her chair she concluded with an impassioned, 'There would be riots on the streets.'

Pep exhaled deeply. 'I get the point.' He observed her for a second. 'By the way, did you pop by Ca'n Julia yesterday to pick up the keys from Mr Jay before he left for London?'

Isabel feigned nonchalance as she whisked some errant papers into an orderly pile on her desk. 'Of course.'

He eyed her suspiciously. 'You didn't say anything to him, I hope.'

Isabel clicked her teeth. 'The first time I met him I noticed that his nose showed signs of septum perforation, a sure sign of cocaine abuse. I saw it all the time when I was in the narcotics investigation team in Madrid.'

Pep winced. 'So, what happened?'

She drained her cup. 'I had a private word with him when his wife was out of earshot. Naturally, he was a little taken aback when I told him a few home truths about his marriage and his addiction, but he took it on the chin.'

'And were you right?'

'Absolutely. He told me the affair wasn't serious and blamed the drugs on pressure of work.'

'You're impossible. The poor guy was supposed to be on holiday, not facing the third degree from the woman renting him his holiday villa.'

Isabel carried on, unabashed. 'I've given him the name of a good counsellor in London we used to work with when I was on the narcotics team and said that if he turns things around before next summer, we'll give him and his wife a week's free stay in one of our properties.'

Pep's mouth dropped open. 'How does that make good business sense?'

'It doesn't, so go and take some more bookings.'

Early evening, both telephone lines rang. Pep put one of the calls through to Isabel. It was Tolo Cabot, her old police boss in Palma. He sounded weary.

'So, how are things in the big bad city?' Isabel trilled.

'About as bad as it gets. I really need your help.'

'Why, what's up?'

'We've got a serious situation on our hands. A child abduction.'

She jumped up from her desk. 'Where?'

'On the beach in Pollença port around two o'clock this afternoon.'

Isabel put him on speaker phone and began splitting open a sunflower seed.

'Do you have to do that?'

'What?'

'Crack those damned seeds!'

'It helps me concentrate, you know that. Boy or girl?'

'An eight-year-old Briton named Miranda Walters. She was having lunch with her mother on Pollença beach and simply vanished.'

'Not unless she was a ghost. Witnesses? Surveillance cameras?'

'Nothing much so far. The beach was teeming with people, but no one seems to have seen or heard a thing. We're waiting for the

ANNA NICHOLAS

release of local film footage. I don't like the feel of this, Bel. You know that with this sort of case, time is of the essence.'

'The family has money?'

'Nothing special, so I'd rule out kidnapping. Besides, no one's called demanding a ransom.'

'Dysfunctional parents?'

He let out a husky guffaw. 'Haven't we all? Actually, I don't know much about them yet. The boys from the Guardia Civil are conducting a preliminary interview with the mother and stepfather right now. Understandably, they're very shaken.'

Isabel paused. 'If the Guardia is already on board, why are you getting involved? You're in homicide.'

'It's not that simple. This is about damage limitation. The Guardia and the National Police are being forced to collaborate and central government is sending in the heavies from Madrid tonight. The commissioner has insisted on my involvement – he's already anticipating this ending up as a murder investigation.'

'Ah, your charismatic boss. Still his usual cheerful self, then?'

'Yes, no change there. Look, by some miracle I'm hoping that the child just wandered off and got disorientated and has been taken in by some kindly local. It's highly unlikely that she got into trouble in the water. She'd already swum before lunch and her swimming suit was drying off at the lunch table.'

'Exactly when was she reported missing?'

'It seems that while her mother was paying the bill she took her bucket to fill up at the water's edge and never returned. It happened in a matter of minutes.'

Isabel frowned. 'Sadly, that's often the case.'

'I know. As you can imagine the tourism minister is in a state of apoplexy and the president has demanded an island-wide sweep by all forces. We've set up roadblocks everywhere and land and air searches are underway.'

'Good. And what about the press?'

'It will be on all the news channels tonight. It's going to be a circus. As it is, the international media has already started crawling all over us like a plague of cockroaches.'

Isabel's lips curled sardonically. 'So if the Guardia Civil is involved, does this mean you and the charming Capitán Gómez will form the twin peaks of the investigation?'

'Unfortunately, yes, within guidelines. He's been assigned to the case, but if he steps on my toes, he'll know about it.'

'Have you done an all ports alert? And what about the airport?'

'Come on, Bel, give us a little credit. We've pulled out all the stops. A fly couldn't give us the slip.'

'When did you mobilise everything?'

'As soon as we could. By three o'clock the island was shut down.'

'Not bad, but it might still have been too late,' Isabel replied quietly. 'If the poor kid has been abducted, there's a good chance that she could already be in some kind of safe house by now. Worst-case scenario, concealed in a vessel and already on her way to Morocco.'

'Child trafficking? I hope you're wrong. If any monster touches a hair on that child's head, I'll hunt them down personally.'

Isabel felt for Tolo. She knew that as a longstanding voluntary counsellor at a centre for abused children in Palma, he often struggled emotionally to deal with some of the force's most shocking paedophilia cases.

'How can I help?' she asked.

'Listen, I know you have contacts up in Pollença. I want you to keep an ear to the ground, but I need more than that.'

There was a pause. Isabel breathed impatiently into the receiver. 'Well?'

'I'd like your help interviewing the parents. They're understandably distraught and your English is better than mine.'

'Fibber. You have a myriad of interpreters for that little job.'

'OK, cards on the table – I need you to work on the case.'

Isabel laughed. 'Good try, Tolo, but the answer's no.'

'Will you at least hear me out?'

Isabel crunched hard on a seed. 'I'm listening.'

'The point is that your father's old chums at the Ministry of Interior in Madrid have expressly called for your involvement because of your expertise in this area. They want this case closed fast.'

She let out a humourless laugh. 'They weren't such good chums to my father when his brother disappeared, were they? Now, when it suits them, they want my cooperation.'

'You're a kidnapping specialist who's dealt with several complex child abduction cases. And you happen to be on the island. '

'Serendipity. I'm also pretty hot on narcotics and homicide, but I don't recall your bending my ear every time there's been a cocaine bust or murder in the last year.'

'Are you making me an offer?' he growled.

'Don't be provocative. The reason you haven't sought my help is because I'm no longer on the force. I resigned so that I could have a life. Remember?'

'No, you threw in a great career because you were angry about your missing uncle.'

Isabel studied her bitten fingernails in some disgust. 'Let's not go over old ground. So what's the deal?'

'You get the badge back and become an external consultant on my team.'

'That doesn't sound like normal practice.'

'It isn't.'

'So would I be acting in an official or unofficial capacity?'

'A bit of both, but I'd try to protect you and keep you under the radar.'

Isabel didn't respond.

'If it's about the money, Bel…'

'Don't insult me, Tolo. You know me well enough,' she replied wearily.

'Listen, we need to move fast if we want to find Miranda alive.'

Isabel's thoughts strayed to her last child abduction case back in Madrid. It had been harrowing and involved a six-year-old boy snatched off the street by a seasoned paedophile. The fates had been on her side and she and her team had tracked the man down with the help of CCTV and eye-witnesses. The child had been rescued from his clutches but at what cost? In less than three days the damage had been done. A life irrevocably changed.

Tolo was warming to his theme. 'Think of your success rate with abductions. Remember that last case you handled in Madrid?'

Isabel closed her eyes, trying to blank out the disturbing images that were needling their way back into her consciousness. She held out her left hand. It was quivering slightly. Was it fear?

Tolo uttered an exasperated growl. 'What, do you want me to get down on my knees and beg?'

'Nice idea but a wasted gesture by phone,' she replied. 'OK, I'll do it.'

He breathed a sigh of relief. 'I'm afraid you'll also have to cooperate with the Guardia, but you'll only take orders from me, not Gómez.'

Isabel crunched on another seed. 'No, Tolo. This is how it'll work. If I help you on the case, I take orders from no one. I'm happy to cooperate with both you and the Guardia, but I'll employ my own methods and no one gets in my way. When it's over, I hand in the badge. Understand?'

A grim smile played on Tolo's lips. He was a skilled chess player and she'd just called checkmate. 'Loud and clear. I'll need you to fill in some paperwork.'

'When do we meet?'

'Pollença police station at eight tomorrow morning. After I've briefed you, I'd like you to visit Miranda's mother and stepfather, and the crime scene.' He paused. 'About your uncle. Don't give up hope.'

'As if...'

After the call Isabel sat for a few minutes absorbed in her own thoughts until Furó, perhaps sensing her discomfort, opened a bleary eye and jumped onto her lap. She ruffled the thick fur and cupped his whiskery muzzle in her hand. There was something tragicomic about his face. Above the smooth creamy vanilla hair around his snout, a dark strip of fur masked the eyes, giving him the appearance of a ferrety bandit.

'So what should I do, Furó? Do I still have it in me to help find this child? What if I've lost my touch?'

The ferret offered a grunt and wriggled off her lap.

She stared after his departing tail. 'Thanks for the show of confidence.'

Pep barged in a few minutes later. 'What's up with you?'

She rubbed her eyes. 'Nothing, Pep. I'm just feeling suddenly very tired.'

'Well, look lively. That was your mother on the phone. She's made us fresh *albondigas*.'

'Excellent,' said Isabel, her mood lifting. 'I tell you, Pep, if Paris had ever sampled my mother's meatballs, he wouldn't have given Helen a second glance.'

Pep fixed her with a blank stare.

'You never read about the Trojan War?'

'No, but I've read everything there is to know on football and fashion. So what did the chief inspector want?'

Isabel yawned. 'Come on, let's close up. What I have to tell you is best said over a few glasses of wine and some good food.'

'Fine by me. I suppose Furó will be joining us for dinner?'

As if on cue, the ferret's head popped up from under her desk.

'Of course. Furó wouldn't miss mama's *albondigas* for the world,' Isabel replied.

FOUR

Isabel was idling in a garden chair nursing a glass of *hierbas* liquor while Pep sat across from her, deep in thought. A handful of soft white stars sparkled in a flinty sky above them and cicadas rustled and throbbed in the peppery darkness. An urgent scuffling came from the long grasses and Furó's inquisitive snout briefly appeared before succumbing once again to the secrets of the undergrowth. Pep leant against the table, pulled a candle towards him and whisked a finger quickly through the flame. Isabel did the same, allowing hers to linger a few seconds longer.

'Show-off.'

She laughed. 'You're right. As a kid I got a bad burn trying to beat your sister at that game.'

'Who won?'

'Marga, of course.'

The sound of clinking dishes came reassuringly from the kitchen behind them. Isabel deemed it a treat to dine regularly with her mother, whose ancient house and sprawling garden occupied a quiet corner a stone's throw from the village church. Aside from her delectable home cooking, another bonus was that Florentina always commandeered the kitchen, shooing Isabel onto the shady patio where she could relax without any misplaced feelings of guilt at the end of a long day. Ever since her father had died two years earlier, Isabel had kept a close eye on her mother, popping by to see her every morning and ensuring that she continued to have an active role in the business for as long as she wished.

Florentina called from the kitchen. 'Anyone for coffee?'

Pep hesitated a moment. 'Maybe a small *espresso*, Florentina. *Gràcies*.'

Isabel stifled a yawn. 'Just a *cortado*, mama. Shall I make it?'

'No, you destroy less when you're out of my kitchen.'

Isabel frowned. 'She always says I break things.'

Pep lit a cigarette. 'But it's true! You've just wrecked the office photocopier, and what about breaking the bathroom door handle last week?'

'Shoddy workmanship, that's all.'

'More like you just don't know your own strength.'

He fixed his eyes on her and exhaled a plume of smoke. 'So, are you going to tell me about your call today with the chief inspector?'

She brought him up to speed on her conversation with Tolo Cabot.

Pep's forehead puckered. 'Why do the police have to involve you? Did you really handle some big child abduction cases on the mainland?'

She pulled a lump of melted wax from the candle and sculptured it into a small ball. 'A few.'

'Who do the police think took the girl?'

'You're assuming she was abducted or kidnapped.'

'What else could have happened to her?'

'Who knows? She could have run away, hit her head and lost her memory, drowned or of course...'

'What?'

'Have already known her abductor and gone willingly. There are no obvious witnesses, which in a way simplifies things.'

'How so?'

'Well, a child can't just disappear off a crowded beach in broad daylight without someone noticing.'

Pep looked confused. 'That's ridiculous. The guy could have chloroformed her or spiked her ice cream.'

'You watch too many movies. Tell me how that could happen in full view of so many sunbathers? Anyway, why assume it was a guy?'

He gave a snort. 'It's not likely to be a woman, is it? It's got to be some paedophile or crank.'

'Never assume anything, Pep. All I do know is that with cases of this kind, time is of the essence. The clock is ticking.'

Florentina barged out of the kitchen carrying a tray. She placed it on the table and then stood up straight with hands on hips, tea towel draped over one shoulder. 'What are your plans for tomorrow?'

'Isabel's going to Pollença, so I'm manning the office.'

She turned to her daughter. 'Pollença?'

Isabel threw Pep a warning glance. 'Oh, just checking up on some new clients over there.'

Florentina smiled. 'I can't believe how you've grown the company. Your father would have been so proud.'

Isabel passed a coffee to Pep. 'I think he would have preferred me to stay in the force.'

Her mother shook her head. 'Not Juan, not after what happened with Hugo. Your father gave the police his life, but when Hugo disappeared no one wanted to know.'

Pep shifted uncomfortably in his chair. 'Who is Hugo?'

'Hugo Flores Romero, my father's identical twin. Assumed dead,' Isabel replied.

'I'm sorry,' said Pep. 'You've never mentioned this uncle to me.'

'Why would I?' she replied flatly.

Florentina placed a hand on his shoulder. 'The truth is that four years ago Hugo vanished. He was an investigative journalist in

Barcelona, one of the best, but a difficult man who didn't know when to stop digging.'

Pep frowned. 'For what?'

'The truth,' said Isabel softly.

Florentina pulled out a chair next to Pep and sat down, fanning herself with the tea towel. 'His newspaper told us that he was on the scent of a leading drug baron with connections to notorious Colombian warlord Pablo Escobar, who was killed by government forces back in the nineties. He was into everything from drugs to extortion and murder.'

Isabel turned to Pep. 'But Hugo was also close to identifying a leading ETA operative.'

'You're talking about the Basque terrorist group?'

'They think of themselves more as separatists and freedom fighters,' she replied with a lukewarm smile. 'He could have been targeted by either ETA or some Colombian drug ring.'

'So what happened to him?'

Isabel reached for the sugar bowl. 'We believe Hugo was kidnapped. A woman reported that she'd seen him bundled into a car by two men outside his newspaper offices, but detectives from Barcelona's Mossos d'Esquadra police force claimed she was an unreliable witness. She was a prostitute and drug user.'

She trickled a spoonful of sugar into her coffee and slowly stirred it. 'Before moving to Madrid I was once a deputy inspector in Barcelona, but when I returned to pick up the trail, even officers I considered friends went cold on me.'

'Why?'

'I'm not sure, Pep. Several leading investigative journalists like Hugo had been kidnapped or assassinated by ETA operatives in the past, so perhaps it seemed easier to lay the blame at their door,' Isabel added. 'Case closed.'

'And did you agree?'

Isabel took a sip of coffee. 'No. ETA never claimed responsibility and Hugo's body never turned up. I believe dark forces were at play closer to home – it has the whiff of a cover-up.'

Pep stubbed out his cigarette and began lighting another. 'Surely not within the police?'

Isabel gave a shrug. 'All I do know is that to the end of his days my father desperately tried to uncover the truth.'

'And what good did it do him?' said Florentina. 'Juan died two years ago a broken man, never knowing what became of his brother.'

Pep turned to her. 'But couldn't your husband have used his influence?'

Isabel noted how her mother's face appeared suddenly vulnerable, like that of a child, although the thick dark hair that framed it was threaded with silver, betraying her age. She gave a sigh. 'It was difficult because Juan had been retired from the National Police a few years by then. He might have been Chief Superintendent in Castilla-La Mancha at one time, but that didn't cut any ice when he went looking for answers. It was as if Hugo never existed.'

'So you came here to Mallorca when Juan retired?' Pep asked.

Florentina nodded. 'I wanted to be nearer my family. While Juan tried to trace his missing brother, I set up a small rentals agency with an inheritance from my mother, just to keep myself busy. Isabel had already relocated here from Madrid to start a new post as a detective inspector. Then two years ago Juan died of a heart attack.'

Pep nudged Isabel. 'So is that why you quit the police?'

'I suppose my father's death was the catalyst. That and the fact that Hugo's disappearance was never investigated properly. Besides, the job just wasn't fun anymore.'

'She did it for me too. I couldn't cope running the agency alone,' Florentina added.

Pep stared at them both. 'So you've given up on finding Hugo?'

Isabel raised an eyebrow. 'As I said, Pep, never assume anything. Now that I can afford it, I've hired Emilio Navarro, a private investigator in Barcelona, because one day I intend to uncover the truth. By some miracle, who knows, Hugo may still be alive.'

FIVE

Tolo Cabot was waiting for her in an unmarked car close to the police station in Pollença port. He wore a pale blue shirt under a cream linen jacket, and sipped on a coffee in spite of the pulsating heat outside. Isabel flashed her headlights at him and parked in the nearest space on the other side of Calle de Vicente Buades. From his rear-view mirror, he watched as she walked jauntily towards him. She was undeniably attractive: strong features, good cheekbones, and a haughty nose. He liked the way she dressed, too, always simple and stylish for maximum impact. No jewellery. Not even a watch. If she wore make-up, she could have fooled him. Best of all, she was a hedonist when it came to food – and wine, for that matter. She read a lot. More than him. And despite the unhappy circumstances that had led her to take up the badge again, his heart skipped at the thought of working with her on the case.

She stuck her head through his open window. 'Get moving. I need a coffee and breakfast.'

He held up his styrofoam cup and laughed when she wrinkled her nose.

'Come on, I know a good place. The best *tortillas*.'

Tolo lumbered out of the car and discarded his cup in the nearest bin, then accompanied Isabel briskly along the street. He gave the scrum of photographers and reporters stationed outside the local police headquarters a cursory glance.

'The sooner we find this kid, the better. Look at them. They're already camped outside police HQ in Palma too. All they want is a sensational headline. They have no soul.'

Isabel turned to him. 'Come on. They're only doing their job. Just like us.'

Tolo smiled at her. 'So how's your ferret?'

'He's in good spirits. We went for a swim early this morning and he's spending the rest of the day with my mother. She dotes on him.'

'What does he eat, apart from human flesh?'

She grinned at him. 'Mostly meat and cat kibble. Ferrets prefer a high protein and fat diet.'

'Then your ferret and I have a lot in common. Did you know that in the States they're training them to sniff out drugs? We could do that over here.'

'Well, keep your hands off Furó.'

'You bet. Last time he nearly took my finger off.'

Isabel headed towards a small and scruffy joint on the promenade where the elderly owner greeted her like a long-lost daughter. He grimaced when she asked about business and handed her a copy of *El Periódico*. On the front page under the headline 'Have you seen Miranda?' a pair of blue eyes peered out from the face of a young girl with long flaxen hair.

Tolo and Isabel exchanged tense glances. The owner jutted his chin towards the beach.

'It's going to be the best day to get a parasol and lounger. The beach will be practically empty.'

Tolo looked away, his ears distracted by the hum of a police helicopter circling the nearby hills. 'I'm not so sure. A pack of ghoulish voyeurs will soon be swarming the place.'

The old man shook his head mournfully. 'Poor little girl. Let's hope they find her. So what can I get you, the usual?'

Isabel nodded. 'He'll have the same, but give him a cappuccino with an extra shot.'

Tolo gave her an appreciative glance. 'You remembered.'

'It's not that long since we had coffee together.'

'Too long by my standards,' he grunted.

They sat in the shade of the terrace, overlooking the beach. Tolo scratched thoughtfully at the grey stubble on his chin.

'Forget to shave this morning?' she asked.

His dark eyes rested on her face. 'It's my new look. You don't like it?'

'No, and I think you could do with a haircut. You're turning into an old rocker.'

He chuckled. 'Anything to rile my superiors. At forty-six I feel I have a right to express my inner animal. Actually, my commissioner's told me to smarten up my act.'

'Oh?'

'Apparently, I've now got to report directly to some top honcho at the Ministry of Interior in Madrid.'

'Why?'

'The government wants to be kept in the loop on all developments in the Miranda Walters case.'

'I'm glad the higher echelons are taking this so seriously.'

'They have no choice, Bel. A child disappearance could prove a catastrophe for tourism here.'

'So how often will you need to be in Madrid?'

He raised an eyebrow. 'I've no idea yet, but the big guns from the Guardia and National Police are flying here for a debriefing on the case tomorrow. Lola Rubio, my liaison point at the Ministry of Interior, will be with them.'

'A woman?'

'Apparently she's quite a tour de force within the government. Young, smart and ambitious, by all accounts.'

Isabel fell silent.

'Look, whatever happens, I won't let this be a distraction. Wherever I am, I'll be on the case 24/7 supporting you and my team back at base in Palma.'

'How's your workload generally?'

'We're understaffed and drowning in cases, if you must know.'

Isabel nodded. 'If that's so, I'll keep off your back as much as possible.'

Tolo glanced at the copy of *El Periódico* left on the table.

'That guy gets up my nose.'

'Who?'

'Josep Casanovas. He's a loose canon.'

Isabel smirked, sensing a little macho rivalry. 'A good editor, though. I've never had a problem with him.'

'That's true enough. He was always sniffing around the Palma precinct when you were there. Now we hardly see him.'

'He has his uses. He did me a lot of favours when I was in the force.'

'I know. I also notice that he's always promoting Hogar Dulce Hogar. More favours?'

She shook her head. 'I take some adverts in return for the odd bit of editorial. We need to keep him and other media on side with this case. I should talk to him.'

Tolo shrugged. 'If you must.'

'What about the expat newspaper here?'

'*Majorca Daily Bulletin*? The editor's a good guy, but the British press are on his back too. Like all of us, he wants answers.'

Isabel drummed impatient fingers on the table. 'So what have we got so far?'

'Two witnesses claim they saw a girl fitting Miranda's description leaving the beach with a man at around two o'clock yesterday afternoon.'

'Voluntarily?'

'So they say. Then again, early this morning a French tourist reported seeing two men escorting a young blond girl into a car at around the same time. No doubt there were countless kids fitting Miranda's description on the beach yesterday. The Guardia has been pulling out the stops with door-to-door and street interviews here, but it's thrown up nothing so far.'

'So who's handling what? I don't want Capitán Gómez tripping me up,' Isabel replied.

'No problem. According to my commissioner, we'll be leading the investigation with backup from Gómez and the Guardia.'

He looked at his watch. 'You'll need to fill in some paperwork back at the station. Then you get the badge and you're free to follow your nose. Should anyone, media included, question your role, just say you've been seconded to my department. Hopefully you won't cross paths with Gómez too often. Just leave him to me.'

'Willingly.'

He tapped his briefcase. 'I've got a file of background information for you.'

'You're not coming with me to meet Miranda's parents?'

Tolo shook his head. 'I've got another press conference back in Palma. The commissioner also needs a complete debriefing before the delegation arrives from Madrid tomorrow.'

Isabel eyed him thoughtfully. 'If there's been no word from a potential kidnapper, Miranda's abduction is evidently not about money.'

'True.'

'Tell me about the parents before I meet them.'

A waiter arrived, placing their coffees on the table. Tolo paused until he was out of earshot.

'The parental situation is a little complicated. You'll be meeting Miranda's mother, Jane Walters, and her Mallorcan partner, Marc Got. She's divorced from Frank Walters, the child's father, an artist who's currently away in Switzerland. We've only just managed to contact him and he is flying here tonight.'

Isabel blew on her coffee. 'You told me that Miranda was having lunch with her mother before she disappeared. Was it just the two of them?'

He nodded.

'And what happened after her mother raised the alarm?'

'Staff immediately scoured the crowded beach, but she was gone. '

'So the child must have left in a hurry either alone or in company?' She paused while the same waiter deposited omelettes, crusty bread, olives and sliced tomatoes before them.

'This is a banquet even by your standards,' Tolo remarked.

'It will set us up for the day. You know I can't function without food.'

She poured olive oil on a chunk of bread and took a bite. 'What's the story on the mother's boyfriend?'

He offered a wan smile. 'You're going to like this. Marc Got owns Romeo's nightclub in Magaluf.'

'Where we did that drugs bust, what, three years back?'

'Precisely. He took over the club just over a year ago, but its reputation hasn't changed much and he himself has two previous drug convictions.'

'You think he's involved in Miranda's disappearance?'

He put down his knife and fork. 'Too early to say. He claims he was at his club at the time of the disappearance, but no one can confirm his whereabouts between one and three.'

'How well is his club doing?'

Tolo gulped down a piece of omelette and waved a fork at her. 'We're on to it. Gaspar Fernández, my new deputy, has been making some checks. Do you remember him?'

'Of course. Still got the crazy hair?' Isabel asked.

'No, he's shaved it all off. Wanted to look like a menacing thug. It works.'

'Shame, I loved those curls.'

'Anyway, Gaspar's been going through his recent business transactions and it's not looking healthy. A few rival clubs say Got's in trouble and owes money.'

Isabel took a sip of coffee and found herself distracted by the pungent aroma of ozone and the distant cry of a gull. She tilted her head up at the sky and watched as a grey cluster hovered on the horizon before descending at speed like a falling star in a cacophony of sound. The pewter stain broke up and soon she could identify flapping wings and the slash of yellow beaks as the creatures swooped on a haze of insects suspended above the sea. A sandy beach vanished in a foamy froth of water at the shoreline, beyond which fishing vessels and yachts nestled together in small groups along the marina. Facing out to sea, a lone elderly man with translucent skin was prodding the quiff of a wave with his naked right foot. He seemed thin and vulnerable against the slab of blue sky as he took hesitant steps towards the vast expanse of glimmering water. Isabel tore her gaze from him and trained her eye on the helicopter sweeping the bay.

'How long has Marc Got been seeing Miranda's mother?'

'Since last summer. It seems that she came here on holiday when the divorce went through and met Got at Romeo's in Magaluf.'

'How romantic. And what about Frank Walters?'

'He's got a fiancée living in Switzerland. Apparently, she and Miranda get on famously.'

'So, happy families all round?'

Tolo wiped his mouth. 'So you'd imagine. I just pray this isn't the work of some paedophile ring.'

Isabel pronged her last piece of tomato. 'Contrary to what people expect, most paedophilia cells aren't opportunistic. They prefer to groom their victims over time to build trust. Few would risk randomly snatching a child from a public beach in broad daylight.'

'That's true, but couldn't some predator have already got to her while she's been holidaying here?'

'That did cross my mind, but this doesn't strike me as the sort of action of a typical paedophile ring. It just seems too daring and reckless.'

Isabel rose from her chair and waited as Tolo hurriedly examined the bill and left some notes on the table.

He followed her to the door. 'Let's hope you're right.'

She frowned. 'At the moment there are pieces in the jigsaw that don't quite fit.'

'And what might they be?'

She gave an impatient sigh. 'If I knew that, Tolo, I'd have already solved the case.'

SIX

Mrs Walters sat slumped on a blue sofa in the living room of her holiday apartment, a crumpled tissue raised to her red-rimmed eyes.

'She's my world. I just can't believe this is happening.'

With her gaze fixed imploringly on Isabel, she released a deep sob and covered her face with her hands. 'And it's all my fault. I should never have left her alone on the beach, but, you see, it all happened in a split second.'

Marc Got sat next to her, his tattooed arm draped defensively around her shoulders.

'Someone must have seen something!' he exploded. 'Have you interviewed everyone on the beach yet?'

Isabel remained silent, preferring to let him vent his rage.

'Look, we're both sick of being interviewed. Guardia, police, whatever. They're all useless. Why should you be any different?'

'I used to work with the National Police and dealt with similar cases when I was a detective in Madrid and Barcelona. That's why they've enlisted my help.'

'Well, then, why aren't you out there searching for her, for Christ's sake? If she's been taken by some sicko, they can't have gone far.'

'Unfortunately, it's a big island, Señor Got. But no stone will be left unturned, trust me.' Isabel's eyes wandered to the large diamond winking from the man's left ear and the heavy gold rings encrusted with diamonds on the fourth fingers of both hands. She turned to him. 'You have good English for a Mallorcan.'

He fixed her with an insolent stare. 'My mum was a Brit. Yours ain't bad either – for a Mallorcan.'

'Hybrid Mallorcan,' she smiled. 'Tell me about your mother.'

He shrugged. 'Not much to tell. She came here in the sixties and met my dad when he was just a waiter. By the time he died, he was running a chain of bars.'

'Impressive,' said Isabel.

'This apartment belonged to my mum, but she didn't use it much. I inherited it when she died a few years ago. Jane has been using it as a base for her and Miranda this summer.'

'Why not use your club in Magaluf?'

'To be honest, my flat above Romeo's is a bit pokey.'

'So you're staying here too?'

'I stay at my club during the week and drive up here every Friday night. My manager covers weekends for me.'

'And how do you and Miranda get on?'

He glared at her. 'What's that supposed to mean?'

'Sometimes children find it difficult to adapt when their parents find new partners.'

'Not Miranda. We get on fine and she's been having the time of her life.'

'Do you have any children of your own?'

'No, why, is that a problem?'

'Not for me.'

Mrs Walters looked up. 'She adores Marc and he spoils her.'

He scrunched her arm affectionately, revealing a scabby tattoo of a green lizard on his left wrist. The creature's mouth was open but no tongue was in evidence.

Isabel studied it for a moment. 'That must have hurt?'

'A bit. Thinking of getting one?'

'Maybe a ferret. Just to annoy my assistant. That tattoo looks pretty raw.'

'Yeah, it's not finished yet. I'm having it done in sessions at lunchtime.'

'You go to Marley's in Magaluf?'

He eyed her with interest. 'You know him?'

'Sure. He's the best tattooist on the island. Did you go there yesterday?'

He paused. 'I popped by to get my leg finished.'

Isabel examined the raw red heart on his right shin. The initials J and M were inscribed in blue ink at its centre.

'Marley gave me a tube of Bepanthen for it.'

'What on earth's that?' asked Jane Walters.

'Nappy rash cream,' replied Isabel. 'It's good for healing tattoos. So why didn't you tell the police about visiting Marley?'

Marc Got gave a stiff shrug. 'Didn't seem important.'

'Even if he was a crucial alibi?'

'I didn't think I'd be needing one.'

Isabel puffed out her cheeks, making a mental note to pay a visit to her old chum Marley later on. 'So tell me your exact movements between one and three o'clock yesterday.'

'I already told one of the Guardia blokes. I left the office at one o'clock and went for a walk and quick kip on Magaluf beach. And before you ask, no, I didn't bump into anyone I knew.'

'So what time did you get to Marley's?'

'An hour later. I was only there about thirty minutes.'

Isabel jotted some notes in a small red book and returned it to her pannier. 'You and Mrs Walters share a home in England?'

'Essex. I've got staff running the club in Magaluf, but I come back every fortnight to keep an eye on things out of the season. Summer's flat out so I'm on the island most of the time.'

Isabel turned to Mrs Walters. 'Has Miranda ever wandered off or run away from home before?'

'Never,' she replied.

'Happy at school?'

Mrs Walters stifled a sob. 'Very. She's got lots of friends.'

'How does she get on with her father?' Isabel continued.

'What, Frank? She worships him. We had a fairly acrimonious divorce, but things are much better now. He has access during holidays and takes Miranda off skiing and on exotic foreign adventures with his girlfriend. He has a base in Switzerland as well as England.'

'Is he a successful artist?'

She shrugged. 'He does regular graphic design work for a couple of large corporate clients, but he doesn't really need money. His parents left him a sizable inheritance a few years back.'

'And do you work at all?' Isabel asked.

'I'm a teaching assistant in a local primary school.'

'And your ex-husband is arriving here today?'

She wiped away a rogue tear. 'Yes, from Switzerland. It took them a while to track him down yesterday because he was off painting in the mountains. I don't know what I'm going to say to him. They're very close. He called Miranda only yesterday morning to wish her a happy birthday.'

'Her birthday?'

'She'd just turned eight, which is why we lunched at Café del Mar – her favourite restaurant. She was so looking forward to it and the chef made her a special cake.'

The woman began to cry again. 'Frank will accuse me of being a bad mother, leaving her alone at the table.'

Isabel leant forward. 'Listen, *señora*, no one can accuse you of that. Thousands of mothers would have done just the same. You can't glue yourself to your child all day long.'

Marc Got nodded. 'She's right, love.'

Isabel stood up. 'Mrs Walters, do you mind showing me Miranda's bedroom?'

She gave a snuffle. 'Help yourself.'

Isabel entered a bland corridor, choosing the nearest door when she observed the ghost of a flower drawn in pink felt-tip on its paintwork. 'This is hers?'

Mrs Walters nodded.

Isabel inspected the anaemic rose-tinged walls and drab floral curtains fringing the open window. Somewhere in the distance came the muffled growl of distant traffic, over-layered with the high-pitched yapping of a dog and a child's steady wailing, although Isabel could see no sign of life below the window. It was *siesta* time, when every shutter was clamped shut in drowsy submission and would remain so until late afternoon when the oppressive summer heat gradually began to abate.

Isabel was hungry. She had spent much of the morning in Pollença port interviewing local shopkeepers, bar owners and groups of tourists. No one, it seemed, had seen anything suspicious. Painstakingly she had gone over the scant details again and again until a shadowy pattern began to form in her mind. Isabel had an inexplicable feeling that the answer lay right under her nose, but what was it? In a short while she would pop by Café del Mar, the crime scene, if one could call it that. The owner had agreed to meet her there at two o'clock, but first she'd resolved to telephone young Aina from the bakery in Morells to find out about her dubious nocturnal adventure with the two fishermen on Monday night. It had been preying on her mind and as a friend of the family she felt it her duty to do a little discreet investigating.

Her eyes now settled on the child's empty bed, fitted snugly beneath the window. Perching on the edge of the mattress, Isabel looked around her. A smiling Winnie the Pooh with distended belly sprawled on a heap of pink cushions as if he'd just had a jolly good lunch. Isabel raised the pillow and found beneath it a neatly pressed, white cotton nightdress adorned with pink roses. She lifted it up and breathed in the smell of fabric softener and, perhaps it was her imagination, chocolate. Two well-thumbed books, an Enid Blyton and a Roald Dahl, lay next to a Barbie doll on a bedside table beside a collection of novelty hairclips. Isabel turned the doll over onto her back. Her vacant eyes, partly obscured by a thick fringe, had been disfigured by blue ink and her tightly plaited shiny yellow mane hung primly down her spine. She wore a suggestive pink top over her brittle chest and a minuscule black leather skirt that barely covered her smooth, unnaturally thin legs. Isabel was instantly reminded of Valentina, a Russian prostitute turned informer she'd known in Barcelona during her time with the Mossos d'Esquadra. Whatever had happened to her, she wondered. Was she ploughing the same murky furrow or had she perchance been moved on to a new city by her Russian paymasters to become yet another sad statistic of human trafficking?

Mrs Walters pattered over to her in yellow flip-flops. 'She loves that Barbie. She calls her Susan. She's had her for years, as you can tell.'

'It's her favourite toy?'

The woman gave an involuntary titter. 'Oh lord, no! She and her Pinky are inseparable. It's her horrible old threadbare blue rabbit. She sleeps with him in her bed every night.'

'Why is it called Pinky if it's blue?'

'Only because she's mad about pink.'

'Can I see it?'

Mrs Walters searched the child's bed. 'It'll be around here somewhere. It's quite small.'

Isabel reached for one of the books and flicked through the pages while the woman continued her fruitless search.

'Roald Dahl. A masterful writer.'

Mrs Walters managed a watery smile. 'Her dad gave her that. He used to read to her every night. She treasures it.'

'I see it's a compilation. All my favourite stories.'

Isabel read the inscription on the cover page – *To darling Miranda, all my love, Daddy.*

The woman sat down heavily on the bed having given up rummaging among the sheets and cushions for Pinky.

'Well, I can't find him anywhere.'

'Maybe Miranda took him with her to the beach?' suggested Isabel gently.

'No way. Pinky never leaves her bed. He'll be here somewhere…'

Her voice trailed off as she stared with blank eyes at the hazy mountains beyond the open window.

'It's nice here. So normal. As if nothing bad happened. Like it's all just some horrible nightmare.'

Isabel grasped her hand. 'Miranda sounds like a smart little girl. Can you ever imagine her walking off with a complete stranger?'

'She's a very confident and friendly child, but she'd never go off with anyone she didn't know.'

'Do you have any regular contacts here?'

She shook her head slowly. 'No, just Marc and some of his friends in Magaluf. I've got to know a few shopkeepers and café owners, but that's about it.'

'And did Miranda ever go out alone, maybe to the beach or local shops?'

'Never.'

'Had she made any special friends here?'

'Not that she mentioned. She played with kids she met on the beach, mostly holidaymakers.'

'Did Marc ever take her to Magaluf alone?'

'No. I was always with them.'

'What about your neighbours here?'

'There are two old Spanish biddies in flats on the ground floor. On this level there's just us and an elderly English couple, but they're away. The flats above are being renovated by the landlord so aren't occupied.'

'Could Miranda keep a secret?'

Mrs Walters looked puzzled. 'She and Marc organised a surprise birthday tea for me a few months ago and she managed to keep that quiet.'

'Can you remind me what she was wearing yesterday on the beach?'

'A white tee shirt, pink shorts and flip-flops.'

'Any jewellery?'

'Just her Mickey Mouse red watch.'

'And did she have a bag of any kind?'

Jane Walters touched her chin absentmindedly. 'Sometimes she takes her pink Barbie rucksack if we're going out for the day. I can't see it here, so she must have had it with her.'

'Was she carrying anything else? '

'Not that I remember. She'd wanted to bring her Roald Dahl book, but I thought it would get spoiled so told her to take some comics instead. She doesn't have a mobile phone. If only I'd bought her one.'

'Apart from reading, what else does she like?'

'She loves singing and drawing and chocolate, of course.'

Isabel released her hand and, smiling, stood up. 'I have a sweet tooth too.'

Tears sprung from the woman's eyes as she rose with effort. In a quavering voice she turned to Isabel. 'Are you a mother?'

'No, but I have two young nephews and a god-daughter.'

The woman faltered at the bedroom door. 'Do you think I'll ever see Miranda again?'

'I like to believe in happy endings, like Mr Dahl did.'

'So you think you'll find her?' she persisted.

Isabel paused in the corridor, the book under her arm. 'Can I borrow this for a short while?'

Mrs Walters gave a dismissive shrug. 'Be my guest.'

Before they re-entered the living room, Isabel touched her arm. 'We will do everything we can to find Miranda. I won't let you down.'

'That's an odd thing for a policewoman to say,' the woman replied with a faint smile.

Isabel nodded. 'That's why I'm not one anymore.'

SEVEN

The semblance of a breeze stirred up a few rogue palm leaves that cartwheeled skittishly across the crowded promenade of Pollença port and onto the busy road. As Isabel parked Pequeñito, her mind wandered to Aina Ripoll, who was yet to return her call. She would try again later.

Walking jauntily along the pavement, she acknowledged the grizzly Tramuntanas in the distance, and broad blonde beach that beckoned to her from the other side of the street. The promenade bristled with touristy cafés and bars, their tables occupied by holidaymakers supping cool beers and laughing freely under a ferocious sun. Isabel wondered how many knew about Miranda's disappearance. Had it cast a shadow over their holiday or did they calmly reason that bad things happened even in paradise?

She stopped when she reached the dribble of wetland known as zona húmeda de La Gola. Here an open vein of salty water flowed up from the sea, passed under the promenade and merged with two freshwater streams to form a boggy lake bordered by a frill of impenetrable reeds. The area was under development, meaning that it was steadily losing its erstwhile shaggy aspect and was being spruced up and manicured to include meandering walkways and a visitor centre. Isabel stared out across the expanse of murky water, lost momentarily in thought, until the urgent cry of a gull prompted her to continue on her way.

When the traffic subsided, she crossed onto the opposite pavement that ran along the edge of the beach, at the same time whipping off her sandals and popping them into her pannier. Isabel took in her immediate surroundings – scrawny beach shrubs and a huddle of flimsy wooden cabins housing public lavatories. She looked out across the plain of yellow sand and, with food never far from her thoughts, scooped up a handful, marvelling at how its texture resembled finely granulated couscous. Despite the continued presence of local police and international press roving the area, tourists sprawled on bright blue sunloungers under raffia parasols, while others milled about, evidently enjoying the frisson of excitement that a major crime scene brings.

Café del Mar, a modest, white-washed building sitting beside a clump of dusty olive trees and a thirsty tamarisk, soon came into view. Isabel studied the red roof tiles choked with dirt and sand, and the arched doorway that led into the sombre interior. To the right under a cane roof, a wood-decked terrace cluttered with metal tables and chairs spilled out onto the sand. Isabel stepped on to the decking and examined the menu board that promised speciality dishes of *paella*, fresh squid and grilled sardines. There were no photographers about, but she wasn't surprised. Like a scourge of mosquitoes, they would have already swarmed the place the day before and had their fill. Inside, she discovered a bar and a handful of unoccupied tables, beyond which lay a wide terracotta-tiled corridor, leading onto the beach. A lone customer stood at the counter sipping a beer, mobile phone clamped to his ear. He offered her a cursory glance before carrying on with his conversation in Mallorquí dialect while Isabel scanned the room. A clock above the bar revealed that it was two o'clock, so Isabel gave herself an imaginary pat on the back. Not bad time-keeping for someone who never wore a watch. Overhead a fan purred. A rogue hen with a glossy russet plumage strutted purposefully about the room. Isabel lowered her sunglasses and frowned. So this was where Miranda spent her birthday meal. She resisted thinking of it as the little girl's *last* meal. A door behind the bar crashed open and a portly walrus of a man, wheezing heavily, squeezed into view.

'You're Isabel Flores Montserrat, the police investigator?'

She came forward and shook his huge hand across the counter. 'You must be José Delgado?'

He nodded mournfully. 'What a terrible business. So tragic and of course a disaster for local tourism.'

A moment later he was by her side, pulling despondently at the edges of his voluminous moustache. He nudged the chicken with his foot. 'Excuse Catalina. So can I get you something?'

'A *cortado*, thank you.'

He ushered her to one of the vacant tables and lumbered back behind the bar.

'Miranda's a nice little kid,' he bawled above the hiss of the coffee machine. 'She and her mother often pop by. I just can't believe something like this could happen. Well, not here, anyway.'

Sighing heavily, he slapped two small cups on the table and squeezed his heavy frame into a chair opposite her.

'At least the reporters have gone. *Gilipollas*! One English photographer even persuaded a young tourist to pose in the same chair Miranda had used. She was wearing a white top and pink shorts just like Miranda had done. That wasn't respectful, was it?'

A cluck of disapproval came from under the table. Catalina poked her head out and, fluttering her wings, flew onto an empty chair.

The Walrus grinned. 'She wants to join in, silly old bird. Do you keep chickens?'

Isabel nodded. 'Yes, but I have to be careful because I also keep a ferret and sometimes he likes to chase them.'

'I have about a dozen in my orchard, but Catalina is more of a pet, which is why she comes to work with me. I suppose we have to thank the Moors for introducing them to Mallorca.'

Isabel smiled. 'Actually, I'm more inclined to think it was the Phoenicians. They probably brought them from Persia or perhaps the Romans arrived with Italian hens.'

'Italian?' The Walrus looked disappointed. 'Imagine!'

Catalina flapped back to the floor, rousing her master from his thoughts.

'So, how can I help you?'

'You said that Miranda had visited with her mother before. How would you describe her?'

'A confident child. Miranda would talk to anyone.'

Isabel frowned, remembering a similar comment made by the owner of the British Food Store where she'd popped by earlier.

'Did she seem at all different yesterday?'

He shrugged. 'In what way?'

'Preoccupied or anxious?'

'Not at all. She seemed very excited. It was her birthday, after all, and we made quite a fuss of her. I organised a cake too.'

'What kind?'

'Chocolate. Her favourite. Isn't it everybody's?' He paused for a second and his big doe eyes filled with water. 'I'm sorry.'

Isabel nodded sympathetically. 'You know we have every intention of finding Miranda alive, Señor Delgado.'

'Of course.' He sniffed loudly and with head bowed slapped his arms dejectedly against the sides of his chair. Isabel tried to dispel the image flashing before her eyes of a pair of walrus flippers.

'So, where exactly were they sitting?'

'At one of our beach tables. Miranda had a bucket and spade with her so probably wanted to be near the sand.'

'Had she brought them with her on other occasions?'

'Not that I recall.'

'Can you remember if she was carrying anything else?'

He issued a dejected sigh and rubbed his eyes with chubby tanned fingers. 'A wet swimsuit which she'd hung on the back of her chair. I'm not certain, but I think she had a little rucksack too. Maria, my waitress, might remember.'

'Can I take a look at the table?'

He nodded, pushing back his chair, and barged through the restaurant's interior, out into the sun. Striding towards a wooden table, he frowned when he spotted a battalion of ants, always the curse of the August heat, marching across its surface. Deftly he swept a giant paw across the table, dispersing them all.

He turned to Isabel. 'I hate ants.'

She tapped her chin. 'So this is where they had lunch?'

'That's right. They arrived around twelve-thirty and stayed until two. I brought them over some drinks and Maria served them the dish of the day, which was lamb chops, salad and chips. Afterwards I carried out the cake, everyone sang "Happy Birthday", and Miranda blew out the candles.'

Isabel cocked her head at some nearby tables. 'Were there other customers dining here?'

'Only a German couple and they joined in the singing with us. They left soon after. Do you think that's significant?'

'No. So tell me what happened next.'

'Just before two o'clock, Mrs Walters popped inside to pay her bill. I just remember saying *adiós* and the next minute I heard her calling for Miranda. It all happened so quickly.'

'When was the last time you noticed Miranda sitting in her chair?'

He frowned. 'She got up after she'd eaten a slice of her birthday cake and went to play nearby in the sand with her bucket and spade.'

'Did Miranda eat all her lunch that day?'

The Walrus gently kneaded his moustache. 'I'll have to ask Maria. Give me a minute.'

He plodded off inside, leaving her alone at the table. Isabel stood up and, abandoning her pannier on the seat, set off towards the sea across the scorching sand. She brushed away small droplets of sweat as she marched on, ignoring the burning pain in the soles of her bare feet. At the water's edge she curled her toes around the wet sand, enjoying the coolness of the briny water and the swell of a distant wave that sent hissing foam rushing around her ankles. She closed her eyes for a moment, turned and walked hurriedly back to the restaurant, where the owner and a young waitress stood waiting for her.

'For a moment there I thought you'd gone and disappeared too,' he said in a flat tone. 'You're lucky your basket wasn't stolen.'

'Sometimes you have to have a little faith,' Isabel countered.

He turned towards the waitress. 'This is Maria. She served Mrs Walters yesterday.'

The woman appeared anxious but relaxed slightly when Isabel touched her arm and smiled. 'Just a few things. Did you notice Miranda's appetite?'

'She ate little, but I think she was over-excited because it was her birthday. She got up a few times to fill her bucket with seawater and then would run back to the table.'

'How many times?'

'Well, let me think. I'm fairly sure she went twice. And then just after her mother went to pay the bill I saw her skip off again for the third time.' She paused solemnly. 'But that time she didn't come back.' She lowered her head. 'The next thing I heard was her mother screaming. I was serving on the back terrace but rushed over here to see what had happened.'

'Then what?'

The Walrus resumed. 'We all dashed out onto the beach looking for Miranda. We found her bucket and spade, but that was all.'

'Where were they?'

'Quite close to here.' He beckoned for her and Maria to follow. At a point midway between the restaurant and the sea he stopped. 'By this old tamarisk.'

'So she never took it to the water's edge?'

'Or maybe she did but abandoned it here on the way back?' suggested Maria.

'But she never returned, did she?' Isabel replied a little more tartly than she'd intended.

'No,' the waitress replied.

'Did she bring anything else with her to the restaurant?'

Maria nodded. 'She was carrying a pink Barbie rucksack and she'd draped her wet swimsuit over a chair.'

'Had she brought the rucksack here before?'

'To be honest, I can't really remember, but I don't think so.'

'And her swimsuit. Was it still there after she'd disappeared?'

The Walrus shrugged. 'Did you see it, Maria?'

The waitress shook her head. 'There was nothing left at their table.'

'So we can assume that they were with her when she disappeared.'

'Is that important?' the Walrus asked.

'I'm not sure,' Isabel replied. 'But if she was just off to fill her bucket with water, why would she take her rucksack?'

'Maybe she was worried about someone stealing it,' proffered Maria.

'No one stole mine,' Isabel replied. 'I've always found children more trusting than adults.'

They walked back to the restaurant, sweating with the effort of pounding through hot, voluptuous sand.

He turned to Isabel. 'I suppose, like the Guardia officers, you'd like to examine the kitchens and toilets?'

'I'm not a health inspector.'

The Walrus balked. 'But the Guardia wanted to know about all potential exits.'

'No point,' she said with a shrug. 'Our bird had already flown.'

At the entrance to the restaurant she slid back into her sandals and shook the owner's hand, still marvelling at his bulk and the thick and lustrous droopy moustache that dwarfed his mouth. For a moment she was transported to the North Pole, crunching snow beneath her feet as fat and contented walruses propelled themselves with fast flippers towards the water's edge. To her shame she found herself asking him if he liked fish.

'As a matter of fact, I do. Crabs, shrimps, clams are all favourites.'

As she'd suspected. A human walrus. She nodded happily and pulled her sunglasses down over her eyes. 'I thought as much.'

He followed her onto the pavement and in some bemusement watched as she strode confidently away from him along the promenade.

EIGHT

It was late afternoon by the time Isabel reached Magaluf on the south-west coast. For once she wasn't dreading the visit. In her days as a detective inspector she only really set foot in this most infamous of resorts when trouble was brewing. She remembered once describing it at a press briefing as a Jekyll and Hyde resort, something the British media was quick to pick up on. By day it was innocuous enough, with its swag bag of water and theme parks, mini-golf courses, tacky gift shops, fast-food joints and pubs, but by night it turned into an ugly and menacing landscape seething with scantily-clad, drunken and drugged-up youths, prostitutes, pimps, pick-pockets and dealers. Music pulsated around the streets, club signs beckoned like lewd sirens, and promo girls tottered around the streets in titanic heels and monstrous fake eyelashes promising sex and forbidden pleasures. She remembered the first time she had to deal with the death of a flyer – a term her erstwhile colleagues used for those holidaying youths who, high on drugs or drink, or both, jumped from hotel balconies. Her first flyer was a nineteen-year-old male from Bedford, a town in England she'd never visited. Even if she'd wanted to, she'd never go now, not after seeing the dead boy's face.

And then there were the drug dealers who hung out in ghettos such as notorious Son Barassa, a few kilometres from Palma, whose lethal chemical booty could be purchased in tablet form for as little as five euros a throw. Isabel had experienced more than her fair share of drug raids and seen enough dead teenagers to last her a lifetime. So she was happy this sweltering afternoon not to be on official police business but instead paying a social call on one of Magaluf's more palatable part-time criminals. With the sun dazzling her vision she turned down a shadowy side street towards the sea, deftly avoiding Magaluf's throbbing centre. Already the esplanade and beach were awash with young families and groups of boisterous teenagers, their skin red and peeling after prolonged sunbathing.

Isabel coursed along the road with the sea and vast beach on her left until she spied a red sandwich board announcing Marley's Tattoo Parlour. A furtive blue arrow indicated that the shop could be found in a nearby precinct. With no traffic behind her, Isabel quickly mounted the kerb and left the car's hazard lights on as she set off on foot along the quiet street. Some way off she spotted a female warden and by the slow gait and short black hair guessed that it was Antonia. She had always made it her business to know local traffic duty teams and had continued to do so ever since leaving the force – after all, you never knew when you might need them. So, placing her right thumb and index finger into her mouth, she gave a shrill whistle. A capped head bobbed up, scrutinised her for a few seconds and shortly issued an enthusiastic wave. Pequeñito was in safe hands.

Sauntering up through the paved precinct she passed an Irish pub and stopped at a tourist shop to glimpse a rack of child-sized polyester flamenco costumes. She raised an eyebrow when a label revealed that they were made in China. On the next corner she found the door to Marley's shop wide open and the front desk abandoned. With a grin she tiptoed around to the back room and seeing him engrossed at his desk shouted 'Freeze!' and pounced on him from behind. He lurched back in his chair and let out a cry.

'Jeez, Bel! You scared the living daylights out of me! What the heck are you doing here?'

'I've missed seeing you since giving up the badge.'

'Yeah, right,' he sniggered.

She placed a hand on his bald head. 'Been in a freezer?'

'Just popped next door to get some photocopying done. Lucky sods have got air conditioning.'

Isabel sank into a brown leather sofa opposite Marley's desk and put her feet up. 'So how are things, you old crook?'

He faced her with head cocked and arms tightly folded. She wondered what he was trying to hide.

'Best season for me. Pissed young Brits getting snakes and skulls tattooed on their arses every night. Couldn't ask for more. Mind you, I need the business. Nothing doing the rest of the year. Not enough flights, see, and Magaluf's changing.'

'Is that so?'

'All them politicians dolling the place up, innit? Won't be no place for the likes of me soon.'

'Sorry to hear that, Marley. So have you been busted recently?'

'You know I don't do drugs no more,' he replied tetchily. 'So what d'you want? I doubt you stopped by to check on my welfare.'

She flashed him an enigmatic smile. 'I wondered if you knew Marc Got.'

'Everyone does around here. Especially now his girlfriend's kid's gone missing.'

He narrowed his eyes. 'Why d'you want to know? You're not mixed up in all this, are you? Thought you'd done with the law.'

'Did you see him yesterday?'

'Don't play games, Bel. You know I did or you wouldn't be here. He popped by at about two to have a heart put on his leg. He's mad about that bird Jane.'

'Who else was here?'

'Just me. I can't afford no assistant no more. Sign of the times.'

'Come on, Marley. Marc Got was here for a drop.'

He eyed her coldly. 'I told you before, I'm not in that game no more.'

'Well, I know he didn't just pop by for a tattoo.'

'How's that?'

'Because at first he lied about seeing you at all, which is odd given that you're the only witness to his whereabouts at the time of Miranda's disappearance. Ergo, he was doing something here that he didn't want the police to know about.'

He sighed heavily and got up from his chair. 'Fancy a beer?'

She watched as the gaunt figure walked jerkily over to a fridge hugging the corner of the dimly lit room. His skeletal legs and arms were white and hairless. She found it interesting that he sported no visible tattoos himself, but perhaps that was because he'd coveted another sort of needle for most of his life. She saw a sudden flash of bright light as the fridge door opened and slammed shut. A moment later an ice-cold can was nuzzling her shoulder. She tore back the ring pull and took a sip. 'That's good.'

Marley gulped thirstily from his own can before wiping his mouth with the back of his hand. 'If I tell you what happened with Marc, where does that leave me?'

'Keeping your head down like a wise monkey.'

He tapped the can impatiently before leaning forward in his chair. 'OK. Marc arranged to come round here so as I could tattoo his leg and finish off a lizard on his left wrist.'

Isabel gave him an encouraging nod.

'Anyway, he asked if I'd mind one of Afrim Cana's boys making a delivery. You know that Albanian dude from Son Barassa.'

'You mean the dude who supplies half of Magaluf with coke.'

'I hope you didn't come here to lecture me.'

'And you agreed?'

'No skin off my nose.'

'So what happened?'

'Cana's guy came round when I was finishing off Marc's leg. He gave him a package – quite big.'

'Coke?'

'I guess. Marc did an exchange – passed him a wodge of cash. I went out to the front desk and left them to it, but then I heard them having a bit of a barney.'

'Why?'

'How should I know? Maybe Marc short-changed him.'

'Then what?'

'The Albanian guy mumbled something about Cana being angry and left. Marc didn't say nothing. We sat and had a beer and a smoke together.'

'How close are Cana and Got?'

He shrugged. 'Pretty cosy, I've heard.'

'Would you know if he's ever met Jane Walters and Miranda?'

He nodded. 'Yeah, down at Romeo's club this summer.'

'So how long did Got stay here?'

'Just before three o'clock he paid me and took off.'

She rose to leave. 'Thanks. You've been very helpful.'

'You don't reckon Marc's involved in the missing kid business, do you?'

She flinched. 'I hope not.'

Marley accompanied her to the front door.

'You know he's quite a family man at heart, old Marc. Bit of a rogue, I'll warrant, but he just doesn't seem the type.'

'That's the problem,' Isabel replied as she stepped onto the street. 'People rarely do.'

*

As soon as Isabel arrived back at Ca'n Moix she rang Tolo to update him on her meetings during the day. Recalling that Jane Walters had mentioned that the upper floor of her apartment block was under refurbishment, she wanted to know whether the area had been searched thoroughly. Tolo assured her that it had. Later, while listening to Chopin's Nocturnes, she read through the case notes he had given her about Miranda and created a wall chart in her office as a refuge for her future thoughts and findings. Satisfied with her efforts she went to bed and slept like a baby. She always did and always had. Even during those crazy days in Madrid when heading up kidnapping and murder investigations or high-profile drug busts in Barcelona, once her head touched the pillow, she would sleep. That was why at six each morning she'd jump out of bed with an excitable Furó at her heels and drive down to her local beach for an invigorating swim.

But there was little peace for Isabel that night. She awoke with a start wondering why her alarm clock was ringing when the sky outside was still an unremitting smudge of darkness. She threw out an arm and hit the raised button on her little tormentor, but something carried on trilling. Isabel switched on her bedside light, trying to divine the source of the din, until it dawned on her that it was coming from her mobile phone. She scooped it up grumpily and as she did so, glanced at the alarm clock.

'*Dígame?*'

'Bel. It's Llorenç.'

Isabel frowned. Why on earth was the mayor calling her at this time of night?

'Do you have any idea what time it is?'

'Three o'clock.'

'That's not funny.'

'Look, there's been a murder.'

She rubbed her eyes. 'Where?'

'Here in Sant Martí.'

She was suddenly wide awake.

'What?'

Llorenç sighed. 'I'm afraid old Angel Tulio Mas has been found murdered. His next-door neighbour called Pau at the local precinct to report his death following what appears to have been a violent break-in. Look, I'd like your take on things before the big guns turn up. You know Ca'n Mas, Angel's homestead on Camino Pomar?'

'Of course.'

'I've just got here with a bunch of local officers, and Capitán Gómez and your old chum Tolo Cabot should arrive within the hour.'

'Why involve both forces? Isn't this the Guardia's province?'

'With such a brutal murder I thought two heads were better than one and I don't rate Gómez. We've had many a run-in, as you know. Tolo Cabot is a man I respect.'

She swung her legs over the side of the bed and stood up. 'OK, I'm on my way. Old Mas, who would have thought it? So how did he die?'

'You don't want to know,' he replied crisply. 'On second thoughts, bring your wellies. It's a complete bloodbath down here.'

NINE

As Isabel turned into Camino Pomar she wondered whether she might have inadvertently driven onto the set of a second-rate murder mystery. The headlights of numerous police vehicles parked along the country lane bored into the darkness to reveal Guardia officers in green uniforms urgently issuing instructions to one another. Several were unwinding a band of white tape with the words *'GUARDIA CIVIL NO PASAR'* along one side of the road close to the victim's home. As Isabel approached Ca'n Mas in her little Fiat, she noticed two warrior-like Guardia officers brandishing assault rifles. She stuck her head out of the window.

'Either of you know where I'd find Llorenç Bestard?'

One of them smacked the bonnet. 'Well, if it isn't our Bel. Think this'll make a good rental property?'

'Only for murder mystery weekends,' she quipped. 'So Sebastià, what's the deal?'

He crouched down by the car. 'Someone carved up old Mas pretty badly.'

Another officer walked over. 'Wouldn't fancy being on the clean-up team.'

Isabel was used to the gallows humour of her former colleagues. It was a coping mechanism that she knew only too well. Llorenç appeared, his espadrilles crunching on the gravel and looking more than a little dishevelled. 'No time for chit-chat, Bel.'

She manoeuvred Pequeñito up onto a grass verge beyond the front gate and stepped out of the car. 'I'd better park here. Capitán Gómez would be livid if I contaminated any tyre treads on the drive.'

'A terrible business,' muttered Llorenç. 'In all my years as mayor of Sant Martí, I have never had to deal with such a tragedy.'

They trudged up the gravel path adjacent to the driveway, passing several blue-uniformed local police officers heading in the same direction.

'So our friend Capitán Gómez is on his way?' she asked.

'I had to inform him. He is, after all, the Guardia's local chief. Besides, he can't keep away from a good rural murder.'

'He won't be happy to see me here.'

'Of course not. It's strictly against police protocol, but what do I know? I'm just an ignorant rural mayor who happens to have a savvy former police detective living in his village. I'll just say you happened to be passing and offered to assist.'

She gave him a sideways glance. 'I need to have a quick look at the crime scene before he and forensics turn up.'

Llorenç beckoned her towards the house. 'Be careful not to touch anything – but of course I don't need to tell you that.'

Isabel pulled a sealed plastic bag from her pannier that contained a protective oversuit, surgical gloves and rubber boots. 'I came prepared.'

As they approached the porch, her eyes lingered on the sprawling farmhouse. Despite the patchy light thrown from the open doorway she could see that the property was built from slabs of sooty grey stone and lay between tall and leafy planes and a handful of aged olive trees. On one side, several shabby outhouses spilled onto a vast lawn. Isabel looked up, noting that many of the terracotta tiles around the chimneystacks were broken and in need of repair, but this was typical of a house in the rural areas. Only when a roof resembled a colander would a frugal Mallorcan finally cave in to pressure and barter with local tradesmen to make it good at the lowest conceivable price. The garden curved round to what Isabel imagined was a substantial piece of land, but it was swallowed up by darkness. To the right of the front porch was a double garage and on the other side a dry muddy patch that was evidently used for visitors' cars. She wandered over and squatting on her haunches examined the dark soil with a small torch.

'What are you looking for?' asked Llorenç.

Isabel got to her feet. 'There's some impacted soil here with heavy tyre treads. I'd wager a four-wheeled drive such as a Mitsubishi. What car did Mas own?'

'An old white pick-up of some kind. Let's check.'

Llorenç pulled open the doors to the garage and switched on the light. A scruffy white Toyota truck and a sleek black Mercedes stared back at them.

'Bit of a dark horse,' puffed Llorenç. 'Who would have thought the old rascal owned such a beauty?'

Isabel carefully scrutinised the tread of both vehicles. 'Well, they don't match the ones outside so let's see what forensics come up with.'

They walked back to the porch, where Isabel stopped to pull on her rubber boots before following Llorenç into the spacious hallway. Around them, armed Guardia officers busied themselves patrolling the corridors or spoke tensely into mobiles phones. The entrance to the study, the murder scene, was cordoned off with police tape. Without a thought, Isabel slipped on her overall and gloves and ducked under it. She turned to Llorenç on the other side. 'Where is the housekeeper?'

'Camila Cortez? An ambulance took her to Son Espases Hospital in Palma shortly before you arrived. Apparently, close to six o'clock she'd opened the front door to four hooded men, one of whom forced her into the kitchen at gunpoint and tied her up. She's elderly, so it must have been a terrible ordeal.'

'How did she break free?'

'Luckily Tomas Llull, the next-door neighbour, found her. He'd come round to the house at about two in the morning to complain about the blaring television in Angel Tulio Mas's study. When no one answered the door, he climbed over the back wall and discovered the French doors to the garden wide open and Mas dead on the floor. He rang Pau at the precinct and happened upon the housekeeper locked up in the kitchen below. She was lying on the floor still partially bound to a chair. It appeared to have toppled over while she was trying to break free.'

'Where's the neighbour now?'

'Being questioned outside by one of the Guardia detectives.'

'How did Señora Cortez cope with news of the old man's death?'

'Badly. As you'd expect she was exhausted, badly bruised and in severe shock.'

Isabel's face darkened. She momentarily thought of her own mother living alone in her rambling house with its doors and windows permanently open to any passing visitor.

'I think I've seen her at the church. Is she Colombian?'

'Yes. Old Angel was half Colombian and brought her over here a few years ago. She's never out of the church.'

Isabel walked to the doorway of the study, her eyes widening when she saw on the far wall the Spanish word for thief, *LADRON*, scrawled in massive red letters.

'Tell me that's not blood,' she said in hushed tones.

Llorenç averted his eyes. 'I'm afraid it must be, but we shall have to wait for forensics to confirm it. You'll find poor Angel lying on the floor by the desk.'

Her eyes flitted about the room. Had a bloody murder not taken place in its midst, it could have been described as a comfortable study. Solid white plaster bookshelves, hand finished in the old Mallorcan style, lined two sides of the room, tightly packed with elegant hardbacks that ran in orderly precision from ceiling to floor. A deep recess carved into one of the remaining walls was home to a pair of heavy mahogany bookcases, an elegant drinks cabinet and a small fridge. It was when her gaze briefly fell on the heavy oak desk that she saw the body. Nearby, a brown leather armchair and a dainty mahogany table had been overturned, while sheets of white paper lay artfully on the tiled floor forming the silhouette of a Spanish fan. Abandoned on the tiles an empty tumbler caught her eye, along with a classy gold and black fountain pen. The thought once again crossed her mind that this was all just some hammy and elaborate stage set for an amateur sleuth mystery, except, of course, this was no *pièce de théâtre*, and the slumped body would not be brushing itself down and taking a triumphant bow at final curtain call.

Blood had spattered along the white skirting board and travelled as far as the glass panes of a French door, forming dried crimson tears frozen against the awakening sky outside. Isabel covered her mouth with her hand and swallowed hard. The metallic, sickly stench of congealed human blood was all too familiar to her. She stifled her breath and crouched beside the crumpled figure lying face down on the tiles, frowning when she saw a frail, bloodied hand outstretched as if seeking a last-minute reprieve – a show of mercy, perhaps, or even entry to some inviolable magic portal? A viscous black liquid that had seeped from several puncture wounds in the grey shirt now oozed from under the belly like an alien creature, forming an abstract and craggy halo. It had evidently been a savage and frenzied attack. For a moment she studied the partially obscured inert and waxy face. She was unable to see the expression in the glassy eyes, but the mouth hung open as if it had perhaps uttered one last agonising scream before death silenced it forever. Isabel felt a sudden uncontrollable urge to gag but forced herself to absorb every detail of the scene before her.

She rose shakily and blinked hard before moving across to examine the tumbler abandoned on the tiles. Kneeling on the floor, she swivelled the heavy glass in her gloved hands, noting that a few drops of amber liquid clung to the bottom, most likely lager by the odour. She frowned and headed for a low rectangular glass table crammed with photographs and bijou *objets d'art*. Examining each image without touching the frames, she reminded herself that she shouldn't really be there at all. Still, one small picture captured her attention. Stealthily she checked that no one was observing her from the hallway and quickly slipped it into her pannier. On the top of the drinks cabinet she discovered another tumbler that also appeared to have contained lager, although a different brand, as the residue was darker and smelt richer. A sudden thought struck her. She made her way to the dinky designer fridge and with gloves firmly in place spent a few seconds examining the contents of bottles and cans of drink. With care she scrutinised the floor, bookcases and a wastepaper basket containing two spent bottles of beer – one, a Club Colombia, the other sporting a San Miguel label – and finally the French windows. They lay wide open and the semblance of an aromatic breeze wafted in from the dark, velvety garden. Llorenç appeared in the doorway and studied her sombrely.

'Any thoughts, Bel?'

'Looks like Mas had a drinking companion last night.'

'I asked the housekeeper about that. Apparently, they had no guests all day. We have to assume it was his killer.'

'But four assailants arrived at the house?'

Llorenç gave a helpless shrug. 'Maybe only one was thirsty.'

Isabel tapped a finger to her lips. 'It's odd that a murderer should sit having a cosy drink with his victim prior to committing the deed. Seems like Mas knew his killer.'

'Who can say?'

'He looks so pathetic and vulnerable,' she replied. 'I'm wondering what kind of a madman would inflict such injury on an old man.'

Llorenç rubbed his forehead. 'We haven't had a murder up here in years. The last time was when two drunken Spanish Civil War veterans had a brawl and one of them wound up dead. We're a close community. This kind of thing just doesn't happen here. It makes no sense.'

Isabel turned to him. 'Murder rarely does.'

She took refuge in the musty hallway. 'So what had old Mas done to deserve such punishment?'

'Why do you say that?'

'Look at the word on the wall: thief.'

'Are you saying this was a revenge attack? That old Angel had stolen something from the murderer?'

Isabel looked glum. 'Maybe. On the other hand, it could just be a red herring, but even at subliminal level it tells us something.'

'Does it?'

'Well, for one thing it's written in Castilian Spanish, not Mallorquí, so that could point to it not being a local.'

'Or to a local faking their origin?'

'Indeed. It's there to create diversion and fear, so we are inevitably dealing with a devious mind and an organised personality.'

'How so?'

'Look at the script. The physical attack was violent and yet whoever wrote that word did so with a steady, almost scholarly hand. Hardly the work of a crazed killer.'

'So what are you saying?'

'Just that this points to it being a premeditated murder, not a random break-in.'

Llorenç emitted a groan. 'I just pray that it wasn't one of our own citizens. It surely has to be an outsider.'

'Don't count on it. At any rate, the wounds inflicted seem very deep. That indicates real hatred, a savagery that only comes from unbridled passion. Would you know if he had any enemies?'

Llorenç shook his head. 'I can't imagine why. He was deeply religious and lived a quiet life here.'

'No sign of a murder weapon?'

He gave a grim nod of the head. 'Not yet.'

'I'd like to have a quick look around the house.'

Llorenç nodded. 'Be my guest, but make it snappy.'

'Would you know where the kitchen is?'

The mayor organised for a local police officer to escort her. She followed him down a narrow staircase to a large basement kitchen. Nothing seemed out of place. Isabel briefly studied items on the marble work surfaces and examined the contents of the fridge and bin. To the rear of the room, French doors opened onto an enclosed patio lined with large terracotta pots of flowers and herbs. She followed the officer around the house, nodding once she'd given a cursory glance to each room. When she returned to the hallway, Llorenç was waiting for her.

'It doesn't look like a robbery, does it?'

Isabel stepped into the study and took one last look at the inert body of the elderly man. 'The rest of the house certainly seems to be in order.'

She hung her head for a few moments, the impact of what she'd just witnessed suddenly hitting her. Excusing herself, she strode out onto the drive, ripping off her overall, gloves and boots and stuffing them into her pannier. Retching several times, she breathed in the cool early morning air, grateful for the overriding smell of thyme and rosemary. She wished she hadn't come. With longing, her eyes were drawn to Pequeñito sitting serenely beneath a carob tree. She wanted to go home where she felt safe, away from the smell of death and pain. But suddenly she was aware of someone calling and spun round to find Capitán Gómez of the Guardia grinning at her, his green uniform immaculate and his matching reptilian eyes bright despite the groggy hour.

'Lost the stomach for murder, Isabel? I'm not quite sure what you think you're doing here anyway. This crime scene is off limits to anyone but authorised personnel.'

She crossed her arms and offered him an innocent smile. 'I just happened to be passing.'

He offered a rasping laugh.

'Actually, I needed to have a word with Chief Inspector Cabot and was told he was here.'

'I doubt that, as this is a rural crime, so Guardia Civil jurisdiction. Tell me, do you normally seek him out at this godforsaken hour? You'll have the rumour mill going.'

'Well, he's a dab hand at blocked drains, and one of my holiday villas...'

He interrupted her. 'Always the joker. Tolo mentioned that you'd been seconded as an adviser to his investigation team – a highly irregular move – but I can't think for a moment why you assume that gives you automatic access here. This has nothing to do with the child abduction investigation in Pollença.'

Llorenç appeared at his side. 'Ah, my dear chap. I'm so relieved that you've arrived. Isabel was passing by after a late swim in the port, and seeing the police cars, thoughtfully stopped to offer assistance.'

'What luck! Even more miraculous is that her hair has remained perfectly dry despite a nocturnal baptism.'

He saluted and stalked off towards the house while Isabel exchanged a complicit wink with Llorenç. She was suddenly aware of a grim-faced, thickly set man wandering past them in what appeared to be a dressing gown and slippers. Llorenç nudged her.

'That's Tomas Llull, the neighbour who discovered Mas. He's probably going home to bed.'

'I doubt he'll get much sleep,' Isabel mused.

Moments later a blue saloon car drew to a halt at the mouth of the driveway and Tolo Cabot stepped out. He headed towards them, letting out a sigh when he saw Isabel.

'What are you doing here? This is Guardia territory. If Gómez sees you...'

'He already has, but it's OK,' snapped Llorenç. 'As mayor of Sant Martí I sought Bel's advice in the absence of senior police personnel.'

Isabel fixed Tolo with a cool stare. 'I'm not sure you're supposed to be here either.'

'Touché.' He turned to Llorenç. 'But I'm grateful you called me. My chief wants to make sure this murder has no connection with Miranda's disappearance.'

'How can it possibly be connected?' asked Isabel.

'Look, in the space of two days a child goes missing and an elderly man is murdered, both on the same side of the island. It's a long shot, but it's best to be sure.'

Isabel shrugged and gave him a sly smile. 'Well, good luck with Gómez.'

Tolo grimaced. 'I won't be long.'

She watched as he followed Llorenç into the house. No doubt the Guardia chief would be furious to see his nemesis. Neither force enjoyed warm relations locally.

She wandered slowly down the drive in time to witness a media circus developing on the narrow country road. A group of officers were frantically blowing whistles at TV and radio crews as they attempted to park their vehicles at the entrance to the property. Isabel wondered how the media had got wind of the crime so quickly. Someone must have tipped them off, either a police mole or member of the public. Par for the course. A few reporters were sneakily trying to gain access to the driveway on foot, but the Guardia team were having none of it. One furious officer was remonstrating loudly with a journalist who'd rolled up on a clapped-out vintage yellow motorbike. Waving his arms dramatically in the air, he pushed the man's shoulder and forced him to do a U-turn. The *moto*'s exhaust spluttered and popped as it reluctantly joined the convoy of rejected vehicles parking some distance from the house. Isabel raised an eyebrow when she recognised that it belonged to Josep Casanovas, editor of *El Periódico*. She made a mental note to call him.

Seemingly woken by the din, locals still in sleep attire were beginning to cluster about the driveway with fear-filled eyes, nudging each other as a new character took central stage. Isabel observed them carefully, deciding that at this early hour they must be nearby neighbours uprooted from their beds by the unnatural sound of sirens, traffic and urgent voices. There was a collective gasp when the stern-faced judge arrived along with a police court commissioner and a plain-clothed police officer led by an enthusiastic sniffer dog. She recognised the judge as Jorge Baltazar, an ambitious yet rational individual who had evidently been put officially in charge of the investigation. The military police might be charged with doing all the footwork, but it would be Baltazar who would sign warrants and make decisions on the case. Next came Nacho Blanco, *médico forense*. When he saw Isabel he stopped in his tracks and rushed over to embrace her.

'So the rumour is true, you are back on the force?'

She accompanied him to the entrance of the house. 'News travels fast. Actually, I'm only assisting with the child disappearance.'

'Then what are you doing here?'

'Just sticking my nose in where I shouldn't.'

'Have you seen the body?'

She nodded. 'My local mayor tipped me the wink.'

'I'd be interested to hear your thoughts.'

'I'll call you tomorrow.'

'That would be best. I imagine Capitán Gómez won't welcome your presence here.'

'That's an understatement.'

Nacho grinned and ambled towards the house with several *criminalistas* from the Guardia's forensics unit. Isabel was pleased to see Nacho again. With his gold ear stud and glossy mane of dark hair drawn back into a ponytail, he was a far cry from the intense and often inflexible forensic doctors she had worked with in the past. She yawned and rubbed her hands together because although it was the height of the summer, there was an icy chill in the air. As she was debating whether to wait for Tolo or to return home, she heard crisp footsteps approaching across the gravel and turned to see Capitán Gómez glaring in her direction.

'I suggest you head off, Isabel, as you are continuing to trespass on a Guardia-controlled crime scene. I'll tell lover boy that you left.'

Before she could issue a retort, Tolo appeared in the emblazoned doorway and, slowly pulling a leather case from his pocket, lit himself a slim cigar. He smiled sardonically. 'We're on our way, Gómez. Do send my regards to Maria.'

When they were some distance from the house, Isabel turned to him.

'I thought Paula was the name of Gómez's wife?'

Tolo flicked some ash onto the dry muddy track and ground it underfoot. 'It is.'

'Then who is Maria?'

'His mistress,' he replied.

TEN

As Isabel walked into her sun-scorched office she was surprised to find Pep, in an unguarded moment, kneeling on the floor, stroking the back of Furó's head. He scrambled to his feet.

'He was whining.'

She gave a knowing smile. 'Of course, Pep.'

His face darkened. 'Have you heard the terrible news?'

Isabel picked up a pile of unopened mail and began rifling through it. 'About what?'

'Angel Tulio Mas! Jesus at Bon Día told me he was stabbed to death in his own home last night. I didn't know him but saw him around the village occasionally. He said it was a robbery and that there were four suspects.'

'I'd say considerably fewer, myself.'

He grunted in disappointment. 'So you already know about it? Did Rafael tell you?'

'Actually, I haven't had time to pop by Bar Castell this morning, which is why you are going to buy me a *cortado* and croissant after you've dropped off this photo at the chemist.'

She delved in her pannier and yanked out the small gilt frame that she had secreted from the home of the murder victim.

Unpinning the back, she released the image and passed it to him.

'When you get there ask Beatriz to have this enlarged as quickly as she can and with as much detail as possible.'

'Who are these men?'

She shrugged. 'I think it's Angel Tulio Mas taken many years ago. I don't know about the others.'

He hesitated at the door. 'Where did you get this?'

Isabel offered him a pert smile. 'From the study of Ca'n Mas. And before you ask, your future father-in-law rang me in the middle of the night requesting my presence over there. That picture caught my eye.'

'So you just nicked it?'

'I have every intention of returning it. By the way, don't breathe a word of any of this to my mother.'

Pep pulled a face. 'So did you see the body?'

'Don't be so ghoulish. Now get going.'

With a frustrated shake of the head, he sloped off down the stairs while Furó dutifully followed Isabel into her office. Pep had left a neat pile of daily newspapers on her desk, but the lead story in *El Periódico*, written by her old chum Josep Casanovas, caught her immediate attention. It referred to Francesc and Felip Torrens, the fishermen brothers she'd seen two nights previously in Port Soller. The report detailed how they'd been found badly beaten, one at their home, the other in a secluded part of the Tramuntanas. Both were undergoing emergency treatment at Son Espases Hospital. She rang Josep and was greeted like an old friend.

'What a coincidence. I was up your way early this morning at the crime scene of that poor old guy, Angel Tulio Mas. Looked like a robbery gone wrong – as usual, the Guardia's giving little away. What's your take?'

'I'm not sure what to think just yet,' she replied.

'You knew him?'

'I saw him in church occasionally.'

'Yeah, I heard he was religious. Lucky his elderly housekeeper survived. Apparently, she'll be allowed home from Son Espases tomorrow.'

Isabel tried to contain her impatience. 'Actually, Josep, I'm interested in a lead you wrote about the Torrens brothers.'

With a confidential tone, he told her all he knew of the case.

'So, to conclude, the Guardia thinks it could be drug related as the attack's got all the hallmarks of Afrim Cana's gang about it. Still, we'll have to wait for the brothers to recover before we can find out what really happened. So, why the interest?'

'Just idle curiosity. Look, are you up for a beer some time?'

'For you, always. How about Monday evening?'

'Perfect. I'll swing by your office.'

He hesitated. 'Actually, I fancy coming over to Soller. Let's meet at Café Paris.'

Isabel replaced the receiver and, scooping up a handful of sunflower seeds from a colourful bowl, crossed the room and perched on the window ledge. Her hens were pecking away at the dry soil while Carlos the cockerel strutted about, crowing manfully. She crunched on a seed and reflected on her conversation with Josep. Felip Torrens had been discovered unconscious in woodland near the Cuber Reservoir while his younger brother, Francesc, had been found trussed up in a hessian sack at the brothers' home in Morells village. Why had they been in different locations, and if Afrim Cana's boys had assaulted them, what had been the motive? There was only one way to find out. She dialled Aina's number again and was surprised when the girl answered.

'Hi, Bel, I've been meaning to return your call, but things have been a bit difficult the past few days. My boyfriend Felip and his brother...'

'I know what happened, Aina. We need to talk.'

There was a snuffle. 'Bel, I haven't done anything wrong. You must believe me.'

'I do, but it's urgent we meet.'

'I'm working with my mother at the bakery this afternoon.'

'I'll pop by.'

After the call, Isabel jotted down some thoughts in the little notebook that she kept with her at all times and turned to Furó. 'Life's getting complicated, isn't it, old boy? Too many threads and yet…'

She was startled by the telephone's high-pitched ring. It was Nacho, calling from the Institute of Forensics.

He sounded tired. 'I hear you're going to be joining the Mas investigation team?'

'Whoever gave you that impression?'

'This morning, Tolo told me that you'd been seconded to work on both the Angel Mas and Miranda Walters cases.'

'That's news to me.'

He gave a cynical grunt. 'So what did you make of the crime scene?'

'There was little evidence of a struggle. The killer made a lazy attempt to knock over furniture, but I'd guess the old man was drugged before death and wasn't able to put up much of a fight.'

'My thoughts entirely. At this stage I'd estimate death occurred between six and seven o'clock. It looks as if the victim fell on his front and was stabbed repeatedly in the back with a sharp knife with a blade of approximately twenty-five centimetres, before one final thrust in the heart finished him off. Be helpful if the murder weapon is found.'

'That's highly unlikely. And it was Mas's blood on the wall?'

'Correct. Most likely daubed with a gloved finger.'

'Neat work.'

'Yes, I noticed that too. The killer took time over it. Evidently a cool customer.'

'What about the two tumblers?'

'Both contained lager, most likely from the two bottles found in the wastepaper basket. We're waiting for fingerprint and content analysis.'

'So did Mas share a drink with his killer or were they just placed there as a tease?'

'We'll find out soon enough. Hopefully Monday at the latest.'

He hesitated. 'The victim certainly appeared to have been drinking beer shortly before he died. It had spilt on his shirt and chest – the odour was unmistakeable. We'll be analysing the stomach contents later. I'll be back in touch tomorrow.'

Pep burst into the office with a *cortado* and a large croissant wrapped in a paper napkin that he placed triumphantly in front of Isabel. 'By the way, I nearly forgot. Have you read the front-page story in *El Periódico* about the Torrens brothers? '

'I most certainly have, Pep.'

'So you were right. They were up to something on Monday night!'

'Actually, it was in the early hours of Tuesday, to be exact. I've just arranged to meet Aina this afternoon.'

'So why do you want to see her?'

'To find out what they were doing out at sea. I think they may have stolen something that didn't belong to them.'

'Like what?'

'You'll recall that I saw them packing two dry tube bags into their car in the port on Monday night.'

Pep gave an urgent nod.

Isabel took a bite of her croissant. 'I think the bags contained drugs. A lot of contraband is still hidden in obscure sea caves off the coast.'

She took a sip of her coffee and nibbled absentmindedly on her croissant.

'While you popped out I had a brief chat with Josep Casanovas at *El Periódico*. He thinks that the drug dealer Afrim Cana might have been involved in the assault on the Torrens brothers on Wednesday night.'

'And you told me that on Tuesday afternoon Marc Got, Mrs Walters' boyfriend, was seen arguing with one of Cana's stooges at Marley's tattoo parlour?'

'I'm impressed, Pep. You do listen. I'll make a detective of you yet.'

He shrugged unhappily. 'So you think the cases are connected?'

Isabel jumped up and rapped on her wall chart. 'This is what I call my "join the dots" diagram.'

Pep studied the two large circles respectively labelled Tuesday and Wednesday and pushed out his bottom lip. In each one Isabel's neat hand had created bullet points with timings and each floating circle on the shiny white surface was connected by a dotted line.

Isabel addressed him. 'On Tuesday, just before four o'clock in the morning, I saw Aina and the Torrens brothers acting suspiciously in the port, while later the same day at two o'clock in the afternoon Miranda disappeared from Pollença beach. Meanwhile, Marc Got, her mother's boyfriend, visited Marley's tattoo parlour between two and three o'clock, giving him a firm alibi, but was seen by Marley having a tiff with one of Afrim Cana's drug couriers.' She pointed to another circle. 'Then on Wednesday between six and seven in the evening Mas was murdered and the Torrens brothers were attacked later that night, possibly by Afrim Cana's thugs, according to Josep Casanovas.'

'But none of it makes any sense.'

'Not yet, Pep.'

He pointed to a series of handwritten sentences on the other side of the board. 'What are those?'

'Unanswered questions. For example, on Wednesday, Maria, the waitress at Café del Mar in Pollença, told me that Miranda had a little bucket with her which she filled three times. On the third occasion, she appears to have dumped the bucket on her way to the shoreline. Why?'

'Maybe it was too hot and she got bored with the idea.'

'In which case why not return to the restaurant where her mother was waiting? And why bring her Barbie rucksack along to the restaurant?'

'Little girls like to carry bags.'

'But the waitress didn't think she'd seen it with her before. In Miranda's bedroom, Pinky, her favourite little toy rabbit, was missing. Where is he?'

Pep scratched his head. 'Heaven knows, Bel. Maybe he's stuck under her mattress or in a drawer.'

'Or maybe she decided to take him with her that day.'

'Meaning what?'

'That perhaps she had agreed a rendezvous with her abductor and had taken her favourite belongings with her, knowing she would not be returning.'

'That's ridiculous!'

'Is it?'

'But why would she willingly walk off with an abductor?'

'I don't know, Pep, but it seems to me that she may have deliberately waited for Mrs Walters to pay the bill before ditching her bucket. I think it was an agreed sign. That is why on the final journey to the water's edge she took her rucksack and belongings with her.'

Pep studied her face intently. 'Did she bring anything else to the restaurant?'

'She was wearing a Mickey Mouse watch and had placed her wet swimsuit on a chair. It was no longer there when the waitress cleared the table.'

'So you think Miranda agreed a time with her abductor?'

'Or abductors. So, you see, it's really a question of joining the dots. An enormous puzzle that we need to solve as quickly as possible.'

'Do you think Miranda was duped by a paedophile ring?'

'No, but I think she was duped, nonetheless. Why else would she abandon her mother?'

For a few minutes they both sat in deep thought, until Isabel broke the silence. 'I've also been having some thoughts about Aina and the Torrens brothers. Do you think your father would lend us his boat tomorrow night?'

Pep eyed her suspiciously. 'Why?'

'I'd like to retrace Aina's boat trip with her and I'd like you to join us too.'

'I'm not sure that's a good idea. You know I get seasick.'

Isabel smiled. 'You'll be fine, Pep. I'm a good captain and the forecast for tomorrow is excellent. It will be calm seas.'

Pep shot her a concerned glance. 'But they might have gone miles out to sea.'

'In that old tug? I doubt it. They'll have stayed close to the coastline.'

'OK, I'll call my father. But what do you hope to find?'

'I'll know that when I find it, Watson.'

He offered her a blank stare.

'And before you ask, go and look it up. Watson, that is.'

Some time later Pep answered a call and came bounding into her office. 'It's your chief inspector on the line.'

'I don't own him, Pep.' She grabbed the phone. 'What news?'

'I'm OK, thanks. Glad you asked,' replied Tolo.

She smiled into the receiver. 'So, Nacho Blanco tells me I'm now working across two cases. Want me to do your job too?'

'Apologies. He caught me just as I was leaving an emergency meeting at the regional government earlier this morning. The president wants our force and the Guardia to put all differences aside and to work closely on the Miranda and Mas cases. My team will be taking the lead on both investigations, with backup from the Guardia.'

'That must make Capitán Gómez happy.'

'Ecstatic. Naturally, he's not in the best mood, though fortunately he's busy with some case involving two fishermen brothers.'

'I know them.'

'Why am I not surprised? Anyway, I hope you're OK to offer us some additional time? Your local knowledge with the Mas case could prove invaluable and the mayor and local officers trust you.'

'Flattery will get you into hot water, Tolo.'

'My chief thinks that Miranda's abduction and Mas's murder could be related somehow.'

Isabel gave a sniff. 'And you?'

'I'm not at all convinced, but I like to keep an open mind.'

'So how did your meeting go with the big guns from Madrid?' she asked.

'As well as can be expected, and Lola Rubio was particularly impressive. She's a quick thinker and on the ball. We'll be working closely on developments regarding Miranda Walters.'

'And what about your existing case load?'

'Gaspar Fernández will keep on top of things back at base while I oversee my various teams and liaise with Madrid. You will have a free rein to concentrate on both cases. Naturally, my team will be at your disposal and they'll keep you in the loop on any new intel. Same with forensics.'

'I'd appreciate that.'

'Our regional government reiterated how critical it is that we find Miranda as soon as possible, as well as the killer of Mas. The president urged me to pull out all the stops.'

'As if you wouldn't.'

Tolo gave a hollow laugh. 'Politicians are all the same. It's about damage limitation. You know the game.'

Isabel sighed into the receiver. 'I need to update you on a few developments. Can we meet?'

'Unfortunately, I have to fly to Madrid later for another briefing with Lola Rubio and her team at the Ministry of Interior and won't be back until Saturday. Is it urgent or can it wait?'

'Saturday would be fine,' she replied.

'In that case, how about we catch up over supper that night?'
Isabel paused.

'Unless you've got plans?'

'Not at all. Come round to the house and I'll cook something.'

Tolo smiled to himself. Isabel's cooking was legendary. Never had an invitation sounded so good.

*

Isabel and Pep strolled along the narrow aisles in Bon Día, the only grocery store in Sant Martí. It was noon and shoppers milled about the tightly packed shelves while a queue of disgruntled holidaymakers had formed by the counter where Jesus, the tubby owner in crumpled tee shirt, shorts and flip-flops, mopped his brow and deliberated over every item that passed before him. The air conditioning had packed up and he was in a sullen mood, barking at the tourists in badly spoken English. His teenage daughter, Lourdes, stood by the till packing items into plastic carrier bags, a beatific smile planted on her lips. Isabel pondered the shelves before throwing a handful of Chupa Chup lollies into the basket along with several packets of sunflower seeds.

Pep remonstrated. 'This is ridiculous. You've already eaten two Chupa Chups today. Your teeth will fall out and then you'll need to spend a fortune on implants. I was reading in a magazine that they cost...'

He stopped mid sentence when a couple appeared next to them and began piling sweets and chocolate into one of the store's decrepit metal baskets. Reaching up to one of the higher shelves with a pale lean arm, the woman grasped a packet of chocolate biscuits and studied the label while her unkempt and bearded companion yawned at her side. Pep nudged Isabel before stepping forward.

'Mr and Mrs Fox, I'm happy to see you again. May I present my boss Isabel Flores Montserrat, owner of Home Sweet Home!'

Isabel flashed them a smile. 'I'm sorry I wasn't able to welcome you personally the other day, but I do hope you are both enjoying your stay with us.'

'I'm Sarah, by the way, and this is my husband, William,' the woman replied in soft French tones. 'Everything's perfect and the house is ideal for my husband's writing.'

Isabel briefly inspected Mr Fox. The eyes were lost behind mirrored shades. 'Are you an author?'

'You could say that.'

'What kind of book are you working on, if you don't mind me asking?'

'Another bestseller, I hope,' he replied in a thin, reedy voice. She couldn't trace the accent.

'I wish you luck. I am an avid reader, Mr Fox. Do you write fiction?'

He paused for a second. 'Crime. This'll be my sixth novel.'

'How exciting. What is your most recent title?'

'Last Chance.'

'And what about the name of the new one?'

He hesitated. 'Now that would be telling.'

She smiled. 'Well, I will certainly look out for your novels.'

Irritably, he pushed a lock of dull brown hair away from his eyes, pinioning it under the brim of a tatty panama. 'I really wouldn't bother. They're a bit violent, you know, sort of gritty. Not a girl's kind of book.'

'What a shame,' she replied and fixing her gaze on their basket added, 'I see you both have a sweet tooth like me.'

The woman thrust a delicate hand through her cropped brown hair, a pretty silver bracelet tinkling at her wrist. 'Yes, indeed. We all have our little vices.'

'By the way, I saw your beautiful yacht in the port the other night. *Monique La Magnifique* is a wonderful moniker.'

The woman smiled. 'It's named after my mother. William and I love sailing.'

'Then we have another thing in common. So do I.'

Isabel watched as they disappeared down the aisle, a smile playing on her lips.

'He's a bit grumpy, isn't he?' whispered Pep.

When Isabel failed to respond, he issued an impatient sigh. 'What's so funny?'

'Oh, just people. There's something odd about that pair.'

'In what way?'

She patted his arm. 'I'm not entirely sure, but I intend to find out.'

Pep groaned. 'Oh, not again. You know some things, Bel, are really best left well alone.'

ELEVEN

After a late lunch, gorging herself on a bowl of Florentina's gazpacho and a plate of plump globe artichokes, Isabel washed her face under the kitchen tap and headed up to the office. Pep was in a fractious mood, unhappy that on Angélica's orders he'd just quit smoking and that the air conditioning unit had packed up. Uncle Idò had promised to fix it, but was yet to pop by. In her office, Isabel threw her car keys and mobile phone into her pannier and was about to head out when Pep put a call through to her. It was Marley.

'I've just got sniff of something interesting.'

Isabel gave an impatient cough. 'What might that be?'

'I've heard on the grapevine that Afrim Cana was expecting a shipment of cocaine on Tuesday, but when his guys got there, they found part of it missing.'

'Where was the drop?'

'Don't be daft, Bel. Even my best informants don't have that kind of intel. All I know is that it was dumped somewhere off the coast on Monday night, meaning that some chancer must have stolen part of it before Cana's boys got there. He'll be swimming with the fishes if they find him.'

'Or *her*, of course.'

'Nah, doubt it was a woman. Have to be some sailor to navigate the sea caves off that part of the coast.'

Isabel issued an exasperated tut. After all, she had been negotiating the island's querulous waters by boat ever since her late teens.

'One more thing. Marc Got popped by last night and told me that he and Cana had gone into business together. He seemed pretty chuffed about it.'

'Thank you, Marley. That's very helpful.'

'You owe me, Bel.'

Pep looked up as she headed for the door with Furó.

'By the way, my father says the boat's all ours tomorrow night.'

'Excellent,' she replied and hurtled out of the house, offering a friendly salute en route to her neighbour Doctor Ramis, who was pruning a lavender bush in his front garden. Isabel walked purposefully towards Pequeñito, parked in a shady side street, and ushered Furó into the passenger seat. Moments later, she looked up to see Marga running in ungainly fashion in flip-flops towards the car.

'Bel! Wait! Are you heading into Soller?'

'I'm going to Morells, but I can drop you off on the way.'

'You're a saint! We're completely out of fresh towels in the salon, so I need to pick up a batch at the laundry. I can get the bus back.'

'Hop in.'

'I tell you, standing up all day in this heat is murder.'

Although a woman of robust build, Marga was voluptuous and alluring, with her henna bob, full lips and fig-brown eyes. Isabel peered down at her friend's swollen ankles and winced.

'When you get home tonight, dunk your feet in a bucket of iced water, pour yourself a glass of *tinto* and watch a good film.'

'In my dreams!' she scoffed as she shooed Furó into the back seat.

En route, Marga turned to her. 'Are you popping by the bakery in Morells?'

Isabel nodded.

'In that case, can you get me a cream *ensaïmada*? Tomeu's mum is round tonight and it'll be an easy dessert.'

'As it happens, I'm buying one for mama too.'

'And I'd like extra icing sugar on top.'

Isabel winked at her. 'The calorie-free version, then?'

'Talking of calories,' she replied. 'When is the next council meeting about the Nit de Foc? Pep told me he was going to suggest serving canapés at our own village event.'

Isabel shot her a pained expression. 'It's next Monday, but I've warned him that his culinary suggestions won't go down well.'

'Poor Pep! He'll never win against the retrogrades of Sant Martí. Mind you, I'm a true Mallorquina. Give me *sobrassada* sausage over fancy canapés any day.'

As they coursed along the mountain roads, Marga suddenly prodded Isabel's arm. 'Your mother tells me that something's going on between you and this Tolo Cabot. Is that true?'

Isabel shot her a warning glance. 'Why does my mother have to read romance into everything? Do you think either Tolo or I have a second to even think of such nonsense?'

Marga pushed out her lower lip. 'Well, he seems quite keen on you by all accounts. I know he's a bit old, but isn't he single?'

Isabel fixed her eyes on the winding road ahead and indicated when she saw the sign for Soller. 'He's forty-six, hardly old.'

'Well, then, what's holding you back?'

'The poor man's a widower with a busy job. Apparently, when Blanca died Fabio was only ten years old, and so he devoted himself to his son's upbringing and his work.'

'Isn't the boy at university in Madrid now? He's hardly a babe in arms.'

'That's not the point. The last thing Tolo needs is another woman in his life.'

'Why ever not?'

'Because he's a workaholic. He's happy with his life as it is.' She paused. 'Just like me.'

'And what about that handsome editor at *El Periódico* who was always sweet on you?'

'Josep Casanovas? Don't be ridiculous!'

Isabel roared into Soller and turned into Carrer d'Isabel II, cursing when a hire car did an elaborate manoeuvre in front of her.

Marga rattled on. 'I read that Casanovas is standing for mayor of Forn de Camp and that he's inherited a lot of wealth too. He'd be a good catch.'

Isabel gave a sigh. 'Look, can you just stop matchmaking? The only thing on my mind at present is finding Miranda alive and apprehending the killer of Angel Tulio Mas.'

'Why not leave it all to the police?' Marga protested.

'Because Tolo needs my help. We urgently need to find Miranda, and as for Mas, I think everyone in Sant Martí would sleep better knowing that his killer was caught.'

She parked up in front of Lavanderia Sa Llimoneta. Inside the brightly lit interior, Rachel, the owner, looked up from the counter and recognising the car gave a cheerful wave.

Marga stepped onto the cobblestone pavement and cocked her head at Isabel. 'This morning *El Periódico* suggested that Mas was killed by a gang of violent robbers, possibly foreign?'

Isabel revved the engine. 'Don't believe everything you read, especially the imaginative prose of Josep Casanovas. Who knows, maybe an old enemy caught up with Mas. Perhaps he even deserved to die.'

Marga looked visibly shocked. 'No one deserves to die, Bel.'

Isabel shrugged. 'Sometimes I'm not so sure.'

With a wave, she zoomed off up the street.

Some twenty minutes later she arrived in the quaint and tranquil honey-hued village of Morells. Isabel patted Pequeñito's scorching bonnet and strode across the quiet square towards a modest shop squeezed between two larger terraced properties, one serving as a Tabac and the other the local *ferretería*, the ironmonger's. Halfway across the *plaça*, she paused at the bubbling fountain for a gulp of water and to collect her thoughts. She was fond of Aina, a bright girl who had scored the highest grades in science for her year group and had more recently impressed the island's university with her zeal for palaeontology. It would be unfortunate if the talented student had got herself into a spot of serious trouble.

Their families had long-standing ties. Isabel's mother, Florentina, belonged to the same needlework group as Juana Ripoll, Aina's mother, and together with other elderly volunteers in the valley, made children's costumes for the annual Moros i Cristiàs fiesta in Soller. Isabel often popped by the bakery in Morells to buy one of Juana Ripoll's famed family-size *ensaïmadas*, the snail-shaped pastries that gave a passing nod to the island's Moorish heritage.

Swinging open the door, Isabel nodded to Aina behind the counter. '*Hombre*! How do you put up with the heat in here? It's like an Arab bath.'

Aina pulled a face and wiped her hands on her white overall. 'I'm just helping out because I don't have any lectures today. Poor mama is stuck in the oven room, which is far worse.'

She yelled through to the back of the shop. 'Bel's here. Can I pop out for a few minutes?'

A petite woman with wiry grey hair and dark, gentle eyes bustled out from behind a pair of striped cotton curtains, beads of sweat clinging to her forehead.

'Good to see you, Bel. Take your time.'

Aina followed Isabel and an exuberant Furó to the local *torrente*, the river, that in the summer heat had been reduced to a sluggish trickle. It was siesta time and nothing stirred save the cicadas and flittering hummingbirds. Taking a seat together on a wooden bench flanked by plane trees, they watched as Furó disappeared hastily into nearby reeds.

Aina drew a fan from her handbag and whisked it impatiently through the air. 'Even here in the shade, it's scorching.'

Isabel turned to her. 'I heard what happened to Felip and his brother Francesc. Do you know who could possibly have wanted to harm them?'

Aina agitatedly flicked her fan. 'I've no idea. They don't have any enemies.'

'Were they doing drugs?'

'Why do you ask?'

Isabel frowned. 'When the Guardia found Felip near the Cuber Reservoir, they discovered traces of cocaine on him.'

'Who told you that?'

Isabel touched the girl's hand. 'I have contacts from my time in the police force. If you know something, Aina, you must tell the truth.'

'What do the police know?'

Isabel decided to test her theory. 'Well, they reckon that Felip and Francesc might have come across a consignment of cocaine smuggled onto the island, and helped themselves to part of it. Perhaps it was hidden in a sea cave...'

Aina instinctively tapped the fan against her lips, leaving Isabel in no doubt that her hunch had paid off.

'The police also think that the gang expecting the delivery wasn't too happy and came after them. They wonder how Felip and Francesc were found out.'

Aina sat in miserable silence while Isabel observed her.

'Of course, the boys might have tried to find a buyer for the drugs and attracted some unwelcome attention.'

Aina unconsciously bit her lip.

'The prison sentences here are pretty hefty for narcotic offences and, of course, anyone associated with an offender can wind up in jail.'

'How?' she squeaked, suddenly fixing Isabel with startled eyes.

'Withholding information, being an accessory to a crime. You know how it works.'

'It's true,' Aina blurted out. 'Felip and Francesc stole the drugs and tried to sell them.'

Isabel nodded encouragingly.

'And where did they find them?'

'Last Monday night when we were hanging out at the Devil's Horn Caves.'

'Up the north-west coast? Aren't they out of bounds to the public?'

'Yes. The caves are of archaeological interest. We were stupid to have gone. It was Felip's idea.'

'Why there?'

'No reason, just a sort of dare.'

'Had you been there before?'

Aina's baleful eyes sought out a clump of pale lemons, now past their best, hanging from a tree to her left. 'No.'

'So what happened?'

She hesitated. 'We sailed up in their dad's trawler, anchored and hung out on deck drinking a few beers and listening to music. Then Felip and Francesc went exploring while I stayed on board.'

'Didn't you want to go too?'

She shook her head. 'I didn't fancy taking a dive that late.'

'Then what?'

'They swam back to the boat and told me they'd come across a pile of wooden boxes full of bibles.'

'Bibles?'

The girl pushed her long dark hair back behind her ears and gave a nervous laugh.

'At first they thought some crazy religious nuts had left them in the caves, but when they opened one, they found a hollow containing a packet of cocaine.'

'Where exactly did they find this haul?'

'Quite deep in the caves.'

'Did they give you the exact location?'

'They described it to me.'

'So they decided to steal the cocaine?'

She shrugged. 'Well, finders keepers and all that. They took back some dry tube bags from the boat and loaded them up with as much stuff as they could carry.' She paused for a second. 'To be honest, I'd never seen cocaine before.'

Isabel gave her a doubtful smile. 'What happened next?'

'Felip stowed the bags away below deck and we all changed into dry clothes.'

'How did yours get wet?'

'Sorry. I meant only Felip and his brother. I told them I didn't want anything to do with it, so once we got back to the port, they just dropped me off at my house. I don't know what they did with the drugs, but Felip bragged about going to Son Barassa to find a buyer.'

Isabel shook her head. 'Silly boy. He'd have been way out of his depth. Did he mention any name?'

'Not that I remember.'

'And when did you last see them?'

'I haven't seen either of them. I've ignored Felip's phone calls and have stayed late at the university library every night. But on Wednesday morning I decided to have it out with him and to end our relationship once and for all.'

'So what did you do?'

'I went round to their house. It was raining hard and as I couldn't get an answer I tried the back door. That's when I saw through the living room window a closed sack lying on the floor and realised that someone was inside.'

'So what did you do?'

'I smashed one of the windows with a rock, untied the sack and found Francesc inside.' She paused, her eyes welling with tears. 'I untied him and got him some water before calling the emergency services.'

'And what about Felip?'

'As you know, they found him unconscious near the Cuber Reservoir.'

Isabel got to her feet.

'Come on, you'd better get back to your mother.'

'You won't say anything, will you?'

Isabel sighed. 'You are a vital witness, Aina. I'm afraid you can't wash your hands of all this.'

'But I've told you everything I know!' she remonstrated. For the second time in their conversation Isabel noticed Aina's eyes flickering to the left. Not conclusive proof that she was fibbing but at least a good indication of fabrication.

'All the same, what you do know is critically important and could even put you at risk from the people who hurt Felip and Francesc. It's against the law to withhold information.'

Furó suddenly came crashing out of the undergrowth, causing both of them to start. He padded around the bench making impatient snuffling sounds until they got to their feet and headed back along the path to the village.

As they neared the bakery, Aina began sobbing. 'So what should I do now?'

'Come clean with your parents. You owe them that much.'

She dried her eyes on the sleeve of her overall. 'What happens now?'

'I'll speak with some contacts and get back to you. You'll be needed for more questioning and you'll have to tell the truth.'

'The Guardia interviewed me when I found Francesc and now they want to interview me again tomorrow,' she replied tremulously.

Isabel contemplated the blue sky and watched as a swallow flitted across the trees, closely followed by another. Perhaps they'd be allowing themselves a brief pit stop in S'Albufera wetlands before continuing their long migratory journey south.

She turned to Aina. 'It would be helpful if you pretended to be ill tomorrow. Get your mother to put off the Guardia. Don't go into the university.'

Aina bit her lip. 'OK, but won't I get into trouble?'

'No more than you are already,' Isabel replied.

Once inside the warm premises, Aina dutifully parcelled up a family-size cream *ensaïmada* sprinkled with a thick layer of icing sugar for Marga and in a separate box, one for Florentina. Isabel handed over some notes and shoved the change into her pannier, giving Aina a peck on both cheeks. At the door she hesitated. 'By the way, I need you to keep tomorrow night free.'

Aina looked up expectantly. 'Why?'

'Because you and I are going on a moonlit boat ride.'

*

Uncle Idò stood in the doorway of Bar Castell with his nose tilted, sniffing the air like a wary fox. He watched Rafael bustling about the tables with an overladen tray of glasses, and wondered where the devil his niece was. Crossing the room accompanied by Perro, his quivering *ca rater*, he cocked his head towards some elderly stragglers playing cards and greeted them with a gruff *'Uep'*.

'We're honoured,' said Rafael with mock gravity as he spun round to face Idò. 'Your old chum Jordi finally thrown you out?'

A few of the old faithfuls sniggered and bent to pat his small black dog. Idò gave a grunt and flapped a leathery hand in the air.

'I'd be up here more often, my old *amic*, if you didn't have all those damned stairs.'

'A likely story,' grumbled Rafael. 'Anyway, if you're looking for Bel, you'll find her taking the air with her young trainee.'

Idò shuffled over to the terrace and glimpsing Pep's beetle-black locks gave them a sharp tug from behind.

Pep spun round. '*Hombre*! What was that for?'

Idò chuckled and took a seat next to Isabel, smiling when she leant over to give him a peck on the cheek. Perro disappeared under the table.

'So, uncle, how's your day been?'

'Could have been worse.' He stared across at Pep. 'By the way, I popped by Ca'n Mayol on Tuesday morning to top up the pool. Didn't think much of that Englishman we've got renting it.'

Pep tutted. 'Señor Fox? I told you he didn't want to be disturbed.'

'Hold your horses, young man,' Idò replied, dabbing at his craggy face with a crumpled handkerchief. 'With this heat, I've got to keep an eye on all the pools. He'd be the first to complain if the water turned green. The wife was friendly enough, but he just barged past me, got in his car and drove off.'

'You'd have been more useful fixing our air con in the office,' Pep goaded.

'Pah! Air con is a waste of good money.'

Pep frowned. 'So are you going to sort it out or not?'

'All in good time. *Poc a poc.*'

Isabel grinned. *Poc a poc* – little by little – was one of her favourite Mallorcan platitudes. She took a sip of her cava and beckoned to Rafael. 'Bring him a glass of red, will you?'

Rafael winked and plodded off towards the bar.

She turned to her uncle. 'You were right to check on the pool, Idò, but let's just give them some space. Actually, with all that's going on, they're the least of our problems.'

Idò gave a solemn nod. 'You're talking about the murder of poor old Mas? Strange business.'

'That's what I wanted to see you about,' she replied.

He leant back in his chair and gave a grunt. 'Always an ulterior motive! No such thing as a free drink in my family.'

On cue, Rafael arrived with a glass of *vino tinto* and the customary bowl of olives and toasted almonds. Isabel yawned heavily and rubbed her eyes.

'Want a kip?' quipped Idò.

'I was over at Ca'n Mas with Llorenç in the early hours. It's been a long day.'

He took a sip of wine. 'So I heard. I thought you'd given up all that police stuff?'

'I'm just helping out my old friend Tolo. I'd rather keep my involvement quiet.'

Idò issued a snort. 'You think this lot won't find out?' He jerked a thumb towards the swell of customers in the bar. 'You're not in Madrid or even Palma now, my girl. Half the village will already know, and by tomorrow, the rest will too. That's rural Mallorca for you.'

Pep popped an olive into his mouth. 'You have to understand that we islanders are very nosy and love intrigue.'

Isabel poked his arm. 'I have Mallorcan blood too, you know.'

Idò grinned. 'It's true. I tell you, Pep, when my little sister Florentina met Juan I was a bit wary given that he was a mainlander, but he turned out to be a really decent fellow. Besides, he came from La Mancha, where they produce the best Manchego.'

Isabel gave her uncle a nudge. 'Tell me about Angel Mas. How well did you know him?'

Idò shrugged and dropped his voice. 'He was an odd one. His father was Colombian, worked in a bar here and met a local girl. They married and set up home in Sant Martí. Angel was the only child. He was brought up here but left for Colombia when he was about eighteen. Came back in his fifties to reclaim Ca'n Mas when his parents died.'

'So what did he do in Colombia?'

Idò shrugged. 'Who knows, but he returned wearing a fancy suit and opened an account at Banca March. That tells you that he'd done OK.'

'So what? Even I've got an account there,' sniffed Pep.

'Bel must be paying you too much,' Idò growled.

Isabel interjected. 'I heard Mas was religious.'

Her uncle nodded. 'That's right. When he returned here, he told us he'd found God and had been helping street children in Colombia. He was always going back there, sometimes for long periods, and then about two years ago he returned with Camila Cortez, an elderly housekeeper, and became a recluse. He never left Sant Martí again. As for her, she's always at mass, clogging up the pews. Just ask old Padre Agustí.'

'So what's your take on his murder?'

Idò scratched an ear. 'I reckon it's got to be about money. He was always tight. I wonder if he kept a stash of loot that someone knew about.'

Isabel dropped her voice. 'But the killer wrote the word "robber" on the wall in his blood.'

Idò held up his glass and peered at the rich red fluid. 'So I've heard. All I can tell you is that he wasn't all he seemed. No one warmed to the man. Even as a child he was a loner.'

'Maybe because he was half Colombian he felt alienated?' suggested Pep.

Idò drained his drink. 'Never! In those days we Mallorcans welcomed foreigners more than Spanish mainlanders, the *forasteros*.'

'Some things never change, then?' said Isabel with a wink.

He broke into a grin as the village's diminutive mayor strode towards them, clutching a bottle of lager.

'Terrible business about this child abduction and now old Mas!' Llorenç declared mournfully. 'A difficult fellow, but he didn't deserve that.'

He hurriedly made the sign of the cross and, leaning on Isabel's chair, took on a confidential air. 'Thank you for coming to Ca'n Mas this morning.'

Isabel noticed a mischievous sparkle in his eye.

'We certainly got Gómez's goat, didn't we?' he said.

'He's not all bad,' Isabel replied. 'He just likes to do everything by the book. Thankfully, Tolo's more flexible.'

Llorenç nodded slowly. 'Indeed. A good man and the safest pair of hands at the National Police. What a terrible night it was. As mayor of Sant Martí I have no choice but to get involved in local matters, however unpleasant, but this was a particularly nasty murder.'

Isabel drained her glass. 'Have you any theories?'

Llorenç squatted by her chair. 'I think Angel might have ruffled a few feathers. Not long ago, a police officer told me he was surprised to see him hanging around that sink estate, Son Barassa. It's a notorious haunt for dealers, as you know, so if he was thumping the bible there, he was asking for trouble.'

'And what did you make of him?' she replied.

'A cold fish. Not much to like. Always shabby in those old clothes of his and never gave a penny for the village fiestas. And to think he had that fancy car in his garage! So much for religion.'

Idò turned to them and issued a grunt in agreement. 'Holier than thou and yet a face like a poker.'

Pep stifled a guffaw. 'So he'll be sorely missed?'

Llorenç rose to his full height of five feet and five inches and took on a solemn air. 'Yes, indeed, Pep. As a citizen of Sant Martí, he will be greatly missed.'

Isabel tapped Idò's arm. 'By the way, please don't tell mama that I was at the murder scene today.'

'My lips are sealed,' said her uncle. Then, turning to her with a sly wink, he whispered, 'All the same, you should know that it was your mother, in fact, who told me.'

TWELVE

Uncle Idò knelt on the floor in Isabel's office, amidst a sea of metal panels and tools. Pep hovered close by, muttering in disapproval whenever Idò removed yet another part from the faulty air conditioning unit's cavernous interior.

'What's the point of pulling it apart? You obviously don't have a clue what's wrong with it.'

Idò sat back on his haunches. 'Well, I don't see you offering to help. These new fangled machines are just like modern cars, with their fancy engineering and navigation systems. Can't make head or tail of them anymore!'

With a sigh Pep returned to his desk while Idò, like a child concentrating on a complex jigsaw, painstakingly put the offending unit back together. He gave a frustrated tut when it failed to work. 'There's nothing wrong with it, that I can see. I've examined everything.'

Isabel appeared from her room and turned on the television.

Pep looked up. 'What are we watching?'

'Tolo's just called. The press conference he gave in Madrid about Miranda Walters is coming up on the news shortly. We should watch.'

Idò wiped the sweat from his brow. 'How about a nice glass of lemonade for us all, Pep? You'll find a trug of my lemons in the kitchen.'

Reluctantly, Pep disappeared down the stairs, reappearing soon after with three glasses brimming with juice. Bel was mid phone call and nodded gratefully when Pep deposited a glass in front of her. She finished the call and turned to him.

'That was Professor Bauzá, an old friend of mine at the Balearic University.'

Pep frowned. 'How do you know him?'

'An old chum, Pep. Now, let's concentrate on the news.'

All three of them watched the screen keenly as Tolo came into view, addressing a room full of media. He solemnly outlined the timeframe and events leading up to the abduction of Miranda and concluded with a public appeal for information. He assured the gathered throng that both the Guardia and National Police were fully cooperating on the case.

'Why aren't the parents at the press conference?' asked Pep.

Isabel shrugged. 'Tolo told me that Jane Walters was too frail to attend and that Miranda's father, Frank, was admitted to hospital yesterday after collapsing at his hotel.'

'A heart attack?' Pep exclaimed.

She shook her head. 'Luckily only a panic attack. Tolo has arranged for me to interview him tomorrow at the Palma precinct, so hopefully he'll be well enough.'

'Poor things must be stressed out of their minds,' Idò chipped in.

Isabel frowned at the television screen, suddenly aware of an attractive blonde in a well-tailored suit hovering in the background behind Tolo. At the end of his briefing the woman leant forward to whisper something confidentially in his ear. Tolo gave the blonde a fleeting smile and issued a nod. As if echoing her thoughts, Pep turned to Isabel. 'Who's that good-looking blonde standing next to Tolo?'

Isabel's fingers tightly gripped the stem of her glass as she turned away from the screen.

'I imagine she is Lola Rubio, Tolo's liaison point at the Ministry of Interior. She's just a civil servant.'

'Lucky him!' Pep's smirk faded as he heard a loud crack and saw Isabel's glass crash to the floor.

'I must have gripped the stem too hard,' Isabel mumbled.

'What's new? You break everything!' He rushed from the room to get a cloth.

Uncle Idò chuckled as he helped his niece gather up the shards of sticky glass. 'You just don't know your own strength, my girl.'

Isabel attempted jollity. 'It must be all my swimming.'

She leant heavily against the air-conditioning unit and gasped as it slid on its rollers and crashed into a nearby wall. Pep stood in the doorway with a wet dishcloth and cheered when the machine rumbled into life unprompted and began churning out cool air.

'Look, Idò, where you failed, Bel's succeeded! She may be as clumsy as a bull in a ring, but she's also got the magic touch.'

Idò gave an indignant sniff and then pointed to a scowling sky beyond the window pane. 'It's started to rain, young Pep, so perhaps you won't be needing that wretched machine after all.'

With a wink to Isabel, he picked up his toolkit and shuffled out of the office.

*

A sultry slate sky shrouded the valley, doggedly imprisoning the sun's rays until mid-afternoon, when a sudden burst of sunlight flooded the orchards and fields, prompting locals and tourists alike to take to the streets without umbrellas. Isabel had briefed Pep about her proposed visit to Ca'n Mas to interview the housekeeper, Camila Cortez. She would feign a flat tyre outside the property, knock at the door and ask the old housekeeper whether she could make a phone call. Once inside, she'd stage a call to Pep in which she'd tell him about the flat tyre and ask him to pick her up on his *moto*. Taking his cue, Pep would arrive at the pre-arranged time of five o'clock, an hour after she'd left the office. She calculated that this would give her more than enough time to informally question the housekeeper. But why, Pep had wanted to know, was she creating such an elaborate smokescreen? In some exasperation, Isabel had explained to him that she wanted to gain the housekeeper's trust and not to interview her in the guise of police consultant.

At four-fifteen, Isabel turned into Camino Pomar. It was a fairly narrow, muddy track with patches of decaying asphalt and large potholes brimming with dirty water from the recent downpour. Her progress was further impeded by a flabby back tyre on Pequeñito's left side which she'd surreptitiously deflated some metres back along the road. She parked and tapped the steering wheel sympathetically. 'Sorry about the tyre, Pequeñito, but needs must. As soon as Pep arrives, we'll have you pumped up again.'

The little car's engine continued to pant with the heat long after Isabel had removed the ignition key and stepped onto the empty road. For a moment she stood still, deep in thought, before tilting her head up at the fiery sun. It was hard to imagine that only a few hours earlier a churlish black sky had unleashed a violent storm, chilling the air while rain lashed the fields, orchards and cobbled streets.

Now she found herself cocooned by orange, lemon and olive groves, beyond which lay the hazy skeleton of the Tramuntana mountain range. In the far distance she could hear the ghostly toot toot of the valley's historic electric train as it trundled along the meandering railway track that curled up into the hills. It would cross the 'cinc-ponts' viaduct before passing through thirteen cool, dark tunnels on its one-hour journey to Palma. To the south, the creamy tips of the twin towers of San Bartomeu, Soller's ancient church, poked through a froth of trees like the straight horns of a mountain goat. She stood admiring the familiar view, basking in the warm, still air. Cicadas hissed in the tall grasses and the smudgy green tail of a *garriga*, the island's harmless field snake, slithered between cracks in the shimmering asphalt.

From the shade of a carob tree, she watched as an emerald lizard scuttled across the hot road still shiny with rain into the crevice of a stone wall. There wasn't a cloud in the sky or even the feeblest of breezes and no one stirred, as it was still siesta period. She looked up and down the empty road and could just make out the russet-tiled roof of Ca'n Mas peeping from behind a crop of shaggy pines. She set off towards it, hopping over pools of water and scraping her shoes free of mud when she reached the grass verge at its entrance.

Standing at the foot of the drive she marvelled at the sunny and tranquil scene before her, a far cry from the night of the murder when dark shadows, police searchlights and fearful faces had created a feeling of terror and foreboding. In that gloomy atmosphere she had been oblivious to the lush, mature trees that lined both sides of the gravel track and the elegant flourishes of the circular courtyard at the front of the house. With approval, she saw that it was bordered by fine sculptures and giant terracotta pots overflowing with corn-blue plumbago and white oleanders. Isabel paused to admire the abundant avocado, almonds and carob trees and tall, willowy cypresses that contrasted sharply with the stunted palms huddling by the front gate like abandoned orphans.

She strolled up to the courtyard, fashioned from small pebbles, towards the arched doorway. With wary eyes, a plump ginger cat observed her approach and skulked behind a stone pillar as she leant forward to pull the ancient brass bell. The clanging was louder than she'd expected and seemed to reverberate throughout the *finca*. She waited a few moments before turning the door handle, unsurprised to find it open. Few people in the rural areas locked up their homes, including Isabel, who in the summer months kept her doors and windows unbolted. After all, what sane person would want to be a prisoner in his own home? She conceded that at night, locking doors was a wise precaution against dubious visitors such as feral cats, bats, genets and rats, although she always welcomed hedgehogs inside. Even Furó would treat the prickly little creatures with a certain degree of civility and respect.

She stepped into the cool, dark hallway, where a mahogany grandfather clock grunted methodically at the far end of the room, its polished face giving nothing away.

'*Hola*! Anybody home?'

She took in her surroundings, reminding herself of the layout; the study to her left and the sturdy stone staircase that lay ahead of her. The door to the basement kitchen slowly opened and a woman with the startled eyes of a bushbaby peered up at her. A bluey-grey bruise had spread across her right cheekbone and around the elbow on the same side, while a large plaster covered part of her forehead. Isabel glimpsed the shapeless black dress overlayered by an unflattering nylon overall, obligatory wear for many elderly matriarchs in the valley. The woman's thin white hair was cut short and brushed back primly against her head. With arthritic knees she climbed the short flight of stone steps and leant against the wooden banister, catching her breath. Isabel broke into a reassuring smile.

'*Bon día, senyora*. I am Isabel Flores Montserrat from Sant Martí.'

The woman nodded expectantly.

'I'm sorry to disturb you, but my car has a flat tyre. I wonder whether I might use your telephone to call my assistant? Foolishly, I've forgotten my mobile phone.'

The old woman's face relaxed and she reached forward to shake Isabel's hand. 'Please come in. I am Camila Cortez. What beautiful wavy hair you have.'

Rather self-consciously Isabel fingered a dark curl. 'At least it protects my head from the sun. I never need to wear a hat.'

The woman smiled. 'But you should in this heat. Please, follow me. You can use the telephone in the study.' She hesitated a moment. 'Or maybe in the kitchen. The study is in a bit of a mess.'

Isabel gave a polite titter. 'Oh, that's no problem. My office is always chaotic! Is it this way?'

The housekeeper pushed open the study door and pointed towards a heavy oak desk. 'Make yourself at home. If you are from Sant Martí, you may know what has taken place here.'

Isabel nodded slowly. 'Yes, I heard the terrible news. It is the reason I hesitated to knock at your door when I realised that it was Ca'n Mas. I'm so sorry to see that you have injuries.'

'Nothing too serious, thankfully,' the woman replied. 'It's nice to have a visitor in this lonely house. For the last few days I've been in hospital while the forensic and cleaning teams were here.'

Isabel touched her arm. 'This must have been so dreadful for you.'

She nodded. 'I've always been a light sleeper, but now fear keeps me wide awake into the small hours. All the same, life must go on. Please feel free to use the telephone and I'll organise some cold drinks. You look so hot.'

With a tinge of guilt, Isabel rang Pep's mobile as pre-agreed and spoke loudly. 'Ah, hello, I'm afraid I have a flat tyre and am parked in Camino Pomar near to Ca'n Mas. I wonder if you could pick me up?'

Pep hissed into the receiver. 'Why are you telling me this? We've already agreed the plan.'

Isabel took a deep breath and blundered on, ignoring the confused clucks at the other end of the line. Why was the boy such a fool? Did he ever follow instructions?

'Forty minutes? OK, I'll wait here. I'm calling from Ca'n Mas because I forgot my mobile. Please ring the bell when you arrive if I'm not at the car. *Gràcies*.'

ANNA NICHOLAS

She replaced the receiver, pretending not to have noticed the woman hovering with a tray in the doorway. Camila Cortez gave a polite cough and entered the room, ushering Isabel into the brown leather armchair that she remembered only too well from her last visit. Isabel shuddered as her mind conjured up an image of the elderly Mas sinking comfortably into the very same hollow of the worn seat. She avoided focusing on the section of tiled floor where his body had lain.

'So is your assistant able to collect you?'

Isabel noted the soft Colombian accent, the way she sibilated her words. 'Indeed, but I'm afraid he is on an errand, so it could be some time before he gets here. I can wait for him in the car.'

'Not at all! You must stay here in the cool. Here, have some home-made lemonade.'

Isabel took a sip. 'Mm. This is so good.'

'An old Colombian recipe,' she replied. 'Señor Mas said it was the best he'd ever tasted.' She fumbled for a small crucifix around her neck and made the sign of the cross. 'He was such a fine, religious man.'

Isabel placed her glass on the tiled floor. 'His death must have been so upsetting for you. Have the police made any arrests?'

The woman shook her head. 'Not that they've told me.'

'The newspapers believe that it was the work of opportunistic robbers, but what do they know? Then again, it seems strange that his killers apparently wrote "ladrón" on the wall.' She dropped her head and sighed. 'I wonder why they would dare to call such a good and law-abiding man a thief?'

Camila Cortez looked visibly shocked. 'Señor Mas was very devout. He'd never have stolen from anyone. How did you hear about that?'

Isabel offered a resigned smile. 'I'm afraid people gossip. It's the talk of Sant Martí.'

'I don't know anyone in the village apart from Padre Agustí and Jesus, the owner of Bon Dìa. That way I avoid lies and gossip.'

Isabel picked up her glass and took a sip. 'Yes, people invent all sorts of stories. Some have even suggested that he stole something, maybe money.'

The woman shrugged. 'If he stole anything, I didn't know about it. Señor Mas didn't seem to need money.'

Isabel offered a reassuring smile.

'He never seemed to want for much, but we lived frugally.'

'Did you notice if anything was stolen that night?'

'Nothing that I could see.'

Isabel leant forward in her chair. 'And did you recognise your assailants at all? Might they have come here before that night?'

She lifted a quivering finger to her lip. 'Not at all. A black car showed up out of the blue and four hooded men in sunglasses came to the door. It wasn't locked. I thought they were tourists seeking directions.'

'Did you receive many visitors?'

'Oh, no. Señor Mas and I lived a solitary existence here. He rarely left home except to attend Sunday mass and spent much of his time alone, reading and praying.'

She took a sip of her lemonade and twisted a handkerchief agitatedly between her fingers. 'You see it all happened so quickly. I just remember one of the men dragging me towards the basement staircase. I cried out for Señor Mas, but he didn't come to my aid. I thought perhaps he'd fallen asleep.'

'When had you last seen him?'

'Lunchtime. He didn't like to be disturbed when he was in his study.'

'What happened next?'

'In the kitchen the man tied me to a chair and locked the door from the outside.'

'What a terrible ordeal for you.'

'You cannot imagine. I thought I was going to die and prayed for salvation. When the man never returned I tried to release the tight ropes binding my wrists, but as I struggled the chair tipped over. I fell on my right side and stayed like that on the cold stone floor until our neighbour, Tomas Llull, found me.'

'Did he pop round regularly?'

'No. In truth there was no love lost between him and Señor Mas. Last Saturday he came here shouting and swearing and Señor Mas ordered him to leave.'

'Why was he so angry?'

'I don't know, but he mentioned something about Señor Mas denouncing him to the council of Sant Martí.'

'Well, whatever their past grievances, thank heavens he saved you that night.'

The old woman nodded. 'Yes, thank God that he chose to visit at such a late hour.'

'And why was that?'

'He told me that he was woken by the sound of the television in the small hours. I couldn't understand how that was possible, as Señor Mas rarely used it. I trembled at what might have happened to him after the men burst into the house.'

Isabel eyed her intently. 'How did your neighbour gain entry?'

'I can't recall exactly. I think he entered the study by the French windows, which were rarely locked.'

'Perhaps Señor Mas was already dead by then and the killers used the television to cover the noise of his screams.'

Camila Cortez put a tremulous hand to her mouth and closed her eyes. 'I don't want to think about it.'

Isabel rose to her feet. 'Your boss certainly liked his books.'

She browsed the shelves of one of the robust bookcases fashioned from white plaster. 'Many religious tomes, I see.'

Camilla Cortez sighed and dabbed at her eyes. 'Yes, he was a holy man. Always reading from the Bible and giving to the poor of Colombia.'

'Are these photographs of him?' asked Isabel, indicating the rectangular coffee table choked with framed images and curiosities that she remembered from her last visit.

A faded smile crossed the woman's lips. 'Yes, they bear testimony to his work. You'll see him with the Colombian holy sisters and children from the Catholic orphanages of Bogotá.'

Dutifully, Isabel bent down to study a few. One showed Mas in a sunny location, with palm trees in the background. He was as she'd remembered him, a balding elderly man with tough little peppercorn eyes and crinkled, sun-ravaged skin. With his arms tightly folded, he stood between two smiling nuns both attired in black habits. His gaze was cold, although the lips smiled like an upturned boomerang.

'Are those nuns from the Saint Francis Order?'

She studied Isabel with approval. 'Yes, they are indeed.'

'He certainly seemed to have a lot of friends.'

'Yes, he will always be remembered in Colombia.'

'And what about his family? Are there any pictures of them?'

'Señor Mas was all alone in the world. His parents died many years ago and he never married. I don't think he had any living relatives back in Colombia.'

Isabel returned to her chair and finished the dregs of her lemonade. 'So when will you return home?'

The woman bowed her head. 'Soon, I think. Señor Mas pulled strings with Padre Agustí to keep me in the valley. Once the police no longer need my assistance I will return to Colombia. At least I have a nephew there, Salvador, a good boy who is finishing his law degree at the Pontifical Javeriana University in Bogotá.'

Isabel nodded enthusiastically. 'Quite a reputation, as I recall.'

The elderly woman beamed. 'Indeed. It was established in 1623. A solid religious institution.'

'Do you have other family in Bogotá?'

She gave a forlorn shake of the head. 'I will need to build a new life there again. God was good to find me this position.' She uttered a heavy sigh. 'And now it's gone, just like that.'

They sat in silence for a while until the old woman tapped the arm of her chair and smiled across at Isabel. 'Now I realise why I know your face. I have seen you at mass in Sant Martí.'

Isabel nodded. 'Yes, I try to pop by when I can.'

'And you work in the village?'

'I run a small rentals business with my mother.'

'What a good girl you are. Your mother must be so grateful to have such a caring, religious daughter.'

Rather embarrassed at this undeserved accolade, especially when it came to religious fervour, Isabel rose and asked to view the gardens. Camila Cortez sprung to her feet with surprising vigour and led her from the front passageway out into the sunshine. She took her to admire the lemon and almond orchards and herb and vegetable patch of her own creation at the back of the house. Swollen, purple aubergines hung low and kissed the earth, while a row of fat, ripe tomatoes jostled for prominence amid clumps of herbs and the last of the season's potatoes and onions. Isabel was on the point of visiting the chicken coop when the angry whine of a *moto* sounded on the drive and came to rest by the front porch. The housekeeper raised an eyebrow as they strolled across a gravel path to greet Pep.

'Is this your assistant?'

Isabel gave an apologetic smile. 'I'm afraid so. He has a love of monster bikes.'

Pep stood on the threshold like an invincible Ajax with toned olive skin and bulging biceps bristling beneath short tight sleeves, his eyes hidden behind dark shades.

'What a strong lad you are,' commented Camila Cortez. 'Your mother must be proud.'

Pep grinned. 'I do my best.'

'And are you devout too?'

Struck dumb for a second, Pep shot an anxious glance at Isabel and began nodding enthusiastically. 'Yes, like Bel, I try to catch mass whenever I can.'

As Isabel turned to go, the old woman offered her a peck on both cheeks. 'I have to remind myself that God works in mysterious ways and that it is not for humankind to question his purpose. Look how he has brought me two new friends when I was feeling so alone.'

And with a cursory nod she wished them good day and closed the door. Pep nursed his bike down the drive and out onto Camino Pomar.

'I see what Idò meant about her being a religious nut. So did you find anything out?'

'Perhaps. I also had a chance to look more closely at the titles in Mas's study. Aside from religious tomes, there were a lot of books about the occult. I wouldn't want to stay alone in such a creepy house.'

'Nor would I,' shuddered Pep. 'Camila Cortez is some brave old lady. So, tell me how you managed to deflate your tyre?'

'I just took the valve cap off and released the air with the point of my pen. I thought it better to make it authentic in case she came over to see the car.'

Pep took out his pump and knelt down by the wheel. 'It shouldn't take long.'

As Isabel pondered her meeting with Camila Cortez, a battered grey Land Rover pulled out of the drive of the neighbouring farmhouse and lumbered towards them, bouncing over the uneven terrain. The driver stopped parallel with the car, his engine purring, and leant out of the open window. 'Can I help?'

'*No hay problema,*' smiled Isabel. 'Just a flat tyre.' She studied his face for a second, recognising him from the night she attended the crime scene. 'You live next door to Ca'n Mas. What a business!'

He nodded. 'I'm Tomas Llull. I found Angel's body that night. Poor old housekeeper was screaming her head off. It was like a horror movie.'

'Did you know him well?' asked Isabel.

'No, and we weren't exactly on good terms. The old devil recently denounced me for building a *casita* in my field. Only a tiny tool shed really.'

'You didn't have planning permission?'

He shrugged. '*Que va!* Who bothers these days? If he hadn't reported me to the local council, no one would have been any the wiser. Now I've just been issued with a hefty fine.'

'So how did you discover the body?'

'I sleep at the back of the house. That night I awoke with a jolt when I heard the TV blaring from Mas's study. It was about two o'clock and as I was pretty annoyed, I went round to the front of the house and rang the bell. No one answered, so I got a ladder and climbed onto the back wall between our gardens. That's when I saw the French windows to the study wide open and Mas's body lying on the floor. All the lights were on.'

'Did you notice if Mas had any visitors that day?'

He turned off the engine, seeming grateful for a chinwag. 'Not really, although late afternoon while I was in the front garden I saw a black Mitsubishi heading up the drive. I didn't pay much attention because I've seen it often enough.'

'Oh?'

'It was the only car I ever saw visit Ca'n Mas. It was a Shogun. Must have seen it pull in there at least a couple of times a month. There was a guy sitting in the driving seat.'

'Anyone else in the vehicle?'

He shook his head. 'No, he was alone.'

'And did you mention this to the Guardia?'

He chortled merrily and restarted the engine. 'I don't talk to the police on principle, let alone the Guardia. I told them how I came across the body and untied the old housekeeper, and that was it.'

Isabel offered him an *adéu* and a wave as he drove off.

'Just fancy that.'

Pep squatted back on his heels and peered up at her. 'What?'

'Llull just said he'd seen a black Shogun the night of the murder, the same that he'd seen at Ca'n Mas many times before.'

Pep shrugged. 'So what?'

'So, my dear Pep, what I want to know is why the housekeeper told me that she'd never seen the car before that night, and why she claimed that four masked men attacked her when apparently, there was only one person in the car.'

Pep frowned. 'But why would she lie?'

'A good question, Pep,' replied Isabel, 'a very good question indeed.'

*

Pep and Isabel returned to the office to sort out a mountain of problems created by their various holidaying tenants. A Dutch couple had managed to lose the key to their house, while an hysterical English woman had manhandled a kitchen tap to such a degree that the top had shot off with the ferocity of a champagne cork, causing a violent torrent of water to gush all over the floor. While Isabel rallied the local plumber and attempted to keep the sodden client calm, Pep had set off on his *moto* with a spare key for the Dutch couple. A moment later, two of the cleaners had bustled into the office, complaining of torn sheets in a seafront apartment rented by Germans, and to top it all, a French woman was threatening to sue over an ant invasion in her bedroom and a voyeuristic gecko lurking in the lavatory. Before five o'clock Pep jumped ship, promising to meet Isabel at his father's boat at the agreed hour. Some time later, as soon as the telephone stopped ringing, Isabel switched off the lights in the office and set off in her car towards the nearby mountain town of Valldemossa.

*

Professor Toni Bauzá sat across the desk from Isabel, thoughtfully studying the yellowed jaw of a long-extinct creature that had once roamed the island. Isabel allowed her eyes to wander around the professor's academic lair. She coveted the heavy mahogany bookshelves lining one side of the room that were laden with scientific tomes and an assortment of fossils, rocks and bovid skulls. Through the grubby windows of the university block, she could see pastureland and the Tramuntana mountains beyond. The sun still glimmered on the horizon, but soon it would be evening. The professor gave a discreet cough.

'You see, Isabel, there was a time when anyone could ravish our land, pluck valuable artefacts from the soil and sell them to foreign buyers. Now we are more cautious, which is why the Devil's Horn Caves are off limits to anyone but approved university personnel.'

'But do the remains of myotragus still have a value for international collectors?'

'Where there is interest, there is always value. It might have died out more than three thousand years ago, but myotragus was a fascinating creature, a scientific phenomenon, really, because it only ever lived on Mallorca and Menorca. Of course, we have to thank the English for putting our little mouse-goat on the map.'

Isabel sat back in her chair. 'You're talking about Dorothea Bate, the English fossil hunter who first discovered myotragus in 1909?'

'You're well informed. Indeed, the very first specimen discovered is still held at the Natural History Museum in London.'

'So, getting back to Aina, you're saying that she lied to me about not having previously visited the caves because she'd already been there on one of your scientific digs?'

He wore a glum expression. 'She is one of my most promising students, so naturally I am disappointed to think of her betraying the university in this way. Whatever could have possessed her to act so irresponsibly? Do you think she sailed to the caves in the hope of discovering some valuable myotragus artefacts?'

'I imagine she was goaded on by her boyfriend, who thought he might make a fast buck if they found anything of worth.'

'How serious is her offence in the eyes of the law? It would be a tragedy if her academic career should be cut short through one thoughtless act.'

'That rather depends on Aina. If she cooperates fully with the police, she may be let off with just a caution. Of course, you could make all the difference.'

The elderly professor nodded thoughtfully. 'Perhaps you might care to elaborate?'

A smile played on Isabel's lips. 'Yes, I most certainly would.'

*

Picking up the copy of Roald Dahl stories that Mrs Walters had leant her, Isabel settled on a chair on her patio with a glass of red wine and bowl of salted almonds. Thirty minutes later her mobile phone rang. Her heart leapt when she heard Tolo's voice.

'Sorry to call so late.'

Isabel laughed. 'The night is but young. Well done on the press conference this morning. I thought you did a great job.'

'Coming from you, I'll take that as a compliment. It's been full on over here in Madrid, but at least I can escape tomorrow afternoon and head back to Mallorca. Anything to report on your side?'

'It can wait until we meet tomorrow evening.'

'You're still planning to interview Frank Walters earlier in the day?'

'Of course. Why do you ask?'

'We've just received some crucial video footage which Gaspar Fernández would like to show you while you're at the Palma precinct.'

Isabel listened intently.

'A bar owner in Pollença port with a direct view over the esplanade has just handed in a CCTV film which clearly shows Miranda.'

Isabel felt a frisson of excitement. 'Where?'

'Gaspar has only just watched it. Apparently, Miranda can be seen hurrying towards a side street at eight minutes past two – soon after her mother raised the alarm.'

'On her own?' Isabel almost shouted.

'No,' he replied.

'Well, who was she with?'

'That's the puzzling part. She was holding hands with a woman. A woman with long blonde hair.'

THIRTEEN

Seawater gurgled and hissed, chasing Isabel's moonlit footprints across the wet sand as she walked briskly along the beach, Furó at her side, towards the harbour. She carried a holdall and pair of docksiders in one hand and her faithful pannier in the other. Every now and then she'd stop to greet the briny foam and watch mesmerised as her feet were hungrily gobbled up without trace. Furó hung back, sniffing enthusiastically at the cool dank sand as he pattered in her wake. There was still a clutch of tourists drinking in the bars, but most had long departed from the port for their beds or more lively nightlife elsewhere. It was midnight and a cool breeze had finally replaced the fiery heat of the day.

When Isabel reached *El Cargol*, she smiled to herself. It certainly wasn't the fastest vessel in the world, but it didn't deserve the name 'Snail', either. Pep's father, Pedro, had once jokingly told her that it made slow progress but always safely reached its final destination. Aina was already on board, perched on a side bench and talking in hushed tones with Pep. Agilely, Isabel followed Furó up the gangplank and briefly contemplated the night sky. The moon hung like a smooth white peppermint drop above the craggy peaks of the Tramuntanas, and to her right the gaunt and elderly Punta de Sa Creu lighthouse cast a dim golden beam across the bay.

The old fishing vessel sat like a comfy slipper in its berth, flanked on either side by similarly battered but seaworthy craft, most reeking of stale fish and sporting scars from countless precarious voyages on the high seas. The gently bobbing turquoise boat to the right was named *El Papagayo*, and was owned by the eponymous owner of Jordi's bar in Sant Martí. It bore the knocks of a disastrous fishing trip in which a sudden maelstrom had sent the boat crashing onto rocks and Jordi flying overboard, tangled in nets and gaping like a halibut. The old rogue often recounted tales of his fishy heroics to unsuspecting tourists drinking late in his bar.

On the other side sat *La Princesa*, a scrawny vessel eaten away by rust that made a few weekly forays out into the bay hunting for the luscious *gambas rojas* that had locals salivating at the very whisper of the name. Isabel glanced at the tranquil moonlit water. It was going to be a fairly straightforward sail, even though she'd have liked a more seaworthy companion than Pep at the wheel. Although his father had a reputation for being one of the most experienced sailors on the coast, Pep had failed to inherit his father's masterly skills. Instead, he suffered persistent bouts of seasickness on choppy voyages, which proved an endless source of amusement to his family.

Aina and Pep now crossed the deck to greet Isabel. She observed that both appeared jittery and alert. Pep was no doubt anticipating with some trepidation the rolling motion of the waves, while his new companion would be dreading a return to the spot that could prove her potential fall from grace. Pep bent down to stroke Furó as he excitedly nuzzled his shin.

He turned to Aina. 'This is Furó. He and I share the same office.'

She smiled and gave the ferret a pat on the head. 'I bet he's good at taking bookings.'

'There's no stopping him,' Pep smirked.

The boat suddenly began to judder. In some alarm, Isabel looked towards the cockpit.

'Who's fired up the boat, Pep?'

'*Tranquilo*! My father insisted on coming along. He thought you might need a reliable pair of hands on board.'

Isabel laughed. 'Pedro must be psychic.'

She disappeared along the deck and settled Furó into the warm and brightly lit galley below. Then she headed back towards the bridge, while Pep and Aina carried on chatting as they drew up the fenders.

In the cockpit Isabel found Pedro engrossed in a map. He was a more weather-beaten version of his son, with the same dark olive skin, black eyes and lean build. He grinned when he saw her and leant forward to share a hug.

She punched his arm with a soft fist. 'Didn't trust me handling the boat alone, eh?'

'More like I didn't trust Pep as your co-pilot.'

'So how long should it take us to reach the caves?'

'About an hour. As we're heading for a restricted zone we'll need to keep an eye out for the coastguard, but at this time of night things are pretty quiet along that stretch of water.'

'That's good, because we need to keep under the radar. If my nemesis Capitán Gómez at the Guardia finds out about this trip, I'll be in deep water – no pun intended.'

Pedro threw her a wink and gently manoeuvred the boat out of its mooring. Soon, boisterous dark water began urgently slapping the sides of the vessel as they headed into the inky void beyond the bay. He turned to Isabel.

'You know the Devil's Horn Caves are supposed to be labyrinthine.'

'So I've heard.'

'Pep didn't explain the exact purpose of the trip but knowing you, I doubt it's a moonlight sightseeing tour.'

She smiled. 'In truth, this whole adventure might turn out to be a waste of time. I'm going on a hunch.'

'Pep tells me that you're back with the National Police?'

'Only for a short while.'

Pedro nodded. 'He mentioned that you were assisting with two investigations. I hope this trip throws up some leads for you.'

'I really appreciate your help tonight, whatever comes of our little adventure.'

He grinned. 'At worst, we'll have had a pleasant evening sea voyage.'

As the boat nudged into the open sea, Isabel stepped down from the bridge and sought out Aina. She was sitting hunched up by the prow, wiry bronzed arms hugging bare knees, ebony hair fighting the breeze. Pep was nowhere to be seen, but Isabel imagined he'd taken refuge in the galley below.

'So, Aina, I'm going to need your help once we reach the caves. I'll need the exact location where Felip and Francesc found those bibles.'

'But they may not be there anymore.'

'I'm pretty certain of that.'

'So what are you hoping to find?'

'A missing link.'

'But I just stayed on the boat that night. I can't lead you through the caves.'

Isabel scanned the coastline as the boat suddenly picked up speed. Black viscous waves danced about them as the vessel nosed gently northwards, the towering cliffs a permanent shadow on their right. Before them, a slash of moonlight ran like a satin ribbon far across the water, melting away as it brushed the smoky horizon. Isabel sat down next to Aina.

'Why don't you tell me what really happened that night?'

The girl flinched. 'What do you mean?'

'You've not told me everything.'

Aina's pale face twitched imperceptibly. 'I have.'

Isabel rubbed her eyes and yawned. 'You said that Felip and Francesc discovered the bibles, but I think you were there too. You slipped up when you told me that you all changed out of your wet clothes. Therefore, you must have swum from the boat with them in order to explore the caves. '

Aina said nothing.

'You claimed never to have been to the Devil's Horn Caves before, but today I spoke with Professor Bauzá, your supervisor at the university, and he said that you'd recently accompanied him on a field trip there.'

Aina looked visibly shocked. 'This will mean the end of my university career.'

'Not so fast. Just tell me the truth.'

She began to sob. 'It was all Felip's idea. I'd told him that some collectors would pay good money for specimens of myotragus, so he persuaded me to take him to the caves. He was broke and I need funds to continue studying.'

'But instead of coming across any prehistoric bones, you found a much more lucrative haul of cocaine.'

'Felip and I had explored the caves on our own while Francesc kept watch. When we found the bibles full of cocaine I told Felip we shouldn't touch them, but he insisted they'd be worth a fortune and that he'd find a dealer.'

'So you took them?'

'He filled two dry tube bags with the drugs and got me to carry one back to the boat. Francesc helped get them on board. Then we sailed back to the port.'

'That's when I saw you.'

'How?'

'I was taking a moonlit stroll with Furó and happened to see you arguing with Felip and Francesc before you all drove off.'

'So you've known all along.'

'I only knew part of the story. So tell me the rest.'

'There's nothing more to tell.'

Isabel sighed impatiently. 'Come on. I can tell you're holding something back.'

Aina let out an exasperated gasp. 'OK, you win, Bel. Just before we found the cocaine, I discovered part of a cranium and jaw belonging to myotragus. It was a near-perfect specimen and I decided to hide it from Felip.'

'You intended to sell it to a collector?'

'I admit that was my immediate thought, but when I got home I changed my mind.'

'How much might it have fetched?'

'One thousand euros or more.'

'So what did you do with it?'

'In the end I couldn't betray Professor Bauzá after all he'd done for me. It's stored safely in my university locker.'

'Good. That simplifies everything,' Isabel replied.

'It does?' said Aina in a brighter voice.

'Tomorrow I think you owe the professor an apology – and what better way than to present him with your find?'

Isabel left Aina with her thoughts and strode along the deck with deft feet to join Pedro in the cockpit. It was a clear night and the weathered craft methodically skimmed the waves, coaxed along by a tangy breeze. Isabel and Pedro stood pensively together at the wheel, only occasionally glancing upwards to admire the splash of white stars staining the sky. A moment later their attention was rudely diverted as a seasick Pep lurched up to the bow and, without ceremony, was violently sick over the side of the boat.

*

More than an hour passed before Isabel stepped from the cockpit out onto the deck. To her right an immense and craggy cliff puckered with small caves and dark mysterious fissures kept pace with the moving craft until it curved gently away from the open sea towards the northern tip of the island. Pedro stood at the helm, Pep at his side, gently nosing the old fishing vessel landward. The engine emitted a steady whine as the boat picked up speed and coursed towards a circle of half-submerged rocks that sprung up from the waves like chipped and blackened teeth. Pedro pointed to a small cove beyond, shouting instructions to Isabel above the drone of the engine.

As the boat ploughed towards the shore, Aina rose unsteadily to her feet, exploring the rocky coastline with impatient eyes. This was familiar territory, and the telltale landmarks were indelibly printed on her mind. She studied the deep gash that split the towering rock face from its midriff to its watery base and stared fearfully into the black void beyond. At the entrance to the tiny cove, she recognised El Cuerno del Diablo, the Devil's Horn, the gnarled and ugly lump of decaying rock that jutted out above the sea, its tip rising defiantly towards the sky. Just a glimpse of it triggered a deep sense of unease in her. Pep walked unsteadily along the wooden deck and joined Aina at the bow while Pedro, with Isabel's assistance, continued to coax the craft towards the shore. A few minutes later the engine slowed and changed tone, its propeller spluttering and churning up water.

'Where's the best place to anchor?' Isabel shouted against the wind.

Pedro shrugged. 'I'm turning into the cove now. Let's take a look.'

Isabel waited until the vessel had entered the wide cave, chugging through gently murmuring waves until the seascape behind them resembled an idyllic diorama. A short distance ahead on the far side of the cave she spotted a fist of yellowing grasses that appeared to mark the beginning of a vertical path carved into the rock face.

Isabel turned to Pedro. 'This seems to be the perfect spot. We can easily swim to that path from here.'

Aina now appeared, raising her voice against the juddering of the engine. 'This is where we moored last time.'

Once Isabel had anchored the boat, she joined the others on deck. Pedro switched on the boat's powerful deck lights, illuminating the dark caverns and craggy rocks around them.

He stared down into the black water. 'I've lowered the tender. Which of you wants to row it over with the equipment?'

Pep stood apart, a towel draped over his shoulders. 'I'm not swimming, that's for sure.'

Isabel patted him on the shoulder. 'Why don't you take my holdall and pannier across in the dinghy and Aina and I can tether it on the rocks?'

'OK, but I'm not feeling up to crawling around in any caves after my bout of seasickness.'

'Don't worry. You can stay with Pedro and keep watch. Aina, Furó and I will go.'

The two women removed shorts and tee shirts to reveal swimming costumes beneath. Isabel nudged Aina. 'Are you ready?'

The girl nodded and launched herself off the side of the boat, diving into the bobbing waves. A moment later her glistening head popped up and she swam quickly to the rocks, Isabel following closely behind with Furó. Pep was already settled in the dinghy and rowing his way over to the bank. As he drew nearer, he gathered up the bowline and stood up unsteadily.

Aina called over to him. 'Throw me the painter and I'll attach it to a rock.'

'The what?'

She rolled her eyes. 'The rope in your hand!'

Once the dinghy was safely berthed, Aina hauled herself up the steep rock face that she had climbed previously, this time with Isabel and Furó following closely behind. Deep indents in the surface allowed them both to find their footing with relative ease and soon they had reached a narrow and stony path on the rock's summit that led to three deep chambers in the cave's interior.

'How was the water?' Pep asked, staring up at them from the dinghy.

'Invigorating,' Isabel grimaced. 'Now hand me up that holdall.'

The dinghy rocked violently as Pep rose clumsily to his feet with the bag and stepped onto the glistening base rock. Leaning down, Isabel grabbed it from him and removed two sets of dry clothes, backpacks, towels, headlamps, torches and rubber-soled shoes. The women quickly changed and switched on their lights in the gloom. When they were both ready, Isabel called out to Pep.

'There's a cow horn in my pannier. If you have a problem, just give it a blow. It would wake the living dead.'

Pep looked up at her from the water's edge, a forlorn expression on his face. Even in his misery he looked chic in branded black shorts, pristine polo shirt and red espadrilles.

'How long will you be?'

'Maybe an hour,' suggested Aina.

'But then again, that all depends on what we find or who we run into,' Isabel said mischievously.

'Don't joke around. So what am I supposed to do?'

She shrugged. 'Stay by the dinghy or go and have a beer with Pedro.'

'I'm feeling too queasy; besides, my father says he's got to bleed the injectors. I'll just get in his way.'

'In that case, I suggest you stay put and act as lookout.'

He eyed her in some alarm. 'For what?'

'Who knows? Just keep your wits about you.'

They were swallowed up in the darkness before Pep could think of a suitable reply. He stepped cautiously back into the dinghy and located Isabel's pannier. Sure enough, inside lay the smooth creamy hued cow horn. Picking up the curved curiosity, he chuckled. As if he was going to blow on a bugle, like some mad old Viking. He waited until the sound of their footsteps had faded before pulling a slim flask from his pocket, unscrewing the lid and taking a hearty glug of its contents. As soon as the brandy hit home, he felt a reassuring fiery warmth in his belly and brightened up. He made himself a comfortable nest in the small craft and, pulling a towel over his chest, settled down for a nap. From his father's boat he could hear the stutter of the engine, the whoosh as it fired and then silence as it cut out. With Pedro's muffled curses floating on the breeze, he smiled happily to himself and closed his eyes.

Aina indicated to Isabel that they should take the second chamber and together they clambered slowly over the rocks and sharp boulders, hugging the walls until they came to a partially covered passage. Taking off their backpacks and switching on their torches, they squeezed along sideways, their bodies scraping the rough and uneven internal wall. Meanwhile, Furó scuttled ahead, snuffling happily as he pattered along the cool, dank passageway. Soon they arrived in an open area where the roof of the cave widened. Tiny rivulets of water ran along its surface, trickling like sweat down the jagged and impenetrable rock face and onto the silt below.

'This is where we focused our dig when we came with Professor Bauzá. We found a few samples of the animal's femur but nothing of great value. No teeth, no craniums. We should have gone further.'

'So where do we go from here?'

Aina adjusted her head torch and stood and surveyed the shadowy outline of the chamber, getting her bearings. A fat crab scuttled past and disappeared into the unremitting darkness. 'Just follow me.'

She strode on until the roof narrowed to the extent that it was impossible to continue walking. Getting down on her belly, she crawled along to a large seam in the rock. 'It's through here. There's a small tunnel beyond. It's body width only, so take it easy.'

Pushing her bag ahead of her, Aina hoisted herself along with Isabel in pursuit, her slim frame feeling restricted in so confined a space. Once through, the roof broadened and they were able to straighten up. The air was chilled and the seeping walls clammy and cold to the touch. Isabel edged her way along the rock face in the obscurity, her headlight awakening devilish shapes that skipped and danced around the moist limestone boulders. Before long a large opening appeared, below which lay a sizeable pit.

Isabel surveyed it. 'That's quite a drop. Maybe seven metres?'

Aina nodded. 'We never got to go down there on my field trip. Professor Bauzá thought it too risky and said there was evidence of flooding. Still, it was dry enough when Felip and I visited on Monday night.'

Isabel pulled a tightly rolled cable ladder, bolts and carabiners from her backpack. Locating two crevices spaced roughly a foot apart, she used a steel hammer to drive a pair of hanger bolts securely into the rock floor. Next, she attached carabiners before fastening the ladder ropes to each one. She tugged the ladder to ensure it was firmly secured.

'Yours is much stronger than the one Felip rigged up for us. Do you always come so well prepared?'

'I used to go canyoning and rock climbing when I was a student, so I learnt the hard way.'

Clipping Furó into a secure harness, Isabel strapped him to her chest and slowly lowered herself down, the ladder swaying slightly and scraping the rocks. Aina blinked hard, her eyes trailing Isabel until she was gradually subsumed by the suffocating darkness.

Isabel released Furó at the base and walked about the gloomy interior, her headlight emitting a sickly glow.

'What can you see?' Aina shouted.

'Some tunnels. Come down, but take it easy.'

'I wish I didn't have to go down there again.'

Isabel peered up at her. '*Animo*! We won't take long.'

Aina cautiously made her way down the ladder and joined Isabel and Furó in the wide circular chamber. A thin stream of water trickled down from a deep fissure to their right.

The pit radiated five tunnels from its centre, two impossibly narrow to contemplate. Aina flashed her head torch at the largest of the three, which was all too familiar to her, and beckoned to Isabel.

'This is the one where we found the bibles. There's not a lot of room down there, Bel, so go slowly.'

Aina got on her hands and knees and entered the same tunnel that she had taken before. This time she was more comfortable with the terrain and before long arrived at the spot where the crates had been piled. Now there was just an empty space and the earth had been brushed clean of prints. She ran her hand through the shingly soil and sat back on her thighs.

'Everything's gone, Bel, as you expected.'

Isabel flicked her hand torch around her and nodded. What had she honestly hoped to find down there?

She turned to Aina. 'Let's just have a quick look at the other two accessible tunnels.'

Together they headed back to the central chamber. Aina, wishing to make amends for her erstwhile bad behaviour, offered to examine them alone. 'I think I'm skinny enough to crawl down any narrow passages.'

'I don't want you to go in deep, just have a glimpse around the entrances for any sign of disturbance.'

While Aina set off to explore the other tunnels, Isabel carefully examined the central chamber. It was pleasantly cool and the sour, slightly musty aroma rising up from the rocks reminded her of caving expeditions she'd made when studying at the University of Barcelona. She hadn't tackled many caves on this part of the coast, but she knew the north-east side of the island well. Although on her youthful forays she'd never found any evidence of myotragus, she had at least come across Roman coins, old pieces of pottery and even a Neolithic flint. She moved slowly around, peering at the craggy boulders, and dipping her fingers into small icy pools of water that had formed between rock crevices. The caves were a marvel to her, although she regretted that so many witless creatures from the island's past had found themselves imprisoned in their inky depths, with no hope of escape. She recalled that thousands of myotragus bones had once been uncovered in a sea cave in the west of Mallorca. Over several centuries the animals had fallen through a large fissure into a deep pit, their bones forming an ivory mountain to be picked over by archaeologists and palaeontologists of the future.

Having made a brief tour of the cavern and found no evidence of footprints or recent human activity, she pushed her backpack against a smooth section of cave wall and sat down with legs crossed in front of her. She could hear Furó scuffling about in the darkness, grunting animatedly whenever he discovered something of interest. She was disappointed that her nocturnal expedition was turning out to be a waste of time, but then, what, in reality, had she expected to find? Something that would prove that Afrim Cana or his thugs had visited the caves hot on the heels of Aina and the Torrens brothers. Even though the trip had so far achieved nothing, she didn't regret being out on the open sea, surrounded by glittering waves and a dark marbled sky, full of flirtatious stars.

Aina suddenly appeared, rubbing dust and soil from her shorts. 'I'm afraid the tunnels are blocked. All I found were a few bat bones.'

Isabel stood up and called to Furó. 'Never mind, Aina. It was worth a try. Come on, we'd better head back. '

Aina climbed the ladder while Isabel looked on and whistled a few bars of her favourite sea shanty. When Furó failed to emerge at the sound, she followed the beam of her head torch to where he was pattering about the rocks. He growled at the intrusion of light and stepped back, unmasking a shallow well of broken shells and decaying insects. As Isabel crouched to stroke his head, she noticed a cigar butt poking out of the tiny cemetery of invertebrates. Using a stick, she flicked the charred brown stub inside a plastic specimen bag and held it up to the light in some wonderment. Could this easily overlooked offering hold a clue? Carefully storing it in her backpack, she attached Furó's harness to her chest and, gripping him tightly, climbed slowly up the ladder. Aina greeted her at the top, a look of relief on her face.

'You took your time!'

Isabel smiled. 'I can't be certain, but I think my clever little ferret has just found something of potential interest.'

'What is it?'

'A cigar butt. It has seen better days and who knows how long it's been down there, but it's still dry. There's a chance that forensics could get a print from it and...'

Isabel's voice trailed off as her ears responded sharply to a bizarre and ghostly sound echoing through the tunnels. Now what in heaven's name was that?

Aina eyed her anxiously. 'What is it, Bel? Whatever is that noise?'

Isabel stood still and bristled as her ears quickly identified the source. It was the cow horn.

FOURTEEN

Isabel released Furó from his harness, and hastily rolled up the ladder and returned it to her rucksack before hurriedly heading back to the boat. Her idea of bringing the cow horn along had been more for fun than in case of a genuine emergency. Had she tempted fate? She hoped that Pep was pulling her leg by blowing on the instrument, but the urgent repeated tooting that she now heard persuaded her otherwise.

Aina scrambled after her, Furó squeezing between both their bodies to take the lead.

'Bel, do you think Pep and Pedro really *are* in trouble?'

Isabel looked back at her companion. 'Hopefully not, but better safe than sorry.'

They retraced their route along the lean, silent tunnels, coughing when showers of dislodged dirt and dust exploded on their heads. When they arrived back at the water, a strange sight greeted them. A small motorboat had appeared and was bobbing up and down a short distance away from Pedro's trawler. On board two young men sat huddled together, while Pedro stood over them with a shotgun. Pep, drenched to the skin, was securing their hands with ropes. His abandoned dinghy sat alongside the craft.

'What on earth's going on?' shouted Isabel as she ran towards the water's edge.

Pep looked across at her. 'It's a long story. Can you swim over here and take hold of the dinghy?'

Isabel scrutinised the captives from the bank. They were dark-skinned and scrawny and evidently exhausted. She hazarded that they hailed from West Africa. Pulling off her shoes, she quickly donned her swimsuit behind a rock and letting out a gasp at the iciness of the water, swam over to the dinghy. Carefully levering herself onto the edge with numbed fingers, she slithered inside and rowed it over to the bank to collect Aina. After loading their belongings and dry tube bags onto the small craft, they made for Pedro's boat. Isabel secured the dinghy to the vessel's side before they both clambered up the metal ladder and onto to the deck. Aina pulled a large towel out of one of the bags and handed it to Isabel, who was shaking with the sudden chill.

Hastily changing into dry clothes, Isabel watched as Pep fired the engine of the captives' motorboat and gently guided it over the choppy water to his father's old vessel. The friskiness of the waves made it difficult for father and son to transfer the shuffling prisoners up the ladder and onto the deck, but after several attempts the task was accomplished. Pedro handed his shotgun up to Isabel.

'Better you take this. It's my old hunting companion. I brought it along tonight as a precaution.'

'Does it work?' quizzed Isabel.

'Sure, but I didn't bring any bullets. Mind you, they don't know that.' He grinned and looked across at the unsmiling young men slouching despondently on the deck. Isabel intimated for them to sit down, the gun at her side, while Aina studied them with wary eyes.

'They look very malnourished,' said Pedro. 'I'll fetch them some food from the galley.'

He disappeared below while Pep clambered aboard, having hoisted the dinghy up by the derrick into its berth. With chattering teeth he gratefully took a towel from Aina and wiped his face.

'So what happened?' Isabel asked.

'I was in the dinghy napping when I suddenly heard my dad calling to me. Before I could say anything, he'd killed the lights on the trawler and we were plunged into darkness. That's when I heard the sound of a distant engine and a small craft entered the cave.'

Pedro returned to the deck and placed a tray of bread, cheese and serrano ham, together with bottles of water and cans of beer by the two men. He untied their hands and watched as they began drinking and eating hungrily.

'Carry on,' urged Aina.

Pedro took up the story. 'I was up on deck when I heard distant voices coming from the sea so went below and unlocked my gun. By the time I'd got back up on deck and had alerted Pep, these guys were turning their motorboat into the cave. I waited until it was level and then blinded them with the searchlights and kept the gun trained on them. Neither tried to escape.'

Pep butted in. 'Then I rowed the dinghy across, picked up my father and we took control of their craft. I decided to sound the cow horn as you instructed.'

'Well done, Pep,' said Isabel with a grin. She'd never have believed that the horn – a random memento from a holiday in Switzerland – could have resonated so far.

Pedro carried on. 'There was nothing on board. Just two thin blankets, empty plastic water bottles and a couple of torches.'

'I wonder what they planned on doing here,' Isabel mused.

He shrugged. 'Who knows? Neither seems to understand Spanish.'

'Nor English,' added Pep.

Isabel gave a small groan. 'We need to call the Guardia coastguard patrol and arrange to hand them over as soon as we reach Soller port. I'll have to do a lot of explaining as this is their jurisdiction.'

'Won't they be pleased that we've caught some potential smugglers?' asked Pep.

'We can't be certain of that. They could be refugees for all we know,' Isabel replied. While Pedro set off to the bridge deck, promising to alert the Guardia, Isabel crouched down beside the two men and began speaking in hushed tones. Pep couldn't make out what she was saying and looked on, mystified. At first the men didn't respond, but finally the younger one spoke. His companion looked up and, seemingly reassured by Isabel's response, also began talking animatedly for some minutes. Isabel replied and, patting the man reassuringly on the arm, stood up.

'What language are they speaking?' Pep interrupted.

'Portuguese Creole. They're drug runners from Guinea-Bissau who travel by boat between West Africa and the Spanish coast every month.'

'So what are they doing here?'

'Nothing. They were sent from Valencia to assess another cave slightly further along the coast that might serve as a new drop-off point for future cocaine shipments. They only came by here for a brief rest. They're exhausted.'

Pep raised an eyebrow. 'Well, they certainly got more than they bargained for.'

Soon Pedro was coaxing the vessel out of the cave and into the black night.

Aina stumbled towards them, holding fast to decking rope as the engine began to hum and the boat was suddenly buffeted against the peevish waves. 'You speak their language?'

'Just a little,' Isabel replied.

Pep stared at her in some surprise. 'When on earth did you learn to speak Creole?'

'A long time ago. I spent a year in Senegal, Sierra Leone and Guinea-Bissau. It was part of a covert operation when I worked in narcotics in Madrid.'

'You never cease to amaze me,' he replied.

'Good. Long may it continue.'

Isabel glanced across at the glum figures sitting hunched on the floor of the deck. 'These men are just runners. No doubt they got sucked into the drug trade in their teens like so many of the youths in their country. It's easy to judge, but most live in poverty and just don't want their families to go hungry.'

Pep pulled on a jersey and gripped a rail as the boat dipped and rose sharply. He watched as Aina yawned and headed for the warmth of the galley and was tempted to join her.

He turned to Isabel. 'Do you think they knew anything about the cocaine stash?'

'They've denied it, but we'll hopefully find out more when they're questioned back at base. My Creole's not good enough, but I know just the man for the job.'

'Who?'

'Gaspar Fernández, Tolo's deputy. He's half Bissau-Guinean.'

The wind whimpered and the frisky waves licked at the sides of the boat as they headed back towards Soller port. With the motorboat tethered behind, Pedro lowered the speed to ten knots and stayed on the bridge deck, his eyes fixed on the black sky before him. While Isabel remained with the captives, Pep slunk off to the galley to lie down, his seasickness apparently having returned. Shortly before the harbour came into view, he returned with a cool can of beer and handed it to Isabel. 'I think you could do with this.'

She pulled back the ring and took a long sip. 'You're right. It's been a long night.'

Some minutes later the boat entered the silent harbour. On the dock, evidently anticipating the arrival of the old vessel, stood three sombre coast guard officers. The two captives would be handed over to them and taken to the cells for the night. As the boat drew to a halt, the men caught sight of Isabel on the deck and, smiling, gave her a friendly wave.

Pep nudged her. 'That's lucky. Those officers seem to know you.'

'True, but they're the least of my problems,' Isabel replied. 'Just wait until Capitán Gómez gets wind of our illegal little caper at sea. He might just make me walk the plank.'

FIFTEEN

Isabel walked into the cool *entrada* of Ca'n Moix, frowning when she heard heavy music thumping from the floor above. Tiptoeing up the staircase, she gently pushed open the door to find Pep jiggling about in the middle of the room. With arms extended above his head, he was yelling in unison with the blaring radio 'I can't get noooo satisfaction'. Isabel watched in amusement as he performed a pirouette and found himself facing her. He stopped abruptly and rushed to turn off the music.

'Ah, Bel! I was just letting off a little steam.'

'So I see. What are you doing here so early on a Saturday?'

'Catching up on some work.'

She raised an eyebrow. 'I'm impressed. After last night's aquatic adventure, I thought you'd be having a lie-in.'

He grinned. 'Actually, it's good to be free of Angélica this morning. She's always on my back about something.'

'Just wait till you're married.'

Pep pulled a face. 'That's not going to happen anytime soon. Luckily, she's gone off to Soller market with her mother and then they're driving into Palma to shop at El Corte Inglés. That should mean I'll have the whole afternoon to watch the Barça football game.'

Isabel laughed. 'Well, once you've collected our new guests from the airport, why don't you head off home?'

'I will. I'm on my way to pick them up now. What about you?'

She gave a sigh. 'I have to go to the precinct in Palma to interview Frank Walters later this morning. At least he's out of hospital following his collapse. I'll also give forensics the cigar stub that Furó found.'

'What about our captives? Are they still being held by the Guardia?'

'I called Gaspar Fernández when I got home last night. He's going to try to calm the waters with Gómez and offer to question the two runners today, given his fluency in Creole.'

As if suddenly remembering, Pep grabbed an envelope on his desk. 'Here's that enlarged image you wanted. I just popped by the chemist and picked it up. Beatriz said it's rather old, so the quality isn't too good.'

With a cheery *adéu* he grabbed the keys to Idò's car and set off down the stairs. Isabel smiled after him, pleased to see how industrious her apprentice was becoming. Yes, young Pep had come a long way in a short time and was becoming a real asset to the business. He might have a penchant for playing loud music and dancing inelegantly at his desk, but it was a small price to pay considering his growing dedication and enthusiasm for the job. She entered her office and stroked a sleepy Furó before closely inspecting the photo of Angel Tulio Mas under the sharp rays of her desk lamp.

She tutted loudly. 'You are not all you appear to be, are you, Señor Mas?'

Then, plucking a Chupa Chup from the colourful bowl in front of her, she slowly unwrapped it and popped it into her mouth. A minute later she reached for the telephone. 'Of course!' she yelled in Furó's direction. 'Why didn't I think of it before? I know just the man to call.'

*

A desultory mob of press photographers hung about the sun-scorched porch of the police headquarters in Palma. Most looked hot and uncomfortable as they nursed plastic water bottles and bawled into their mobile phones. Having parked her *moto*, Isabel ignored them and skipped up the front steps with her crash helmet swinging from one hand. She dismissed the lift and made her way up the stairs to Tolo's department where Corc, his highly strung, agoraphobic assistant, rushed forward to greet her.

'Ah! Senyora Flores Montserrat! It's always a pleasure to see you, but if you're here to see the boss, I am afraid you will be disappointed. He is not due back from Madrid until later today.'

Isabel smiled. 'Actually, I'm here to see Gaspar, and do call me Bel. I'm not one for formalities.'

'*Molt bé*! Bel, it is.' He gave a titter. 'You know the boss always wears a new tie when you visit.'

'I'm sure that's not the case, Corc.'

'Oh, but it's true.'

Flustered and overcome with excitement, he inadvertently kicked over his wastepaper basket in his hurry to alert Tolo's deputy to her arrival. As he scrabbled around on the floor, picking up discarded knots of used paper and plastic cups, a nearby door shot open, revealing a tall and sinewy figure with a head as smooth and brown as a cocoa bean. He broke into a toothy grin. 'What's going on here, then?'

Seeing Isabel, he came forward to give her a kiss on both cheeks.

'So you've got the badge again, eh?'

'Don't goad me, Gaspar. It's a temporary measure.'

He hooted with laughter. 'Good luck with handing it back again. The boss is enjoying having you on board.'

'I'm not surprised. It means he can go off gallivanting to Madrid, hobnobbing with his superiors.'

'You're telling me! There's some young bird called Lola Rubio who's never off the phone to him. He tells me she's a bigwig at the Ministry of Interior.'

Isabel swallowed hard. 'I'm sure it's vital that they keep in regular contact on the abduction case.'

'Absolutely. Poor old Tolo's on the frontline, having to fend off the media. Not great when we've got so little to go on. Talking of which, I've got that video set up for you in my office.'

Isabel followed Gaspar into the sparse room while Corc scurried off with their coffee order. When they were seated, Isabel turned to him.

'How did you get on with Gómez this morning?'

Gaspar grabbed the TV control and paused the first still of the video. 'Well, apart from railing about you breaking the rules by entering the Devil's Horn Caves last night, he seems none the wiser as to why you were there in the first place and I didn't enlighten him.'

'So he thinks I just set off on a moonlit boat ride?'

'He's not buying that either. He knows you were up to something, but he hasn't worked out what yet. Be warned: he's on your tail.'

'What about the African runners?'

'He was fairly cooperative on that front, probably because no one in his own team speaks Creole. He's allowing us to interview them here at the precinct tomorrow at two o'clock, if that's alright with you? So much for Sunday off, eh?'

There was a knock at the door and Corc entered with two cups. Wordlessly and with trembling hands, he placed a *cortado* in front of Isabel and a cappuccino on Gaspar's desk. He scuttled out of the room and quietly closed the door.

'He's still a bit jumpy, isn't he?'

Gaspar rolled his eyes. 'Don't go there, Bel. He's a complete hypochondriac and he drives Tolo mad. You know that he only got the job here because his dad is Minister of Fisheries.'

'A case of calling in the favours.'

'Too true. His old man is best friends with the police commissioner.'

Isabel yawned. 'Let's see this video, because I've got to interview Frank Walters in thirty minutes.'

Gaspar glanced at his watch. 'Eleven o'clock, isn't it? Spot on, Bel. How do you do that?'

'Do what?'

'Know the time without wearing a watch.'

'Magical powers, my old friend.'

Gaspar laughed and pointed the remote control at the TV. A moment later, a grainy black-and-white film flickered on the screen. Isabel sat forward on her chair, riveted by the image before her. A slim, fine-boned woman with a mane of blonde hair had come into view. She wore dark shades and walked purposefully along what Isabel recognised as the busy promenade in Pollença port. Her heart missed a beat when the camera focused on the little fair-haired girl whose hand she gripped. Miranda wore shorts and a tee shirt with some kind of detail around the neck. Tiny flowers, perhaps? A watch was visible on her left wrist. Isabel replayed the film several times and on the fourth viewing, hissed across at Gaspar, 'There! In Miranda's left hand. Can you see something?'

Gaspar hovered by the screen and peered at the still frame. 'It could be anything.'

'No, you're not looking carefully. It's something soft. A small toy. Look at the way her hand is curled protectively around it.'

'Maybe. I'll ask Forensics if they can get better definition.'

'I'll hazard that it's Pinky, her little blue toy rabbit.'

Gaspar nodded. 'Is that significant?'

'Yes, it is. Miranda's mother said she always slept with the toy. If it proves to be Pinky, that will back up my theory that Miranda planned on absconding that day.'

'But why?'

Isabel stretched out her arms. 'I'm working on it, Gaspar.'

He replayed the image of the woman. She was sporty-looking, with fashionable yet simple clothing.

'What do you think of her? Is she wearing a wig?'

Isabel nodded. 'Seems like it. She's also quite composed for an abductor. She's holding the kid's hand, but it doesn't look as if any force is being applied. They could be mother and daughter with their matching blonde hair. Probably the idea.'

'So, working on your theory that the child might have known her abductor, who is she? We've cross-referenced with Interpol, but nothing has come up yet. We showed the video footage to the Walters and Marc Got last night and all categorically deny knowing who she was.'

Isabel replayed the tape. 'The woman is, what, one metre seventy? Good physique. She obviously works out. Any identification on the clothes?'

'The tee shirt is from a popular high-street chain in the States and the jeans are Levis, but that's about it.'

'Is that a bracelet she's wearing?'

Gaspar studied the screen. 'Yes, and she's also sporting a watch and earrings. None of them are distinctive, so it won't be easy to identify them.'

'It looks like Miranda is carrying her Barbie rucksack,' Isabel replied. 'I expected as much.'

Gaspar eyed her curiously.

Isabel continued. 'Her body language is relaxed. She doesn't seem afraid of the woman, which suggests Miranda knew her. If not, how did the woman persuade her to leave her mother's side that day?'

Gaspar shook his head helplessly and scratched his chin. 'And what was the motive? The whole case is puzzling. The Guardia has conducted hundreds of local interviews and done detailed searches in the area, but it's as if they were invisible.'

They both sat in silence, contemplating the last still showing the interwoven hands of abductor and child. Isabel shifted uneasily in her chair when Corc blasted into the room, forgetting to knock. He bobbed his head contritely. 'Sorry to interrupt, Sir, but Mr Walters has just arrived for Bel. I've sent him to the meeting room.'

With a stoic smile, Isabel rose to her feet and headed for the door.

*

Frank Walters sat nursing a cup of black coffee, his eyes fixed glassily on some distant point beyond the window of the bland meeting room. His fair hair, cut casually in long layers, framed a gaunt and pale face. With effort he turned to Isabel.

'So the police have made no progress whatsoever?'

Unobserved by the man sitting opposite her, Isabel's fingers danced impatiently on her knees beneath the table. 'Mr Walters, I understand your frustration, but it's been less than five days since Miranda's disappearance and our teams have been working around the clock. We already have video footage of the suspect and have alerted Interpol, international security forces and the media. The police and Guardia have been following up hundreds of calls from the general public and hopefully some of those will bear fruit very soon.'

'But you still don't know the identity of this woman and whether she was working alone.'

'Not yet, but I have every confidence that we will any time. Tomorrow artist's impressions of the woman will appear in all local and international press. It's highly likely that there'll be a significant public response.'

'Do you think this is the work of a paedophile ring?' he whispered.

'No.'

'How can you be so sure?'

'In truth, I can't be, but I've handled such cases before and this feels different.'

'How reassuring,' he said curtly.

'For one thing, Miranda appeared to know the woman on the beach.'

'That's impossible.'

'On the day of your daughter's disappearance, I believe you spoke with her by phone?'

'I rang early morning to wish her happy birthday and said that I'd give her a present when we met.'

'Had you arranged to see her soon?'

'Her plane tickets were already booked for next Saturday. She was coming to Switzerland for a week's holiday before school started. I had all sorts of things planned for her visit.'

Isabel smiled across at him. 'I hear you're an artist, Mr Walters?'

'What of it?'

'Sounds like a great line of work. What is your specialism?'

'Nature, mostly.'

'You live between Sussex in England and Vevey in Switzerland?'

'That's right.'

'Both inspirational places for an artist, I'd imagine.'

'I spend most of my time in Switzerland because that's where my work is.'

Isabel took a sip of water. 'And how has Miranda been since your divorce?'

'It wasn't easy at first, but now that Jane and I have new partners, the situation has improved.'

'What's your fiancée's name?'

'Sabine Labelle. She and Miranda get on famously. Only last month we took her to Disneyland in Paris. I have something…' Fumbling in his pocket, he withdrew a battered brown leather wallet and pulled a photo from it. The image showed a couple at a restaurant table, an angelic little blonde girl wedged between them, all smiling happily to camera. The woman's face was framed by a halo of wild auburn curls and her startling lavender eyes studied the lens intently. Isabel cradled the happy family in her hands for some moments before slowly passing it back to Frank Walters.

'She's not called Labelle for nothing.'

He offered a tentative smile. 'Yes, I'm lucky. Sabine is beautiful, as her name implies.'

'Is she coming over here?'

He sighed. 'I wish. I wasn't able to speak with her until today. She's been on a sailing holiday near Corsica and her mobile was out of range. The police managed to track her down early this morning and contacted her on the boat. Apparently, she's had a bad bout of food poisoning and needs to rest for a few days.'

Isabel nodded sympathetically 'By the way, I nearly forgot. I have something for you.' She rumbled about in her pannier and pulled out the Roald Dahl book that she had taken from Miranda's bedroom. The man stiffened, his pale blue eyes rooted to the cover.

'Mrs Walters kindly lent it to me. All my favourite childhood stories. I believe you bought it for Miranda?'

He took it from her and hugged it protectively to his chest. 'I've been looking for this everywhere.'

'Oh?'

He stared at her reproachfully. 'It was her special book. I wanted it to be there for her when she returned.' His voice cracked and he stifled a sob. 'Jane had no right to give it to you.'

'I apologise. It was just that there was a particular story I wanted to re-read,' Isabel replied.

The man's voice was icy. 'With all due respect, I think your attention would be better spent finding whoever abducted my precious daughter. And about this woman in the video – have you nothing to go on at all?'

'We're already following a number of leads,' Isabel replied.

'Such as?'

'Potential sightings and also information gathered from the video.'

He stared at her intently. 'Can you be more specific?'

'For example, the woman in the video was evidently wearing a wig.'

'A wig? How can you be sure?'

'With enhanced imaging, it's incredible what one can discover.'

'Let's hope so.' He nodded slowly and began to rise from his seat. 'Look, I think I'd like to return to my hotel, if that's OK, and look in on my ex-wife. She's not in good shape.'

'Of course. We'll inform you of any new development. The next few days will be critical.'

He gave a terse nod of the head.

Isabel offered a stiff smile. 'How is the hotel in Pollença, Mr Walters? Comfortable, I hope?'

'It's adequate. At least the ring fence of Guardia officers keeps the press scrum at bay.'

Isabel accompanied him to the corridor and waited until the lift doors closed behind him before returning, deep in thought, to the meeting room.

*

Nacho was waiting for Isabel in his cramped office and smiled as she entered. She noticed that his gold ear stud had been swapped for a small silver hoop.

'I heard that you were in the building, but I see that I'm at the bottom of the pecking order.'

'Why's that?'

He offered her a seat in front of his overladen desk. 'Well, I presume I'm last on your to-do list before leaving the precinct?'

Isabel winked. 'Actually, I was saving the best till last.'

Nacho pulled a heavy manila file from the top of his towering in tray. 'I think you could just be right.'

She eyed him intently. 'How's that?'

He waggled a piece of paper at her. 'Your visit is timely. I've just received some conclusive results from our toxicologist about Angel Tulio Mas. It seems that before he was murdered he was poisoned with a substance known as burundanga. The powder comes from the Solanaceae plant family that grows in Colombia. Although, of course it grows here in Mallorca too.'

'I know about burundanga, or devil's breath, from when I worked in narcotics. It contains high doses of the chemical scopolamine. The fact that it's colourless and has no smell or taste means it can easily be slipped into a drink.'

'Bravo! It's also appropriately known as *borrachera*, drunkenness, because it stupefies its victims and makes them passive. It's from the nightshade family and rather deceptively has very pretty white or yellow flowers.'

'And if I'm correct,' Isabel added, 'it was used by Colombian tribesmen to dope the wives and slaves of their fallen chieftains so that they'd voluntarily follow their masters into death.'

'How very civilised of them. It's estimated that in Bogotá it's used in about five hundred crimes to stun victims every year.'

'Hardly surprising, since it's cheap and easy to come by. But why did the murderer use burundanga rather than sedatives such as GHB or roofies?'

Nacho nodded. 'They'd be easier to come by, unless of course you happened to know someone who could get hold of a ready supply of *borrachera*.'

'I wonder if it was used to get Mas to reveal something before he died. Since it can act like a truth drug, some victims become zombie like and do anything demanded of them.'

Nacho shrugged. 'I can't comment on motive, but I can tell you that the drug was disguised in a glass of Club Colombia, a very traditional beer produced in Bogotá. There were traces left in the glass and in the victim's stomach.'

'Mas might have been given the drug purely to render him impotent,' she suggested. 'It would have been so much easier to kill him if he was immobilised.'

Nacho offered her a bleak smile. 'Quite.'

'What about the two discarded bottles in the wastepaper basket?'

'No traces of the drug in either. You might be interested to know that the other tumbler found at the crime scene contained San Miguel lager and that fingerprints of an Albanian named Afrim Cana were evident on the glass. He has a lively criminal history.'

Isabel's eyes sparkled. 'Afrim Cana? And were his prints on Mas's tumbler?'

'No. The glass was wiped clean but his prints were everywhere else in the room and in the hallway.'

'And the bottles in the bin?'

'Both bottles had the victim and Cana's prints on them.'

'How very careless. Any thoughts about the tyre treads on the drive?'

'Hopefully we'll have the results back on Monday. If they belong to Cana's car, it looks like you could have your man.'

Isabel stood up and removed a small plastic bag from her pannier. 'Can you take a look at this for me? I'm after any DNA or fingerprints, and the brand and approximate age of the specimen.'

Nacho swivelled the bag in the air. 'I'm not a miracle worker, Bel, although I am a cigar man myself.'

Isabel kissed him on both cheeks and headed for the stairs. Down in the lobby she called Gaspar, giving him an update on the latest forensic evidence from Nacho and suggesting that she interview Afrim Cana the following afternoon after they'd both questioned the African runners. Now that the Albanian could be firmly placed at the murder scene, she was keen to speak with him.

In some haste she left the station and headed for the motorbike parked under the shade of a bushy olive tree. She would just have time to pop by Son Espases Hospital en route back to Sant Martí. Isabel was in high spirits. Several pieces of her mental jigsaw were slotting into place and tonight she would be seeing Tolo. She looked forward to spending an evening in the company of her old and trusted friend. They would have much to discuss over good food and exquisite Mallorcan wine.

SIXTEEN

Son Espases Hospital sat like an exotic spaceship on an unprepossessing lump of barren landscape on the outskirts of Palma. Rather incongruously, its nearest neighbour was an ancient monastery that by comparison seemed rather staid and scholarly. Isabel squinted up at the contemporary medical block with its slab of sky-tinted windows and wiped the perspiration from her forehead. She thought back to her solitary swim earlier that morning in the cool and briny waters of Soller's horseshoe bay, with its panoramic vistas and old Sa Creu lighthouse. Even now, a thin white tidemark of salt stubbornly remained on her bronzed forearm like a ghostly tattoo. She was glad that she'd borrowed Pep's motorbike – so much easier than Pequeñito to manoeuvre in the narrow, crowded streets of Palma. Indicating left, she turned with care into the hospital's asphalt entrance. If so much as a tiny scratch appeared on the paintwork, Pep would never let her hear the end of it, especially as she had taken the bike without his permission.

She decided against the underground car park and deposited the *moto* in a restricted zone out of bounds to the public, leaving her orange helmet swinging from the handlebars. In the lobby a busy receptionist directed Isabel to the third floor, but it was some minutes before the lift finally arrived. As the doors opened, an elderly man leaning on metal crutches eyed her hopefully. She smiled and offered him a cheery *'Bon día!'*

He responded with a heavy rural Mallorquí burr that even Isabel found difficult to comprehend.

'You know I've had both hips replaced and now my knees.'

Isabel nodded politely. 'Then it's good you're up and about already.'

He gave a throaty cough. 'The doctors are replacing my lenses next and then I need a triple bypass.'

'And a new head and arms?' she teased.

He hesitated for a moment, deadpan. 'No, *guapa*, not yet. Well, not that they've told me.'

On the fifth floor she walked along the quiet corridor and having reached the designated room, knocked robustly on the door and waltzed in. Felip sat propped up in bed, a patch over his right eye and his left arm and leg in plaster. At his side sat Francesc, his right leg also in plaster and resting on a small plastic stool. His eyes, one still badly bruised, were trained on a football match unfolding on a nearby television screen. Both looked at Isabel in surprise.

'Hey, Bel, long time no see! What on earth are you doing here?' Felip grinned. 'Brought me some chocolate?'

She closed the door softly behind her and switched off the TV. 'I heard you had more of a preference for coke these days.'

Felip shot her a nervous look. 'Not funny, Bel.'

His brother got up and hobbled over to her on crutches, planting a kiss on both cheeks. 'Good to see you, but I'd rather wanted to see that match.'

Isabel sighed. 'No time for that. We need to talk.'

'About what?' asked Francesc.

'The mess you're both in.'

'What's it to you anyway?'

'Look, I'm just trying to help – as a friend, not an ex-cop. Tell me what happened after you tried to sell that cocaine haul to Afrim Cana.'

He frowned at her. 'What cocaine haul, and who's Afrim Cana?'

'It seems like you're suffering from amnesia as well as broken limbs. Let me refresh your memory. On Monday night you and Francesc made an unauthorised visit to the Devil's Horn Caves with Aina Ripoll in the hope of finding myotragus bones to tout on the internet. Instead, you came across a stash of cocaine hidden in crates of hollowed out bibles.'

'How do you know all this?' asked Francesc.

'Keep quiet!' hissed his brother. 'Has Aina talked to you?'

Isabel smiled at Felip. 'Just as well, given your temporary memory loss.'

The two brothers eyed her intently as she continued.

'The day after you returned from your little boat ride, you attempted to sell the drugs in Son Barassa. Unfortunately for you, Afrim Cana, the man who was expecting the shipment, got his hoods to follow you home. Having got you to own up, they took you, Felip, to the Cuber Reservoir. Why was that? Had you hidden the cocaine there?'

'We can't remember anything about that night,' he replied, averting his gaze.

Isabel pulled up a chair on the other side of his bed. 'I'm right, aren't I? It was Afrim Cana's boys who beat you both up?'

'We don't know who they were,' said Francesc petulantly. 'They were masked. Three of them broke into the house, attacked us and took Felip as hostage. All they wanted was the cocaine stash we'd found.'

'They left me for dead near the mountain refuge hut where I'd stashed the drugs,' added Felip. 'Damaged my right eye and broke my left arm and leg.'

Isabel stretched out her arms. 'A few broken bones won't kill you.'

'Easy for you to say,' huffed Francesc. 'Look at me! They broke three of my ribs, my right leg and nearly ruptured my spleen.'

'What is this, a competition?' Isabel took a bag of sunflower seeds from her pannier and began splitting the shells open with her teeth. 'Next time, don't mess with drugs,' she said with a shrug. 'Now, if you don't want to end up in the clink, I suggest you revise your story to the police.'

The two young men sat in stubborn silence.

'We didn't steal anything,' blurted Francesc. 'The boxes were there for the taking.'

Isabel laughed. 'Good try. No doubt Cana's guys ordered you to keep shtum, but since he's being brought in for questioning in connection with another serious crime, I'd advise you to tell the truth. That's if you don't want to be implicated.'

Felip stole a glance at his brother and bit fretfully on his lip.

Isabel munched on a handful of seeds. 'I like your swashbuckling, masked raider version of events, but it doesn't really hang together, does it?'

The two brothers remained silent.

Isabel clapped her hands together. 'I'm sorry you don't want to play ball, because after Aina gives evidence – and Cana, for that matter – you'll both be facing a long stretch in the slammer. Don't say I didn't try to help.'

She rose slowly. 'Of course, my heart goes out to your parents. How racked they'll be to see you both put away for years. Imagine the gossip in Morells!'

Turning the television back on, Isabel gave them a smile. 'Enjoy the match.'

As she opened the door and headed into the corridor, Felip called out to her. 'Wait, Bel! Come back. We'll tell you what you want to know.'

*

Isabel tore into Sant Martí and parked Pep's *moto* under a carob tree close to the town hall. Before preparing dinner for Tolo, she needed to water the garden and pop round to see Florentina. Midway across Plaça de Sant Martí, she caught sight of Padre Agustí heading for the church. She caught up with him and was rewarded with a benign smile.

'My dear Bel, how nice to see you. These days you never seem to have time for a chat. I take it you won't be coming to the service tonight?'

Isabel shook her head. 'Forgive me, *padre*, but life's a little frantic at present.'

'What about tomorrow? Surely you have time to make a Sunday service?'

'I promise to do my best, but I'll be working most of the day.'

He shook his head, the fine wispy hair rising like strands of white candyfloss in the soft breeze. 'And when, I wonder, did you last grace the confessional box?'

She raised an eyebrow. 'Ah, now you've got me. Actually, *padre*, I wondered whether you might be able to help me?'

'I'll try.'

'It's about Angel Tulio Mas.'

The priest lowered his head and made the sign of the cross. 'Such a devout Catholic.'

'Indeed. I just wondered whether I could show you an old photo of him?'

Withdrawing the image from her pannier, she passed it to the priest. He took a pair of ancient tortoiseshell reading glasses from a pocket in his cassock and studied the photo closely. 'That's Angel, but he was much younger then. I remember the three men with him. It was back in the seventies. They were on a Catholic pilgrimage from Colombia. A priest and two of Angel's former work colleagues.'

Isabel nodded encouragingly. 'What did you make of them?'

The priest jutted out his lower lip. 'It was a long time ago. I remember that they came to the Sunday service and we had a brief conversation afterwards. They seemed very pious men, like Angel.'

'Do you see the hand gesture they're making?'

The elderly man hung his head over the image for some moments and returned a puzzled look. 'The sign of the horns, if I'm not mistaken.'

'Do you find that strange?'

He gave a little shrug. 'I once met an American pilgrim on the Camino de Santiago who told me that the Texas Longhorns football team used it as a good luck symbol. Perhaps Angel and his friends were all sports fans back then.'

'They're using their left hands and the thumb is hidden. That's supposed to be a sign of recognition between members of the occult.'

Padre Agustí reared back in horror. 'No, that's not possible! Angel was a pillar of the church. In fact, Angel by name, angel by nature.'

'And what about the cross around the other man's neck?'

The old man peered closely again at the image. 'It looks normal enough to me.'

Isabel returned the photo to the envelope and popped it in her bag. 'I hope you're right, *padre*.'

'Can I help you with anything else?'

'How about identifying the other men in the photo? Now that would take a miracle.'

He gave her a bemused smile. 'A miracle won't be necessary. They would have signed my church visitor's book, and I have kept every single one since the end of the sixties when I first took over the diocese.'

Isabel kissed his cheek. 'You're a saint.'

The old man made an involuntary sign of the cross. 'Alas, that I will never be. I'll have a rummage in my archives tonight.'

She patted his arm gratefully and set off for home, pausing at the gate to answer her mobile phone. It was Josep Casanovas from *El Periódico*.

'Hey Bel, got a minute for an old admirer?'

She broke into a smile. 'Ah, Josep! I hope we're still meeting for a drink on Monday?'

'Of course. It'll be the highlight of my week. In truth, I was just calling to catch up on a bit of gossip. I hear you've been reinstated. Working on the Mas murder case and the abduction of Miranda Walters?'

'News travels fast.'

'So it's true?'

'I'm just acting as a sounding board for the National Police, nothing more.'

He laughed. 'That's not what I heard. So you're working with both Cabot and Gómez? You're a glutton for punishment.'

Isabel's brows knitted. 'You've got good moles.'

'I'd hope so. I pay them enough.'

'I'll pretend I didn't hear that. So how can I help?'

'I'm doing a news piece in tomorrow's edition about the video footage showing the female abductor. Any new intel yet? I can't get any sense out of Gómez's or Cabot's teams.'

'That's because there are few leads.'

'No wonder the goons have roped you in. They obviously haven't a clue how to solve either case.'

'Come on, Josep. Give them a break. It's been less than a week since everything kicked off.'

'Well, if they want help, why haven't they released a video still to the media? A digital image of this woman would obviously be much better than a police sketch. Doesn't Cabot want us to help him trace her?'

'Of course he does. I'm sure he has his reasons.' Isabel stood doubtfully in the shade of the porch. 'I'll have a word with him, but please do me a favour and cut him some slack. He and his team are working like demons at the moment and they're very understaffed. Your mischievous headlines aren't helping.'

'I'm a newsman. If they don't feed me, I just have to draw my own conclusions. You know how it works.'

'If you do a fair report in tomorrow's paper, I'll have a word with Tolo and see if we can offer you an exclusive story.'

He laughed. 'I'll see what I can do. In the meantime, do remind Cabot that it takes two to tango.'

SEVENTEEN

Isabel returned from Palma and caught the telephone on the third ring as she stepped into the abandoned office. It was Julian Mosquera, a detective with the Colombian police force and one of her old contacts. Before she set off for her habitual swim earlier that morning, she'd left him an answerphone message, not expecting an immediate response.

'Julian, that was quick.'

A warm voice flooded the line. 'We Colombians don't mess about. No Mallorcan *mañana* over here. As promised I ran a check on your murder victim, Angel Tulio Mas, but nothing showed up on our system. We've also had no luck in identifying the other three men in the image you faxed across. Some names would help.'

'I'm working on that.'

'All the same, I have something that might interest you...'

Isabel held her breath.

'By luck, when I mentioned the name to my deputy he seemed certain that he'd come across it before. Then he remembered. It was a death notice he'd read in Bogotá's *El Espectador* newspaper last week. We've checked our sources and it appears that others were also placed in *Bogotá Today* and *El Colombiano Times* in Medellín on two consecutive days.'

'Which?'

'Thursday and Friday.'

Isabel reached into her pocket and popped some sunflower seeds into her mouth. 'So these notices appeared on the two days following the murder. That was fast work. The big question is, who placed them? To the best of my knowledge, Mas doesn't have any living relatives.'

Julian Mosquera gave a hearty cough. 'You chewing on something?'

'Sunflower seeds.'

'Healthy.'

'Are you smoking?'

'Impressive. You've got the ears of an owl. I'm smoking a very fine – and unhealthy – Cuban cigar. Anyway, we contacted the advertising desks of each of the newspapers. All we've established so far is that last Thursday a Colombian guy handed over the wording and image to each one and paid in cash.'

'Can you send me a copy of the ad?'

'We've just scanned and sent it over.'

'Hold on.' Isabel woke her computer from its temporary slumber and studied her e-mail messages. 'Just got it, Julian.'

She opened the attached file and read the death notice out loud. '*In memory of the great Colombian benefactor and devout Catholic, Angel Tulio Mas, whose untimely death at the age of 78 occurred on 13 August in Soller, Mallorca, Balearic Islands, Spain. May the souls of the faithful, through the mercy of God, rest in peace.*'

'Is the accompanying black-and-white photo a true likeness of the murder victim?'

Isabel examined it closely and frowned. 'No, it's nothing like him. Do any of the newspaper offices have CCTV? Might there be footage of the man who placed the ads?'

'We're on the case. By the way, can you send me a copy of the old guy's fingerprints?'

'Sure, I'll have them sent over to you today.'

When Isabel finished the call, Furó emerged from his basket and jumped onto her lap. He looked at her expectantly.

'What do you want, my little friend? Food?'

The ferret nuzzled her hand and uttered an impatient whine. Dropping him gently to the floor, Isabel set off to the kitchen to prepare him some dinner. She felt a buzz of excitement following her call with Julian Mosquera. If her theory were correct, solving the death of Angel Tulio Mas would open a Pandora's box of secrets and deadly deeds. Of that she was certain.

*

Isabel was sitting on a wicker chair on her terrace, her bare feet curled up under her. A plump candle flickered on the table, affording just enough light by which to read her latest crime thriller. She took a sip of red wine and placed the book on her lap, tilting her head heavenwards, where a sprinkle of tiny stars throbbed in a velvety sky. From the citrus orchards she heard the screech of a scops owl, its persistent one-note cry reminding her of the ghostly sonar pulse of a submarine. A baby gecko sped across the linen tablecloth and disappeared into the unremitting darkness just before Furó padded out of the house and slunk away into the shadows for a spot of night prowling.

She glanced at her book and frowned at the sudden memory of her impromptu meeting with William Fox and his wife Sarah at Bon Día on Thursday. She had returned to the office and immediately ordered his most recent book online. It was entitled *Last Chance* and was only available in English. Isabel wasn't bothered because she usually preferred to buy English or American novels in the original language. It was the same with foreign films, which she couldn't bear to watch dubbed into Spanish. All the voice-overs appeared to be performed by just one couple – a hysterical woman with a shrill cry and a man with a deep husky tone. *Last Chance* would arrive by courier in a few days, giving her enough time to polish off the book she was currently reading.

She yawned. It had been a long day and she needed to unwind, to disconnect from the flurry of thoughts that occupied her mind. She had become absorbed in her temporary new role with Tolo and felt a twinge of guilt that she was not pulling her weight at work. Pep hadn't complained about the hours she now spent away from the office, but she had to be careful not to place too much pressure on him. It was the height of the summer season and he was working around the clock as it was. Her anxious thoughts wandered to Miranda Walters. Where was she and was she still alive? She felt certain that this was no typical abduction by a paedophile ring, but how could she be certain? Was her instinct correct or was she just trying to comfort herself? A fantastical theory was forming in her mind, which if proved correct, required a great deal more spade work. Lost in her thoughts, she gave a little gasp when she heard the insistent ring of the front doorbell. With glass in hand, she lingered in the kitchen a moment to breathe in the delicious cooking aromas before heading for the *entrada*. Tolo was standing on the porch, clutching a chic gift bag.

'Am I disturbing you?'

She wedged herself in the doorway. 'Yes, make it quick. I have a houseful of important guests and the president needs his glass refilled…'

'Then get your butler to do it.'

'If only he wasn't off duty.' Isabel smiled as she welcomed him inside. 'You took your time.'

Tolo apologised, bending slightly to kiss her on both cheeks. 'My flight was delayed, as you know, and then the commissioner asked me to pop by the office for an update.' He closed the front door. 'What is the time, anyway?'

'Nine-thirty, I'd hazard. Time for a glass of something, although I'm already one ahead of you.'

In the kitchen she poured him some red wine and, topping up her own glass, led him out onto the patio and pulled over another wicker chair. She placed a bowl of home-cured green olives, local bread and *alioli* dip between them. 'So, how are you?'

He inhaled the wine and murmured his approval. 'ÀN Negra? Pushing out the boat, aren't you?'

'A gift from a satisfied rentals client. 2005 was a good year.'

He took a sip. 'Distinctly hedonistic and intense.'

'Aromatic yet woody.'

He grinned. 'With a hint of red fruits and possibly cinnamon.'

'Violets too, I'd say. So, how was Madrid?'

'Endless press briefings and meetings with politicians and civil servants. God preserve us.'

She watched as he spread the garlicky *alioli* onto a slice of bread. 'And how's it working out with the woman from the Ministry of Interior? I can't recall her name.'

'You mean Lola Rubio? She's good news. Quick on the uptake and a shrewd operator.'

Isabel took a long sip of wine and beamed. 'It must be good to be home.'

'I'm not so sure. It's been a heavy few days. In the midst of everything else, my department's been dealing with a brutal wife-killing in Palma and the death of a pensioner at the hands of an arsonist in Manacor. Added to which I've had the international press on my back all day and that swine Casanovas is writing his usual imaginative prose. Did you see the lead story in *El Periódico* today?'

'No.'

He pulled a rumpled newspaper out of his slipcase and slapped the front cover. 'Listen to this: *"Police at a loss to find suspect in child abduction case,*"' He gave an indignant sniff and continued. '"*Leading the investigation, Chief Inspector Tolo Cabot, known for his unconventional policing methods, admitted that four days into the case the Policía Nacional was no closer to finding Miranda Walters' abductor…*"'

Isabel gave a sigh. 'Well, maybe it's worth throwing Josep a few titbits to keep him on side. As it happens, I'm meeting him on Monday.'

Tolo's face clouded over.

'Just for a quick beer and catch-up.'

'Rather you than me.'

'When he rang me, he mentioned the video footage of the female abductor. Do you intend to release a still of the woman to the media?'

'I was holding back, as Miranda's abductor won't know how much is disclosed on the tape. Good to make her sweat.'

Isabel shot him a glance. 'True, but publishing an image of the woman could get a good response from the public. On balance, though, I agree with you. Let's keep them guessing.'

'Them?' asked Tolo.

'I don't believe the woman was acting alone.'

'How come?'

'I have a theory I'm working on. Patience.'

He tapped the cover of her open book. 'I wish I had more time to read.'

Isabel shrugged. 'You have to make time, *amigo mío*, if only to stay sane.'

'So bring me up to speed on the latest developments.'

Isabel nodded. 'But first let's eat. You must be famished. I've made spinach and cod croquetas followed by paella with freshly caught Soller prawns.'

Tolo clapped his hands together. 'You are a wonder. How have you done all this when I'm working you to the bone?'

'As you know, I have special powers.'

He laughed and handed her the bag he had brought. Isabel pulled out a bottle of 4 Kilos, one of her favourite Mallorcan wines, and an elaborately wrapped box of handmade truffles from La Pajarita Bomboneria, a historic sweet store in Madrid. She examined it for a moment. 'These were always my guilty pleasure when I worked on the mainland.'

'I remember you telling me, so I hunted down the store.' He shook his head and chuckled. 'Actually, I asked Lola if she knew of it, but she said that she never ate chocolate or desserts. A bit of a fitness freak, I gather.'

Isabel wafted into the kitchen, placing her trophies in her dark larder, trying to dispel from her mind a stubborn image of a slender Lola Rubio performing cartwheels in the street, a stick of celery wedged between her perfect teeth.

It was gone midnight when Isabel slapped a bottle of *hierbas*, the island's famed liqueur, on the table and poured each of them a generous dollop of the greeny-gold liquid. Tolo rattled the ice in his glass and looked across at her. 'I've been thinking about Afrim Cana. He has to be our lead suspect in the Mas case. He was at Ca'n Mas on Wednesday evening drinking beer with the victim. His prints were all over the study, on a tumbler, and on two beer bottles found in a bin. And if you're proven right and the car treads match his Mitsubishi, he's got a lot of explaining to do. He's currently enjoying a night in our cells, so he'll be on top form when you interview him tomorrow.'

'But what about motive? And why leave such an obvious trail? Remember, too, that Cana's prints weren't on the tumbler Mas drank from, only on his own.'

'We know from your chat with the Torrens brothers that Cana's thugs attacked them and reclaimed the cocaine. It's highly probable that they're the same ones who entered Ca'n Mas, tied up the old housekeeper and kept watch while Cana bumped off Mas.'

'But why? We don't even have proof yet that Mas and Cana knew one another.'

Tolo sighed. 'What about the neighbour, Tomas Llull? He'd had a rift with Mas over his illegal *casita*. His story seemed a bit woolly and his prints were everywhere.'

Isabel shook her head. 'He's just a rubbernecker who's enjoying the media circus. As I said, I think there is more to Mas's history than meets the eye. I'm hoping Padre Agustí can identify the three men in that old image. Julian Mosquera is going to run a check on Mas's fingerprints and find out who posted those death notices in the Colombian press. All roads seem to lead to Mas's past.'

Tolo glanced at the enlarged black-and-white photo lying between them and picked it up. 'Even if your theory is correct and Mas turns out to be the devil incarnate, how does it help us?'

'In Mas's study I noticed a lot of books about the occult and all of the men in this photo are making the sign of the devil's horn. Why, I don't know, but it's no coincidence that the cocaine shipment was found at the caves of the same name.'

'So what are you saying? That Mas was involved in the drugs trade with Cana and was into some kind of devil worship?'

'That's my thinking.'

Warming to the notion, Tolo looked up with bright eyes. 'And perhaps if they were partners, Cana killed the old man that night when he discovered that part of the shipment had gone missing, believing that Mas had double-crossed him. That would explain why "thief" was scrawled on the wall in Mas's blood. Maybe Cana is into the occult too and was following some bizarre ritual?'

'Tempting, but I don't think Cana would have made it so easy for us. It strikes me that the murderer of Mas is an opportunist, someone who perhaps tried to use the theft of Cana's cocaine assignment as a perfect alibi. If Cana could be framed for a crime he didn't commit, the real perpetrator could get away scot-free.'

Tolo issued a frustrated sigh. 'We need results, fast. I can only keep the media at bay for so long – and the commissioner and Judge Baltazar, for that matter.'

Isabel got up and walked over to a stone pillar and leant her back against its cool surface. 'We have a murder investigation full of blind alleys and yet things are gradually falling into place – just as they are in the kidnapping case. I just need time to think.'

'Time isn't on our side,' he mumbled.

Yawning he got up and clasped Isabel's hands in his own. 'I'm sorry if I don't sound grateful, Bel, because that's not the case. I know how hard you're working on both investigations. It's just that four days have passed and yet we seem to be throwing up more questions than answers. I just want these cases solved quickly and with as positive an outcome as possible.'

'You and me both,' she smiled. 'Then hopefully you'll get off my back and I can resume a normal life.'

He removed his jacket from the back of his chair. 'Don't count on it.'

Isabel turned to him. 'If Miranda did know her abductor, there's every chance she is still on the island.'

'I just hope we find the poor child alive.'

Isabel was on the point of answering in the affirmative but held back.

'Me too,' she replied softly. Stretching her arms above her head towards the star-encrusted sky, she fixed him with serious eyes. 'You do trust me to solve both these cases?'

'I can't think of a safer pair of hands.'

'Thank you.'

He looked weary. 'I've overstayed my welcome.'

'Not at all.'

He led the way through to the *entrada* and stepped out onto the porch, breathing in the crisp night air. Gazing up at the ice-white stars he turned to hug her goodbye, suddenly pausing, a rosy flush staining his cheeks. 'Fabio is visiting from Madrid for a few days and tomorrow we're having dinner in Palma. We wondered whether you'd be free to join us? He always asks after you.'

Isabel stumbled over her words. 'Thank you. I'd love to see Fabio, but I'll be working at the precinct for most of the day and will be dining with my mother later. Please do send him my love.'

His voice betrayed a trace of disappointment. 'Of course. We'll just have a father and son supper instead.'

Grappling in his pocket he pulled out a slim *puro*, one of his favoured cigars, and lit it slowly. Isabel watched as he released ghostly white smoke into the dark night and headed up the silent street. At the corner he stopped and looked back at the house, a smile forming on his lips when he saw Isabel still lingering in the porch, the light from the *entrada* forming a brilliant halo about her head.

EIGHTEEN

Isabel opened her eyes and focused on the uneven white plaster ceiling above her head. Fine cobwebs hung from the old pine rafters like thin strands of spittle, trembling and fluttering under the forceful blast of the whirring fan. Propping herself up on a pillow, she observed the smokey-green hills beyond the open window, ignoring the animated snuffling of Furó in his basket. In some frustration, he jumped on the bed and began nuzzling her.

'OK, you win. So much for a Sunday lie-in.'

Yawning, she disappeared into the bathroom, emerging some minutes later fresh-faced and with her hair whipped up into a makeshift bun. She knotted an orange sarong over her yellow bikini and with a towel slung over one arm slipped on some worn espadrilles, while Furó danced at her feet. As Isabel stepped into her leafy street and headed for Pequeñito, parked under a tall plane tree, she marvelled at how cool and fragrant the air was at so early an hour. Furó curled up contentedly on the passenger seat as she wound down the windows and turned on the CD player. On the open road she sang along to the Habanera from Carmen and turned to the ferret.

'You know Georges Bizet called this aria "love is a rebellious bird". He was right.'

Furó offered her a blank stare and snuffled excitedly as she swung into a parking bay close to Repic's empty beach. There wasn't a soul in sight, although she could hear the rumble of a truck in the distance and the melodic sound of sheep bells tinkling from the hills beyond. She glanced up at the steep and winding track that led to the summit of Sa Muleta, where the stoic old Cap Gros lighthouse kept watch over the sea. In winter and spring when the water was icy and unforgiving, she and Furó would make the arduous ascent on foot early morning, sprinting to the top where they would breathe in the sharp briny air before running back down to the beach. The huddle of restaurants flanking the paved esplanade remained closed, although a delivery van hovered outside the entrance to Es Canyis, its tail lights blinking. A young man appeared from the back of the building carrying two empty crates, jumped in the driver's seat and drove off up the quiet street. A few stray yellow-legged gulls streaked the pale sky, while others, cawing wildly, dived into the frothy white waves in search of prey. Isabel guessed it was about six-thirty. Time for a swim.

Before her, the sea glistened in the rocky bay and disappeared around the headland like a never-ending bale of rich blue silk. After stretching out on the sand, she performed three erratic handstands before running headlong into the sea. She emitted a loud shriek as the cold water hit her midriff and Furó's disembodied head suddenly bobbed up in front of her like a mirage. A low haze now hung over the mountains, indicating that it was going to be another humid day. Isabel aimed with decisive strokes for the middle of the bay, her mind casting back to her supper with Tolo the night before.

On balance she should have perhaps elaborated on her suspicions and hunches and admitted that in just a few more days she thought she might bring him the answers he so desperately sought. But at this stage, without hard proof, what was the point? No, it was far better to put her theories to the test, her strategies quietly in place and let events unfold while the police and Guardia concentrated on the day-to-day distilling of public information.

She flipped over onto her back and allowed her body to float gently on the surface of the water under the first rays of a bright sun. On the beach she wrapped a towel about her and whistled loudly until Furó's head appeared above the waves, the frothy spume forming a white ruff around his neck. She dried hurriedly and with the ferret at her heels strolled to where mallards, geese, baby egrets and Muscovy ducks formed an animated gathering at the mouth of the estuary where Soller's main river embraced the sea. She often wondered how such a rarefied assemblage had found its way there, and could only conclude that many of the birds must have at one time been domesticated.

Her thoughts turned to Tolo again. He would be having dinner with his son later and she could have been there. After joining the National Police in Palma she had got to know Fabio when he returned to the island during the long university holidays. Now he had just one year left of medical training in Madrid before taking up a junior post at a hospital in the city. Tolo was immensely proud of him and Isabel had always enjoyed the young man's company. So why had she declined to join them?

Aside from her mother and Marga, Tolo was her most trusted confidant and if she was honest, her feelings for him perhaps crossed the line of friendship, not that would she let it be known. The fact was that since relinquishing her role at the Palma police precinct, Isabel and Tolo had remained close friends, totally at ease in one another's company and always relishing their time together. At weekends Isabel habitually cooked paella or steaks on an open fire up at his *olivar*, an inherited olive grove, that occupied a strip of mountain land on the outskirts of the village of Esporles, and they would sit talking into the small hours. And yet there seemed to be an unspoken understanding between them, a desire not to jeopardise their perfect camaraderie by taking the relationship in a new direction. Now they were working together again, just like old times, and surely, the last thing either of them needed were complications? She blushed involuntarily.

'What am I thinking of, Furó? There are no complications.'

The ferret nuzzled her leg and, panting, lay down adoringly at her feet. She laughed.

'You're right, I have you. What more could a girl want?'

She walked back along the seafront towards Pequeñito, stopping to admire the gleaming yachts en route. The statuesque *Monique La Magnifique* stood out from the rest, its beautifully polished wood and chrome glinting in the sun. She heard shuffling footsteps and turned to see an elderly fisherman.

'Been swimming, Bel?'

She smiled. 'It's always a nice way to start the day.'

He nodded and pointed at the yacht, wiping his brow with an old cap. 'Beautiful craft, isn't it? I watched the young skipper navigating it in on Monday night. A real pro.'

Isabel frowned. 'A young man, you say?'

'Well, anyone's young by my standards,' he cackled. 'About thirty. A born sailor.'

Isabel's brow furrowed. Had the Foxes not sailed the yacht themselves? And if they'd employed a skipper, where was he now?

Half an hour later she was back in Sant Martí and, having deposited Furó at her mother's house, made her way to Bar Castell. At the counter, Rafael cocked his thumb towards the terrace and spoke to her in hushed tones. She strode through the main bar, acknowledging various locals with a brief nod before finding herself blinded by sunlight on the open terrace. Having successfully fished her shades out of her pannier, where they lurked under a bumper packet of sunflower seeds, she headed for the only occupied table where, she surmised, a hearty breakfast had not been enjoyed.

The table's tall and angular occupant was now on his feet, ducking out from under the cream parasol and leaning forward ingratiatingly to shake Isabel's hand. She was slightly thrown off balance, more used to his normal attire – the sharp green ensemble of the Guardia Civil, comprising fastidiously pleated trousers, painstakingly polished black shoes and olive green shirt. In an attempt at levity, during the summer months the sleeves stopped short of the elbow, although the rank of the wearer was never in doubt. On both shoulders the status of *capitán* was determined by a strip of sage braid studded with three fiery gold stars, and on each lapel of the formal green jacket emblazoned in gilt was the national emblem of the Guardia Civil: the Royal Crown of Spain and coat of arms. Capitán Gómez had more than once felt it necessary to remind Isabel of the famous historical pledge of the elite military corps, *El honor es mi divisa*, honour is my emblem, perhaps to underline his moral superiority, or, Isabel pondered, his own insecurity in that regard. The man who now studied her through impenetrably black shades that perfectly matched his short military thatch wore a white linen shirt and beige chinos. Neatly laced shoes peeked out from below the hems of his trousers like two shiny black beetles, and a stylish and expensive sports watch clung to his wrist. His smile radiated bleakness.

'Wet hair? So the fable's true. You really do rise for an early-morning swim every day.' He paused. 'I'd be more careful, though. Your routine and breakfasting habits appear well known by locals.'

'Then it's lucky I'm not a spy.'

'It's not just spies who prefer to avoid unwelcome attention.'

Isabel pulled out a chair opposite him. 'The locals respect my privacy, whereas you, Capitán Gómez, are invading my private space on a Sunday.'

'Please, call me Álvaro. After all, we are supposed to be temporary colleagues.'

Rafael plodded out onto the terrace and stood defensively by the table.

'Your usual, Bel?'

She nodded slowly and stared across at the military police chief. 'I'm having *tostados*. Want to join me?'

He shook his head. 'Just another cappuccino for me. I only do fruit before midday.'

Rafael wandered off, a disgruntled look on his face.

Isabel stared across at Álvaro Gómez and observed the lean fingers resting on the table, their perfectly manicured nails, as smooth and pink as the heart of a conch. 'So, what can I do for you?'

'I thought it might be helpful for us both to catch up alone without Cabot playing go-between. Forgive me, but I'm not entirely sure that I understand your new consultancy role. It seems that you have carte blanche to carry out your own line of investigation without referral to either Cabot or me.'

Isabel offered him an elusive smile. 'Best to ask Tolo's paymasters in Madrid.'

'Ah, yes, I've heard you have powerful admirers in the Ministry of the Interior. Of course, it helps that you had a father with an impeccable track record in the force. And naturally, your own meteoric rise is well catalogued. An inspector before you'd even reached your third decade. What a feat, Isabel.'

She took off her sunglasses and placed them in front of her.

'And your point is?'

'I'm just curious that you threw in the towel so soon. I know about the unfortunate kidnapping of your Uncle Hugo and death of your father, but surely that wasn't the real reason for giving up such a promising police career to become, what, a glorified housekeeper to foreigners?'

She offered him a blank stare.

'I've thought about it and wonder whether at a subliminal level you felt your exceptional run of luck might peter out. That the golden girl with the stash of solved cases under her belt might be rumbled. That, at the end of the day, all those successes might just have been a gift from lady luck.'

Isabel enjoyed the moment.

'If I'd known you were so keen on amateur psychology, I'd have lent you a few of my old university tomes.'

The shades remained in place, only the mouth twitched.

Isabel continued. 'Interesting what you say about luck. I've always liked to think I've made my own.'

Rafael reappeared with another cappuccino, a *cortado* and a basket of toasted chunks of bread smeared with fresh tomato pulp and olive oil. Casting a wary eye in the military chief's direction, he deposited them on the table and left.

'Are you going to eat all that?'

Isabel reached for some salt and a paper napkin. 'Just watch me. You see, I only do carbohydrates before midday.'

The gaunt face gave way to an alligator smile. 'Touché.'

She whipped the sugar around in her coffee cup and took a sip. 'So, what is the real purpose of your visit?'

'Cards on the table, I'm not happy about your involvement in the kidnapping or murder case, which in my opinion should have been a matter purely for the Guardia with support from Cabot's team.'

'Your superiors and the presiding judge, Jorge Baltazar, don't seem to agree.'

'Maybe not, but I'm the one on the frontline and I dislike such interference. I don't enjoy sharing, for that matter.'

'That figures. You were the eldest of what, three or four kids?'

'Four. How did you know that?'

'Just a hunch. You had your own private fiefdom before the others popped up?'

'For seven years, actually.'

'Must have been tough, especially as they weren't even your own flesh and blood.'

He paled. 'Have you somehow managed to access my personal data?'

'Wouldn't need to. You mentioned once in passing that your mother was widowed when you were four and that you were her only child. She obviously remarried – a widower, I'd hazard – and acquired some stepchildren. All younger than you.'

He didn't reply.

'It must have been hard not to feel resentment and territorial at that young age.'

'I didn't resent them,' he replied coldly.

'Your mother, then.'

'She had to secure our joint future. Remarrying was her best option.'

'And yet ironically it left you feeling more alone and insecure than ever.'

He removed his sunglasses to reveal a pair of steely green eyes. 'You're wide of the mark, I'm afraid, Isabel, but ten out of ten for trying.'

'And of course it explains your attitude to women.'

He glared at her across the table. 'That's enough.'

'Very well. Besides, if I told you any more, I'd have to charge you.' Isabel crunched on her toast and observed him coolly.

'We can all play at amateur psychology, Capitán. Sometimes, we might even get it right with a bit of… what did you call it, luck?'

Álvaro Gómez stroked his face absentmindedly, an erratic tic needling his left cheek. 'Returning to the subject in hand, I don't want you muddying the water in my own investigations. You had no right to interfere in the Torrens assault case.'

'That was never my intention. I believed that the cocaine haul that the brothers and Aina Ripoll discovered at the Devil's Horn Caves might have a direct impact on the Mas murder investigation.'

'And has it?'

'You'll know from Gaspar that we're interviewing the two drug runners this afternoon and also Afrim Cana. I hope that our findings might shed further light on the matter.'

'And Gaspar mentioned that you speak Creole too. Is there no end to your talents, Isabel?'

'I'll leave that for you to decide.'

'Our joint superiors, in their eternal wisdom, seem to feel that combining our efforts will speed up the process. I'm not so sure. It seems to me that my force has been left to do all the tedious legwork while you and Cabot's team hog the limelight.'

'Neither Tolo nor I are looking to score brownie points, Capitán. We just want to find Miranda and the killer of Mas as soon as possible.'

'You think the two cases are related?'

'No.'

'Neither do I, so we agree on one point.'

'So what is your take on the Mas murder?'

'I think it's quite straightforward. The old man's housekeeper opened the door at around six o'clock to four masked men, one of whom fitted Cana's build and profile. He tied up the old woman and shared a cosy drink with an unsuspecting Mas before murdering him. His three sidekicks must have kept watch. As you know, Cana's fingerprints were found on a glass and all over the study, and the tread marks on the drive will most likely match his vehicle.'

'But what was the motive?'

He shrugged. 'Hopefully you'll discover that when you interview Cana this afternoon.'

'And you honestly think he'd be foolish enough to leave his prints everywhere and yet studiously clean Mas's glass after killing him? It's madness.'

'Few people are in a particularly sane state when they commit murder, Isabel.'

She leant forward. 'In the spirit of cooperation, I want you to look at something that might be of interest.'

She pulled an image from her pannier and passed it to him. He scrutinised it closely. 'Who are these people?'

'It's Mas and three of his religious cronies.'

'And where did you get hold of this?'

'Let's just say lady luck put it my way. Take a close look at their hands.'

He issued an impatient grunt. 'Is it some kind of thumbs up sign?'

'No. It's the sign of the devil's horn. You extend the forefinger and pinkie and hold down the middle two fingers with the thumb. Like this.' She gave him a quick demonstration.

'And what is so significant about the gesture?'

'Normally it's a fairly harmless sign to ward off bad luck or it's meant as a crude insult, but its use here is distinctly odd.'

'I don't follow.'

'If you look closely, you'll see that one of the men is wearing a dog collar, and another a bizarre cross which appears to have a black pentagram at its heart. It's known as the devil's cross. It therefore becomes a defiant and mocking gesture against Catholicism, the supposed religion they all represent.'

Gómez ran a hand across his forehead. 'I'm glad you've found a use for your criminal psychology degree, but you're reading far too much into what is probably a symbol of male camaraderie.'

She sat back in her chair. 'Have it your own way, but when I visited Ca'n Mas, I noticed a significant number of books on the occult in the study. Is that normal for a holy man?'

'Better to know one's enemy, wouldn't you say? You have a fertile imagination, which of course is part of your charm.'

Isabel slapped down her empty glass. 'When I've got something tangible, I'll let you know and then you can thank me.'

A smile hovered on his lips. 'I'll look forward to that.'

'And once we have concluded both cases, you won't have to worry about me anymore. I'm just passing through.'

'In the meantime, I want your assurances that I will be kept apprised of all developments. And that also means anything you personally might discover using your, how should I say, unusual methods.'

He paused before adding, 'I'm willing to cooperate and even tolerate your presence if it gets the job done.'

Isabel crunched ferociously on her last piece of toast. 'Very magnanimous of you, Capitán.'

'As for that poor abducted child, it's surely the work of a paedophile ring.'

'I don't think so. Luring a child off a beach in full view of hordes of holidaymakers wouldn't be easy. It's most likely someone she knew.'

'To the contrary – I think a crowded beach would serve a potential abductor well. People would be too busy to notice anything much, so I don't concur.'

She shrugged. 'It's a free world.'

'And now I must press on.' His eyes lingered on her face for a moment. 'By the way, how do you know Aina Ripoll, the girl who tipped you off about the cocaine stash at the Devil's Horn Caves?'

Isabel stood up and slung her bag over her shoulder. 'Her parents own the bakery in Morells. They sell the best *ensaïmadas*. Nice family.'

'Do you know everyone around the valley?'

'I try to make it my business. Don't you?'

He rose to his feet, and suddenly gestured to her left hand, where there was an absence of rings. 'Still searching for your white knight? Don't leave it too late, Isabel. I wouldn't want you to become a lonely old woman.'

She threw him a radiant smile. 'I've heard that white knights aren't all they're cracked up to be. And in this village one might get old, but never lonely.'

They walked through to the bar where Rafael stood wiping a beer glass. He nodded at Capitán Gómez. 'Ten euros.'

'I'll pay,' Isabel said, waving a note in Rafael's direction.

The military police chief snapped at it like a hungry crocodile and, pressing it purposefully back into her hand, said, 'My treat.'

Bending low, he kissed her fingertips and headed for the door, pausing only to slap a crisply folded note from his wallet onto the counter before sauntering out of the bar.

NINETEEN

Isabel took a long sip of coffee and cast her gaze at the dingy white walls around her and at the grubby tiled floor. Although a freestanding fan whirred incessantly from a corner of the room, the heat was cloying. She was in need of a good Sunday *siesta*, but there would be little chance of that today. The two suspects sat before her, both with eyes downcast and hands folded loosely in their laps. Isabel was not enjoying the desultory tone of the interview, not helped by her rusty Creole. Earlier Gaspar had been called to attend a serious incident on the outskirts of Palma, so she was having to muddle through on her own. She leant forward.

'So, let's recap to make sure I've fully understood. Your names are Jawara and Allie and you're both natives of Guinea-Bissau?'

They nodded.

'And together you got involved in drug running in your early teens and have been working for different drug traders for the last ten years?'

The younger of the two shifted in his chair and cocked a thumb at his companion. 'Allie introduced me to them. I only got involved because my mother was poorly.'

The other man opened his mouth in protest, exposing a set of crooked yellow teeth. 'You're a liar, Jawara. You wanted money for yourself not just your sick mama.'

Isabel held up a hand. 'So your specific task was to handle cocaine distribution around the Spanish coast and the Balearics?'

Allie laughed. 'Yeah, but we're just small fish. There are big ships with cocaine and other drugs leaving Guinea-Bissau, Senegal and Sierra Leone all the time. They go all over Europe.'

'Have either of you ever heard of Afrim Cana?'

'No,' replied Allie, while his companion shook his head.

'Listen, if you cooperate with me, I can make sure you walk free. Understand?'

Allie gave an irritated sigh. 'Hey, man, we only heard about some big shot Albanian guy here in Mallorca who was running a drug op, but that's all. No one told us his name so we can't say if it's this dude, Cana. We're just runners. They don't tell us nothing.'

'Is this Albanian involved in the Devil's Horn Caves operation?'

'I might have heard that from someone,' Allie replied evasively.

Isabel sat quietly for a few minutes. 'Do you get paid well for what you do? It must be dangerous work.'

Jawara sniggered. 'Don't make me laugh, man. We get paid peanuts doing the dirty work for the guys who make all the money.'

His companion nodded. 'Yeah, that's right.'

'So why do it?'

'Better than being back in Guinea-Bissau. Everyone's hungry or dying.'

'So how long have the Devil's Horn Caves been used for drop-offs?'

Allie answered. 'About five years.'

'Have either of you come across a Colombian named Angel Tulio Mas?'

Jawara avoided Isabel's gaze while his companion offered a nervous shake of the head.

'No, we don't know about no Colombian.'

'What happens to us now?' asked Allie. 'We want immunity.'

'And I want some hard facts and names, so what is to be done? I suggest you spend the rest of today jogging your memories and then we'll talk further,' Isabel replied. Wishing them good day, she left the room. She would be interviewing Afrim Cana in less than an hour but first wanted to telephone Gaspar and update him on her meeting with the drug runners. And there was also the small matter of taking Furó for a quick walk. Corc was keeping an eye on him in the reception area, but she felt that her lively ferret might enjoy attending her next interview.

After a quick phone call with Gaspar, Isabel strolled along the Paseo Marítimo, Furó padding enthusiastically along at her side. She was enjoying the gentle sea breeze and the accompanying sharp whiff of ozone that cut through the humid air, offering a little respite in the pulsating heat. Gaspar was investigating the fatal stabbing of a British holidaymaker in El Arenal following a pub brawl in the resort but had promised to interview Jawara and Allie later that day. With his fluency in the Creole language Isabel was confident that he might extract more crucial information out of the two young men than she had.

As she made her way to the police interview room with Furó dallying along the corridor behind her, one of the officers on duty gave her a wry smile. 'I'm not sure how the commissioner would feel about a ferret interviewing a suspect, but as it's Sunday, I'll turn a blind eye, Bel.'

'Well, we like to play good cop, bad cop.'

He gave a chuckle. 'Just so you know, Cana doesn't speak much Spanish. He's better in English.'

'So I heard.'

With a complicit wink, he opened the door and promised to pop back with some coffee. Afrim Cana offered Isabel an insolent stare as she entered the room and pulled out a chair opposite him. Taking a bag of sunflower seeds from her pannier, she addressed him in English.

'Want some?'

He ignored her, although he kept a wary watch on Furó, who emitted a series of growls as he busily explored the spartan room.

'He's bored. Do you like ferrets?'

Afrim Cana's mouth formed a snarl. 'Filthy creatures.'

'Be careful what you say. He's bitten my assistant for less. Seems like you've run out of cigarettes.'

He looked down at the stub of his hand-rolled cigarette and pinched it hard as if it were a tiresome insect. With some impatience he flicked it to the floor and began tapping his fingers on the table.

'I have nothing to say.'

He allowed his eyes to wander upwards to the small barred window in the airless room.

'Have you ever read Franz Kafka?'

He frowned at her.

'Freedom,' observed Isabel, 'is so important to the human state. Consider the grim monotony of prison life. Day after day in a stifling cell, straining to see just a tiny square of blue sky. Imagine listening for the sharp and transitory cry of a passing gull, the kiss of a breeze, the rumble of traffic. Such a sad way to witness the passing of the seasons, don't you think?'

Silence.

'Well, Mr Cana, if you're not feeling talkative, I can go for a coffee and leave you and my ferret to become better acquainted.'

The Albanian shifted uncomfortably in his chair and in broken English, replied. 'My lawyer say under Spanish law I only need speak in front of Judge Baltazar, not police.'

'Correct. But if whatever you say has to be corroborated in front of a judge, why not answer my questions now? You can always deny everything later. I'm not recording our chat and I'm not taking a witness statement.'

'So why should I speak to you?'

'Why not, if you've got nothing to lose? I might even be able to help you.'

'I want a cigarette.'

Isabel waggled a packet of Marlboros in his direction. 'All yours, if you cooperate.'

He nodded. She flicked the packet towards him and watched as he stuffed a cigarette hungrily between his lips and ignited it with a stylish silver lighter.

'Impressive.'

'You smoke? Know Davidoff, St James's Street, England?'

'No.'

A rattle in the throat, followed by a busy cough. 'I buy there. Good cigars.'

'I hear that Marc Got has given you a share in his Magaluf club. Is that true?'

He shrugged. 'Maybe.'

'Why would he do that? I've heard the club's not doing too well.'

Cana's beefy shoulders rose impatiently inside his costly black jacket. 'Marc had some financial problems, OK? So I help him. In return he give me thirty percent of club.'

'And how do you help him, exactly?'

He blew out a plume of smoke. 'I supply dancers and promo girls for his club and do his marketing.'

'Is that your main business?'

He grinned. 'Yes. I am marketer and entrepreneur. I make much money in Albania.'

'One of the lucky few. And, of course, drugs make for a very lucrative business. Do you supply them to Marc Got?'

'I never even seen drugs.'

'So why do you live in Son Barassa and hang out at dives like Son Gotleu?'

Afrim Cana smiled sardonically. 'I never go Son Gotleu – it's bad place, full of heroin junkies. Son Barassa has friendly community.'

Isabel couldn't suppress a smile. She was enjoying the game. 'It's also the cocaine capital of the island.'

He puffed out his bottom lip. 'Really? I don't know this.'

'Have you ever heard of the Devil's Horn Caves?'

'No.'

'Did you meet two brothers named Felip and Francesc Torrens last Tuesday?'

'I never heard of them.'

'I think you have. They tried to sell you back your own cocaine, didn't they?'

He shook his head. 'As I said, I don't do drugs.'

'Do you know a man named Angel Tulio Mas?'

Isabel observed him carefully.

'I read in newspapers that he was murdered this week.'

'You knew him?'

'He was a religious man. Sometimes I gave him money for his charitable work in Colombia.'

Isabel resisted the urge to laugh. 'Did you visit his house last Wednesday evening?'

'Maybe.'

'At what time?'

'About six o'clock.'

'Why?'

'Angel and I often prayed together.'

The door to the room opened and an officer placed a *cortado* in front of Isabel, silently motioning for her to speak with him beyond the confines of the room. She stepped out into the corridor and after a hurried conversation cursed under her breath, nodded and returned to the room.

Isabel tore open the small sugar packet placed on her saucer and stirred the crystals into her coffee. 'Remind me what car you drive?'

'A Shogun. The police already know this.'

'Colour?'

'Black.'

'Did you murder Angel Tulio Mas the night you visited him?'

'No. We were friends. I had beer with him and left.'

'Did you visit alone?'

'Yes.'

'At what time did you leave?'

'Maybe six-thirty or later, I don't remember exactly.'

'What did you do after you left?'

'Met some friends.'

'So you have an alibi? Someone who can confirm your whereabouts?'

'I had drinks with three neighbours in Son Barassa.'

Isabel laughed. 'In that case we might as well get a witness statement from the three wise monkeys. Who opened the door to you at Ca'n Mas that night?'

'Angel.'

'Did you attack and tie up his housekeeper?'

He laughed. 'She's old woman. I'm not a monster. Why would I do that?'

'I don't know. You tell me.'

'Listen, I visit Angel for a social drink and leave. I never see that old housekeeper.'

'How often did you visit Señor Mas?'

'Maybe once a week for prayers and a chat.'

'So what did you talk about? The missing cocaine shipment?'

He sighed impatiently. 'I told you. I know nothing about drugs.'

Isabel took a sip of coffee and sat back in her chair. 'Then let me fill you in. Colombia is the largest producer of raw coca. In the past the traditional drug route used to be northwards to the Caribbean and then on to Europe and America. Now, drugs are often sent over the eastern frontier into Venezuela and flown by old aircraft such as DC-9s or Boeing 727s across the Atlantic to West Africa.'

'Fascinating.'

'And small countries like Guinea-Bissau make ideal transit points because they have little ability to police their airspace.'

'Really?'

'In fact, in West Africa there are many young men from impoverished backgrounds who risk their lives by becoming drug runners. Two such men washed up on the north-west coast of Mallorca on Friday night. They were found at the Devil's Horn Caves.'

'I don't know this place.'

'Unfortunately, it's a restricted zone and out of bounds to the public and yet, would you believe, some unknown persons have been using it for some years as a drop-off point for cocaine.'

He grinned at her. 'Shocking.'

'The latest drop was contained in bibles, so perhaps they were good religious dealers or merely had a sense of humour. What do you think?'

'I couldn't guess.'

'I have a theory that I'd like to share. I think you and Angel Tulio Mas were in the cocaine business together. You went to Ca'n Mas that night to tell him that part of your shipment had been stolen. I don't know whether you argued or fought and I don't know whether you killed him, but it won't be long before I find out.'

The Albanian remained mute.

'The good news is that the forensics team has identified your fingerprints all over his study and soon we'll know whose car tyre tracks were in the drive that night. I'm guessing they'll belong to a Mitsubishi Shogun.'

Afrim Cana didn't flinch, although Isabel noticed from the corner of her eye that his polished black loafer jerked under the table.

'So what happened that night? Did you go to Ca'n Mas with the intention of poisoning and incapacitating the old man before you knifed him to death? Was it a deal gone sour? Did you go to recover something he'd stolen from you?'

Cana jumped to his feet. 'I want my lawyer. You have no right to hold me here.'

Furó gave a low hiss.

'How odd,' mused Isabel. 'Furó normally likes Albanians.'

'I want to leave.'

'Just one last thing. Did you drink the same beer that night?'

Afrim Cana stubbed out his cigarette. 'As always, Angel drank Club Colombia and me, San Miguel.'

'Just one?'

He drummed his fingers against the wood. 'Yes, just one.'

'You're free to leave.'

Cana rose to his feet in some confusion. 'I can go?'

'Yes, but as they say in the movies, don't leave town.'

TWENTY

At the head of the enormous mahogany table in the mayoral office, Llorenç was gesticulating wildly like an impassioned conductor. It was Monday morning and before him sat his twelve disciples, who each had a critical part to play in the forthcoming Sant Martí festivities. Across the *plaça*, the quivering hands of the geriatric clock that graced the bell tower of Sant Antoni suddenly struck ten and chaos briefly ensued. Clashing discordantly with the clanging of the bells, ten deep and cavernous booms resonated around the room, causing the diminutive mayor to cover his ears. His companions stoically gritted their teeth until both bells and clock came to an abrupt halt. Pep resumed his animated speech. As the youngest member of the committee, he valiantly attempted to put forward a case for serving cocktails and canapés at the village event rather than the usual more traditional Mallorcan fare. As he finished, the mayor's brow crumpled like that of an old bulldog.

'What's wrong with serving up *sobrassada* sausage and *coca*?' he thundered. 'They're surely everyone's favourites?'

Murmurs of approval came from the assembled throng.

'Since I was a babe in arms, Sant Martí has served the same fare at every celebration. Even during the gruelling Spanish Civil

War, my grandparents and their contemporaries kept the tradition going in the village, albeit in clandestine circumstances. If Franco's henchmen had discovered the truth, all of them would have been taken out and shot!'

Pep reared back in his chair. 'Oh, come on! Shot for serving *sobrassada*?'

Llorenç relished the moment. 'Indeed, young man, but what would you know about deprivation? Here in Mallorca, Franco tried to strip us of everything we held dear – our language, our culture, our very roots.'

Jesus from Bon Día nodded his head vigorously. 'He's right. If you were caught speaking Mallorquí, you'd cop it, and eating *sobrassada* or *coca*, who can say?'

The mayor crossed his arms and fixed his beady eyes on Pep. 'It seems to me that you are merely proposing change for change's sake?'

Pep rolled his eyes. 'I thought it might just bring a fresh touch to the evening. Even in Palma they've started serving canapés.'

'What kind of canapés?' barked the eponymous owner of Jordi's bar.

'Things like smoked salmon and caviar on little squares of black bread, or tartlets of anchovy and *aioli*...'

His voice was drowned out by heckling and laughter.

'Food for *maricones*!' yelled the elderly Jordi excitedly, until he noticed that Alfonso, the much-loved village artist and token gay of Sant Martí, was casting him a sour glance. He caught his eye and mouthed an apology before rising to his feet.

'Can you imagine if I started serving up fancy bits on sticks in my bar? I'd be the laughing stock not only of this village but the whole of the Soller valley!'

More laughter.

Llorenç gesticulated to Jordi to take his seat. 'The point is, young Pep, that here in Sant Martí we do not follow the crowd.

THE DEVIL'S HORN

We take pride in the customs that have formed the backbone of community life: that is our strength. For good reason we are the envy of Fornalutx and Biniaraix and other villages in the valley. Over the centuries we have suffered earthquakes, plague, civil war and poverty, but never once did our forefathers give up, nor did they forget the heritage that defines what Sant Martí is today.'

Fierce applause broke out.

'*Bravo*!' yelled a buxom *señora*, wiping a tear from her eye.

'Well said,' another cried. 'Llorenç, you are wasted as the town's *batle*. You should be in the senate in Madrid!'

Llorenç smiled modestly and held up a hand to silence his admirers. 'And that is also why for three years running we have won the award for most traditional village in the whole of Spain. Soller might think it's the king of the valley and Fornalutx the prettiest, but little Sant Martí gets all the accolades. They cannot compare with our village, which is why the townspeople envy us from the bottom of their hearts. We are the veritable jewel in the valley's crown.'

Pep sighed deeply and shook his head. He saw no reason to continue arguing with these old fossils who lived in an eternal time warp. Alfonso cast a sympathetic glance in his direction and winked, but it did little to lift his mood. He vowed to himself that one day he would move to Palma, where he'd open his own rentals agency or perhaps even go into private detective work with Isabel. Maybe with Llorenç's daughter Angélica on his arm he himself could aspire to be mayor of the village one day. That would shake the old fogies up. Anything was possible. For now he'd bide his time.

'So,' said Llorenç. 'We must plough on with the agenda. Lest we all forget, the Nit de Foc is but a week away. We are unanimously agreed on the food. *Sobrassada, pa amb oli* and *coca*?'

The door swung open and Isabel appeared, her hair still damp and cheeks flushed from an early-morning swim.

'Apologies, but I had to make some important calls.'

Llorenç leapt from his seat and ushered her to a chair left vacant at his side.

'Our very own sleuth in the valley,' he chuckled. 'Who would have thought that our Bel, a mere slip of a girl and citizen of Sant Martí, would be showing the men in blue and green how to do their jobs?'

Isabel gave an awkward smile as everyone indulged her with nods of approval. 'I hope I haven't missed too much.'

'Not at all,' replied Llorenç magnanimously. 'We've only just got started. Now we shall move on to entertainment for the night.'

He turned with a wolfish smile to the hapless young man sitting directly opposite him. 'So, Pep, tell us, any more bright ideas?'

*

Isabel and Pep were halfway across the *plaça* when she heard a feeble cry. Turning, she saw Padre Agustí attempting to flag her down from the stone steps of the church. She decided to wait while Pep made his excuses and headed back to the office.

'Padre, how are you?'

He gripped Isabel's hands in both of his. 'Good news! I discovered the names of Angel's three Colombian friends.'

Isabel felt her head buzzing.

'Ah, here we are.' He unfolded a piece of paper from his pocket and examined the orderly handwriting. 'The priest was Padre Paz García, and his two friends were Cruz Ramírez and Andres Moreno. When I found the visitor book, I noticed that I'd made a note in the margin by their names. I'd written "The Brotherhood".'

'What does that mean?'

He offered a puzzled frown. 'I've really no idea. I presume that they were all part of a religious brotherhood in Colombia.'

Isabel took the paper from him and carefully stowed it in her pannier.

'Padre, I don't know how to thank you for this.'

'I do,' he beamed. 'I shall expect you at confession next Sunday.'

She squeezed his shoulder affectionately. 'Now that's an invitation I couldn't possibly refuse.'

On the corner of her street, Isabel stopped abruptly at the modest house owned by hypochondriac pensioner Señora Coll, the village postmistress. In the absence of a formal post office, due to the tiny population of Sant Martí, she had fulfilled the role from her own home for more than twenty years but was now finding the task onerous. Lately she had decided only to open shop before noon and accompanied the processing of post and parcels with heavy sighs and mournful headshaking. As Isabel stepped onto the porch, a small elderly woman was exiting the premises. It was Camila Cortez. Isabel smiled and touched her arm. 'How good to see you again, Señora. I am still dreaming of your heavenly iced lemonade.'

Camila Cortez's face filled with pleasure. 'Then you must come and visit me again some day. It is so lonely now without Señor Mas.'

'As it happens, I would like to meet with you on a confidential matter. Might you be free later today or tomorrow?'

'Alas, this afternoon I am being re-admitted to Son Espases Hospital for a scan. Can you come to Ca'n Mas on Wednesday morning?'

Isabel nodded. 'Of course.'

The old housekeeper smiled and patted Isabel gently on the arm, then walked slowly along the path, the handle of her worn black handbag grasped tightly in both hands.

Seated behind a large mahogany desk in the dark interior sat Señora Coll. She was wearing a white nylon overall draped over a floral dress. Isabel pulled a clump of envelopes from her pannier and handed them to her.

'How are you today, Señora Coll?'

The elderly matron shook her head miserably as she began selecting stamps for the bundle of post. 'Terrible, as usual, Bel. What with the stress of this job and the heat, it's a wonder I'm still alive. And don't mention all the foreigners queuing up for stamps this summer and not a word of Spanish between them. If it wasn't for Doctor Ramis' magic pills, I'd have faded away long before now.'

'Perhaps you really should retire and hand over the baton to someone else?'

'Retire? Impossible! There's no one here that I could entrust with such a role. No, this is my burden, one which I must bear until such time as the good Lord dictates.'

Isabel stifled a grin and nodded sympathetically. 'Well, that's a relief to us all.'

*

In the office Pep smiled when he saw that Isabel was clutching a paper bag. 'So you've got your fix?'

'And yours.' She pulled two plates from a cupboard, placing a chocolate croissant on one and handing it to him.

He gave a murmur of delight. '*Gràcies*. My favourite, but don't tell Angélica. She's said that we've both got to lose weight before the wedding.'

Isabel stared at him in astonishment. 'You're getting married?'

He licked a chocolaty finger. '*Qué va*! In her dreams. She says she'd like us to marry next year, so I just smile and say nothing. As if I'd give up on life so soon.'

Isabel laughed. 'Well, don't string her along, Pep. Get some *cojones* and tell her it's far too soon to think about marriage.'

'Rather you than me.'

She grinned. 'Sorry that you lost your battle at the meeting this morning.'

He tutted. 'To be expected. Nothing much changes in this village. By the way, I have a bone to pick with you. You stole my *moto* over the weekend and you damaged it.'

'Don't be so dramatic, Pep. I merely borrowed it. You left the keys in the office and I had to get to Palma quickly.'

'I needed it this weekend.'

'What for? You have a car.'

He looked away. 'It doesn't matter now.'

'So what was broken?'

'The right wing mirror.'

Isabel nodded. 'Ah, yes, it seemed a bit faulty. When I parked it, the silly thing dropped off. I put it back, though.'

Pep smirked. 'Yeah, the wrong way.'

Isabel was about to reply when the telephone rang. She wiped her greasy fingers on a paper napkin as a strangled cough ricocheted down the line. 'Is that you, Tolo?'

He sneezed into the receiver. 'Apologies, I have hayfever. It always comes at this time of the year.'

Isabel curled the cable around her fingers. 'My grandmother used to take freshly squeezed lemon juice with honey. It always worked for her.'

'I'll stick with antihistamines, if it's OK with you. I'm not a great one for home remedies.'

'More fool you.'

He gave a hoarse cough. 'Any news?'

'My local priest has identified the three men in that image with Mas. I'm sending the names to Julian Mosquera today.'

Tolo's fountain pen hovered momentarily over a network of stars and hearts that he had unwittingly doodled on the blotting pad in front of him. 'Good work, Bel.'

'Padre Agustí said that they were from a brotherhood in Colombia.'

'What kind, I wonder?'

213

'One,' said Isabel ominously, 'that might prove not quite as godly as Padre Agustí might like to think.'

There was a pause. 'I'm off to Madrid again today. Lola needs to catch up with me on a few fronts, but...' Tolo sneezed loudly while Isabel nibbled irritably on a nail.

He continued. 'I wanted you to know that we've just had a hopeful lead in the Miranda case. A local woman from Pollença has just called my department to report a potential sighting.'

'Why has she only just come forward?'

'She went on holiday last Tuesday and only returned today. When she caught up with local news she called us immediately.'

'So what did she see?'

'She claims to have bumped into a young woman with long fair hair just off the esplanade in Pollença port. She said that the woman was holding hands with a little girl with a pink rucksack strapped to her back.'

'Anything else?'

'It seems that they stopped by a blue Clio. The window was apparently down and the driver, a slim young man with short brown hair, was urgently beckoning the woman and child to get in the car.'

'We need to check out every Clio and rental car company on the island.'

'Gaspar and the team are on the case, but it's going to take time. It's possibly the most popular car in Mallorca.'

'There may be a faster route than that. How about we give Josep Casanovas an exclusive for tomorrow? I'm meeting him for a drink later.'

Tolo frowned. 'I forgot you were drinking buddies.'

'Just seems like an ideal way to get him on side,' Isabel replied.

'I'll leave it in your capable hands,' he replied. 'There was one other thing about Miranda.'

Isabel waited.

'According to the witness, the child was clutching a toy. She said it was a little blue rabbit.'

TWENTY-ONE

Isabel was sitting back in her chair, eyes closed, one foot gently tapping the cool marble floor beneath the desk. She listened intently to the deep husky throb of guitar strings, the sudden cascade of bittersweet plaintive chords that wafted from the speakers like an intoxicating musk until, with maddening predictability, the door to her office flew open and Pep yelled, '*Olé!*'

'Is that all you can say?' Isabel bawled over the sound of excitable strings. She jumped up from her chair and lowered the volume on the CD player.

'You don't say "*Olé*" to the *Goyescas*!'

'The what?'

Isabel massaged her temples and let out an exasperated sigh. 'Surely even you've heard of Enrique Granados?'

Pep scratched an ear. 'Vaguely. Is he a guitarist?'

A voice boomed behind him. 'Guitarist? Only the greatest Catalan composer and pianist who ever lived.'

Isabel clocked the whiskery visage of her next-door neighbour, Doctor Ramis, popping up from behind Pep's shoulder.

'Sorry to interrupt, but the front door was open. I wondered whether I might leave some medication for Señora Coll. She was due to pick it up from the surgery an hour ago but hasn't turned up.'

'You shouldn't pander to her hypochondria, Doctor Ramis,' scolded Isabel. 'There's nothing wrong with her stomach. She just has too much time on her hands.'

'I know that, which is why I prescribe her my very own peppermint pills,' he replied with a wink, placing the brown glass bottle in her hands.

Isabel laughed when she read the tiny black letters inked on the label. '*Panacea pancita*? Panacea for the tummy? You old fox! So, how will she know to come here?'

The portly doctor tapped his prominent, rosy-hued nose. 'I've left a note to that effect on my front door.'

Pep observed him keenly. 'So where are you going?'

'Off to lunch, of course. A medical man cannot possibly function without food.'

'Nor can a dogsbody like me, but I doubt I'll be allowed out of the office today.'

Doctor Ramis patted Pep's shoulder sympathetically. 'I'll leave you to your taskmaster, then.'

As he turned to leave, the door to the main office sprung open and Florentina appeared like a genie from a bottle.

'Not so fast! I've just laid out lunch in the kitchen.' She turned to Dr Ramis. 'You'll join us won't you, Miguel?'

'*Pues*, Florentina, I was on my way to Bar Castell, but if you insist…'

'I most certainly do.'

'And what exquisite delicacies are on the menu today?'

She shrugged. 'Snails, Russian salad, stuffed squid, garlic prawns, and cod and jamon serrano croquettes.'

Doctor Ramis' eyelashes quivered as he faked a swoon. '*Basta*! I can't bear any more. Florentina, I genuflect at your culinary shrine.'

'Me too,' Pep piped up.

Doctor Ramis kissed her hand and caught Isabel's eye. 'Perhaps poor Señora Coll can join us too if she turns up? After all, she's a poor lonely widow with bouts of dyspepsia…'

'Aren't we all,' replied Florentina with a chuckle. 'Come on, Pep, help me dish up downstairs.'

Isabel barged past Pep and raised her hands in the air.

'Mama, this is an office not a canteen. Pep and I have important work to do.'

Florentina gripped the doctor's arm. 'You know, Miguel, my daughter promised to give up police work and then I found out from Pau, that sweet young officer at the town hall, that she'd been sniffing around old Mas's place with that police chief in Palma she used to be sweet on…'

'God give me strength,' muttered Isabel as she resolved to give Pau an earful for tipping off her mother.

'Examining the corpse of an old man. Imagine! I thought she'd done with all that, but it's in the blood, Miguel. Her father was the same. And now she's getting drawn into that abduction case too. What is a mother to do?'

Doctor Ramis pulled at his moustache. 'Cook and eat, my dear Florentina. That is the only solution.'

Isabel watched as they trooped down the stairs, her mother's sharp *'venga'* ringing in her ears. She peered round her office door, and smiled to see Furó asleep in his basket despite the uproar having taken place around him. Relieved to have a few moments to herself, she walked over to her busy whiteboard and scrutinised the growing number of scribbled notes and headers scrawled with marker pen. Coloured post-it stickers with jottings had been slapped onto different sections, each one segregated from the next by heavy black lines. Images of Angel Tulio Mas, his three brotherhood cronies, Miranda Walters and an assortment of newspaper cuttings from the British, international and local press had been clipped on to the easel's frame. Isabel stood thoughtfully in front of the sea of information. What was she missing? A floorboard creaked and she smiled when Idò bounded in from the main office.

'So you've been summoned to lunch too?'

He nodded and pointed to the board. 'Any further developments on the Miranda case?'

'A witness claims to have seen Miranda and a blonde woman getting into a blue Clio driven by a man. It's quite a breakthrough.'

'What would a couple want with her? Maybe they don't have a child of their own and decided to run off with her.'

'She went willingly.'

'You're sure about that?'

She nodded emphatically.

'And what about Mas? Are you any closer to identifying the killer?'

'Or killers, Idò. There's a Colombian connection and I suspect dark arts are at play.'

Her uncle eyed her glumly. 'Be careful, Bel.'

She squeezed his arm. 'Come on, I'm a big girl now.'

He gave her an uncertain smile. 'Still, for your mother's sake, don't take risks.'

As the sound of distant chatter rose up from below, Idò cocked his head absentmindedly towards the door. 'You know your mother sent me up here to fetch you.'

'OK, let me turn off the music.'

Idò held up a hand. 'Wait, this is "El Amor y la Muerte". The guitar arrangement is good, but being a traditional old fool I still prefer the piano original. Sometimes I wonder if Granados hummed this piece as he attempted to rescue his wife in the English Channel. You know that when their boat was torpedoed by a German U-boat during the First World War he could have saved himself, but instead...'

'... he tried to swim to her and they both drowned. Yes, and he had a lifelong fear of water. Perhaps he had a premonition of his death. I wonder if old Mas did too.'

They stood quietly in thought until an exasperated shout from Florentina had them both scrambling for the staircase.

*

Florentina and Idò sat on Isabel's treasured leather sofa sipping glasses of ice-cold limón granizado while Furó slumbered between them.

'It's good, but it needs more sugar.'

Florentina bashed Idò's arm. 'No, it's perfect. This is our grandmother's recipe.'

'*Exacto*, and I remember as a kid that it was always bitter because she never sweetened it enough.'

'She didn't want our teeth to drop out.'

Pep, who sat propped up against Isabel's desk with legs outstretched and locks gelled to perfection, tapped the floor impatiently with his foot. 'It's great lemonade, Florentina.'

Idò thrashed the arm of the sofa, causing Furó to growl in his sleep. 'And what would you know? Always rotting your teeth with those fizzy drinks!'

'At least my teeth are real, Idò.'

Isabel turned to face them. 'Can you all stop bickering? I can hardly hear myself think.'

Florentina drained her glass and stood up. 'Well, I'm off for a siesta. I've eaten far too much.'

'It was an excellent lunch, mama,' said Isabel, softening, 'but before you go, can I ask you all a favour?'

Idó sniffed suspiciously. 'Well?'

'When are you due to check the pool at Ca'n Mayol?'

'Thursday,' he replied. 'And Pep's coming to help me.'

Pep tutted. 'I hope Mr Fox isn't about. He's a misery.'

'I'd like us all to go,' said Isabel. 'You too, mama. You can give the kitchen a light clean while we're there.'

'Why?' asked Florentina. 'That's not part of their rental agreement.'

'It doesn't matter. I just need you to act as a diversion while I take a quick look about the place.'

'Whatever for?' replied Florentina, alarmed.

'I'm not sure yet, but I think I'll know when I get there.'

*

Isabel sat under a parasol outside Café Paris in Soller's main square. It was early evening and yet the sun was still pounding. From her chair she watched as a gaggle of local children, evidently enjoying their long summer holiday, sold home-made cakes from a makeshift stand by the town hall. Some elderly matrons were circling the table, gently pressing the sponge cakes and nodding in approval. Nearby a sleepy Guardia officer puffed on a cigarette, flicking the ash onto the cobbled street as he watched the children do a brisk trade. He called over to them and a second later a little girl presented him with a *magdalena*. The officer ruffled the child's hair before taking a healthy bite from the little sponge cake. Isabel smiled to herself, enjoying the wilful flouting of EU legislation: minors trading without a street licence, the flagrant disregard for health and safety regulations, and best of all a military police officer smoking while on duty. With effort she forced herself to sit upright and focus on the lean and handsome visage of Josep Casanovas. He gave her a laconic smile.

'You were miles away.'

'Sometimes it's good to reflect on what good fortune one has. This place and the people are special.'

He laughed. 'You know, Bel, the first time I met you I knew you were special, so it makes sense that you live in a special place.'

Isabel sipped on her lager, marvelling at how unctuous Casanovas could be. 'And because I'm so special, I hope you will be able to do me a small favour.'

A faint frown passed across his lineless brow, quickly replaced by a grin as he swished back his mane of subtly highlighted hair. He rested his chin on his hands and studied her intently. 'Anything for you.'

'Tomorrow I'd like you to run a headline story about the brilliance of the police team handling the abduction case, heaping praise on Álvaro Gómez and Tolo Cabot, as well as Tolo's deputy, Gaspar Fernández…'

Josep fixed his seductive grey eyes on her. 'Are you mad, Bel? I can't stand Cabot. You never know what's going on in that crazy head.'

'That's very true,' smiled Isabel. 'If you do this for me, I'll give you an exclusive.'

'I hope it's more exciting than the images of Miranda and her female abductor we eventually got from Cabot. The quality was appalling.'

'It was the only video we received.'

'So, what have you got for me?'

Isabel told him about the new eyewitness who had come forward in Pollença and watched as his eyes lit up.

'You reckon the blue Clio is a hire car?'

'Most probably. I'd like you to put out an appeal for information. It'll be quicker than going through the normal channels. Time isn't on our side.'

'And what can I say about you in my report?' he asked.

'*Nada*. I don't exist as far as the public is concerned. I am invisible.'

'Not to me,' he simpered.

The young waiter ambled over to their table. 'Another San Miguel, Bel?'

Isabel nodded. 'Maybe one more for the road. You too?'

Josep Casanovas smiled. 'Any excuse to stay longer in your company. So, when are we going to have time for a relaxing dinner?'

Bel sighed. 'As soon as you deliver the goods, Josep.'

He pulled out his notebook and beamed. 'In that case, Bel, let's map out the story.'

*

At eight o'clock Isabel and Furó found themselves in deep undergrowth playing chase with a field rat. Isabel stopped to catch her breath.

'He's gone, Furó. Game over. Let's go back to the car.'

The ferret made a strange gurgling sound and set off purposefully along a rocky track heading into the hills. Isabel issued a sharp whistle. 'Come on! Mama's cooking paella and I don't intend to miss it.'

Furó hesitated, panting hard.

'You see, you need water. Don't be so stubborn.'

Defiantly he wriggled into the long grasses and disappeared. It was still light, but a circle of dull cloud sat like a ball of putty above the horizon, partnered by a whimsical breeze. Isabel turned abruptly when she heard the sound of approaching footsteps. A woman was talking animatedly in French on her mobile phone. Shamelessly eavesdropping, she waited to see who was heading her way and smiled when Mrs Fox appeared from behind a clump of rocks. In some surprise, the woman hurriedly cut short her call.

Isabel stepped forward to greet her. 'How nice to see you again. I hope you are enjoying your stay at Ca'n Mayol and that your husband's writing is going well?'

'It's wonderfully tranquil and William is making good progress with the book.'

'I see you're a walker like me.'

The woman offered a tentative smile. 'Yes, it's good to stretch one's legs. Are you walking far?'

Isabel shook her head. 'I'm on my way home, if I can persuade my companion to join me.'

Isabel turned on the track and whistled a tune.

'That's a nice song.'

'It's an old Mallorcan sea shanty. It normally has the right effect.'

The woman reared back as a ball of fur bounded towards them. 'Oh, heavens! Is that a ferret?'

'Don't worry, he's quite friendly.'

'You don't like dogs?'

Isabel laughed. 'Of course, but ferrets have their own charm. So do you have everything you need? We'll be over to change the sheets soon, probably Thursday.'

'Thank you, but please can you call us first? My husband hates unexpected visitors when he's writing.'

'I understand.'

Isabel turned to her with a smile. 'I meant to ask before, do you skipper your own yacht?'

'*Monique La Magnifique*? Of course, my husband and I are both keen sailors. We don't need hired hands.'

Isabel clicked her fingers at Furó, who promptly followed the two women back to the woodland car park, sniffing the hedgerows as he trotted along.

'This is my car,' Mrs Fox announced as they arrived at a black Golf. 'I look forward to seeing you again.'

Isabel watched as the woman briskly fired up the engine. The vehicle stalled. In some exasperation she restarted it, revving so hard that the sound sent birds fluttering from the trees. With her eyes trained ahead, she swung out of the car park. Just as Isabel reached Pequeñito, she was hit by a sudden thought. Mrs Fox's silver bracelet swam before her eyes. Where, she wondered, had she seen it before?

TWENTY-TWO

As Isabel entered Bar Castell she heard Rafael yelling animatedly into his mobile phone. She could tell by his pained expression that he must be conversing with his elderly widowed mother, who as everyone knew was woefully deaf. Every Friday he would call her to make laborious arrangements for his customary weekend visit. It had been some years since the old lady had relocated to Es Plà, the agricultural heartland of the island, to be nearer her ninety-year-old sister-in-law, but it might as well have been the moon as far as Rafael was concerned. After all, he was a Sant Martí local for whom the centre of the universe would always be Soller, and Mallorca's other towns and villages merely satellite planets of the Soller solar system.

The day hadn't begun auspiciously for Isabel. On the way back from her habitual swim in the port she had had a spirited altercation with Angélica, Pep's girlfriend, which she was trying to distance from her mind. Picking up a copy of *El Periódico* on the counter, she read the lead story and smiled. Josep Casanovas had been true to his word. She fumbled for her mobile and left a message of thanks on his answerphone. Next she called Tolo.

'I see that creep Casanovas delivered the goods. What did you have to do for him?'

She laughed. 'You wouldn't want to know.'

'Then don't tell me. We've already had thirty calls this morning and one is a hot lead. A car rental agency in Magaluf hired a blue Clio to a man fitting the suspect's description the day before the kidnapping. The car was never returned.'

'Do they have the guy's licence details?'

'The licence was in the name of a John Gilbert. It turned out to be fake.'

'What about a credit card?'

'The guy used a cloned card. According to the agency, card cloning, or skimming, is becoming quite a problem for hire car companies.'

'Damn. Anything else?'

'He said the guy was clean-shaven and in his thirties. Wore jeans and dark shades.'

'It's a start. In fact, it's got me thinking.'

He gave a dry laugh. 'That's ominous. I'm afraid I have to cut you short. You've caught me on my way to a press briefing.'

'Some things never change,' muttered Isabel.

She stepped out onto the empty terrace and briefly observed Sant Martí's tranquil *plaça* below before taking a seat under a parasol. An excitable bee waltzed about mid-air, before finally landing on her outstretched arm. She examined it closely, her mind still occupied with thoughts of Rafael's deaf mother. Of course, as any fool knew, bees didn't have ears, but they did at least sense vibrations just as a worm or an ant might, for that matter. She remembered as a child examining a dead ant with a magnifying glass until her father had put her out of her misery and declared that ants didn't have ears. Now she sat deep in thought working her way through an A to Z of animal, amphibian and reptilian life, reminding herself which creatures failed in the ear department. She'd passed snakes and reached turtles when her mobile phone rang, jarring painfully with the doleful chiming of the church clock as it struck eight. She caught the phone on the last ring.

'*Diga?*'

'It's Emilio Navarro. I have news.'

Time froze for a split second. She felt her heart thud against her chest. With all that had been going on, she'd let thoughts of Uncle Hugo slip from her mind. Hiring Emilio, a private investigator in Barcelona, to uncover the truth about her uncle's disappearance had allowed her to take her foot off the pedal. But in handing over the baton to another experienced pair of hands, had she somehow relinquished responsibility? She had been impressed with Emilio's track record when they'd first met and felt that he could be relied upon to pick over the carcass of the investigation with objectivity and a certain clinical ruthlessness. He was forty-eight, a former Spanish military officer and police detective who had worked in covert operations in Europe and South America. When she'd met him in his pokey office above a hairdresser's shop in a shabby district of Barcelona, he had chosen his words with meticulous care, as a dandy might his wardrobe. And yet his searing analysis of the criminal underbelly of South America coupled with his background in narcotics surveillance had assured her that he was the man for the job. Lean and fine boned, he had dark eyes that sagged at the corners, perhaps weighed down with all they had been forced to witness during his years undercover in countries where savagery replaced the rule of law.

Isabel had been distracted that day by a livid scar that ran from just below the investigator's right ear to the base of his neck. Emilio had caught her eye and smiled laconically. The scar, he told her, was a salute to the nine months he had spent as a prisoner of the FARC rebels in Colombia back in 1997 when he had been chained up in a coop along with a group of the country's paramilitaries. Although he'd managed to escape, he never explained how he had received the scar, or how he'd been captured by the guerrilla group in the first place.

She wondered why he was calling her now. It was barely a month since she'd given him the brief, and although she needed to know what had happened to Hugo, she dreaded learning of his death. She braced herself.

'So tell me.'

'You recall Daniela Sánchez, the woman in Barcelona who testified four years ago that she'd seen Hugo being abducted?'

'Of course.'

'She was found dead in her flat yesterday. Dosed up on a cocktail of drugs. Apparently, the local police discovered quite a cache of cocaine and heroin lying about the place.'

Isabel emitted a small gasp.'What are they saying?'

'Suicide. She was a known user and also took medication for depression.'

'Will there be an investigation?'

'Very unlikely. She was a prostitute with no relatives and a drug history.'

'What's your take?'

'I'm keeping an open mind, but it's suspicious. Where would she find money to buy so much smack? She didn't have a pimp. But that's not the most disturbing part of it.'

Isabel momentarily lost her grip on the mobile phone and watched in irritation as it landed on the terracotta tiles. Hastily she clamped it back to her ear with a shaky hand.

'Bel?'

'Sorry, go on.'

'Last Tuesday she called me. She sounded drunk but said she'd remembered something significant. On the night your uncle had been dragged into a black car, she'd noticed a sticker of a yellow, blue and red flag on the back windscreen. It matched one she recently saw on a television show. It was the flag of Colombia.'

'Why didn't she tell this to the police at the time?'

'She said it completely slipped her mind until she saw the same flag on TV last week.'

'This could be crucial to the case.'

'There's more. We agreed to meet at a local bar last night because she had recalled some other details about the abduction, but she never showed. Now I know why. I heard about her death only this morning.'

To her embarrassment, Isabel found tears welling up in her eyes. She gripped the edge of the table and gulped hard.

'Where does this leave us?'

Emilio sighed. 'On a positive note, it means that I can follow one particular line of investigation. At some stage I'll need to go to Colombia.'

'If you do, I'll be coming with you.'

'First let me do some more digging here in Barcelona.'

'Will you tell the police about all this?'

He hesitated. 'At this stage, I'd rather not. I'm not sure whom to trust.'

'Within the police?'

'All I'm saying is that I'd rather keep my powder dry.'

Isabel pinched her nose and attempted a level tone. 'Hey, Emilio, don't take any risks – and watch your back.'

He emitted a hollow laugh. 'I do. Every damned day.'

Watch his back or take risks? Maybe both, Isabel surmised. She replaced the mobile in her pannier and cupped her eyes with her hands, unaware of Rafael's presence. He walked softly over to her and squeezed her shoulders.

'Ánimo, amiga mía.'

She gave him a watery smile.

'And now I will resurrect your soul with a perfect *cortado* and the sweetest *ensaïmada* pastry in the whole of the valley. Nothing comforts better than calories and a decent coffee.'

*

Before heading for the office, Isabel made a small diversion up Camí Vell, a cobbled track off her street, where she booked a haircut at Marga's salon. By the time she arrived at Ca'n Moix, the sun was sizzling in the sky and all she could hear was the sound of hissing cicadas and buzzing bees. She opened the front gate and addressed the wild borders of bushes, gaudy flowers and long yellowing grasses.

'Shh! I can hardly hear myself think.'

As if acknowledging the final sweep of a conductor's baton, the garden suddenly ceased to throb.

'Thank you, my friends.'

A wide-brimmed straw hat hovering like a flying saucer on the other side of the wall caught Isabel's attention.

'Doctor Ramis?'

'Ah, Bel, I was just taking heed of your words and trying to tiptoe around my garden as quietly as possible.'

She clambered through the undergrowth and stood on an upturned plastic crate that she kept by the wall specifically for the purpose of neighbourly engagement.

He smiled up at her. 'By the way, did Señora Coll pick up those pills yesterday?'

'Yes,' Isabel replied. 'She said they were a lifesaver.'

'Excellent. Another satisfied customer. So what have God's little helpers done to offend you this morning?'

'I've not had a good start to my day.'

'That makes two of us. What's ruffled your feathers, *reina*?'

Isabel whisked a strand of damp hair from her face. 'On the way back from my swim Pequeñito broke down by the Monumento roundabout, and while I was waiting for Chico...'

'Young Chico, the mechanic?'

Isabel nodded impatiently. 'Well, anyway, Furó spotted a little brown *ratero* sniffing about the roadside and chased him.'

'Did he gobble it up?'

She tutted. 'He gave it a tiny nip on the leg, but as I called him off, I recognised the dog immediately. It belonged to Angélica.'

'That awful yappy hound? It's more like a flea on a lead.'

Isabel laughed. 'When I returned, Angélica shouted at poor Furó and even threatened to denounce me. It's her own fault for letting her mutt roam so far from Sant Martí.'

Doctor Ramis grinned conspiratorially. 'Still, I suppose it's better not to upset the mayor's daughter, especially a particularly spoilt one. Where's Furó now?'

'I left him here in disgrace while I went for breakfast at Bar Castell.'

'Quite right.'

'Tell me about your difficult morning.'

Doctor Ramis gave a sigh. 'A new traffic warden has been posted here from Soller and had the audacity to give me a ticket. Tough as an almond shell, with eyes the colour of steel. She must be from the Peninsula.'

'Perish the thought that she'd be a Mallorquina!' Isabel teased. 'Where were you parked?'

'On the *plaça*. I was just popping by Bon Día to get my baguette and when I returned to the car, the silly girl accused me of illegal parking.'

'Rather stating the obvious.'

'Quite. And as I pointed out to her, all of us locals park on yellow lines. Besides, my indicators were flashing to show I would return imminently.'

'We can't have a traffic warden issuing tickets to locals. Whatever next?' Isabel grumbled.

'*Exacto*. In Soller, you can't even smoke in a bar nowadays thanks to the new tobacco laws. At least Pau sensibly turns a blind eye and we locals can carry on smoking in Jordi's bar.'

Isabel shook her head. 'I'll speak with Llorenç. Tear up that fine.'

As she turned to go, Doctor Ramis called out.

'I nearly forgot. A parcel arrived for you today. By its feel it must be a book, but I have no idea what the title is.'

'I'm glad your curiosity didn't get the better of you.'

He handed it to her over the wall. 'I wouldn't dream of opening another person's mail.'

She gave him a wink. 'It's a crime thriller by William Fox, a British author who's renting one of my properties.'

'And the book's title?'

'*Last Chance.*'

'Sounds a bit gloomy,' he replied. 'I doubt I shall be borrowing it if it's in English. Besides, as you know, I prefer historic tomes, especially those about the Spanish Civil War. And now I'd better adjourn to my waiting room. Rather a full house today.'

Isabel waved as he pottered back into his hallway, clutching a pair of secateurs and a trug brimming with lemons. Doctor Ramis lived in a timeless universe, a fact that his doting patients seemed to accept with good grace. Instead of cursing and fighting to get to the head of the queue – and how pointless that would have been with no receptionist in situ – they would arrive with happy diversions – newspapers, card games and embroidery, even cups of coffee and *ensaïmadas* from the local bars – until the good doctor called them to his consulting room, one after the other.

Entering the velvety cool of her *entrada*, Isabel listened for a discordant disco beat, but the house was still. On her desk lay a bag of Chupa Chup lollies, together with a note from Pep explaining his absence. He and Uncle Idò had gone to fix a faulty swimming pool filter at a rental property in the village of Biniaraix and he had taken Furó along for the ride. It seemed that Pep and her ferret were becoming firm friends. She smiled and unwrapped one of the lollipops. Had he really gone to Bon Día just to buy one of her favourite indulgences? But wait. Isabel froze and fixed her gaze on the brightly coloured packet. Then scuffing her head with her hand, she gave a frustrated laugh, recalling a recent encounter that had now taken on new significance. Why ever hadn't she thought of it before?

For the next few hours she worked diligently at her desk, picking up the telephone in Pep's absence and answering the many e-mails flooding her inbox. Chiding herself for placing so much responsibility on Pep's young shoulders during the last frenetic week, she resolved to allocate more time to her agency work early in the morning and late at night, when she could put her onerous assignments for Tolo briefly aside. Isabel heard the telephone ringing in the main office. She was surprised to hear Nacho Blanco's voice.

'Good news, Bel. We've just had confirmation that the tyre tracks on the drive of Ca'n Mas belong to Cana's Shogun. With his fingerprints all over the study, there's surely enough to hold him in custody?'

'It's not that simple. When I was at the police precinct on Sunday, an officer interrupted the interview to advise me that Cana's wily lawyer had just raised bail. We still don't have a murder weapon and as you said yourself, Cana's DNA has not been found on the corpse of Mas or on the tumbler containing burundanga. I need something more.'

'I have something else. We've been able to analyse that cigar butt you left me. It's a Zino Platinum Crown cigar from a shop called Davidoff in St James's Street, London. One cigar would set you back a fistful of euros.'

'Any DNA traces?'

'Sure,' Nacho intoned deeply. 'I'm happy to confirm that the cigar belonged to Afrim Cana.'

*

At seven-thirty that evening, Julian Mosquera telephoned from Bogotá. He sounded breathless.

'You OK, Julian?'

'I've just run up two flights of stairs. Our elevator's out of action again. I'm going to make you happy. I've found out quite a lot about the three guys in that image with Angel Tulio Mas, and they're a pretty nasty trio.'

Propping the phone under her ear, Isabel grabbed a handful of sunflower seeds and began furiously dissecting each one in turn. 'Go on. I'm all ears.'

*

Having waited with growing impatience for Tolo to return her call, Isabel strode about her office debating whether to hold fire or take matters into her own hands. It was already nine-thirty and the sky was darkening outside her office window. What Julian Mosquera had told her had set her mind whirring and her pulse racing. It had all but confirmed a shadowy theory that had dogged her thoughts since the killing of Mas. Tomorrow morning she would be visiting Ca'n Mas and would have some stern questions to ask of the elderly housekeeper, who for whatever reason appeared to be withholding vital information. She also urgently needed to re-interview Afrim Cana. Throwing caution to the wind, she resolved to drive over to his abode on the notorious sink estate, Son Barassa, without Tolo's blessing. True, Cana's lawyer would have much to say on the matter and Tolo might chastise her, but instinct told her that time was of the essence. She hesitated and dialled Tolo's mobile number, killing the line when she heard the answerphone message. Cheerlessly, she gave a sigh. Her former boss no doubt had a lot on his mind right now, not least the athletic Lola Rubio in Madrid.

She observed Furó napping in his wicker basket and decided to drop him off at her mother's house en route to Son Barassa. Her mother would want to know where she was going at that time of night and in a flash of inspiration, she thought of Josep Casanovas. Yes, she would feign a late supper in the port with the smooth editor. Picking up her bag and car keys she paused momentarily by the sofa where her new purchase, *Last Chance*, sprawled on the brown leather. Carefully examining the cover, she noted down the publisher's name on a scrap of paper before hastily dialling a UK number on her mobile phone.

*

A windswept and litter-strewn parcel of bland terrain greeted Isabel as she rode into Son Barassa under the setting sun. Ahead of her she could see a huddle of dreary and squat one-storey terraced houses, some no better than hovels, their faded white facades pockmarked with holes and broken windows. On the roofs, concrete slabs and plastic sheeting had replaced rows of missing red tiles, while crude white satellite dishes jostled for space. High above them, an ugly cat's cradle of slack pylons and low-slung cables seared an ominous grey sky, scarring the distant mountains, while at ground level, barefooted, sullen children, their faces covered with grime, played listlessly in the squalor.

Revving Pep's *moto,* Isabel set off down the uneven track into the heart of the shantytown. Soon after she arrived at her prize, a sizeable dwelling at the end of a terrace. The front door, painted an electric blue, sported no name or number, but a sign daubed with the words **LARGO DE AQUÍ!**, Get away from here, had been nailed to a wooden post by the porch. She remembered the property from her days in the police force. It was known as the drug hub, and it was owned by Afrim Cana. Although the drug dealer owned lavish properties in other parts of the world, he appeared to spend much of his time in his dishevelled Mallorcan lair. Parking a little distance from the house on a stretch of scrubland, she killed the engine and removed her helmet. A grubby communal yard sprawled before her, strewn with decaying supermarket trolleys, decrepit and soiled mattresses, scrap metal and abandoned washing machines.

In the gloom, Isabel had the uncomfortable sensation that her every move was being monitored. Standing with her back to the motorbike she became aware of several ragged youths nearby. Silent as stones they observed her steadily and sombrely from their muddy perches. She knew that locals referred to them as *gitanos* – gypsy kids – whose statelessness made them a despised and afeared group. They had a reputation for lawlessness, aggravated robbery and petty theft, and most had never received any kind of education. One of the children, a boy of no more than ten, sidled over to her, his narrow black eyes full of menace, and placed a tanned paw on the motorbike's leather seat. Isabel sprang forward just as the child lashed out at the bike's back tyre and in one agile move had his hands in cuffs behind his back. He stared at her in fury, wriggling violently as he tried to set himself free. The others moved forward protectively, a little unnerved and uncertain as to what to do. Isabel smiled at them all and reaching into her pannier pulled out a bag of Chupa Chup lollies. Briskly she handed them around and, releasing her captive, suggested that if they guarded her bike she would reward them with euros. One of the teenagers shrugged and, discarding the lollipop wrapper at his feet, gave a nod. 'How much?' he asked.

'Five euros each.'

A sullen girl slunk over to her. 'And a ride on the *moto*?'

Isabel nodded. 'If time permits.'

'You buying drugs off Cana?' she asked.

'You know him?'

'He's big around here. Be careful or he'll slit your throat.'

Isabel frowned. 'Is he home?' The word jarred.

'Haven't seen him all day,' the girl replied.

Isabel walked through the small huddle of youths, an inexplicable cold and sickly dread gripping her stomach. The sun had set and the sky, now overlayered with coppery clouds, had visibly darkened and a few drops of rain began to fall. In the distance the jagged peaks of the Tramuntanas, like a row of sharp and discoloured teeth, poked through low-lying cloud, stifling the horizon. A wild breeze gusted in, whipping up dust and grime and shaking the branches of the squat palm trees with such ferocity that their leaves rustled like raffia skirts.

Striding towards the dilapidated property, Isabel knocked robustly on the front door and waited. The windows had long since lost their panes and were boarded up with cheap plywood, while over the front door a moss-choked drainpipe hung down dejectedly, disgorging a thin stream of rusty water. After a moment Isabel pushed against the door and was surprised when it swung wide open. The hot and muggy passage before her was enveloped in darkness, although she could hear a gentle creaking as the wind raced inside, upsetting a pile of old newspapers stacked near the entrance. Isabel pulled out her torch and took a few tentative steps forward. She called out, but no one returned her greeting. As she edged further along the corridor a gut-wrenching smell filled the air and the creaking loudened. A frenzied buzzing could be heard and as the light of Isabel's torch hit its mark, she gave an involuntary cry. Staring at her with bulging, cloudy eyes, Afrim Cana's distorted face came into view. His body was swaying gently in the breeze, a swarm of excitable flies clustered about his neck, which had been compressed by a taut ligature. Tremulously she raised her torch, shining it on the thick wire that had been affixed to a beam.

With haste she retraced her steps, covering her nose and mouth as she stumbled into the dark night. The children watched her dispassionately before one of them stepped forward and demanded money. Slamming the front door shut, she thrust a fifty-euro note into the boy's clammy hand and watched as he and his urchin companions sped off across the bleak scrubland in the descending rain. Isabel huddled in the flimsy porch and pulled out her mobile phone. She spoke urgently into the receiver and when she'd finished the call, dialled another number.

Tolo's voice was hoarse. '*Diga?*'

Isabel strained against the wind and rain. 'It's me.'

'Bel, forgive me for not returning your call earlier, but I've been stuck in meetings all day with my superiors. Are you OK?'

'I'm at Son Barassa. I got here too late.'

'What are you talking about, Bel?'

Isabel could hardly make out a word Tolo was saying as the rain drummed against her face and thunder steamrollered the sky. 'I've called Gómez for backup. The Guardia will be here any time.'

Tolo bawled into the receiver. 'What on earth has happened?'

'It's Afrim Cana. He's been murdered.'

TWENTY-THREE

Tolo sat at the table in Isabel's kitchen, observing her as she toyed listlessly with a piece of toast. It had been long after midnight when Capitán Gómez, his officers and the forensics team had finally departed from Son Barassa following Isabel's discovery of Afrim Cana's corpse. Exhausted, she had finally got to bed in the early hours, only to be woken at six o'clock by an urgent telephone call from Julian Mosquera. She had called Tolo immediately and he had driven straight over to Ca'n Moix. They sat together in her tranquil, sunny kitchen while Mrs Buncle stood clucking at the open door, ever hopeful of being offered a crust of bread.

Tolo turned to Isabel. 'Not hungry? Gómez told me this morning that you'd got soaked in that storm. I hope you're not sickening for something.'

Isabel managed a smile and threw a chunk of bread in her hen's direction. 'I'm just a bit tired, that's all.'

'You did well to involve Gómez last night at Son Barassa. As you rightly deduced, the area comes under Guardia jurisdiction. He had only good things to say about you.'

She raised an eyebrow. 'Well, that's a first. What a night. I wasn't Cana's greatest fan, but I'm sorry that he met such a violent end.'

Tolo gave a grunt. 'Many would disagree.'

'True, he destroyed a lot of lives. Live by the sword, die by the sword, eh?'

'All the same, no one deserves to be tortured to death. So who killed him and why?'

Isabel took a sip of her coffee. 'First, let me tell you about my interesting call from Julian Mosquera earlier this morning.'

'I'm all ears.'

'Apparently, the fingerprints of Mas I sent him match those of Enzo Ortega, a Colombian supposedly murdered back in the late nineties in Medellín.'

'You're telling me that Mas had assumed another identity?'

'It gets better. Yesterday Julian gave me the results of a background check on the three men in the image that I took from Ca'n Mas.'

Tolo looked at her expectantly.

'They were all members of the Diablo Brotherhood set up by Pablo Escobar, the Colombian drug baron, way back in the late sixties.'

'So not a religious brotherhood, as poor old Padre Agustí had imagined?'

'Far from it. This was a clandestine organisation with a carefully guarded list of powerful members, the most feared and ruthless of Escobar's drug associates in Medellín. The devil's horn symbol was the brotherhood's secret sign. The group dabbled in the occult and performed satanic rituals on their enemies.'

'And who were they?' he asked.

'Members of the judiciary, politicians or senior police officers. In fact, anyone influential who refused bribes and tried to take Pablo Escobar down.'

'They were killed?' asked Tolo.

'Tortured and butchered to death, as well as their families. When Colombian security forces finally tracked down and killed

Escobar in 1993, senior members of the Diablo Brotherhood fled to safe houses in Bogotá or left Colombia for Venezuela, the States or Europe.'

'And our friend Mas was one of them?'

'Colombian police records show him to have been one of the most ruthless of the brotherhood members. Mas invented Ortega and created a convincing paper trail for him. He was evidently quite the master of disguise and in Ortega mode, transformed into a bearded, bespectacled older man who relied on a silver walking cane. He donned a black wig and had even altered his eye colour with the aid of tinted contact lenses. Meanwhile, as Angel Tulio Mas he has only ever been associated with acts of benevolence in Colombia and in the rest of the region.'

'This is quite incredible.'

Isabel nodded. 'During the nineties he must have covered his tracks carefully and when the brotherhood dissolved, put out word that Ortega had been killed. A charred body with no teeth or prints turned up in a burnt-out car in Medellín but with Ortega's ID conveniently still legible in a barely damaged wallet in the glove compartment. He was given a hasty burial by the state. There were a lot of vengeful killings in the drug wars in Colombia around that time. No one had time to question ethics or identities.'

'And what about his three conspirators?'

'Their names are Cruz Ramírez, Andres Moreno and Padre Paz García. The latter – apparently another former saintly benefactor in Bogotá – is definitely deceased.'

'And how did he die?'

'Shot down in a blaze of gunfire in Medellín,' Isabel replied.

'Nice,' muttered Tolo. 'What about Moreno and Ramírez?'

Isabel offered him a faint smile. 'Cruz Ramírez was released from prison a week before Mas was murdered and can't be traced – he's probably using a false identity – and Andres Moreno seems to have fallen off the planet shortly after Escobar's death. Some assumed he'd died, but Mosquera learnt from an informer that he'd recently resurfaced in Bogotá and was asking questions about Ortega.'

'How recently?'

'Two weeks ago.'

'God knows, they could be anywhere.'

'I doubt that very much, Tolo. They're both here on the island.'

'How can you be so sure?'

'I think both recently discovered that Mas, whom they had long believed to be dead under his assumed name of Ortega, was in fact still alive. So they came here to reclaim something: a possession that he had stolen from them.'

'But which of them got here before the murder?'

'That's the sixty-million-dollar question. Perhaps both.'

'I'll get my team to check passenger names on all incoming flights from Colombia to the Spanish peninsula in the last three weeks.'

Isabel gave a shrug. 'Good luck with that. Remember these guys use false passports and know how to avoid detection.'

Tolo tapped the table impatiently. 'What of those death notices about Mas in the Colombian press?'

Isabel nodded. 'Using images of Ortega to accompany them was presumably a ruse to expose the fact that Mas went under another name. Whoever placed those ads probably hoped to alert his old cronies and enemies to the fact that he had been alive all these years when everyone assumed it was his body that had been cremated in that car fire.'

'But if Cruz Ramírez and Andres Moreno already knew of his dual identity and had found out that Mas was still alive, what was the point of the ads? They'd have already arrived on the island a few weeks earlier.'

Isabel gave him a quizzical look. 'How do you know both men were here before Mas was murdered? Perhaps only one was aware of Mas's identity while the other remained in the dark and arrived after his murder, having been made aware of his duplicity by the death notices.'

'If that's the case, we need to establish whether it was Moreno or Cruz who arrived here before the murder. That way we'll know who Mas's killer was.'

Isabel got up and threw some more bread to Mrs Buncle. 'We also need to know who placed those death notices.'

'And what exactly did Mas steal from his brotherhood comrades?' asked Tolo.

'That remains a mystery, but I know a woman who'll be able to fill in some of the blanks.'

'Who?'

'Camila Cortez. I think she knows a lot more than she's letting on.'

'Then we must re-interview her immediately.'

'All in hand, Tolo. She had to return to Son Espases Hospital for a scan, but we've arranged to meet on Monday.'

Tolo smiled at her in some admiration. 'Always ahead of the game, Bel.'

She turned to him. 'Make sure to put out an all ports and airport alert, but we can't let the media in on this yet. For the moment, we need Moreno and Cruz to believe that they're still under the radar.'

'Do you think they're working together?'

'I doubt it. I imagine each wants to claim the booty for himself, whatever it is.'

'But who's to say that either is still on the island?'

Isabel sighed. 'That all depends on whether either has got his hands on the prize yet, but I doubt that.'

'Your reasoning?'

'Afrim Cana died in vain. He was tortured last night because his killer or killers thought that he'd taken whatever it was that Mas had stolen years ago. Whoever despatched him must have been convinced of that, which is why he was murdered so violently. If he'd played the game, he'd have only got a bullet between the eyes.'

*

Isabel stood in the gloomy study of Ca'n Mas examining a hand-painted vase, the sole occupant of a glass cabinet in the far corner of the room. Camila Cortez, sombre in her black pinafore and white apron, shuffled over to her.

'You know that's a Picasso?'

Isabel raised an eyebrow. 'How did Señor Mas acquire it?'

She handed her a glass of lemonade and gave a sad smile. 'It was a gift from a great art collector in Colombia in recognition of the loyal support Señor Mas had given to his foundation for street children over the years.'

'Did your boss collect much art?'

'He was a very cultured man. There are beautiful paintings in every room, but he loved books most of all.'

Isabel glanced over Mas's collection of occult titles on the shelf before her.

'I can see that.' She took a long draught of lemonade. 'Still as delicious as ever. Now, *señora*, we need to have a serious chat.'

The elderly woman settled in an armchair and fretfully studied Isabel's face.

'Señora Cortez, I haven't been entirely honest with you. Although it's true that I run Hogar Dulce Hogar, I am also assisting the National Police with the investigation into the murder of Señor Mas.'

'I don't understand.'

'The truth is that I was once a police detective here and on the mainland and so they asked for my help. I didn't tell you when I visited before because I wanted you to speak in an unguarded manner.'

'I see.'

'I hope you'll understand my motives.'

The woman sighed. 'Thank you for being so candid.'

'I'm afraid the forensic institute has now confirmed that Señor Mas was stabbed to death with a twenty-five-centimetre hunting knife. It was a Swiss brand and used with considerable force.'

The old lady made the sign of the cross and visibly crumpled. 'Dear God. I don't think I can bear to hear anymore.'

'I appreciate that this is painful for you, but I need your help. Are you happy to talk to me?'

'Of course.'

Isabel pulled out a file and leafed through some sheets of paper. 'I have a copy of your original signed police statement in which you claimed that you had opened the door to four hooded men the night of Señor Mas's murder. You said that they arrived in a large black vehicle and that one of the men tied you up and locked you in the basement. None of them were known to you.'

The old woman bit her lip.

'Yet when I spoke with Tomas Llull, your nearest neighbour, he told me that on the evening of the murder he saw a Shogun with a single occupant arriving at Ca'n Mas. Furthermore, he claimed to have seen the same car at the house many times before. In fact, the treads of the car belonged to a drug dealer named Afrim Cana. Ever heard of him?'

Camila Cortez sought comfort from the tiny gilt cross about her neck.

Isabel continued. 'I interviewed Afrim Cana on Sunday. He told me that he had visited Ca'n Mas alone on the night of the murder and had spent less than an hour praying with Señor Mas. He denied seeing you when he called. His story is rather at odds with your own, isn't it?'

The housekeeper dabbed at her eyes. 'You must ask him to tell you the truth.'

'That's no longer possible as he was murdered last night.'

Camila Cortez put her hands to her mouth. 'This is all my fault. God will strike me down.'

Isabel sat forward in her chair. 'Why don't you tell me what really happened that night?'

The woman took a small sip of her juice. 'I have tried hard to protect Señor Mas's reputation since we arrived in this village. He was once a man of God – you can see all the evidence of that here.' With a trembling hand she pointed to the coffee table laden with images of Angel Tulio Mas in the company of nuns and other beneficiaries of his largesse.

'When I began working for him in Colombia, all I knew was that he was a religious man and great benefactor. I was grateful for the job and we had a traditional master and servant relationship.'

Isabel offered an encouraging nod.

'One night in Medellín, several years after I took the job, Señor Mas told me that some dangerous drug dealers had targeted him after he had publicly condemned their evil practices, and that we would need to leave immediately for Bogotá and go into hiding. We stayed for two years on a remote estate out of town. I was forbidden to leave and supplies were delivered. I didn't mind because it had a small chapel and a priest would come to deliver a Sunday service.'

'You were, in effect, a prisoner.'

'I didn't see it that way. It had beautiful grounds and I had all I needed.'

'So when did you come to Mallorca?'

'Two years passed and he told me that he wanted to return to the town of his birth in Soller and would like me to continue in his service. I was happy to be appreciated and to travel to a country of devout Catholics.'

Isabel resisted the urge to smile.

'And where does Afrim Cana fit in?'

'At first everything went well and we moved to this lovely house that once belonged to his parents. We went to church and prayed together and lived a quiet life. But suddenly all that changed when this man you talk of, Afrim Cana, began visiting. Every week he would arrive in a big black car, often with three other men. While they stayed by his car he would spend time in the study with Angel.'

'Did they pray or drink together?'

'Señor Mas enjoyed a bottle of Club Colombia lager, his favourite, and sometimes a glass of good red wine with Padre Agustí. He did the same with Afrim Cana. One day the door was left ajar and I heard them discussing shipments of drugs. I was concerned.'

'Did you challenge him about it?'

'No, it was not my place. I convinced myself that Señor Mas must be trying to help the wayward young man to see the light.'

'A regular hero,' muttered Isabel.

'In time I came to fear that Señor Mas might become contaminated by Afrim Cana, but he continued to go to church and prayed so I was reassured.'

'You saw Cana the night of the murder?'

'No. I was aware of the front door opening, but I was busy working in the kitchen downstairs.'

'What were you doing?'

'Making fishcakes. That was at about six o'clock. It must have been nearly an hour later that I was aware of a terrible commotion and shouting. I crept out of the kitchen and stood on the dark staircase wondering what to do. But then I heard a terrible scream from the study and someone crying and yelling as if in pain. It sounded like Señor Mas, but there was also loud background noise blaring from a television.'

Isabel sat quietly taking notes in her little red book. 'Carry on.'

'I stood paralysed with fear outside the study, too cowardly to enter. I'm not sure how long I was there, but all of a sudden a man appeared from the study. He had furious eyes and held a knife to my throat. He told me that I would die unless I told him where the diamonds were.'

'Diamonds?'

'That is what he said.'

'And did you know anything about them?'

'I never heard Señor Mas talk about diamonds.'

'Did you recognise the man?'

'Yes, even though he had aged. His name was Andres Moreno. He had visited the house of Señor Mas in Medellín many years ago, often in the company of another man, Cruz Ramírez, and a priest named Padre García. At the time I assumed they were religious colleagues.'

'And it was Andres Moreno who tied you up in the kitchen that night.'

She lowered her head. 'Yes, it was. I knew it was wrong to incriminate Afrim Cana, but Andres Moreno threatened to kill me if I didn't say that I'd been assaulted by Cana and his thugs that night. He seemed confident that Afrim Cana would be implicated because his fingerprints would be found in the study and his tyre tracks on the drive.'

'But of course Cana came alone – something your neighbour verified.'

'That was my mistake. I told Andres Moreno that Cana always left three of his men guarding the car.'

'And how did Andres Moreno know that Cana had just visited Señor Mas?'

'He told me that he had entered the back garden that morning and decided to bide his time. His intention was to force Señor Mas to tell him where he'd hidden the diamonds that he claimed were his.'

'Did he explain how he had acquired these diamonds originally?'

'No.'

'And did he mention why he had waited until now to fly to Mallorca to find Señor Mas?'

She paused. 'His belief was that he had died in Medellín many years ago under the assumed name of Enzo Ortega. He said that everyone thought he had died in a car fire because Enzo Ortego's identity card was discovered in the vehicle. He had since learnt that the man who perished was in fact a local vagrant.'

'Did you know that Señor Mas masqueraded as Enzo Ortego?'

Camila Cortez shook her head in some bewilderment. 'It came as a terrible shock.'

'Presumably Andres Moreno waited that night until Afrim Cana had left before breaking into the study?' Isabel asked.

'He didn't need to. The French doors were always unlocked. We didn't worry about security here.'

'Did he confess to killing Señor Mas?'

She covered her eyes and began weeping. 'Yes. He told me that Señor Mas was barely conscious when he entered from the garden. He said that he had been drugged.'

'What happened next?'

'Andres Moreno said that he asked Señor Mas to reveal where he'd hidden the diamonds and he had pointed to the false bookcase.'

'What false bookcase?'

'It is where Señor Mas kept important papers and his safe.'

'You never mentioned this to the Guardia.'

'I feared reprisals from Andres Moreno. To continue, he said that he'd found the door to the safe wide open and its contents gone. When he couldn't get Señor Mas to talk, he just killed him.'

Camila Cortez sniffed loudly. 'Andres Moreno assumed that Afrim Cana had overpowered Señor Mas with a powerful drug and stolen the diamonds. He asked me where he lived. As if I would know.'

'It seems that Moreno found him without your help. Do you know what the safe contained?'

'Señor Mas would never have let me know of the contents. He was a private man.'

'Show me the safe.'

Isabel looked out of the French windows, which were drawn back to reveal a mature garden and orchard of lemon trees, heavy with fruit. As sunlight spilled into the room Camila Cortez halted at one of the bookcases and peered at the titles before her. Then, carefully, she removed two leather-bound books from the third shelf, exposing an ornate brass handle. Pulling on some surgical gloves, Isabel stepped forward and depressed it. A moment later the middle section of the bookcase swung open, revealing a substantial recess behind. She removed a small torch from her pannier and shook it vigorously.

Camila Cortez offered a bleak smile. 'We have Michael Faraday to thank for that sort of device.'

Isabel turned to her. 'Indeed. The Faraday flashlight was a marvellous invention. That's why I use this modern version which doesn't need batteries.'

The old woman watched as Isabel carefully probed the recess. 'I remember studying Faraday's law and electromagnetic induction many years ago in Bogotá.'

Isabel wiped some sweat from her forehead. 'He was a British physicist, wasn't he?'

She nodded.

Isabel removed a bundle of documents and shoved them into a plastic file. Shining her torch into the depths once more, she became aware of a safe set far back into the wall. The heavy door lay slightly ajar, but there was nothing inside. She inhaled deeply and frowned. 'I'm going to need forensics to examine this.'

Excusing herself, she stepped out into the garden to call Tolo. She arranged for the forensics team to return to Ca'n Mas and also for Camila Cortez to be driven to the Palma police precinct to sign a revised statement. She had perverted the course of justice and might have to pay the consequences, but that was not for Isabel to decide.

She returned to the study and picked up her pannier. 'Señora Cortez, has Andres Moreno been in touch since Wednesday night?'

She shook her head. 'When he locked me in the kitchen, he said that he would know if I ever talked to the police. I am so scared.'

'Don't worry. We'll give you police protection here at the house. Has anyone else been here since the murder?'

'I have few visitors. A lost tourist called at the house yesterday, but that's all. I offered him a glass of lemonade.'

'Could you describe him?'

She shrugged. 'He was in his sixties, I'd say. He had white hair and wore sunglasses and a wide-brimmed hat. He spoke good Spanish.'

'Did he ask any questions?'

'Not really. I explained that a murder had taken place at the house and he was very sympathetic and understanding.'

Isabel walked slowly towards the hallway, deep in thought.

'What will happen to me now?' the housekeeper asked.

'You gave a false statement, which is a serious offence. Your best bet is to plead mitigating circumstances – in other words, that your life had been threatened.'

'I have always been a law-abiding citizen so will put my faith in God's grace.'

'In which case, let's hope that he hears your prayers.'

*

By the time Isabel returned to the office a note had appeared on her desk, rather like an egg laid by an invisible hen. This time it was from her mother, confirming arrangements for Thursday morning. She had advised the Foxes that she and agency personnel would briefly visit Ca'n Mayol to change the laundry and clean the pool. Isabel yawned. She was still feeling the effects of her long and unsettling night at Son Barassa. After a few hours working at her desk, she received an unexpected call from Capitán Gómez. He sounded animated. 'In the spirit of cooperation between our two forces, I bring good tidings, Isabel. A few hours ago two of my officers were alerted by walkers to an abandoned blue Clio parked on remote forestland not far from Lluc monastery. We must assume that Miranda's abductors dumped it there and switched it for another car.'

'When will forensics have any results?'

'They're at the scene now.'

'Well, Capitán. I appreciate the update. Please keep me in the loop.'

'Likewise,' he replied.

No longer able to keep her eyes open, Isabel decided to have a siesta but not before making a long-distance call to an old detective contact at Sûreté de Quebec, the French Canadian police force. Sometimes, she mused, it paid to have a friend in every port.

By the time she awoke from her refreshing and much-needed slumber it was seven o'clock in the evening and Pep had already left the office. She sat back in her swivel chair and crunched on a sunflower seed, her eyes trained on Furó, who lay curled up in his basket.

A little later, she popped into the main office for a file and noticed that the answerphone's red light was flashing furiously. Pressing the playback button, she became interested when she heard a plummy English accent. The woman announced herself as Sophie Barnes of Platinum Publishing and explained that she was returning Isabel's call. Dialling the London telephone number, Isabel hoped that as the UK was one hour behind Spain, the woman might still be at work. She was in luck. An elegant voice purred down the line.

'Ah, Miss Flores Montserrat. I was so sorry to miss your call yesterday. My assistant mentioned that you were hoping to invite one of our crime writers, William Fox, to a Mallorcan literary festival this autumn?'

Isabel pulled a face. She felt bad lying, but it was a necessary evil. 'Yes, we would love him to present his new book at the festival, and of course there would be a generous fee.'

The other woman sighed. 'Ah, such a shame. William moved to New York a year ago and is rarely in Europe now. He has some serious health issues, but all being well he'll be back to promote his new book at Christmas.'

Isabel was momentarily lost for words. 'That is indeed a shame. By the way, what is the title?'

'Well, I can give you that news hot off the press. It's called *Brutal Maze*.'

'One final thing – would you be kind enough to e-mail me some biographical material and an up-to-date image of Mr Fox that I can circulate to our literary committee? I can't find much via Google, only photos of him when he was young.'

The woman laughed. 'I'm afraid you won't. Mr Fox is a notoriously private man, but I can e-mail you a new image that we'll be issuing as part of *Brutal Maze's* promotional campaign. I'll do that before I leave the office tonight.'

Isabel thanked her and replaced the receiver. She smiled to herself. No, she hadn't lost her touch. Her instinct had been right all along. But if the man renting Ca'n Mayol wasn't the real William Fox, as she had suspected, who the devil was he?

TWENTY-FOUR

Pep sat outside Café Sa Plaça in Fornalutx nursing a weak *cortado* while he lazily scrolled through his mobile phone messages. Several locals stopped to pass the time of day and a huddle of teenage girls, delighted to see a well-known stud in their village, greeted him with enthusiastic hugs. Pep took all of this in his stride. He knew he was *guapo*, a handsome beast, and quite a catch for any girl in the Soller Valley. But he was already taken. Angélica and he had been childhood friends and everyone acknowledged that they were a couple-in-waiting. Pep didn't mind; after all, she was a curvaceous belle with a mane of raven hair and the only child of Llorenç Bestard. Although she was given to sulking bouts, Pep had to admit that she was a dab hand in the kitchen, capable of rustling up a decent *paella* or steaming pot of *arroz brut*, his favourite rice stew, in next to no time.

For all that, since his recent evening boat ride to the Devil's Horn Caves, he found his mind wandering back to Aina like a drunk to a favourite bar. During their eventful evening he had discovered a shared love of fashion and a guilty ambition to rise above the expectations of their parents and to escape the shackles of village life. The encounter had left him confused about his feelings for Angélica and uncertain about the future. Since then, he and Aina had enjoyed a few clandestine phone calls and had already met for a discreet drink in Palma. Of course, Angélica was none the wiser, nor Isabel for that matter. Magdalena shuffled out of the bar and, grinning, tipped up Pep's chair.

'Hey! Give a guy a break.'

She winked. 'Look lively, your boss is here.'

Pep looked up and flinched at the sight of Isabel's wild hair clipped back with a pair of wooden clothes pegs when the rest of her ensemble – tailored navy shorts and orange linen top – seemed so stylish. He rose and planted a kiss on both her cheeks while Magdalena bustled over.

'Your usual, Bel?'

Isabel flashed her a smile. 'Perfect, *reina*.'

Pep pulled off his shades. 'Been hanging out the washing this morning?'

'Good observational powers. You have the makings of a sleuth.'

'Yeah, and being a good sleuth, I noticed that some clumsy thief nicked my *moto* again yesterday and returned it with a scratch.'

'It must have been those narrow lanes near Ca'n Mas. Apologies.'

'What's wrong with Pequeñito?'

'His engine needs a rest in this heat. Besides, your *moto* is much faster.'

He gave a snort. 'Lucky my cousin's a mechanic. He's nicknamed you King Kong because he says you don't know your own strength.'

She fondly recalled the famous Hollywood film and how the giant gorilla was able to pick up cars in his bare hands and scale skyscrapers. Surely there were worse sobriquets?

Pep yawned. 'I could have met you back in Sant Martí.'

'It's no bother. Besides, Ca'n Mayol is closer to Fornalutx. So, did the new German clients arrive here on time this morning?'

'They're German – of course they arrived on time! Their taxi was here on the dot of nine and so I drove them up to Casa Sirena and settled them in.'

'It's such a popular house for renting. Mind you, it's got a beautiful garden and one of the best pools in the valley.'

Pep nodded. 'It also helps that it's outside the village, away from snoopers.'

'Snooping is part of the fabric of village life, Pep, as you often remind me. It has its uses.'

Magdalena placed a strong *cortado* and a plate of *tostadas* in front of Isabel.

'So why have you got pegs in your hair?' Pep asked.

Isabel gave a mock frown. 'As your sister can't give me a haircut until Friday, desperate measures are called for.'

Isabel poured olive oil on her toast and generously sprinkled the tomatoes with black pepper and salt. 'By the way, we need to talk about William Fox. He is not all that he seems. I thought it best to warn you before we set off for Ca'n Mayol with Florentina and Idò.'

Pep issued a groan. 'Don't tell me! He's a drug addict with a mistress, or perhaps he's murdered his mother.'

Isabel gave him an arch smile. 'Of course, you could be right on both fronts, but I've just discovered that William Fox, the author, is in bad health and currently residing in America, meaning that our William Fox is an imposter.'

'And how on earth have you deduced all that?'

Isabel took a long sip of coffee.

'I'll admit that I was suspicious about him from the start. Something seemed phoney about that couple when we met them in Bon Día last Thursday, so I ordered one of his books via Amazon hoping that it might throw up a clue and searched for current images of him on the web, but I couldn't find any.'

Pep stared at her. 'Go on.'

'I knew something didn't add up. Then my police contact Julian Mosquera in Colombia called me yesterday about Mas. He told me that he had been part of something called the Diablo Brotherhood and had worn a heavy disguise and gone by the name of Enzo Ortego. That was it! I thought about how our William Fox kept his shades on when we met him in the grocery store and about his long unruly hair and beard. He'd obviously seen one of the only existing images of the author on the web when he was a young hippy and tried to copy the look.'

'I wonder why there aren't any current images of William Fox.'

'According to his London publisher, he guards his privacy.'

'You've been in touch with his publisher?' Pep exclaimed.

'I spoke with his editor, Sophie Barnes, and pretended that I wanted to invite the real William Fox to a book festival here in Soller.'

'How could you tell such a fib?'

'To find out the truth, of course! Anyway, Sophie told me that he was in America and wouldn't be back in Europe for some time. She e-mailed me this too.'

Pep leant forward and examined the paper she waggled in front of him. It showed a plump elderly man with cropped grey hair and a moustache.

'Is this the author?'

'Yes.'

'He doesn't look anything like our Mr Fox.'

She pushed away her empty plate. 'I know.'

'Could there by any chance be two crime writers of the same name?'

'Possibly, but certainly not writing books with identical titles.'

Pep shrugged. 'So the guy's masquerading as a well-known author. So what? Maybe he's just a sad delusional fan or a failed writer trying to live the dream.'

Isabel smiled. 'I don't think so. Today, when we go over to Ca'n Mayol, I need you to keep alert – and don't say a word to the others.'

'That house gives me the creeps. I'll be on my guard alright, just in case a ghost jumps out.'

Isabel laughed. 'I think you should be more concerned about the living, Pep.'

'So why can't Idò and Florentina know about all this?'

'I'd rather they acted as naturally as possible so as not to raise suspicions. I'll fill them in later.'

'What exactly do you want me to do?'

'Nothing. Just be observant around the house and grounds and we'll compare notes afterwards.'

Isabel strolled into the café to pay Magdalena and came back out into the sun. She looked across the *plaça* and waved at Juan Albertí, the former mayor of Fornalutx, and Sari, an old childhood friend of hers, who were supping coffees outside Bar Deportivo.

She joined Pep back at their table.

'As we're not being picked up by Idò and Florentina for another thirty minutes I'm going to pay a brief visit to Es Turo restaurant to pick up some of their home-made *croquetas*.'

He nodded. 'OK, I'll see you back at the car park – and don't be late.'

As Pep turned to go, Isabel grasped his arm. 'One other thing. I know you were out of the office yesterday, but you may have read in the newspapers that Afrim Cana was found murdered in Son Barassa. He was tortured and choked to death with a metal cable.'

'What?' Pep goggled at her, his mouth hanging open in shock. 'How come you leave that till last? Who killed him?'

'So you didn't see the news?'

'I've been a bit preoccupied,' he replied.

'Hm. Would-be investigators must always stay alert.'

'Were you there?'

'Of course. I discovered the body.'

Pep rubbed his forehead. 'Why am I not surprised?'

Isabel ignored him. 'There is a strong Colombian connection. I think Cana's murderer is an old enemy from Mas's past.'

Pep remonstrated. 'But if that's the case, why kill Cana?'

'It's likely that Mas kept something of great value at his home and that whoever killed Cana thought he might have stolen it.'

'What was it?'

'A stash of diamonds.'

'So this psycho killer of Cana and Mas is still at large in Mallorca?'

'Actually, I think there might be two psycho killers on the loose – possibly three.'

Pep stood motionless. 'That's just great. I hope they're not heading up to Sant Martí.'

Isabel patted his shoulder. 'I'm afraid that is exactly where I think they'll be heading.'

'That's not funny, Bel. We don't want murderers up here.'

'No? But didn't you tell me that a grisly murder might relieve the boredom of village life?'

Pep rolled his eyes and, flopping back in his seat, pulled out a packet of Marlboro Lights.

'I thought you'd given up?'

'So did I, until I started working for you.'

Isabel popped on her shades and planting a kiss on both his cheeks pressed her lips to his right ear. 'Just keep your wits about you.'

He watched as she breezed across the *plaça* with a smile on her face. He wondered what it would take to change her perennially cheerful demeanour.

*

Florentina made the sign of the cross as Idò jammed his foot on the brake and swerved into the drive of Ca'n Mayol.

'What driving! Thank heavens we all have guardian angels,' she muttered.

Isabel threw open the passenger door. 'Next time we go in Pequeñito.'

'No way,' replied Pep. 'It's slower than a snail. That's why you keep nicking my bike.'

He strode onto the path and looking up at the ancient *finca* before him gave an involuntary shudder. The frontage had been gobbled up by yellowing creeper and the windows were hidden behind dark shutters. A black Golf covered in grime sat on the grass verge by the front door.

'It's very quiet. Perhaps they've gone out?' suggested Idò.

'Without the car in this heat?' scoffed Pep.

Florentina shrugged. 'Maybe they decided to have a nice walk?'

Isabel breezed past them and slammed the door's brass knocker, then hoped that it wouldn't inexplicably fall to the ground. King Kong indeed. After a while she heard the sound of a woman's light cough and a key turning in the lock. Mrs Fox's pale face peered out from behind the door, her green eyes wincing as sunlight engulfed her.

Isabel offered a cheery greeting. 'Well, Mrs Fox, you've got the whole cleaning team today.'

'I assumed you'd just be leaving clean sheets. My husband is very busy writing upstairs and doesn't want to be disturbed.'

Isabel nodded. '*No hay problema*. We'll keep away from his study.'

Mrs Fox shrugged. 'I've already stripped the beds, so there's no need for you to go upstairs.'

'In that case, we'll just clean downstairs and Idò and Pep can take care of the pool,' replied Florentina.

Somewhat hesitantly the woman ushered them inside. Before them a wide grey marble staircase with ornate mahogany banisters curled up to the two floors above. Isabel had been renting out the property to holidaymakers for a few years and knew its every nook and cranny. On the first floor there were five ensuite bedrooms and a handsome study overlooking the rear garden and orchard. A converted attic of one large bedroom and an adjoining bathroom were found on the level above. Such a spacious house squirreled away on a private lane in the middle of rolling countryside normally attracted large family gatherings, which was why the Foxes were an anomaly.

The elderly owners had no wish to sell their home, which had been in the hands of the Mayols for more than three hundred years, but neither did they want to live in so remote a spot as they grew more infirm. Instead, they relocated to a flat in Palma and sought Isabel's help with rentals when their own efforts failed. They had explained that local rumours about hauntings made it difficult to let the property to villagers. Over the years, various Mayol family members claimed to have seen a young girl with brown hair and dressed in a white gown roaming barefooted about the rooms. The elderly couple suggested that the child ghost might possibly be an ancestor who had perished in the terrible plague of the seventeenth century but there was no historical evidence to back the theory. All Isabel knew was that she had never had a problem renting the property to foreigners and none had ever reported any sort of paranormal activity. Mind you, she made sure not to enlighten them of the ghostly gossip at the time of booking.

Mrs Fox glanced anxiously at Isabel.

'Can you just concentrate your efforts in the kitchen and garden?'

Isabel nodded reassuringly. 'We'll be gone before you know it.'

Mrs Fox swept them all along the corridor in the direction of the kitchen.

'Just make yourselves at home. All I ask is that my husband is left in peace.'

'I only have clean sheets for one double,' grumbled Florentina in Mallorquí dialect, rounding on her daughter. 'What other beds is she talking about?'

Isabel turned to Mrs Fox. 'I'm sorry, but we only thought to bring one set of sheets. Do you need more?'

The woman shook her head and tittered. 'Excuse my use of English. I get confused. Of course we're only using one bed – my mistake.'

Isabel mollified Florentina while Idò and Pep stepped out into the extravagant garden beyond the kitchen. A vast and lonely pool greeted their gaze, its surface sallow under the sun.

Idò placed his hands on his hips. 'Heavens! We need to get some chlorine in there fast.'

Pep stopped at the blue tiled edge and peered into the water. A few crisp leaves floated past, caught on a gentle current, while a pink lilo slowly pirouetted round and round like a drowsy ballerina. With the sun boring into his back, Pep knelt down and trailed a finger in the tepid water before rising up and surveying the rugged Tramuntanas before him.

'Well, get to it!' growled Idò. 'We need the chlorine and nets from the poolroom. No time for dreaming, boy.'

Pep issued a grunt and trudged off across the tiled patio towards a *casita*.

Back in the kitchen, Isabel and her mother waited until Mrs Fox had retraced her steps and could be heard mounting the marble staircase.

'She's an odd one,' remarked Florentina. 'Obviously hasn't a clue about keeping house. This kitchen's in a right mess.'

Isabel squeezed her arm. 'We can't all be as perfect as you, mama. Now, can I leave you to clean up here?'

'And where might you be going? I smell a big rat.'

Isabel pressed a finger to her lips. 'I smell one too. I won't be long.'

She slunk out of the kitchen and re-emerged almost thirty minutes later wearing a troubled expression.

'What's up?' hissed Florentina.

'Nothing. Are you nearly finished here?'

'I like that. You swan off while I'm left slaving away and expect me to have the place spick and span faster than a lizard sheds its tail!'

Isabel shooed her out into the garden and spoke to her in hushed tones. 'I think some strange things are going on here. I'll tell you more in the car. Come on, let's find Idò and Pep.'

Florentina flipped the old dishcloth she was carrying onto her shoulder and wordlessly followed her daughter across the gravel to the pool house. Pep and Idò were sitting on the parched grass chatting.

'Seems like I'm the only one working today,' grumbled Florentina. 'What a family!'

'I'll have you know that Pep and I have been working like dogs. We've cleaned the pool and swept out the garage, and put the sprinklers on in the orchard. It's been non-stop.'

'So we're all done?' asked Isabel.

The men rose slowly and shook themselves down while Isabel looked up at the ivy-clad exterior of the old house. As her eyes lazily roamed the stone façade they suddenly froze at a first-floor window where the pale face of a young man appeared. A second later it had vanished and Isabel was surprised to find herself shivering, her arms covered in goose pimples despite the intense summer heat. Her mother placed a comforting hand on her arm.

'Are you OK, Bel?'

Before she could reply, Pep turned to Florentina. 'I saw it too, a ghostly face behind the window.'

Idò gave a guffaw. 'It must be Mr Fox.'

Pep shook his head. 'No, it was a young man.'

On the drive Mrs Fox reappeared. 'Thank you for coming. We'll no doubt see you again next week.'

'Yes, indeed,' smiled Isabel. 'By the way, do let us know if you have any visitors coming to stay and we'll be happy to make up some of the other beds.'

'You don't need to worry. My husband won't tolerate another soul in the house while he's writing – apart from me, that is.'

Isabel slid into the front passenger seat and peered out of the open window. 'I can understand why authors need complete peace when they write. It must be so important for the creative process.'

Mrs Fox nodded. 'So true. I believe you enjoy reading?'

'Oh, yes. In fact, I've just ordered a new book called *Brutal Maze*. It's a thriller.'

The woman shrugged her shoulders. 'I'm afraid I don't know of it. There are so many new books around. It's hard to keep up.'

Idò started the engine and headed along the drive while Isabel waved from the car. Mrs Fox stood perfectly still, watching their progress from the front steps with serious eyes.

Pep suddenly broke the silence.

'So, you all heard what she said. There is no one else staying at Ca'n Mayol – so how do you explain that mysterious face at the upstairs window?'

'To be honest, Pep, I can't,' sighed Isabel. 'But if Ca'n Mayol is hiding the sort of dark secrets I think it is, any right-minded ghost would be shaking in his boots.'

*

It was afternoon by the time Isabel arrived back at Ca'n Moix. To her surprise, she discovered Josep Casanovas standing on the porch, holding a bunch of triffid-like sunflowers.

'Bel! What perfect timing. I just popped by to lure you out for a drink.' He stepped forward, placing his load in her arms. 'I couldn't think of a more appropriate flower. Like you, they are strong, bright and beautiful, and I know for a fact that you find their seeds irresistible, as I find you...'

Isabel cut him short, whisking the flowers up to her nose, despite their lack of fragrance.

'It's so good of you, Josep, but it really wasn't necessary. It should have been me buying you flowers for your newspaper's support.'

He stepped forward and offered her a lingering kiss on the cheek just as she spied Florentina and Doctor Ramis peering around the gate, their mirth evident from their conspiratorial grins. In a flash they had gone, no doubt eager to creep up the good doctor's garden path in order to eavesdrop. In some desperation she edged towards the front door, keeping the flowers in front of her as a barrier.

'Much as I'd love to join you, Josep, I have some urgent work deadlines.'

He dropped his head in disappointment. 'But surely we could have a quick beer in the *plaça*?'

She shook her head. 'I really...'

He took her arm. 'Oh please! I've come all this way, and don't forget I moved heaven and earth to get you and your police buddies that front page coverage the other day.'

With some reluctance Isabel placed the flowers against the front door. 'OK. A very swift drink in Bar Castell.'

She hurried him down the path, briefly turning her head as she passed Doctor Ramis's house to see whether he and her mother were lurking in the garden. As she had suspected, both were crouched by the wall, sharing animated whispers and giggles amid the creeper. Uttering a subdued growl she strode ahead, resolved to have strong words with her prying scholarly neighbour and matchmaking mother on her return.

*

Having placated Josep Casanovas by spending an hour in his company at Bar Castell, Isabel drove to the home of one of her cleaners to collect a batch of laundered bed linen. On her return to the village she parked her car on the edge of the *plaça* and popped into Bon Día to buy some groceries. It was just as she emerged, laden with shopping bags, that she noticed an apparition, thin and weasel-faced, looming over the windscreen of Pequeñito. Striding across the *plaça*, Isabel noted the official dark blue uniform, cap and gaudy yellow fluorescent jacket.

'Can I help you?' she asked.

A curtain of lank brown hair met her gaze, followed by a sharp nose and a pair of cold brown eyes. 'I am issuing you with a ticket for parking on a yellow line.'

Isabel dumped her bags at her feet. 'I was only gone for a second and left my indicators on. What's your problem? I live here.'

The small weasel's mouth puckered angrily. 'I wouldn't care if you were the mayor himself. You are breaking the law.'

With venom she ripped a page from a small pad and slapped it under one of Pequeñito's wipers. Angry black words ran illegibly across the parking ticket, together with a fine. Like the imprisoned wing of a bird, the ticket began flapping frantically in the breeze.

'You must pay this fine within two days at the *ajuntament* or you will be charged double. The building is over there.' The woman wafted a hand in the general direction of the town hall.

Isabel folded her arms. '*Gràcies*, but I am already well acquainted with the town hall's whereabouts. You're not from around here, are you?'

'I don't have to answer that.'

'Something to hide?'

The weasel's lips twitched. 'I am from Madrid. Is that a big enough city for a country girl like you?'

'It rings a bell. But maybe it proved too big for you since you've ended up here in a tiny *pueblo*.'

'It wasn't my choice,' she replied furiously. 'Circumstances change. I gave up a good job in the accounts department of El Corte Inglés because my husband decided we should move here. Now look at me.'

'And what does he do?' Isabel asked.

'No business of yours.' She hesitated then huffily continued. 'He's the sales manager of a hotel in Palma, but we live with his mother in Soller.'

'So you're angry at being uprooted and doing a job you feel is beneath you. And you resent living with your mother-in-law.'

She turned red. 'What is it to you, anyway?'

'You know, life could be more pleasant if you were a little nicer to people. Let us locals go about our business. Occasionally turn a blind eye and bend the rules and you'll make friends.'

'Just like that?'

Isabel examined the ticket for a moment and tearing it into tiny fragments threw it to the wind. The traffic warden took a sharp intake of breath and her small mouth ruched in displeasure.

'Yes, just like that,' said Isabel with a smile. 'See you around.'

She got into her car and, waving at the mystified weasel, set off up the road.

*

Replete and yawning heavily, Isabel wandered back along the dark street to Ca'n Moix with Furó snuffling along behind her. Having gorged on home-made *croquetas* and *tumbet*, a local speciality of aubergine, potato and peppers, followed by Florentina's mouth-watering *lomo con col*, pork with cabbage, she was feeling mellow and at one with the universe. At supper she decided to tell her mother and Uncle Idò about the duplicitous William Fox. Idò advised caution while Florentina bewailed the fact that police work would be forever in her blood. As Isabel stood on her porch admiring the mountain peaks floating in soft cloud, she could hear the blunt but insistent bleat of her mobile phone. Cursing, she knelt down on the smooth paving stones and shook her bag upside down until the little object tumbled out in a flash of electric blue light. She held it to her ear and was surprised to hear Capitán Gómez's doleful voice.

'Death seems to dog us, Isabel. I'm afraid we have made another rather grizzly discovery in Banyalbufar. Some walkers have just stumbled across a male corpse.'

'Whereabouts?'

'Beyond the road, Camí des Molí, there's a rather nice stretch of forestland and a cliff from which our victim appears to have plummeted. The body had become ensnared on the rocks below.'

'Have you alerted Tolo?'

'Naturally, but, rather tediously, he's back in Madrid.'

'Any identity on the victim?'

He intoned deeply, 'Nothing at all. His face and hands appear to have been soaked in acid post death, so we may never find out who he was.'

'What about his teeth? Can't we get dental records?'

'I'm afraid that the victim has no teeth.'

'How come?'

'Looks like he wore dentures, but they've been removed.'

'Any idea of age?'

'We're guessing that he was a man in his sixties judging by hair colour and skin tone. According to forensics the man was tortured prior to asphyxiation with a wire ligature. Sound familiar?'

'Seems like someone played hangman a lot as a child.'

Capitán Gómez gave a dry laugh. 'I have left the most important thing until last. Forensics suspect that the victim was of Latin American origin, perhaps Colombian. Care to join us down here?'

Isabel puffed out her cheeks. 'OK, give me an hour. I'm on my way.'

TWENTY-FIVE

Isabel finished her breakfast in Bar Castell and examined the violet sky above her. There was a spit of rain in the air and the sun wore a dirty grey beard of cloud. She predicted that there would be a storm that night and hopefully rain. During the summer her vegetable patch was constantly thirsty because the little water still finding its way to the homes of Sant Martí now dribbled feebly from the taps like muddy cocoa, spilling brown tears into the kitchen sink and on the white ceramic basins in the bathrooms. There was hardly enough to fill a kettle, let alone water a garden. During the last week severe water shortages had meant that *agua potable* needed to be delivered to the village by truck to fill the communal tank and the mayor had advised all residents to use the minimum of water possible. As for the tourists, most remained blissfully unaware of the constraints being placed on their hotels, grumbling to the management whenever their parched showerheads gasped and gurgled like dying men in a desert.

Isabel gave a hearty yawn. Yet again she'd had another late night in the company of Capitán Gómez and a corpse. Nacho Blanco had estimated that the victim had been lying unnoticed at the bottom of cliffs for at least twenty-four hours and had been killed approximately twelve hours beforehand. Isabel had urged the Guardia chief to get his officers to scour hotels and rental apartments in the area in the hope of finding where the body had been treated with acid following death. She returned from the village of Banyalbufar at dawn and immediately called Julian Mosquera, seeking yet another small favour before waking Tolo at his hotel in Madrid. She needed to talk through some hypotheses with him, about both cases. He had listened with interest and in some haste had arranged to return to the island on the first available flight.

With thoughts whirring in her head, Isabel jumped up from her seat and hurriedly paid Rafael at the counter.

'What's the rush?' he called after her.

She jogged down the steps and collided neatly with Llorenç's stomach. The mayor surveyed her with narrowed eyes.

'Just the woman I wanted to see. What's this I hear from the new traffic warden about your tearing up a *multa*?'

'Come on, Llorenç! We don't do parking fines in Sant Martí.'

'This isn't the Wild West, Bel. Even Sant Martí must abide by the law. As a former cop, you should know that.'

'What's a traffic warden doing here at all?'

'She's been hired by Soller town council, and I had to agree to her doing a trial here in the village. So just bring the fines to me and I'll lose them. That's what I'm doing for all the locals.'

'She's a menace. The woman even upset Doctor Ramis.'

Llorenç tutted. 'All the same, your throwing rubbish in the street didn't help matters.'

Isabel put her hands on her hips in indignation. 'I tore up the parking ticket she issued, that's all. A symbol of resistance and solidarity with my fellow freedom fighters.'

Llorenç chuckled. 'Well, my little rebel, she'll be gone in two weeks' time, so just play the game. And don't forget we have a final committee meeting about the fiesta tomorrow. I can hardly believe that the big weekend is nearly upon us. '

Isabel offered him a cursory peck on the cheek and headed off across the *plaça*, stopping on the way to buy some tickets from old man Valls, who was blind and lame but still managed to run his ONCE lottery stall in the square every Friday. Isabel smiled when her mobile bleeped and she saw Tolo's name flash up on the screen.

'How was Madrid?'

'Don't ask. It's good to be back. So, any further news on the victim in Banyalbufar?'

'Not yet, but surely it has to be either Cruz Ramírez or Andres Moreno?'

Tolo sighed. 'Gómez has stepped up protection for Camila Cortez in case the killer returns to Ca'n Mas, but that's hardly likely, is it?'

'I wouldn't be so sure.'

'Don't worry. We're not taking any chances.' He hesitated. 'When you called last night you said things were moving on in the Miranda case. Can you elaborate?'

'As soon as I've put the final piece in the jigsaw. I'm nearly there.'

'OK, but time is running out. Jane Walters is a complete wreck, and tomorrow night Frank Walters' fiancée arrives. It's hardly going to be a happy reunion for them.'

Isabel strode through the *plaça*, wondering whether she should have told Tolo that she was on the verge of a happy discovery and just needed a few more facts to support her theory in the Miranda case. But what if she was wrong? For now she would keep her own counsel. She headed to Camí Vell, where Marga stood in her salon awaiting her old school friend, with scissors at the ready.

*

It was eleven in the evening and Isabel was still working at her desk. She had spent several hours staring at her whiteboard and rereading the notes in her little red book. After taking a phone call from Colombia, Isabel replaced the receiver and sucked thoughtfully on a Chupa Chup. What Julian Mosquera told her had confirmed a few more of her suspicions. Instinctively, she picked up the telephone and dialled the home number of Ca'n Mas. There was no answer. With a sense of dread she telephoned Capitán Gómez.

'A late call, Isabel. Is anything wrong?'

'I've tried Camila Cortez's phone, but she's not answering. Could you get your officers at the house to check on her?'

'The old lady's probably asleep.'

'She told me that she always stayed up late. I've got a bad feeling.'

He gave an impatient sigh. 'Leave it with me.'

Isabel jumped when the telephone rang some minutes later. To her astonishment it was Camila Cortez.

The woman's voice trembled. 'Isabel, remember that lost tourist who turned up here on Tuesday? He's come back. When he knocked, I thought it was one of the Guardia officers.'

'Where the heck are they?' Isabel asked urgently. 'They're supposed to be giving you twenty-four-hour protection. Where is this man now?'

'In the study,' she whispered. 'He is Cruz Ramírez, although I didn't recognise him before. It's such a long time since I last saw him in Colombia. He told me that he had undergone facial surgery.'

'What does he want from you?'

'He is searching for the diamonds in Señor Mas's study. The phone rang and I recognised your number, but he refused to let me answer it.'

'Where are you?'

'In the kitchen. I offered to make him a coffee so that I could call you. I am so frightened about what he'll do to me if he cannot find the diamonds. I don't believe they are here.'

'Nor do I. Try to keep calm, *señora*. I am on my way and have already alerted the Guardia. Just do exactly what Ramírez asks and if you have an opportunity, lock yourself somewhere secure in the house. I'll be with you in a matter of minutes.'

Isabel suddenly heard a gurgle of terror as Camila Cortez hissed into the receiver. 'Isabel, it's too late. He is coming down the stairs.'

In alarm she tried to offer some hurried instructions, but the housekeeper didn't reply. Instead she heard muffled banging, and then the telephone line went dead.

*

Leaving Furó slumbering blissfully in his basket, Isabel grabbed the keys to Pep's motorbike and fled the office. Driving at speed through the dark narrow streets she wondered what gruesome scene might greet her on arrival at Ca'n Mas. She prayed that nothing untoward had happened to the Guardia officers on duty, and that Capitán Gómez had raised the alarm. As she approached the drive, she saw an abandoned military police vehicle and two officers lying comatose on the ground, both bound hand and foot. She killed the engine and crept across the gravel to where they both lay. To her relief both were breathing, though sporting bloodied wounds on their heads. She was about to call Capitán Gómez but discovered that in her hurry she had left her mobile phone in the office. Cursing, she picked up a small rock and gripped it in her right hand, only too aware that she had no weapon and no backup.

As she strode towards the house she was suddenly blinded by harsh headlights as a car careered towards her at full speed. Isabel dived out of the way and rolled onto a muddy verge, before picking herself up and setting off in hot pursuit on the *moto*. As she sped after the silver car as it hurtled left out of the drive, she spied two Guardia vehicles coming into view from the far end of the lane. The cold wind hit her face as she revved the bike, determined not to lose sight of her prize. As the car raced along the narrow lanes with Isabel on its tail, she was aware of flashing lights and the whine of a police vehicle some distance behind her. With her eyes trained on the red tail lights ahead, she wondered where Cruz Ramírez might be heading. Soon he turned onto the steep and curving American Road that led to Soller, following it all the way down to the Monumento roundabout, whereupon he took a left and then a sharp right turn in the direction of the mountain village of Deià.

Isabel shivered with cold as she snaked up the black hill, her heart thudding in her chest. Ahead of her, Ramírez clung to the steering wheel with the tenacity of a leech as he swerved round each tight bend on the precarious mountain road. To their right, a gentle sea glistened in the moonlight, flanked on one side by steep craggy cliffs. On their left, wild and bushy scrubland sprawled across the hillside, a flash of dark olive and pine trees occasionally catching their vision as the headlights chased the shadows on the silent road. Isabel looked in her wing mirror and saw a frantic blue light nudging the slumbering rocks behind her. The shimmering car ahead of her began to lurch carelessly as it spun round every hairpin, its tyres screeching in protest.

Before her, the jagged silhouette of Deià village floated in the still night air, illuminated by a corona of bleached moonlight. Isabel hugged the bike, doggedly pursuing Ramírez, although alarmed when he began increasing his speed, no doubt relieved to find himself on a straight stretch of road. A signpost announcing Ca n'Alluny Museum lay ahead of them, and as Isabel strained to match the car's velocity she was momentarily blinded by two dazzling, flashing lights heading straight towards them from the other direction. She swerved to the left and brought the bike to a grinding halt on the grass verge, jumped off and ran forward. As if suspended in space and time, she watched as the silver car before her rose in the air and with a sickening crunch, rolled over and smashed back down onto the road. Slithering uncontrollably across the tarmac it came to rest with a resounding bang against the stone wall of Ca n'Alluny, erstwhile home of the English poet Robert Graves.

*

Isabel watched as the ambulance set off at speed, its urgent lights illuminating the awakening sky. She stood in a huddle with Tolo and Capitán Gómez at the gates of the museum, dazed by the scene of devastation before her and trembling with shock. Her mind raced back to her early years as a traffic cop in Barcelona when she had often been faced with devastating tableaux of a similar kind on the treacherous high-speed roads. For Isabel, neither time nor memory had erased the repugnant odour of diesel fumes mixed with acrid smoke and charred human flesh that was the stuff of car accidents. Her eyes swept past the twisted metal and debris scattered about her and rested on the distant hills that cushioned the village. The tip of the Teix mountain was now swathed in soft, mysterious mist that hovered over the steep forests of pines, oaks and olives like ghostly plasma. She wished that she were up there now, light years away, from the chaos at ground level.

Her attention was suddenly deflected by the sound of doors slamming and she turned to see one of the green Guardia vehicles gently setting off in the direction of Palma. The silver Audi, its bonnet snarling in a deadly grimace, lay defeated at the side of the road. The driver's door had been ripped from its hinges and lay on scrubland a few feet away along with other debris from the vehicle. The car's metal roof bore a huge gash down its centre, as if sliced by an enormous knife, and yet surprisingly the sole occupant was pulled out, bloody and unconscious, but still alive.

Isabel turned to Capitán Gómez. 'This is Cruz Ramírez. He is barely recognisable from that seventies image taken of him with Angel Mas. Do you think he'll make it?'

He shrugged. 'Let's hope so. His testimony would confirm that the body found in Banyalbufar is that of Andres Moreno.'

'I think we can safely assume that,' replied Isabel.

Tolo sighed deeply. 'It's been a perplexing case, but it's a relief to have found the culprits.'

Without a thought he removed his jacket and wrapped it around Isabel's shoulders. 'You're shivering.'

Capitán Gómez offered him a tentative smile. 'This investigation has been all about team effort, my friends.' He turned to Isabel. 'You, particularly, have played a crucial part in solving this case.'

Tolo acknowledged the gesture with a bemused smile, while Isabel propped herself up against the wall of the museum and stared at them both.

'What about the diamonds?'

Tolo pushed out his bottom lip. 'Did they ever exist? Forensics found no evidence to suggest that the safe contained anything of value. The hidden documents secreted behind the bookcase proved that Mas had substantial funds in several offshore accounts, but there was no mention of diamonds.'

'The way I see it,' Capitán Gómez replied, 'is that as Isabel always suspected, Afrim Cana was not involved in the death of Mas. Perhaps there were diamonds in the safe that night, but I doubt it.'

Tolo turned to him. 'It's unlikely we'll ever know for certain, unless Ramírez pulls through and talks. In the meantime, it would pay to make another complete search of the house and grounds.'

Capitán Gómez fixed his green eyes on Isabel. 'My officers also radioed through earlier with an update. During their search of Banyalbufar today, a local rentals agency alerted them to a holiday flat that had recently been illegally occupied, it seems, by Andres Moreno. It had been broken into and a suspicious neighbour called the agency yesterday to report having seen a man of Latin American appearance exiting the property earlier this week.'

'I wonder how long he'd been staying there,' Isabel remarked.

'Who knows?' replied Capitán Gómez. 'He probably murdered Mas, then Cana and hung around, hoping to return to search Ca'n Mas, but Cruz Ramírez somehow caught up with him.'

'Perhaps Ramírez tracked him down, hoping to find the diamonds on him – that's if they existed. When that proved not to be the case, he probably killed him and returned to Ca'n Mas for a final search,' suggested Tolo.

Capitán Gómez gave a sniff. 'That's as may be. All I can tell you is that the bathroom in the rented flat contained several empty bottles of a common brand of acid cleaner and traces of blood which no doubt forensics will match to the corpse found by the cliff. Two false passports were hidden in a dresser together with a pile of Colombian pesos.'

'Cruz evidently tracked down Moreno there before killing him and treating certain body parts to an acid bath,' added Isabel. 'He probably picked up his trail at Son Barassa.'

'What a way to go.' Tolo sighed. He examined his watch and yawned. 'It's nearly five in the morning. Once I've had a few hours' rest I'll head into the office to write a preliminary press statement.'

Capitán Gómez smiled amiably. 'Indeed. Let's head back to Palma together and work on a joint statement when we've had a chance to rest for a few hours. Isabel, you must get some sleep. I'll organise a Guardia car to take you back home.'

Isabel shook her head. 'Thanks for the offer, but I have a *moto*.'

Capitán Gómez's mobile rang out and in some irritation he pressed it to his ear and walked away from the others.

Isabel turned to Tolo. 'By the way, do you know William Graves?'

'The son of the English poet? No.'

'Well, I do, and I can tell you that he's not going to be at all happy about the damage done to the wall of his father's property.'

Tolo grimaced. 'In that case, I'll leave you to call him with an explanation and an apology. It'll be rectified soon enough.'

Capitán Gómez beckoned to them as he continued to speak curtly into his phone. Isabel grabbed Tolo's sleeve.

'Look, before you agree a joint statement with Gómez, bear in mind a few things.'

'Such as?'

'We still don't know the identity of the young man who placed death notices in the main Colombian newspapers the day after Mas was murdered.'

'Does it matter? Maybe it was a friend or some relative we don't know about?'

'How was the information relayed to them so soon from Mallorca? And where did they get that image of Mas as Ortega?'

'I don't know, but hopefully Ramírez will survive and can fill in some of the blanks.'

'I suppose your commissioner and Judge Baltazar will want a speedy conclusion on this case.'

He offered a grim smile. 'You bet. The good news is that we can concentrate all our efforts now on finding Miranda.'

Isabel was quiet for a moment before turning to Tolo. 'Actually, I really need to talk to you about one of my renters.'

'The strange couple you mentioned when you telephoned me the other night?'

'The same.'

Capitán Gómez wandered back over to them.

'Your chariot awaits, Tolo. As for you, Isabel, go to bed. You look exhausted.'

The captain's mobile phone bleeped again. He took the call and offered the others a relieved smile. 'The two officers injured by Ramírez are both going to be OK. They are being treated at Son Espases now. Camila Cortez is fine too.'

Isabel gave him the thumbs up sign. Tolo touched her shoulder.

'About your renters – can it wait until later this morning?'

Isabel hesitated, noting the dark shadows under his eyes. 'Of course. In the meantime, try to get some kip yourself.'

He kissed her on the cheek and striding over to the Guardia vehicle laughingly called back, 'Chance will be a fine thing.'

TWENTY-SIX

Isabel arrived back at Ca'n Moix just before six o'clock. As it was the weekend there was an air of tranquility about the little neighbourhood and no one stirred. On any other Saturday she might have enjoyed a visit to Soller's bustling market but since working for Tolo, she now had little time for herself. When in the last few weeks had she enjoyed the luxury of finishing a chapter of a book or watched a local football match with her friends? She was close to solving both cases but still needed to tie up a few ends before presenting Tolo with her conclusions. Once resolved, life would hopefully return to normal and she would cut herself some slack.

She stood outside Ca'n Moix and examined the unruly garden. Brambles were straggling into the path of a climbing rose, its few remaining petals now withered and faded. Yellowed ivy clung to the front wall, while tall and bullish weeds dominated the parched lawn.

She shook her head sadly. 'When was the last time I watered you?'

A few lazy insects buzzed in reply, but the garden remained huffy and mute. The sun was just rising over the hills and a cockerel's excitable cry shattered the silent air. On the porch she fumbled for the house key just as the gate clanged behind her and Marga and Pep rushed forward.

Marga hugged her tightly, with tears in her eyes. '*Gràcies a deu*! We heard on the news late last night that there had been a car chase in Deià involving suspects in the Mas case and that there had been a terrible crash.'

Pep turned to her. 'And then your mother called Marga and me in a panic to say that, unable to sleep, she'd come round here an hour ago and found poor Furó all alone. She's been frantic with worry about you!'

'Why didn't you answer your mobile?' demanded Marga.

Isabel wearily opened the front door. 'I foolishly left it in the office last night. I'm surprised mama didn't find it.'

After calling and reassuring Florentina, Isabel enjoyed a soothing cup of coffee and slice of almond cake while she talked Marga and Pep through the evening's events. They continually interrupted, asking detailed questions, until Marga announced that she had to collect her daughter, Sofia, from her mother's house and hurried off, not before kissing Isabel extravagantly on both cheeks.

When they were alone, Pep offered her a smile. 'Well, at least the Mas murder case is resolved.'

Isabel frowned. 'I'm not so sure. I'm close to the finishing line but not quite there.'

'Are you feeling OK?'

'Just in need of sleep.' Isabel walked into her office and hurriedly examined an e-mail with an attachment that had arrived from a contact at the Quebec police force. She hesitated a moment, deciding to open it after she'd taken a shower. Before heading for the bathroom she called the house phone at Ca'n Mas and was relieved to hear the voice of Camila Cortez. The elderly woman assured her that Cruz Ramírez had left her unscathed.

'So, what has become of him?' she asked Isabel.

'He is in a coma and was the only one injured after a car chase.'

The old woman uttered a small cry. 'I saw the news late last night. They talked of a crash and casualties. I was so worried about you. And what of Andres Moreno?'

'A body was found in Banyalbufar which we think will prove to be his.'

'It is the end of a long chapter in my life, Isabel. Tomorrow afternoon I return to Bogotá.'

'I will pop by to say goodbye. What time are you leaving?'

'The taxi is picking me up at three o'clock.'

After replacing the receiver, Isabel took a quick shower and changed into fresh clothes. She gulped down another strong *cortado* before picking up the key to Pep's *moto* on his desk.

Pep stared at her in some concern. 'Where are you going with my *moto*?'

'To Ca'n Mayol.'

'What on earth for? What is this obsession you have with the Foxes? I'll be only too glad when they leave in a few weeks.'

'You don't understand, Pep.'

'I do. You just can't accept that they're just a pair of weirdos. You're as bad as old Idò.'

'What do you mean?'

'He's got a bee in his bonnet about them too. Last night in Jordi's bar he was blathering on about the first day he went over there to check the pool. He said that Mr Fox had seemed in a real hurry when he drove off and that the wife was very nervy. Of course, he spiced up his account for the regulars with our sighting of a mystery man at the window.'

Isabel reached into her pocket and retrieved a handful of sunflower seeds. 'He's a good raconteur, my uncle.'

Pep laughed. 'You don't say! Then yesterday he waffled on about it being suspicious that the Foxes had two cars when they never seemed to leave the house.'

'He's mistaken. They only have a black Golf.'

'Apparently not. Idò remembered that the car Mr Fox was driving the first day he went over there had been blue.'

Isabel flinched. 'Blue?'

Pep frowned. 'So he claimed.'

Agitatedly, Isabel called her uncle's mobile. On the sixth ring he picked up. 'Bel, what a relief to hear your voice! I hear you've been out gallivanting with..'

She cut him short. 'Idò, think carefully. What was the colour of the car Mr Fox was driving on the Tuesday you first went over to Ca'n Mayol?'

'Funny that. I know it was nearly two weeks ago, but I suddenly remembered when we were back over there that I'd seen him driving a blue car. I noticed it wasn't in the garage on Thursday when we visited.'

Pep eyed Isabel quizzically.

'Would you recall the make of the car?'

'I can't honestly be sure,' he replied. 'But at a guess I'd say it was one of those popular brands.'

'Maybe a Clio?'

Idò paused. 'You could be right. The sort of well-worn hire car you see on every street.'

Isabel thanked him and headed for the door.

Pep observed her anxiously. 'What did he say?'

'Wait!' she replied. 'I need to speak with Tolo and Gómez.'

To her irritation, both of their mobiles were on answerphone mode and she didn't want to leave a rambling message. Most likely they were still catching up on sleep or already locked in a meeting with their joint superiors and Judge Baltazar, preparing a press statement on the Mas investigation. She paced about the office in her bare feet, a fan blowing her newly tamed dark curls about her face. Furó eyed her intently, disturbed by her agitated movements.

Pep stood frowning. 'You think the blue car that Idò recalled seeing at Ca'n Mayol is the same one used to abduct Miranda?'

'And the very same one that was found burnt out near Lluc monastery.'

'Don't be hasty, Bel. There are thousands of those cars on the island.'

'It's the last piece in the jigsaw, Pep. It's merely confirmed what I already knew.'

She swayed slightly with exhaustion. 'The e-mail!'

Pep watched in increasing alarm as Isabel darted into her office and sat in front of her computer. A moment later she clapped her hands together and returned to his desk, her pannier over her shoulder.

'What an idiot I am! It's Saturday.'

'What of it?'

'Today's the day that our weirdo friends at Ca'n Mayol intend to leave. We've no time to lose.'

'Please, Bel, slow down!'

She looked up at him. 'Listen, if I'm right, they intend to clear out today. Miranda's future is at stake.'

Pep's eyes bulged. 'Are you *loco*? If, by chance, your suspicions are justified, these people could be armed and dangerous.'

'I don't think so. Anyway, I'll have you on standby here. Please keep calling Tolo and Gómez until one of them picks up. If you get no response in the next thirty minutes, call their duty officers and ask them to send backup to Ca'n Mayol.'

Pep stood his ground, arms folded like a wrathful Greek God. 'I'm coming with you.'

'No way,' said Isabel. 'I'd prefer to park up unobtrusively and do some subtle spying until either the Guardia or police arrives.'

Pep shook his head. 'I'm coming with you, whether you like it or not.'

She rolled her eyes. 'OK, but this is how it'll work. I'll go ahead on your *moto* and you follow in Pequeñito.'

'I don't like you using my bike again. You nearly destroyed it last night.'

She glowered at him. 'Stop whining. Just do as I ask.'

He nodded grumpily.

'Now, when we get there, park some distance from the main track and get hold of Tolo and Gómez.'

Pep stuffed his mobile phone into his pocket, scooped up the car keys on Isabel's desk and whistled in Furó's direction. 'Look lively, we're going on a ghost hunt.'

The ferret issued a low growl and then with a decisive sniff, pattered after him down the stairs.

*

Crouched low behind some oleander bushes flanking the drive, Isabel raised her binoculars and scanned the upper windows of Ca'n Mayol. Not the slightest movement and yet she knew that the Foxes must be home. Although the front door remained stubbornly shut, the windows of the living room had been wedged open, allowing a pair of soft cream curtains to flirt with the breeze. She stole a glance at the driveway, noting that the black Golf had been washed and polished and was now facing in the direction of the road. Although she never bothered with a watch, she calculated that she'd been positioned there for about ten minutes, time enough surely for Pep to have made contact with Tolo and Capitán Gómez or their police teams. She'd told him to stay in the car ready to brief whoever arrived first, while she undertook an advance recce of the building and grounds. Gingerly she rose to her feet and checked about her before sprinting across the drive towards the garage. Once there, she ducked down behind a hefty terracotta pot of rosemary and gazed about her. Silence, save for the methodical clicking of the invisible cicadas in the long grasses. For a moment, she closed her eyes and allowed the sun to caress her face. She hoped that her instincts hadn't betrayed her, that her hunches were not just the product of an overzealous imagination and a series of bizarre coincidences. Believing the coast to be clear, she gradually straightened up. Pep would have rallied the troops by now, so she might as well hold her position, unless of course any of Ca'n Mayol's occupants attempted to leave. Isabel snapped back to the present when she heard a sharp metallic click and turned to see a weapon trained on her. It wasn't the first time she'd found herself staring down the barrel of a gun, but that had been a long time ago. The man now studying her with cold impatient eyes was holding the revolver in his right hand. With interest she noted the youthful, aquiline features and short chestnut hair. Devoid of long hair, beard, moustache and shades, Mr Fox had transformed into the ghostly figure she and Pep had spied at an upper window the previous day. She offered him a jaunty smile. 'What a pleasure to meet you again, Mr Fox, or should I call you by your alias, John Gilbert, or your real name, Jérome Baudoin?'

He pointed towards the back of the house with his gun. 'Move it.'

Isabel stepped cautiously onto the gravel path, stopping to remove a small stone from her left espadrille as she stared up at the sky. 'What a beautiful day. Perfect for sailing, wouldn't you say?'

Robustly she began whistling a few bars of her favourite Mallorcan sea shanty and was immediately silenced.

'Shut up and walk.'

The man shadowed her along the path, his gun close to her head. When they reached the lawn, he nodded towards the kitchen door. 'Get inside.'

Isabel's eyes adjusted to the sudden gloom of the kitchen. The window's dark green shutters were tightly closed, although the back door now swung open. The man directed her towards a chair at the trestle table.

'Sit down with your hands behind your back. Don't try anything stupid.'

Isabel noted the French intonation. The way he hissed the word *stoopid*. She did as she was told and hung her arms behind the back of the pine chair. A moment later she felt her wrists being tightly manacled together with handcuffs and inwardly sighed with relief. The man crossed the room and bellowed into the empty hallway.

'Sabine! Frank! *Vite!*'

He stepped back into the kitchen and eyed Isabel sulkily. 'I had a feeling you would be trouble that day we met in the supermarket in Sant Martí. You were asking too many questions. My instincts are rarely wrong.'

She offered him an encouraging nod. 'Mine neither. I knew you were fake the moment we met.'

He offered her a tight smile. 'And then you found an excuse to come sniffing round here yesterday with your weird little crew...'

'My family, actually.'

'Whatever. Before you left the house I saw you looking at the upstairs windows. Did you see me?'

'Yes. You looked quite different without the disguise, but I knew it was you.'

'I should have been more careful.'

'It only confirmed what I already suspected – that you were the brother of Sabine Labelle, Frank Walters fiancée, and that both of you were posing as the Foxes.'

Jérome Baudoin leant against a marble work surface, the gun resting at his side. 'When you left here yesterday I made a few calls and discovered you were a cop.'

'Former cop.'

'It makes little difference. As they say, once a Catholic, always a Catholic.'

'You shouldn't be so influenced by the Vatican's PR bandwagon.'

There came the sound of hurried feet and Jérome's sister appeared in the doorway.

Isabel greeted her enthusiastically. 'Ah, Mrs Fox, how nice to see you. Although perhaps it's better that I call you by your real name, Sabine Labelle. Another amazing disguise, if I may add.'

The woman appeared speechless as Isabel continued. 'I was puzzled about your surname, Labelle, until I discovered, thanks to a contact in the Quebec force, that it belonged to the French Canadian husband you divorced three years ago, and that your maiden name was Baudoin.'

With a pained expression the woman turned to her brother. 'She knows who we are! Now what do we do? What if she's contacted the police?'

'Be quiet, Sabine. I found her motorbike on the track, so she must have come alone. We need to move quickly, though. Get Frank.'

Isabel examined the woman's pale face now pinched with anxiety as she hovered in the doorway.

'Hurry!' snapped Jérome.

Wordlessly, Sabine left the room. Isabel turned to her captor. 'So, Frank Walters is here already? If I'd arrived any later, I might have missed him.'

'Yes, your timing is impeccable. We were leaving within the hour, but thanks to your unexpected visit our departure will need to be sooner. The question is what we do with you.'

'Release me?'

'I'm impressed that you're able to retain a sense of humour. You're either very brave or very stupid.'

Urgent voices ricocheted along the corridor and suddenly Sabine reappeared, this time with Frank Walters in tow. He appeared ruffled and tired, his gait slow and his eyes bloodshot.

'So, policewoman Isabel doubles up as a rentals agent? How enterprising of you. It was only yesterday that Jérome and I finally worked out that Isabel the police consultant and Isabel from Home Sweet Home were one and the same. Regrettably, we've had sporadic contact using pay-as-you-go mobiles since everything kicked off, so any mutual intelligence gathering has been tricky. As you'll know, all my movements are monitored by the Guardia officers at my hotel in Pollença.'

Isabel felt a sharp pain in her shoulder blade and shifted in her chair to alleviate the pressure. It was some years since she'd been handcuffed in hostile circumstances. During her time at the police HQ in Palma, it had just been for sport. She smiled to herself, remembering how she nearly always outwitted colleagues, freeing herself from the cuffs in a matter of seconds using a trick she'd learnt from her former superintendent in Barcelona.

'So how did you elude the Guardia officers today?' she asked.

Frank Walters sat down opposite her. 'I donned some blue workman's overalls and a cap that I'd found in a basement maintenance room, then used the service lift and left the building via the back entrance. Easy as pie. Sabine picked me up in the Golf on a quiet side road out of the town. We communicated via pay-as-you-go mobile phones we bought in Russia. It's impossible to pick up their signal, so the poor old Guardia was none the wiser. But all that's unimportant. What I really want to know is how you managed to work out so much for yourself. We thought we'd covered our tracks pretty well.'

'Just old police habits. Putting two and two together and making five.'

'Tell me, I'm intrigued.'

Sabine leapt forward and grabbed his arm. 'Frank, we don't have time for this now. We need to leave. She may already have called the police.'

Jérome shook his head. 'I don't think so. Señorita Flores Montserrat seems a bit of a lone wolf, probably born out of arrogance.' He smirked at Isabel. 'Perhaps the real reason why you left the police force so suddenly was simply because you got too big for your boots. I don't see you as a team player.'

Isabel shrugged her shoulders. 'What can I say? You are very perceptive.'

He tapped his lip. 'All the same, if you'd been booted out of the police force why, I wonder, did they invite you back to help on the kidnapping case?'

'It used to be one of my areas of expertise and they needed results fast.'

'It strikes me that you wanted to solve this case all by yourself, rub the local police chief's nose in it and maybe get your job back in the local force. And now it's all backfired.'

Isabel offered a contrite expression. 'You could well be right.'

He waved the gun around in the air. 'So, tell us how much you think you know.'

'I couldn't have a glass of water and a Chupa Chup, could I? I noticed when I was here yesterday that you had quite a stock of them. Presumably for Miranda?'

Frank Walters smiled sardonically. 'At least she's funny.'

Isabel cleared her throat. 'It all began when I met your former wife, Jane Walters, the first time in Pollença. She showed me Miranda's bedroom and mentioned that she always slept with Pinky, her little blue rabbit. It was missing.'

'And the significance of that?' asked Jérome.

'It occurred to me that Miranda might have known that she would not be returning to her bedroom after her birthday lunch so had made sure to take her beloved Pinky with her in her Barbie rucksack.' She paused. 'My other thought was that her abductor had removed Pinky in order to give it to the child later. I therefore worked on the premise that the abductor was known to her. A long shot, I know.'

Frank Walters gestured with his hand. 'Go on.'

'I saw the compilation of Roald Dahl stories you'd bought your daughter – apparently her favourite. I explored possible connections.'

'What do you mean?'

She laughed. 'At a subliminal level you framed yourself, Mr Walters. I'm a great fan of Roald Dahl too, and one of my favourite stories was about the Fantastic Mr Fox, who managed to outwit a group of farmers by digging an underground tunnel right under their noses.'

Sabine cursed. 'You idiot, Frank. Is that really why you suggested the name Fox to us?'

'It seemed as appropriate as any and there was an author of that name. Besides, there was a certain delicious irony about it. Why in heaven's name would anyone make the connection?'

Isabel nodded and looked up at him. 'You're right. It was only by sheer coincidence that I happened to be handling the house rental for your fiancée, Sabine, and her brother, who of course were posing as a couple named Fox. Naturally, the name meant nothing to me at the time, but gradually things began to fall into place. The problem was that I had no evidence.'

She turned to Jérome. 'You too made a big mistake. Aside from your suspicious manner that day when we met in Bon Día – and may I add, your unnatural facial hair – you chose to impersonate William Fox, a well-known crime writer.'

Frank Walters shrugged. 'I'm a fan of his books, and since I'd already suggested the name Fox, it seemed a good idea for Jérome to assume his identity, especially as the author apparently keeps a low profile and there are very few internet images of him.'

Isabel continued. 'True, but after tracking down his publisher...'

'What made you do that?' barked Sabine.

'Because I smelt a rat. I wasn't convinced that Mr Fox – or rather, your brother – was a writer.'

'Why not?' she persisted.

'Because he overacted his role as the recluse. It was too stage-managed. When I did get to speak to the publisher, I discovered that the real author was ill and residing in the States. That confirmed that you were both imposters. And then she gave me the title of his latest book hot off the press, but when I was over here on Thursday and mentioned the title, I realised that you'd never heard of it.'

Sabine cursed silently and stared accusingly at her fiancé. 'This is all your fault.'

Frank Walters threw a glance at Jérome. 'But your brother was evidently a lousy imposter.'

Isabel turned to Frank Walters. 'We were told that you and your former wife Jane were on good terms, but when I dug a little deeper I discovered that at the time of your divorce there had been a bitter custody battle over Miranda and when you lost, you apparently completely backed down. Seemed odd to me.'

He shrugged. 'People change.'

'Maybe, but after such an acrimonious fight, would you have given up on your daughter so easily?'

'I had little choice. Jane held all the cards, or so she thought.'

Isabel shifted again in her chair. Her arms were beginning to ache. Something she would have to rectify but not yet. It was crucial to keep the conversation going until the cavalry arrived. Playing for time was her only hope.

She smiled at him. 'Of course, Miranda gave the game away. The day of the abduction she had a birthday lunch with her mother at Café del Mar. Jane Walters told us that you had phoned Miranda the night before, ostensibly to wish her a happy birthday, but I assume it was to issue some last-minute coded instructions to her?'

A cold smile crossed Frank Walters' lips. 'Keep going.'

'It struck me as odd that Miranda went methodically back and forth to the sea's edge to fill her bucket with water that day until her mother went to pay the bill in the restaurant. At that point the child ran off with the bucket for a third time but never returned. The bucket was left abandoned halfway to the sea, but she'd made sure to take her Barbie rucksack with her.'

'So?' said Jérome.

'So someone had obviously told her to use the bucket filling as a ploy to leave the restaurant without raising any suspicions until the time came when her mother paid the bill inside. At that point Miranda took up the bucket again but this time ran off to her awaiting abductor – a heavily disguised Sabine – ditching it on the way. But she kept the rucksack because she needed it. No doubt it contained some important keepsakes for the trip, such as her swimsuit and more importantly, Pinky.'

Frank Walters sighed. 'Miranda couldn't sleep without Pinky. He had to come.'

'But you presumably told her to leave behind her Barbie, Susan, and the Roald Dahl book, because if they went missing too it might have looked like a pre-planned abduction.'

'Correct. I intended to pick them up some time later when visiting Jane, but the Roald Dahl book was gone because you had of course taken it, as I discovered when we met at the police station.'

Isabel turned to Sabine. 'And you were a perfect abductor because Miranda trusted you. With that blond wig you could have been her mother so no one would have suspected you. Of course, you made a mistake wearing that silver bracelet.'

The woman instinctively touched the delicate trinket about her wrist.

Isabel gave a tut. 'It was careless to have worn it on the day of the abduction. It showed up foggily in video footage and it got me thinking. I'd seen something similar before. When we met in the woods last Monday your bracelet caught my eye, and it was then that I remembered seeing the same one that day we first met in Bon Día. I also recalled that it included the initials SB.'

'How did the initials help you?' asked Jérome.

'Because I suspected from our first encounter that Mrs Fox, or rather Sabine, was French Canadian.' She stole a glance at Sabine. 'I'm afraid your accent and turn of phrase gave you away.'

'How?' demanded Sabine.

'I overheard some of your telephone conversation that day we met in the woods. You were speaking in French, but you used Quebec terms such as *un chum*, not *copain*, meaning boyfriend, and I distinctly heard you say that you'd just taken a walk, but instead of using the noun *promenade* for walk, you used *marche*.'

'What are you, an etymologist too?' Jérome sneered.

'Not at all, but at home my Spanish father often spoke with me in French. He was quite a polyglot. So, to continue, it was a long shot, but I called a chum at the Quebec police force who confirmed by e-mail this morning that your family name was Baudoin and that you were originally based in Montreal. Coincidentally, your mother's name was Monique – hence the name for your yacht.'

'Well, aren't you a clever little sleuth,' replied Frank Walters.

She looked up at Jérome. 'Another little error you made was not donning your disguise when you sailed into Soller port on the night of your arrival. An old fisherman told me that he'd seen a young man skippering the yacht and yet last Monday when I met your sister while walking my ferret, she told me that you had no skipper.'

Isabel observed Sabine.

'You're quite the master of disguise, like your brother. You cut off and dyed your auburn locks and changed the colour of your eyes from lavender to green for your alter ego, Mrs Fox, but then donned a blond wig when you played abductor.'

The woman glared at her.

'What you failed to hide, though, along with your bracelet, were your freckles. They helped me decide that Mrs Fox, Sabine Labelle and the female abductor were just one unholy trinity.'

ANNA NICHOLAS

'We can't all be perfect,' Sabine snapped.

'Ah, yes, and a small thing that bothered me was the amount of Chupa Chup lollies and sweets you had piled into your basket that first day I met you in Bon Día.'

'Sweets aren't just the preserve of kids,' scoffed Frank Walters.

'True, but few adults go for those kinds of sweets. I do, but then I'm just a big kid at heart.'

Sabine twisted her fingers agitatedly. 'Big problem, more like.'

Isabel sighed. 'I can't imagine what kind of story you and Frank Walters cooked up to persuade Miranda to leave her mother that day. But what I did learn from Jane Walters was that Miranda was very good at keeping secrets and liked springing surprises.'

Frank Walters flicked a glance at his watch. 'Time is running short – for you, that is – but I'll tell you this, it was quite simple. I convinced Miranda that Sabine and I would be getting married on Jérome's yacht the following day and that she'd be our bridesmaid. I told her that we wanted it to be a big surprise for her mother and Marc, who would be invited, but that she was needed for rehearsals. She thought she'd be seeing her mother the next day.'

Isabel shook her head. 'How could you tell such a despicable lie to your own daughter?'

'Expediency,' he replied calmly. 'Miranda is my life. There was no way I would let Jane and that druggie oaf Marc Got have custody of her.'

'And the reason you didn't get joint custody according to court records was because of the aggressive and threatening behaviour you displayed towards your wife prior to and during the divorce proceedings. You were your own worst enemy.'

'The judge was a woman. I didn't stand a chance.'

Isabel turned to Sabine. 'So, let me see if I've got this right. Having successfully lured Miranda away from the beach, you drove off in a blue Clio hired by Jérome – using the counterfeit name, John

296

Gilbert – from a car hire office in Magaluf. You then dumped the Clio on a quiet track near Lluc monastery, presumably removing all DNA from the car with a heavy-duty industrial antiseptic, before setting fire to it.'

'Bravo,' Frank Walters replied sardonically.

'Then you transferred to the black Golf you'd hired when you first arrived by yacht in Port Soller. And presumably Miranda has been held captive here ever since. In the attic bedroom, I'd hazard.'

Jérome offered her a contemptuous glare.

'But Mr Baudoin, you slipped up on the day of the abduction. My Uncle Idò came round unexpectedly early morning to clean the pool and yesterday recalled seeing you taking off in a blue Clio. So I imagine that you drove to a pre-arranged remote spot near Lluc monastery where you waited until your sister, Sabine – disguised in a blonde wig – arrived in the black Golf. Then you left the Golf there and both set off for the port of Pollença in the blue Clio. Sabine presumably played sunbather until the designated time of the abduction.'

Frank Walters rested his back against the wall of the kitchen and eyed her furiously.

'I wish you'd stop referring to this as an abduction. Miranda is my own flesh and blood. I had every right to take her.'

'She isn't a possession, Mr Walters.'

He ran a hand through his hair. 'So, why have you come here? Surely not just to prove how clever you are?'

Isabel shook her head. 'I guessed you'd be making your escape today. Sabine was expected to arrive at Palma airport tonight after supposedly holidaying near Corsica. But of course Sabine has been here the whole time. So, who went on holiday to Corsica impersonating you, hiring a yacht and answering to your name when the police eventually made contact with the boat on Friday?'

'You seem to have all the answers, so you tell us,' countered Frank Walters.

'It all came together when Sabine's background was forwarded to me by Sûreté de Quebec, the local regional police force in Canada. I only got to read the file this morning, but I saw that she had an older brother named Jérome and a sister, Cecile, two years her senior, who bore a striking resemblance to her. It was she who posed as Sabine in Corsica.'

'Impressive deduction,' Jérome replied.

'So, you all have no choice but to leave today because if Sabine had never shown up at the airport tonight, the police and the Guardia would have grown mightily suspicious and the whole thing would have unravelled.'

Sabine tore ferociously at a nail. 'She knows too much. It's ruined everything. What are we going to do with her?'

Frank Walters placed an arm around her shoulder. 'Keep calm, *cherie*. Soon we'll be far away from all this. She can't change any of that.'

Isabel raised an eyebrow. 'Oh, really? You think you can all just swan off to some overseas hideaway with Miranda and live happily ever after? Are you naïve enough to believe that she'd never be discovered?'

'It happens more than you think,' replied Frank Walters. 'There are thousands of cases of missing children who've never been found.'

Isabel stared at him. 'You're a fool if you think Miranda would conveniently forget about her mother or forgive you for fabricating such lies.'

Sabine thumped a fist on the table. 'I will become her mother. In time she will learn to forget Jane.'

'Miranda loves her mother. It's too late to reprogramme her.' Isabel bowed her head and sighed. 'You're all delusional. Even if you make it to your yacht in the port and set sail today, the police will track you down.'

'I don't think so,' replied Jérome. 'We have new identities and a perfect safe house. By the time the police cotton on, we'll be untraceable.'

'And where is this safe house?'

Frank Walters attempted humour. 'If we told you that, we'd have to kill you. All the same, we will need to make sure you go undiscovered for at least twenty-four hours. We can't have you blabbing too soon.'

'That's too bad, because I've already alerted the police. They'll be here anytime,' she replied.

Jérome gave a hollow laugh. 'It's evident that you foolishly came alone. I spotted your motorbike hidden in bushes. Curiosity and hubris apparently got the better of you. As I suspected, you wanted to be a heroine and solve the case alone. We'll be long gone before the police learn the truth. And now, we must say our fond farewells.'

Isabel looked across at Frank Walters. 'It's not too late to put an end to this madness. You say you love Miranda, but she will end up hating you if you take her away from her mother.'

'Jane left me no choice. She lied to gain custody.'

'How?'

'She told the court that I was an alcoholic and was given to violent outbursts. She never said that I harmed Miranda, but the implication was that I was a potential time bomb.'

'And were you?'

'A reformed alcoholic, yes, time bomb, no.'

Jérome turned to Frank Walters. 'Go now.'

'Is Miranda ready?'

'She's playing on the upper landing. All her belongings are packed.'

'Good. Take the Golf. I'll deal with Señorita Flores Montserrat and follow behind on her motorbike.'

Sabine eyed her brother fretfully. 'I don't want to leave you here. You've sacrificed everything for us. What if something happens?'

'If for any reason I don't show up at the port in thirty minutes, just get the hell away.'

Frank Walters hesitated at the door. 'What will you do with her?'

'Make sure she's not found for a while. Hurry!'

Sabine embraced her brother before hurriedly leaving the room. He waited until their footsteps had receded before slowly picking up the gun from the work surface. He offered her a pitying smile. 'It's a shame you came here. It would have made life simpler for us all if you'd not been so inquisitive. You're really very smart but also a little too clever for your own good.'

Isabel flexed her fingers. 'So now what? Come on, Jérome, you seem very savvy. I don't know how Frank or your sister persuaded you to get into this mess, but there's still time to put a stop to it.'

'You know nothing about me. Come to think of it, there's still a lot my sister and Frank don't know either. They think new identities just grow on trees. Love's young dream means they'll believe whatever they want to believe.'

'And what about you? I know that both your parents died within a short time of each other.'

'Within a year, actually. Sabine was just thirteen and Cecile fifteen, and I had barely turned eighteen.'

'So, what happened? You went off the rails, got in with the wrong crowd and turned to a life of crime?'

'Something like that.'

'A bit of a cliché, isn't it?'

'Life often is. My parents had been struggling with debts before they both died of cancer. The private clinics in Montreal had sucked them dry of funds and Sabine, Cecile and I were left with a mortgage and only state aid. So I skipped college and through the right contacts ended up working with one of Quebec's most renowned fraudsters. He taught me pretty much everything I know. By the time I reached twenty we owned the house and were in the clear financially. I got Sabine and Cecile through school and university and made sure we'd all be set up for life. I skippered and captained boats with Cecile while Sabine taught. All was fine until she met Frank.'

'And when Frank mentioned that he'd lost custody of his little girl, you offered to help kidnap her.'

'Kidnap? That's a little dramatic. As he said, it was merely a case of taking back what was his. I know what it's like to lose parents at a young age.'

'And what about her mother? You think it was right to break her heart?'

'I did this for my little sister, Sabine. Nothing else matters. When she was thirteen I told her that I would do anything to make her happy and I've kept my promise.'

'But at what price?'

Jérome gave a long sigh and offered her a bleak smile. 'I'm afraid we've run out of time, but I've enjoyed our chit-chat. The most pressing issue now is what to do with you.'

Isabel felt a chill run down her spine. Where were Tolo and Capitán Gómez? Had Pep rallied the troops? If so, where the heck were they? She would have to fend for herself as best she could. As she struggled to release her hands using that old method she had learnt back in her police rookie days, she heard a blood-curdling shriek from the hallway. With her hands now free, Isabel jumped to her feet just as Jérome lunged forward and grabbed her hair. Isabel felt her head yanked forward and cursed when it grazed the edge of the table. Despite the sudden flash of pain, she managed with an upward motion of her elbow to strike Jérome in the chest. As he groaned and relinquished his hold on her, she twisted round and jerked her knee sharply upwards towards his groin. Jérome let out a startled cry and dropped his gun, but before he had time to retrieve it, Pep came hurtling into the kitchen and without a moment's hesitation delivered a cracking punch to his jaw. The man's eyes rolled back in his head and he slumped to the floor. Isabel felt dizzy and tasting salt on her lips realised that the gash on her head was seeping blood. Pep rushed forward to hug her just as the back door crashed open and Capitán Gómez and several armed Guardia officers raced into the room. In a matter of moments, expert hands were firmly guiding her out of the kitchen and into sharp sunlight, while the unconscious Jérome lay handcuffed on the kitchen floor. On the back lawn Capitán Gómez offered her comforting words before running stiffly across the grass and disappearing around the side of the house. As sirens continued to wail from the direction of the lane, she turned to Pep.

'Where's Furó?'

He pointed to some nearby shrubs where a ferret's nose could be seen poking out from the leaves. A paramedic arrived from nowhere and fussed about Isabel's head as she reached across to touch Pep's hand.

'Are you OK? You look as though you've seen a ghost.'

He stared at her with wild eyes. 'I did, of a sort.'

'But what were you doing here? I told you to wait in the car.'

He gave a snort of derision. 'You can blame your damned ferret. I'd only just managed to get hold of Capitán Gómez on his mobile and to speak with Tolo, when Furó suddenly went berserk. He leapt out of the car window, so I had no choice but to run after him.'

Isabel broke into laughter. 'He heard my sea shanty. It's my sign for him to come to me.'

'I might have known! When I finally caught up with him, he was sniffing around the front of the house. I tried to lure him away, but at that moment the front door opened and a little brown-haired girl with blue eyes was standing there in a white dress, goggling at me. I thought it was the child ghost of Ca'n Mayol and shrieked my head off. Next thing I knew, Mrs Fox and Frank Walters came out and tried to jump into the black Golf with the kid. I grabbed him, but he swung a punch at me. That's when Furó sank his teeth into his leg.'

'What happened next?'

'The kid was crying and the woman started hitting me with her handbag, but I managed to wrestle the car keys from her so knew she wouldn't be able to go anywhere. Then I heard police sirens and saw Guardia and police vehicles tearing up the drive. I decided to leave the police to sort out the woman and child while I went looking for you inside. Furó had pinned Walters down on the doorstep and he was yelling in pain. That's when I burst into the kitchen and found you being attacked by Mr Fox.'

'Rather, Jérome Baudoin, brother of Frank Walters' fiancée.'

'You're kidding? How did you work that out?'

'A long story, Pep. As you can see for yourself, Jérome Baudoin was the mystery ghost we saw at the window on Thursday.'

'I take it that the little girl is Miranda Walters?'

'Correct. She'd been kept locked up in the attic all this time. They must have cut and dyed her hair.'

'You were right all along. I should have believed you.'

'But I was only completely certain this morning. I could have got it all wrong.'

He smiled. 'I very much doubt that, Bel. You may be ham-fisted and a slave driver, but you know exactly what you're doing. I'll listen to you next time.'

'Hopefully, there won't be a next time.'

Groggily she looked about her, squinting under the harsh rays of the sun, until her eyes settled on an ungainly figure running towards her. It was Tolo, his face registering conflicting emotions. She couldn't remember a time when she'd been so happy to see him.

TWENTY-SEVEN

Bar Castell was unusually animated for such an early hour. Following the dramatic events at Ca'n Mayol the day before, many villagers were keen to congratulate the newly born heroine of Sant Martí. Isabel politely greeted her well-wishers at her favourite table on the terrace, although she disliked the attention. Rafael disliked it too and soon began shooing them away, saying that his most loyal of clients was exhausted and needed time to recuperate from her ordeal. Despite the odd protest, most turned tail and flocked across the *plaça* to Jordi's bar instead.

Isabel folded her copy of *El Periódico* and tossed it across the table. Josep Casanovas had been true to his word. He had omitted to mention the part she had played in the arrests at Ca'n Mayol and furthermore had written glowing reports on the joint actions of the Guardia Civil and National Police. Isabel finished her coffee and slid a smile to Pep.

'At least there's no mention of your child ghost in the report.'

Pep gave an indignant sniff. 'Listen, if you'd seen her, you would have nearly died of fright too.'

'I'm sure,' grinned Isabel. 'The most important thing is that Miranda is safe and well and reunited with her mother.'

Pep nodded. 'Poor kid. It's going to be hard for her to come to terms with what's happened.'

'One day I hope she'll understand that what her father did was for love. He was a misguided and selfish fool who lost sight of reality.'

'He was crazy to think he would have got away with it.'

'Stranger things have happened, Pep.'

He gave her a quizzical expression. 'You don't honestly think they could have completely disappeared off the map?'

Isabel looked sombre. 'Children do drop off the map every day. Truth is often stranger than fiction.'

'And what about Jérome Baudoin?'

'The federal criminal police in Switzerland got back to me last night after I'd requested a background check on him. They have a specialist unit called Einsatzgruppe TIGRIS, known as the super cops. It turns out that they had been trying to track down Baudoin between Canada and Switzerland, where he relocated, but he proved a slippery fish. He went under numerous aliases and had quite a global network going.'

'What was he involved in?'

'Money laundering and organised crime. They think his sister Cecile was in cahoots with him but that Sabine knew very little about his operation.'

'What'll happen to them?'

Isabel rose from her seat and pulled her pannier over her shoulder. 'I imagine they'll be doing time for some years. As for the mysterious Cecile, she's apparently vanished into thin air, as I'd have expected.'

Pep looked up at her with a bright smile. 'And now we can get back to normality, just in time for the village shindig tonight and the Nit de Foc tomorrow.'

Isabel smiled. 'Yes, we're almost home and dry.'

Pep followed her through to the bar. 'What does that mean?'

'There are still some questions hanging over the death of Mas.'

'They've caught the murderer. What more do you want?'

Isabel shrugged and without thinking touched the white dressing that covered the wound on her forehead. It had only needed five stitches, but it still throbbed.

'I need to tie up some loose ends. Ramírez is still in intensive care, so I won't be able to interview him just yet.'

Pep offered a note to Rafael, but he waved it away, pulling Isabel in for a bear hug on her way out.

'Don't try anything stupid like that again, Bel. No point in being a dead hero,' he whispered.

She offered him an inscrutable smile and sauntered down the stairs towards the *plaça*. Pep tucked his arm protectively under hers as they walked across the village square.

'Why don't you take the rest of the day off? I'll hold the fort. Furó and I can go for a long walk later.'

'You and Furó bonding on a walk, now that's progress! You could probably do with a day off too. I'm only sorry the job hasn't quite panned out as planned.'

He laughed. 'I don't know. I'm getting to enjoy all this action and adventure stuff. Beats picking up people from airports.'

She scrunched his hand. 'I am so grateful for your courageous actions at Ca'n Mayol. You probably saved my life.'

A pink hue suffused his cheeks. 'I don't think so! You were doing fine without me. I just stopped him in his tracks. Besides, I don't think he intended to kill you.'

'Luckily, we'll never know,' she replied.

When they reached Ca'n Moix, Doctor Ramis was standing by his gate, snipping dead leaves with his secateurs. He gave Isabel a wink.

'You've just missed your mother. She was hoping to find you resting in bed.'

'In her dreams,' muttered Pep.

'Well, as your physician, Bel, I would recommend peace and tranquility and lots of sleep.'

'Mmm, nice idea, Doctor Ramis, but I have a few small tasks to finish before the village party tonight.'

He mopped his brow. 'The postman brought you some mail and that charming new boyfriend of yours popped by with some flowers, which he left on the doorstep. Your mother invited him to the event tonight.'

Isabel frowned. 'What boyfriend? Oh, please don't tell me Josep was here?'

'That's the chap,' he replied. 'He told me you'd called him last night with an exclusive about the Miranda case. The poor boy seemed sick with worry about you.'

Isabel plodded up her path and groaned when she saw a massive bunch of roses on the doorstep. Pep let out a guffaw.

'It must be love!'

She gave him a sharp elbow in the ribs. 'If he knew me at all, he'd know that I prefer my flowers alive.'

She gathered up the mail and walked into the house just as her mobile phone rang. It was Tolo.

'Are you in bed?'

'What a thing to ask a woman.'

'Let me rephrase that, then. Are you resting?'

'Of course not. I'm absolutely fine. Any news?'

He breathed heavily into the receiver. 'Miranda's recovering well. I told her mother that you'd played a big part in her rescue and she is eternally grateful to you.'

'So, how did the press conference go this morning?'

'Naturally, a success. Everyone likes a happy ending. Largely thanks to you, tomorrow's international headline news will herald the safe return of Miranda to her mother. We all come out of it smelling of roses. There's only one hitch.'

'Which is?'

'Cruz Ramírez is still in intensive care, so we're going to have to wait before we can wrap up the Mas investigation. That's if he makes it, of course.'

Isabel leant against the cool white wall of the *entrada* and watched as Pep staggered past her towards the kitchen, his face obscured by the gaudy red flowers springing up from his arms.

'I have some concerns...'

Tolo stopped her mid sentence. 'Me too. I don't like loose ends either. Once the housekeeper's left for Bogotá this afternoon we'll do a complete sweep of Ca'n Mas in case those diamonds really do exist and continue to liaise with your contact Julian Mosquera and the Colombian authorities.'

'What'll happen to Mas's house?'

'It seems he left no will, so the State should get it all. Mean old sod didn't set aside so much as a *céntimo* for his housekeeper or the church.'

'Maybe he wasn't planning leaving this world so soon,' she replied. 'How is our friend Capitán Gómez?'

'Still raving about your impetuousness yesterday. Apparently, he's gearing up for the Soller Nit de Foc tomorrow night. He's in charge of policing.'

Isabel laughed. 'God help us all. So has he lost interest in the Mas case?'

'Let's just say he's got more pressing community matters on his mind. Besides, he's decided that the diamonds never existed. Open and shut case.'

'Did Gaspar get anything more from our two drug runners?'

'Nothing useful. They're being deported to Guinea-Bissau.'

Isabel felt a twinge of pity for them, imagining the poverty-stricken existence they would resume on their return. She shook the thought from her head. 'So, Tolo, will you be coming to our village event tonight?'

She detected a slight edge to his voice. 'I'll try, but I'm up against it. There's a debriefing meeting now with Judge Baltazar and the commissioner, so I might not emerge for some hours. Then I've got a mountain of urgent paperwork to complete for Lola Rubio.'

'I suppose you'll be sad not to be working with her now that Miranda's been found.'

'Well, Madrid's not far. I can always pop back if I'm needed.'

When he'd rung off, Isabel dropped the mobile phone back into her pannier and paused for a few moments' reflection. She was disappointed that Tolo didn't seem particularly enthusiastic about the fiesta in Sant Martí, but why should he be? It was her village, not his, and she knew well enough that he was run off his feet. She also had to face facts. There was every chance that he had formed an emotional bond with Lola Rubio while in Madrid. Perhaps the young woman would make him happy. Isabel knew that life hadn't been easy for him losing his wife Blanca to cancer and having to bring up their young son alone. All the same, he had done an admirable job and Fabio was now a credit to him. Try as she might, she couldn't imagine life ever being the same if Tolo were to leave the island for a new life with the ambitious and attractive young civil servant. With a sorrowful sigh, she slung off her espadrilles and pottered into the kitchen, where Pep was still doing battle with the roses that now engulfed the old white sink.

'Do you want me to put them in your office?'

'No. You have them,' Isabel scoffed.

He laughed. 'Maybe you should put Casanovas out of his misery. All the same, my sister thinks he's a good catch and the newspapers are saying he'll soon be the next mayor of Forn de Camp.'

Isabel turned to him. 'Firstly, your dear sister, Marga, would marry me off to a coat stand if she had the chance and secondly, the only newspaper predicting that Josep Casanovas will be the next mayor of Forn de Camp is his own.'

'Still, he's...'

Isabel didn't stop to listen, instead stepping briskly past her patio into the arid garden and making her way along the path to her vegetable patch. She examined the sad display before her with a degree of resignation. The last of the green beans had shrivelled up, the curly kale was yellowed and tufts of bold weed had sprung up between the terracotta tiles delineating the vegetable rows. The truth of the matter was that she had neglected the garden of late, along with just about everything else in her life. Despite the mass of casualties she was given a burst of hope when she noticed a few resilient survivors – a clump of overripe tomatoes and aubergines. She crouched on the ground and filtered the ruddy brown soil between her fingers. It smelt good enough to eat and she lamented the fact that the last fortnight had been so occupied with police work. At least life would return to some semblance of normality now that both cases had been more or less resolved. As Isabel made her way back to the house and began climbing the stairs to her office, Pep appeared on the upper landing.

'Your Colombian pal is on the line. Shall I say you're busy?'

Isabel shook her head. 'No, I want to speak with him.' She waited until Pep had transferred the call to her office then walked in and closed the door. Ten minutes later she re-emerged with her car keys.

Pep offered her a quizzical glance. 'Where are you going?'

'Ca'n Mas. I told Camila Cortez that I'd pop by before she left and now I have completed the circle, time is of the essence.'

Pep gawped at her. 'What circle?'

'Please call Capitán Gómez and tell him to send backup immediately. Don't bother with Tolo. He's stuck in a long meeting with Judge Baltazar.'

Pep failed to understand the significance of her words and with a grin, tutted. 'Here we go again. Is this one of your warped jokes?'

His mirth quickly turned to fear when he saw the look on her face.

'Pep, just do as I ask! I now have conclusive proof that Camila Cortez is the murderer of Angel Tulio Mas.'

He grabbed the telephone and began dialling just as Isabel dashed down the stairs. In some angst he yelled after her, but she was already at the front door. A moment later he heard Capitán Gómez's voice on the answerphone.

*

Isabel sank into the comfortable leather armchair that was once the refuge of Angel Tulio Mas. Most of the furniture in the dead man's study had been covered in dustsheets and the shutters were bolted and curtains drawn. An overhead fan whirred dispiritedly as Isabel bent politely forward to catch every word uttered by the elderly housekeeper sitting across from her. With delicate hands the old woman fingered the crucifix about her neck while fixing her with plaintive eyes.

'It's such a nice surprise to see you even though you promised to pop by. It has been such a wretched period. It will take some time for me to adjust to life back in Colombia, but after such an ordeal and losing poor Señor Mas, I shall be glad to go home today.'

Isabel nodded sympathetically. 'When do you leave for the airport?'

She sipped at her lemonade. 'Actually, I have a cab picking me up any time.'

'Then I mustn't delay you.'

The housekeeper gave a genteel cough. 'Is your lemonade sweet enough?'

Isabel lifted the glass to her lips and nodded. 'Still as good as before.'

Camila Cortez fidgeted in her seat. 'And what has become of Cruz Ramírez? I read in the newspaper today that he killed Andres Moreno.'

'It's true. As for Ramírez, he is still at Son Espases in a critical state.'

The old woman offered a heavy sigh. 'And Andres Moreno killed poor Señor Mas.'

Isabel smiled. 'Why let Moreno take all the credit? After all, it was you who killed Mas.'

Camila Cortez froze, her eyes fixed on Isabel's face. 'What are you saying?'

'Although I had no hard proof, I suspected you early on, Señora. You see, the murder scene was too perfect, Afrim Cana's fingerprints too copious. It was obvious to me that he was being framed, but by whom?'

The housekeeper said nothing.

'The bloody handwriting on the wall was neat and scholarly and to my mind, the work of a woman. I never believed your first account about the four masked men. Both your neighbour, Tomas Llull, and Cana himself disputed that. It was a clumsy stitch-up.'

'Still,' the woman replied in a level tone. 'It bought me some time.'

'Maybe. Of course, when I questioned you later, you accused Andres Moreno of murdering Mas, also mentioning that he had found the old man drugged. That wasn't true. Neither did he tie you up, because he never visited Ca'n Mas, did he?'

The woman raised an eyebrow. 'I'm listening.'

'Andres Moreno only came over to Mallorca after he'd read the death notices about Señor Mas placed in the Colombian press by your nephew Salvador. As it happens, I learnt from the Colombian police yesterday that a man fitting Andres Moreno's description had been caught on CCTV buying a ticket at the Iberia Airlines desk at Bogotá airport, two days after the murder of Mas. He booked a flight to Mallorca via Madrid.'

'He was an evil man.'

'And what of Cruz Ramírez? You waited patiently until he neared the end of his jail sentence in order to involve him in your planned murder of Mas. I assume that some weeks before he was freed, you lured him over here with a letter, presumably a fake one purporting to be from Mas or his alter ego, Ortega.'

'You're good, Isabel. How did you guess that?'

'My police contact in Colombia informed me that the prison authorities had registered that a letter was sent to Ramírez from Spain two weeks before he was freed.'

'That was my handiwork. I penned it as if I were Enzo Ortega saying that he was still alive and wanted to return the diamonds that he had stolen from Moreno and him many years before. I claimed that he had become a religious recluse and had reverted to the name of Mas and that he wanted to make amends, once Ramírez was released from prison. A day of reconciliation in Mallorca was suggested two days after the night I planned to kill Mas.'

'And Ramírez swallowed it all?'

'Surprisingly, he did. He wrote by return to say that he would come here on the allotted day.'

'And what happened when he arrived?'

'He came to the house the night I returned from Son Espases Hospital. He was furious to have discovered that Mas had been murdered and the safe emptied. I told him that the culprit had to have been either Afrim Cana or Andres Moreno, who'd both turned up at Ca'n Mas on the night of the murder. I told him that Moreno had tied me up in the kitchen, but that I had no idea which of them had killed Mas.'

'But Moreno wasn't even on the island at that stage,' replied Isabel.

'Exactly, but I spun a convincing yarn. Then I told Ramírez that Afrim Cana lived at Son Barassa and he evidently found and killed him. It was just a question of time before he caught up with Andres Moreno, who, like a lamb to the slaughter, came over here on the strength of those newspaper announcements.'

Isabel closed her eyes a second, suddenly overcome with tiredness. 'But take me back to the night of the murder. Presumably you waited until Afrim Cana had left before disabling Mas with the poison? There were traces of poison in Mas's glass, so by implication Afrim Cana had given it to him. But that wasn't true. Cana's fingerprints weren't even on the glass.'

'Right again, Isabel. I knew I wouldn't be able to get Cana's prints on Mas's tumbler, but they were all over the study anyway.'

Isabel stared at her. 'But Cana was clever. He'd never have left such a crass trail. And another thing, when I examined the crime scene, I noticed that two bottles of Club Colombia were missing from the fridge in the study and only one of San Miguel. I worked out that six bottles of beer could fit on each shelf in the minibar. On the shelf of San Miguel bottles, only one was missing, but on the Club Colombia shelf, two had gone.'

'Meaning?'

'That you took another bottle out after Afrim Cana had left, slipped in the Burundanga without Mas's knowledge, and poured it into his glass. Within a few minutes he would have been incapacitated and as it acts as a truth serum, he would also have been under your control. Later you got rid of the incriminating bottle.'

'At a municipal tip in Palma, actually.'

'The day you revealed the false bookcase to me, you mentioned Faraday, the British physicist. That was a mistake. It got me thinking.'

'Why, are you interested in science?'

'I studied the humanities mostly, but I'd heard of Faraday. Of course, you might have studied him at school, but it told me that you had a bright academic mind.'

'You flatter me.'

'It just so happens, Señora Cortez, that I learnt something very interesting today from my Colombian colleague. It seems that under your maiden name of Rodríguez you were a pharmacologist and lecturer for twenty-five years at the University of Colombia in both Medellín and Bogotá. Then you met your husband Juan Cortez and took his name. Sadly, he died of cancer within five years of your marriage.'

The older woman's face clouded.

'So, with such a track record, why on earth would you have changed course and opted to work as a humble housekeeper for a man like Mas? The simple truth is that you had discovered that he also went by the name of Enzo Ortega and had headed up the Diablo Brotherhood under the auspices of the drug baron Pablo Escobar.'

The woman stared at her but remained silent.

'I now know that you had only been widowed a year when your brother, Luis Rodríguez, a prominent judge in Medellín, was murdered by Ortega and his Diablo Brotherhood thugs. On the eve of his securing a conviction against Escobar, Mas's boss, he was kidnapped at home along with his wife, Rosa. Their bodies were discovered on wasteland some days later. They'd been tortured using some kind of satanic ritual and then shot.'

Camila Cortez bowed her head. 'Stop. Please.'

'Their young son, Salvador Rodríguez, had luckily been staying with you in Bogotá, or he might have copped it too. Being a devoted aunt you became the boy's legal guardian and sent him to a secure boarding school in Switzerland. Long after Escobar's regime had been destroyed, you financed Salvador's passage through law school back in Colombia. He's just graduated from Javeriana University in Bogotá.'

'My pride and joy,' she whispered.

Camila Cortez dabbed at her eyes as Isabel pulled a piece of paper from her pannier. The top of the page bore the insignia of the National University of Colombia and with it a traditional crest adorned with the university's moto of *Inter aulas academiae*

ANNA NICHOLAS

quaere verum. Recalling her school Latin, she falteringly translated it out loud, 'Among the classrooms of the academy you search for the truth.'

An image of a serious-faced and much younger Camila Cortez stared back at her, below which were listed her academic qualifications and dates of employment.

'I received this scan today from the university's human resources department. By all accounts you were a deeply devout Catholic and a respected pharmacologist, but soon after your brother's murder, you resigned and disappeared off the radar.'

Camila Cortez looked down at her watch and sighed. The dithery, faint voice was gone, now replaced with a measured tone delivered with a soft, educated South American accent. 'Well done, Isabel. As I always suspected, there is more to you than meets the eye. No wonder you were an admirable police officer. I too did some checking on your own background.'

'I'd have done the same in your shoes.'

'So, let me tell you some things you can't know. After the butchering of my beloved brother and his wife, Rosa, I infiltrated the Diablo Brotherhood. My objective was to get close to Enzo Ortega, whom I'd learnt was their killer.'

'Waiting until the right moment when you could kill him. An eye for an eye?'

The woman cursed. 'Don't you understand? My law abiding brother and his wife were tortured to death by Mas and his cronies – Andres Moreno, Cruz Ramírez and Padre Paz García – leaving a young boy, my only nephew, an orphan. Can you even begin to imagine how I felt?'

Isabel observed her quietly.

'I vowed to God that with his sacred assistance I would crush and destroy them all. You see, Isabel, my brother believed in upholding the law at a time when Medellín was like a cesspit of vipers. He was a judge and a man of scruples who would not be intimidated or corrupted. He always vowed to deliver real justice to the people of the city and for those principles he paid with his life and that of his dear wife.'

'I understand,' Isabel replied gently.

Camila Cortez wiped away a tear. 'So overnight, I cast aside my former life and became a cold lifeless thing devoid of emotion and fuelled with hatred. I would have ended it all had it not been for little Salvador.'

'You still had enough love in your heart.'

The old woman gave a crisp laugh. 'Yes, I had a few small crumbs left for him.'

Isabel sat back in her chair. 'So you became a housekeeper to Ortega, or rather Angel Tulio Mas, and having got under the brotherhood's skin, learnt about their operations?'

'Yes. Believe me, they were miserable and lonely years spent first in Medellín and later, after Pablo Escobar was killed, Bogotá. Can you imagine what it was like to live day after day under the same roof as your brother's murderer, patiently biding your time and waiting for the moment to strike?'

Isabel shook her head. 'A living hell.'

Camila Cortez hugged her scrawny torso as if suddenly overcome with cold. 'Yes, it was hellish.' She dabbed at her eyes. 'Excuse me. I have not spoken to anyone of this. You are raking over the nightmares of my past.'

'What happened when you moved over here two years ago?'

'Ortega reverted to his real name of Angel Tulio Mas and kept up the pretence of being a great benefactor, while steadily establishing his international drugs business. Cana became his henchman – you know the rest.'

'Meanwhile, of the other brotherhood leaders, Padre Paz García was murdered in Medellín, Cruz Ramírez sent to prison and Andres Moreno simply disappeared or went underground. How did you hope to round them up?'

'I knew Ramírez's release date. As for Moreno, I learnt that he had run out of funds and resurfaced in Bogotá a month back, so I needed to act quickly.'

'Neither knew that Mas was still alive, presumably?'

She gave a bitter laugh. 'He'd covered his tracks carefully. Mas trusted me implicitly and often boasted about having stolen some diamonds from the other brotherhood ringleaders, so I knew that would act as bait to get them over here. All the same, I never saw the diamonds myself. I'm sure that if they existed, he probably sold them a long time ago.'

'Do continue,' said Isabel, lifting the glass to her lips.

'I had already worked out how to get rid of Mas. I had brought a supply of the drug burundanga with me from Colombia, and I purchased a sharp knife for the deed a few years back in Medellín. But my idea was to devise a plan that would implicate both Ramírez and Moreno in the murder of Mas, not me.'

'How?'

She offered Isabel a bright smile. 'I hadn't quite worked that out, but providence stepped in to lend a hand. That's when I knew God was on my side.'

Isabel listened intently.

'The night I decided to murder Mas, Afrim Cana came to see him alone just after six in the evening. He was in an agitated state and raged that part of the incoming cocaine shipment was missing from the Devil's Horn Caves. I was listening from the hallway as the door to the study was open. I could see that Mas looked sceptical and was probably of the opinion that Cana might be trying to double-cross him. The timing for the deed therefore couldn't have been better, as I realised that the murder might be blamed on Cana, or of course Ramírez and Moreno, once they turned up.'

'You'd sent the counterfeit letter to Cruz Ramírez, but you had to ensure that Moreno came over too.'

'That was why I got my poor unwitting nephew Salvador to post those death notices the next day. I knew it would flush Moreno out.'

'Your nephew suspected nothing?' said Isabel.

'There was nothing to suspect. He is as principled as his father and would never imagine that I would be capable of such subtefuge. I asked him to post them discreetly, paying in cash and to avoid identification. He didn't know of Mas's putrid background, that he was the notorious Enzo Ortega who had killed his father. He genuinely believed that I was in mourning for Mas and wanted to alert any of his relatives and contacts in Colombia. I added the image of Mas as Ortega just to ensure that Moreno would recognise him. Luckily my nephew had never seen a photo of the monster in his dotage. Just a second.'

The woman rose unsteadily and walked stiffly over to a chair where a black leather handbag lay open. She withdrew a small wallet which she examined intently. With a slow gait she came over to Isabel. 'Here, this is Salvador with his parents.'

Isabel felt a stab of pity as she viewed the happy trio. The boy had thick wavy dark hair and large thoughtful brown eyes. His right hand was entwined with that of his mother's and an enigmatic smile played on his lips. Luis, the judge, was statuesque with a handsome face, while the mother was slightly built and wore a beatific smile.

Camila Cortez returned to her seat. 'That photo was taken a few months before my brother and his wife were murdered.'

She offered Isabel a sad smile. 'Good, I see you've finished all your lemonade.'

Isabel clasped her hands together. 'After drugging Mas, I suppose it was easy to force him to divulge the combination to the safe where the diamonds were hidden. Burundanga acts as a powerful truth serum, as you will know as a pharmacist.'

Camila Cortez glared at Isabel. 'No, that part is not true. I had no interest in diamonds. I just wanted to kill him. Plying him with burundanga made the exercise much easier and meant he wasn't able to fight back.'

'And writing *LADRÓN*, thief, on the wall in his own blood was just a dramatic flourish, a red herring?'

'Yes. I had to steel myself for the task. My hands were shaking. In truth, I felt strangely detached as I plunged the knife into him again and again. It was as if I was merely the witness to a brutal murder, like the chorus in a Greek tragedy. I felt no emotion at all.'

'I presume you didn't write the word in Mallorquí dialect for fear of implicating a local.'

'Exactly, I wanted to contain matters.'

'And the reason your neighbour Tomas Llull heard the TV suddenly blaring at two in the morning was because you turned it on at that time, leaving the French windows open so that he could easily access the study. You needed him to find the corpse of Mas, and you tied to a chair in the kitchen.'

'The man's a nosey oaf. Perfect for the task.'

'So you bound your own hands and locked yourself in the kitchen after you'd switched on the TV?'

'Correct. I was organised. I locked the kitchen door from the inside with a key which I hid on my person and even tipped myself off a chair to ensure that my injuries were consistent with such a fall. It convinced the medics at Son Espases Hospital.'

'But it didn't stack up. Why would the killer keep you alive? You would have been a prime witness. All the same, you were an accomplished actress, Señora Cortez.'

'And may I repay the compliment. When you came to Ca'n Mas on the pretence of having a flat tyre, you were very convincing, but after your visit I'd noticed that the image of Mas with members of the Diablo Brotherhood was missing from the table and wondered whether you'd taken it.'

'Actually, I removed it on the day of the murder when I first visited the crime scene.'

'Well, its disappearance concerned me. It was then that I started making discreet enquiries about you. You became a problem for me.'

Isabel smiled. 'I like becoming a problem to lawbreakers, Señora Cortez. It usually means I'm nearing my goal.'

The elderly woman nodded. 'Yes, but I underestimated you.'

Isabel rose. 'Out of interest, how did you dispose of the knife? I assume that on the night of the murder you wiped it down with a substance such as hydrochloric acid to degrade the DNA content. No doubt you hid it in the recess of the bookcase, thus avoiding detection by the forensic team. There was a faint smell of bleach too when I examined the safe, so I knew it had been wiped clean.'

Camila Cortez nodded. 'I wasn't a chemist for nothing. No DNA would have been found.'

'You still had to ditch the knife somewhere safe, so I'm guessing you disposed of it at Son Espases Hospital when you were admitted there.'

'Right again, Isabel. It was risky, but I carried it on my person along with the plastic overall and surgical gloves I'd used for the killing. I used a powerful chemical enzyme I knew about to rid them of all DNA. That's one advantage of being a pharmacist. Then I wrapped everything securely in a bin liner which I threw down a waste disposal chute at the hospital.'

She stood up. 'Time is running out, Isabel, and my car will be here any minute.'

Isabel rose from her seat. 'How do you feel about being responsible for the deaths of three people?'

The housekeeper shrugged. 'Pretty good. In one fell swoop I have orchestrated the demise of Mas, Cana, Moreno and hopefully soon Ramírez. All of them are monstrous, not worthy of mercy. '

'What a web we weave,' muttered Isabel. 'You do realise that I can't let you leave for Colombia?'

She laughed softly. 'Yes, you can, Isabel, because soon you will be fast asleep. Why did you trust my lemonade?'

Isabel walked over to the French windows and fumbled with the shutters.

'Need some air? You must understand that I have to get to Colombia. My lawyers there will seek to protect me from extradition to Spain. I would prefer judgment from the Colombian courts.'

Sharp knocking could be heard from the front door. 'That will be my cab. You will sleep from the effects of burundanga but will be right as rain by the morning. I wish you luck in life, Isabel.'

She watched as the housekeeper walked out of the study. A moment later she heard shouts and a scuffle and Capitán Gómez rushed into the room.

She smiled at him. 'I guess you beat her taxi driver to it?'

'We stopped him on the drive and sent him away. Then we made our move. Are you OK?'

'Señora Cortez thought I'd drunk her spiked lemonade, but I anticipated her game and slipped the contents of my glass into this pot while she was distracted.' She indicated a brass ornament by her chair. 'All the same, I'm not feeling my best. I think I just need some fresh air and a good night's sleep.'

Solicitously, the military captain took her arm and led her out onto the sunny porch.

'So, Pep got hold of you?'

He dropped his voice. 'I could hardly believe what he told me about Camila Cortez. Who would have thought her capable of killing Mas?'

Isabel nodded. 'It's hard to absorb. I need to explain everything to you back at your office.'

In the courtyard Camila Cortez stood forlornly between two Guardia officers, handcuffed and with head bowed. As they led her towards a Guardia vehicle, Isabel touched Capitán Gómez's arm.

'Can I have a minute with her?'

He hesitated, then, relenting, gave a curt nod and walked off to make a phone call.

Camila Cortez offered her a weak smile. 'How enterprising of you to call the Guardia in advance. I should have anticipated that, and also that you wouldn't fall for my laced lemonade.' The woman gave a little shrug. 'As I said before, I underestimated you.'

Isabel lowered her voice. 'Listen, I need you to tell me the truth. I believe you forced Mas to give you the safe's combination before you killed him and that you took the missing diamonds.'

'An imaginative yet erroneous theory.'

'That day I bumped into you in the post office in Sant Martí, I learnt from Señora Coll that you had sent a small package to Colombia the day before.'

'How amusing that you sought clarification from that old busybody. I thought post mistresses were supposed to be discreet.'

'Not in our village.'

'I sent a small gift of an olive bowl to my nephew, nothing more.'

Isabel looked away. 'Be assured, Señora Cortez, that I intend to uncover the truth, however long it takes, and will pass on my findings to the police. Your nephew may well be implicated.'

The woman fixed Isabel with serious eyes. 'Please, before you act, contact Salvador in Bogotá as soon as possible and ask him what he knows about the diamonds. That is all I ask. I may be a murderess in your eyes, but I have honourable intentions.'

'I'll think about it,' Isabel replied.

They stopped at the back doors of the green Guardia van.

'If you promise to call Salvador, I will tell you something you'll badly want to hear.'

Isabel crossed her arms. 'And what might that possibly be?'

The woman checked that Capitán Gómez and his officers were still out of earshot. 'I know about your missing uncle.'

Isabel felt a wave of shock pass through her. 'What do you mean?'

'I'm talking about Hugo Flores Romero.'

Isabel felt her mouth suddenly turn dry. 'You have information?'

'As a gesture of goodwill, I will tell you that until two years ago when I moved over here, he was still alive.'

The woman hesitated, her pale fingers fluttering up to her face as she pushed away a strand of hair. 'Your uncle was briefly held prisoner at the remote estate where Mas and I were staying on the outskirts of Bogotá. He was brought to the house late one night by some of Mas's thugs and kept locked in the cellar for a fortnight. I brought him food and talked to him, that's how I know who he was. All things considered, he was in reasonable shape.'

'Why were they holding him there?'

'I didn't ask and he didn't say.'

'Where was he taken?'

'I don't know.'

'How can I believe you when you have lied and continuously altered your testimony over the last two weeks?'

'Because I've nothing to lose.'

'I need to know more.'

'That's all I have to give.'

The woman stared into Isabel's face and then reached forward and squeezed her hand.

'Have a good life, Isabel. Please try to think well of me.'

Moments later Camila Cortez was directed into the back of the van where, with red-rimmed eyes, she stared out at Isabel from behind the window until the vehicle slowly pulled away. Capitán Gómez finished his call and strode over to his car.

'Who would have thought it, Isabel? That woman played us all for fools. But truth will always out in the end.'

Isabel smiled at him. 'Will it? I'm not always sure about that. What will become of her?'

He removed his shades and gave them a cursory wipe with a pristine handkerchief. 'No doubt the Colombian government will fight to have her returned. Whether the Spanish authorities play ball, who knows? I have a feeling that given her age, the horrendous crimes of Angel Tulio Mas and the hideous legacy of Pablo Escobar and his despicable associates, her sentence will be light, either here in Spain or Colombia.'

'In some ways, that would make me happy. She committed a heinous crime, but the circumstances were exceptional.'

He frowned. 'Be that as it may, Isabel, justice must be served. There can be no exceptions.' Firing the engine, he looked at her from his open window. 'Shall we meet back at Guardia HQ?'

Isabel nodded. 'I just need to call my family to let them know that I'm OK.'

He grimaced. 'And I'd better let Tolo know that no harm has come to you. Like me, he will be unhappy that you recklessly took matters into your own hands – yet again. What are we to do with you, Isabel?'

She watched as he drove off, nodding stiffly at her from the window. Isabel slumped into the driver's seat of her own car and sat deep in thought. She was perplexed by events and the housekeeper's disturbing revelations and yet a small seed of hope had been planted in her heart that possibly, just possibly, her Uncle Hugo might still be alive.

*

Early evening as Isabel pushed open the front door to Ca'n Moix, the first thing she noticed were her mother's house keys sitting abandoned on a chair in the *entrada*. She stood at the base of the staircase and smiled when she heard distant laughter. It had been an exhausting afternoon spent debriefing Capitán Gómez at the Guardia headquarters in Palma. Tolo had called her as she drove home to Sant Martí and had sternly reprimanded her for visiting Camila Cortez alone. All the same, he had sounded greatly relieved to know that Mas's killer had finally been nailed. Although Isabel felt sad that he had decided not to join her at the Sant Martí celebrations that evening, he had at least promised to attend the Nit de Foc fiesta the next day. In her office she discovered Florentina and Idò ensconced on her leather sofa while Pep lolled on the floor with Furó on his lap. It was this unexpected endearing alliance that grabbed her attention most in the comfortable, domestic scenario. In a matter of weeks her beloved ferret had, against the odds, bonded happily with the young hothead. Perhaps their shared adventure over at Ca'n Mayol the day before had served to reconcile any differences. All looked up expectantly as she entered the room.

Isabel gave a smirk. 'I'm glad to see you've all made yourselves at home.'

'How's your head?' asked her mother anxiously as she whirled a teaspoon about her glass of iced coffee.

'I'm fine.'

'To think you might have died yesterday if it hadn't been for young Pep,' said Florentina.

'True. I owe him,' replied Isabel with a wink.

Pep smiled modestly. 'Shame I wasn't with you today. That mad old housekeeper could have killed you too!'

Isabel shook her head. 'She only intended to drug me for some hours in an attempt to flee the island. As a pharmacologist she knew exactly how much burundanga was needed to knock me out.'

Uncle Idò gave a grunt. 'Lucky our Bel was one step ahead of her!'

Pep looked up at Isabel from the floor. 'What I still don't get is why she was so keen to return to Colombia. Doesn't the country have an extradition treaty with Spain?'

'It does, but I imagine Camila Cortez thought she'd be on safe territory and that they'd give her some kind of immunity. Her brother's murder shocked the country at the time and it's likely she'd have been treated more like a heroine than a murderer. Enzo Ortego and the Diablo Brotherhood were greatly feared and loathed.'

'And so you're telling me that that little wisp of a woman drugged old Mas and then stabbed him brutally to death?' asked Uncle Idò. 'It seems hard to believe.'

Florentina gave an involuntary shiver. 'I never liked the man, but I wouldn't have wanted him to meet such a bloody end.'

Isabel raised an eyebrow. 'She was a woman consumed by sorrow who allowed hatred to flourish in her heart. I pity her.'

They sat in sombre mood until the door opened and Doctor Ramis appeared, beaming like a benevolent god.

'Are we all set for the village event?'

Isabel gave a sigh. 'I've only just got home and I've had an exhausting few days. Maybe I'll bow out tonight.'

There was general outcry.

'You will do nothing of the sort, young lady,' said Idò. 'As one of Llorenç's committee members it is your duty to be there.'

'Besides, it'll be fun,' encouraged Pep. 'Even if we will still have the same boring old food.'

Florentina rose hurriedly and surveyed her watch. 'Only an hour until the event and I have to go and help set up the bar in the marquee. Come on, Pep, let's get cracking!'

'What about Idò?' he replied.

Idò feigned an important air. 'Don't worry, I'll be doing my bit.'

'Sure, drinking up half the bar,' Pep muttered.

Isabel yawned and walked towards the staircase. 'I'll have a shower and get changed.'

'Yes, you do that, especially as that charming editor of yours is coming along,' replied her mother.

'What?'

Florentina exchanged a wink with Doctor Ramis. 'When he popped round the other day to leave you those lovely flowers, I invited him along tonight.'

The doctor shrugged helplessly. 'I did tell you at the time, Bel. You must have forgotten.'

Isabel closed her eyes and slowly counted backwards from ten. At the risk of committing matricide and joining the ranks of hardened killers such as Camila Cortez, she uttered a silent curse and marched up the stairs. Even in sunny Mallorca at the height of the summer, it didn't rain but it poured.

TWENTY-EIGHT

It was Monday morning and the elderly church clock of Sant Martí managed ten arthritic strikes and a barely audible discordant half-note before falling dumb. Llorenç stared up at the Roman numerals in some disdain. The clock needed a complete overhaul, which would deal yet another hefty blow to the village's strained finances. With an impatient shake of the head, he kicked off his tatty brown espadrilles and spread out his bare arms in the sun. He grinned across the table at Isabel.

'Surely I'm the luckiest mayor alive? Not only do I have a wonderful job in the most beautiful village in the world, but I also get to have coffee whenever I like with a woman more alluring than Cleopatra herself.'

Isabel crunched on a sunflower seed. 'Don't forget that she had a penchant for asps.'

The mayor smiled. 'Sometimes it pays to play with fire.'

'I'm glad you think so, Llorenç, because Furó's taking a lot of interest in your bare feet.'

The diminutive man drew his legs up as the ferret sniffed enthusiastically at his espadrilles.

Isabel laughed. 'He won't hurt you – it's just that he's got a bit of a foot fetish.'

Warily, Llorenç rested his feet back on the tiled terrace. 'I wanted to congratulate you on your successes in solving both the Miranda and Mas crimes. The police and Guardia may have got all the glory in the media, but I know who did the spade work.'

Isabel smiled. 'I'm happy to stay under the radar.'

'Your secret's safe with me. So, Bel, tonight we celebrate Nit de Foc in Soller, and may I say what a brilliant success our own little event was last night?'

'With you at the helm, how could it have been otherwise?'

He waggled a finger at her. 'You know how to flatter an old man! I'm pleased to see that in the end young Pep came round to our way of thinking regarding the refreshments. He's a good boy but has a lot to learn.'

Isabel pondered exactly what was meant by *our way of thinking*.

'I noticed that your editor friend came too. What's his name, Josep Casanovas? Hopes to make mayor of Forn de Camp next year.'

'So everyone keeps telling me. To be honest, I wasn't entirely happy that my mother invited him.'

'But he has prospects, Bel. You're in your thirties now, it's time to think about settling down.'

'Thanks for reminding me. Actually, I'm quite happy with the single life, Llorenç.'

'Perhaps all it needs is for the right man to knock you off your feet.'

'I have a ferret that does that daily, thanks all the same.'

Llorenç suddenly took on a confidential air.

'Listen, I wanted to have a discreet word with you about Pep.' He cocked his head towards the interior of the café. 'Old Jordi here told me that he spied Pep drinking in Palma last weekend with that pretty girl Aina from the bakery in Morells.

Angélica is still in the dark, but it won't be long before she finds out.'

Isabel shrugged. 'I wouldn't read too much into it. Aina was assisting with the investigation into the murder of Mas. Pep had to liaise with her.'

Llorenç murmured in approval. 'Well, I shall put Jordi right. How impressive it is that you entrusted him with such important detective work. Of course, I never thought for a moment that Pep would be so underhand. I know how he dotes on my Angélica.'

'Absolutely.'

'And how exactly was Aina involved?'

'I really can't discuss that, Llorenç.'

He tapped his nose.

'Of course, discretion is everything. I understand.'

He finished his beer and sat back in his chair. 'I'm glad the uncertainty arising from these two police investigations is over. It simply wasn't good for village morale. Thank heavens the culprits have been brought to justice, although I'm sad about old Camila Cortez. To think she lived so many sorrowful years in the company of her brother's murderer. I suppose there's no news on Cruz Ramírez?'

'Still in a coma, I believe.'

Isabel smiled when Jordi appeared at her side, a tea towel slung over his right shoulder. 'Nice to see you in my bar for a change, Bel. Rafael will be sulking for the rest of the day.'

She looked up at the lofty terrace of Bar Castell and nodded. 'Yes, I will have to do penance next time I see him.'

'By the way, if you set eyes on that thieving uncle of yours, tell him that he still owes me twenty euros from our last poker game.'

Isabel rose from her chair and, kissing Llorenç on the cheek, set off across the *plaça* with Furó following in hot pursuit.

*

Back at the office, Isabel discovered Pep dancing wildly to the Gypsy Kings. A glimpse of her face was enough to have him bounding over to the CD player to kill the sound.

'Just a bit of retro music to get me going,' he proffered.

Isabel cast him a pitying glance as Furó pattered off to his basket.

'I've just saved your *jamón*,' Isabel countered. 'The Sant Martí thought police spotted you with Aina in Palma at the weekend. Your future father-in-law was not amused. You don't deserve it, but I saved your backside.'

'How?'

'I claimed that you had met Aina to discuss important information about the Mas case.'

Pep crossed his arms. 'It's impossible to do anything in this village without some interfering...'

'Steady on. You're not going to tell me it was a wholly innocent encounter?'

Pep blushed. 'All we did was meet up for a few hours.'

'Ah, that's why you were cross that I'd borrowed your *moto* at the weekend. No doubt you wanted to impress Aina with your motorcycling skills on the way to Palma.'

He scrunched up his nose. 'You sound like my mother! Anyway, what's the harm in an innocent drink?'

'None whatsoever, as long as your girlfriend is happy about it.'

'She isn't, as it happens. Look, thanks for covering for me, but the truth is I'm not sure how I feel about Angélica anymore.'

'That explains your recent moodiness. Well, don't make any rash decisions.'

The door burst open and Florentina stalked in. 'About what?'

Pep eyed her grumpily and sloped off to his desk. 'Don't ask.'

Isabel gave her mother a warning grimace. 'Right, are we setting off to the beach? Where's Idò?'

'Here!' He stood in the doorway, a wry smile playing on his face. 'Hey, Pep, I hear from Jordi that you've been two-timing Angélica. She'll be after your hide.'

Isabel faced him. 'And Jordi will be after yours if you don't give him the twenty euros you owe him.'

Florentina turned to Pep. 'What's this, young man? I hope that's not true.'

'Is nothing sacred in this village?' he groaned.

'Of course not!' bawled Idò. 'There isn't a local who couldn't hear a bat wink.'

Isabel picked up a hefty pannier. 'I've got the picnic ready. *Venga!* Pep can make his confession en route.'

'And you, yours,' said Florentina.

Isabel stopped on the staircase. 'Mine?'

'About your budding romance with Josep Casanovas, of course,' replied her mother chirpily.

Pep brightened up. 'Well, that is a turn up for the books.'

With a slight scowl, Isabel thrust the heavy pannier of food and wine in Pep's direction and instructed him to place it in the boot of Pequeñito. He gave a grunt and set off down the stairs, wondering whether he should be doing her bidding on a Sunday anyway. There again, perhaps she was doing him a favour. If he hadn't agreed to spend the afternoon on the beach with her, Florentina and Idò, he would have been lunching with Angélica and her family, and she was still miffed with him over his rendezvous with Aina in Palma. Women, were they ever reasonable?

*

As Isabel squeezed Pequeñito into a tiny space just off the *plaça*, she heard someone calling to her from the pavement. She had just dropped her mother, Pep and Idò off at her home and, unable to find a parking place, had taken her chances parking near the square. To her displeasure, she saw that it was the weasel, no doubt ready to plant a parking ticket on the vehicle before Isabel had even had a chance to exit her seat. She wound up the car windows and jumped out.

'What's wrong with me parking here?'

The young woman shrugged. 'Nothing that I can see, aside from you being on a yellow line again.'

Isabel frowned. The weasel was not in her characteristic traffic warden uniform but was wearing jeans and a tee shirt, with her dark hair loose about her shoulders. She looked almost human.

'Are you off-duty today?' she asked warily.

The woman came over to her. 'I thought you'd be interested to know that I've quit the job. It's not for me.'

'So, what will you do instead?'

'I've been offered a job in the accounts department of El Corte Inglés in Palma. It's like a dream come true.'

Isabel stood in stunned silence. It wasn't necessarily her idea of utopia, but each to their own.

'*Enhorabuena*! I'm very happy to hear the news. And where will you live?'

'My husband has decided that it's too cramped living with his mother, and now that we'll have more income, we can rent a flat in Palma.'

'What a fantastic idea. I suppose they'll find a replacement for you here soon.'

The woman shook her head and laughed. 'I told Soller's town council that the people of Sant Martí were very law abiding and needed virtually no policing. You'll all be safe from traffic wardens here for some time.'

Isabel smiled. How different people could appear when they were happy and free from the stresses of life. '*Gràcies*. Good luck with the new job. Don't forget to come back and visit us.'

Isabel locked the car door and was about to head towards the square when the weasel called after her. 'Aren't you forgetting something?'

She pointed to the ticket machine. Isabel rolled her eyes and fumbled in her bag for her purse, but the woman broke into laughter. 'Only joking!'

Isabel nodded cautiously and carried on her way. Giggling traffic wardens breaking the rules. Whatever next?

In the *plaça* Isabel was unable to avoid Padre Agustí, who floated towards her in his black cassock, a look of grave concern etched on his face. 'Ah, Isabel, what a week it has been in Sant Martí. I can hardly believe that such a devoted parishioner as Camila Cortez could have succumbed to the devil so wholeheartedly.'

'Well, there were rather a lot of devils doing the rounds, Padre.'

He shook his head sadly. 'And as for Angel, what can I say? All we can do is pray for his soul.'

'I'm not sure he had one,' muttered Isabel. 'So, Padre, I hope you'll be joining us for the Nit de Foc celebrations in Soller tonight?'

The old man shook his head. 'Alas, no. I must visit some elderly parishioners and I have a sermon to prepare.'

Isabel smiled as she watched him shuffle off towards the church, stopping dutifully en route to greet various villagers.

A voice interrupted her thoughts. It was her mayor. 'He's quite a trooper, isn't he? Old school and strong as an ox. He'll be with us for some years yet, hopefully.'

Isabel was about to take her leave when he bent forward confidentially. 'How is Tolo? Will he be able to join us at the event tonight?'

Isabel shrugged. 'I hope so.'

'Good, I'd like to congratulate him personally on his fine detective work on these two cases. You're a winning team, and may I say how proud I am of my future son-in-law. Angélica is telling everyone what a hero Pep is. He's turned out to be a fine young man.'

Isabel managed to extricate herself from Llorenç's clutches and arrived home without further encounters. In the office Pep was speaking loudly in English to a client.

He came off the telephone and dramatically banged his head on the desk.

Isabel observed him in some bemusement. 'What's up with you?'

'I've just spent fifteen minutes trying to explain to an English woman how to drive from the Alfabia Gardens to Fornalutx village. She managed to get there this morning and now can't find her way back so she rang Home Sweet Home. It's hardly our job. It seems that it's not just Spanish women who are lousy drivers.'

Isabel laughed and clumped him on the head.

'So are you all set for tonight? I presume you'll be going with Angélica, not Aina.'

He tapped a pen against his notepad. 'Aina has been told by the university that she'll definitely be getting a bursary to study in Barcelona from October. She's looking forward to a new life. Apparently, her professor in Palma was thrilled with some old goat specimen she presented to the university – I think that clinched the deal.'

'I wonder where she found that,' Isabel muttered to herself with a grin. 'And so is everything OK between you and Angélica?'

'Better than ever. She was really jealous about Aina, which was silly because nothing happened between us. But she's had a change of attitude. She just telephoned me from her parents' home to say that I was a hero, having assisted you on the Mas case and saved you from the clutches of Jérôme Baudoin.'

Isabel laughed, assuming that Llorenç had put in a good word. 'Long may it last.'

'By the way, Aina told me that the Torrens brothers wouldn't be going to jail. How come?'

'It's a bit complicated, Pep. Let's just say that Francesc and Felip were very cooperative with the police. Thanks to them, the rest of Afrim Cana's gang will be put away for many years. It will at least stop one stream of cocaine reaching these shores.'

Pep smirked. 'I wouldn't count on it.'

In the sanctity of her own office Isabel e-mailed Julian Mosquera and left a voicemail for Emilio Navarro in Barcelona. He would be interested to learn about her conversation with Camila Cortez and the possibility that her Uncle Hugo could still be alive and being kept captive in Colombia. It corroborated the evidence offered by Daniela Sanchez, the only eyewitness to his abduction, found dead in suspicious circumstances. At four-thirty in the afternoon she received the e-mail reply from Julian that she'd been expecting. It would be nine-thirty in the morning in Colombia. She dialled the telephone number that he'd sent her and on the fourth ring, was greeted by a warm, youthful voice. Isabel hesitated a moment. 'Mr Salvador Rodríguez?'

'*Sí*. I am Salvador. Who is this?'

Isabel settled back in her chair. It was going to be a long call.

*

A crush of people lined the pavements around Soller's broad Plaça de la Constitució that ran from the old church of Sant Bartomeu to the handsome town hall. At the far end, opposite the church, was a raised circular terrace with an old fountain, an area popular with dance troupes and live performers during the summer months, and a haven for children on bicycles and mothers with prams the rest of the year. Now clusters of locals filled the space, all eagerly awaiting the moment when the Nit de Foc's famed *correfoc* would begin. A local group known as Esclatabutzes were responsible annually for staging the dazzling event, which involved spectacular pyrotechnics, dancing devils, lighting and music. Standing on the edge of the square in the company of a crowd of locals from Sant Martí, Isabel looked anxiously about her for Tolo. She had left a message on his mobile phone late afternoon instructing him to meet the group at nine-thirty outside Café Paris but now some twenty minutes later he still hadn't arrived. As more spectators swarmed into the main *plaça*, Isabel attempted to call Tolo's mobile, to no avail. Florentina noted her anxiety and tried to reassure her. She bellowed above the music blasting from giant speakers.

'He'll be here soon, don't worry. When he called the office earlier I urged him to come.'

Isabel frowned. 'He called the office?'

Pep nodded. 'You were in the shower. Florentina told him all about the Sant Martí party last night to whet his appetite.'

Florentina laughed. 'I told him that he'd missed a treat but that nice Josep Casanovas had come to keep you company.'

Isabel stared at her with wide eyes. 'You told him that Josep was with me?'

'Shouldn't I have done?'

Isabel tried to hide her exasperation. 'I'll go and look for him.'

She crossed the road and scanned Avinguda de Cristòfol Colom, which ran down towards the ice-cream factory, Sa Fabrica de Gelats, and the market place. Hordes of cheery locals and tourists were walking towards the square, shepherded by Guardia officers piping sharply on whistles. Cars had been banned from the central zone and barriers had been put in place, although a support vehicle, two fire engines and a Red Cross ambulance were waved through. They lumbered slowly along the narrow streets towards the market, where they would be stationed for the event. After the *correfoc*, the fire crews would aim their hoses at the overheated revellers and saturate them in cold water. Isabel wandered along Calle Bauzá as far as the post office, but there was no sign of Tolo among the merry throng of visitors. Somewhat dejectedly, she headed back towards the square, no longer feeling in a celebratory mood. The previous evening at Sant Martí's own fiesta she had told Josep Casanovas in no uncertain terms that much as she'd like to remain a friend, there could never be any romance between them. He had offered her a well-rehearsed wounded expression, but by the end of the evening had been in high spirits as a gaggle of young women attached themselves to him. She had felt that his state of dejection would be short-lived. But what did any of this matter as far as Tolo was concerned? Surely it would be of no consequence to him whether she was romantically involved with Casanovas or not? To her astonishment, she returned to find Tolo in deep discussion with her mother and Uncle Idò. Extravagantly, Florentina waved her over.

'There you are! I was telling Tolo that you were beside yourself with worry when he hadn't arrived.'

'A slight exaggeration,' Isabel replied.

Tolo winked and gave her a hug. 'Sorry for the delay, but I had the devil's own job – no pun intended – finding somewhere to park. In the end, I left the car on the main Soller road.'

'Mine's just beyond the post office – illegally parked, of course.'

He laughed. 'Let's just hope Gómez and his crew aren't being too assiduous tonight. Can I get you a beer?'

Pep slapped his arm. 'Llorenç is at the bar buying for everyone. You can help me carry them.'

Isabel watched as they made their way over to Bar Bini and began chatting with the owner. Within moments a vast queue had formed behind them. Small boys ran excitedly by letting off firecrackers, while two teenagers sneakily placed a large banger into a can of Cola and ran away as it exploded inches from a group of startled tourists. Llorenç grabbed one of them by the collar and gave him a clip round the ear. 'Do that one more time, Juan, and your father will hear about it.'

The boy looked suitably chastened, mumbled an apology and disappeared into the melee.

Marga now pushed through the crowds with her daughter, Sofia. 'It's bedlam tonight, Bel. This event gets more popular every year.'

Isabel nodded and scooped her god-daughter up into the air. 'Are you going to run through the fire tonight?'

Sofia squealed and giggling, reached out for Florentina.

Marga laughed. 'Come on, are we going into the middle?'

Isabel looked at Pep. 'Please tell me you're not wearing socks?'

He threw down his empty plastic beer cup. 'Of course not. *Venga*!'

Isabel turned to Tolo. 'Want to have a quick race through the fire?'

Before he could gather his thoughts she had grabbed his arm and suddenly they were right outside the town hall, surrounded by laughing revellers running in all directions as robed demons showering hot white sparks chased them from all sides. Isabel and Tolo followed Pep and Marga as they screamed and ducked, laughing uncontrollably when hot cinders slipped into Pep's shoe, causing him to fling it into the crowd. Twenty minutes later, they returned to the group, exhausted but exhilarated.

'I haven't done that since my twenties,' gasped Tolo.

Florentina tutted. 'I never thought I'd see a police chief do anything so daft. You're as mad as our Bel.'

Tolo looked at his watch and turned discreetly to Isabel. 'Would you like something to eat? I'm famished and I have a feeling we've a lot to catch up on.'

Isabel nodded and, freeing themselves from the group, they grappled their way through the crowds in the *plaça*.

'You'll miss the fireworks,' Pep shouted after them.

'You'll miss your shoe,' Isabel quipped.

'We'll see them from the main road,' called back Tolo.

As they walked up Calle Bauzá, Tolo turned to her. 'I've been sick with worry about you all afternoon. Forgive me that I didn't call round earlier, but I was stuck in meetings. I still don't know why you took such a risk visiting Camila Cortez alone.'

'I had to try to stop her from leaving the country, but I needed to be sure of all my facts first. Anyway, I knew she'd never do me any harm.'

'She only tried to poison you.'

Isabel tutted. 'She wanted to knock me out, that was all.'

With a chuckle he linked arms with her. 'Well, I suppose that's OK, then!'

Isabel looked up at him. 'I have to tell you that I called Salvador Rodriguez, Camila Cortez's nephew, this morning.'

He raised an eyebrow. 'I wouldn't let the residing judge know that you did that, or Gómez, for that matter.'

'I know. I'm telling you because this has to remain our secret.'

Tolo sighed. 'He has the diamonds.'

'What? How did you know?'

'I didn't. Just surmising. Like you, I think Camila Cortez drugged old Mas not only to make him defenceless but also to force him to give her the combination of the safe. She must have known they were there all along.'

'Salvador told me that she had sent him a pouch full of diamonds. It was the parcel that Señora Coll, the postmistress of Sant Martí, told me she had sent last Monday.'

'So what has he done with them?'

'He's given them away.'

'What?'

'He sent them to the director of the Medellín orphanage where many of the child victims of the Diablo Brotherhood, the ones whose parents had been murdered by its members, were placed. He told me that as a student he worked at the orphanage every summer and recently agreed to join the board of trustees.'

'Do you trust him?'

'Yes, I do. I also asked Julian to run a background check on the director of the orphanage and to check out Salvador's activity there. The director is as clean as a whistle and has dedicated more than thirty years of his life to the place. They rely on donations and live hand to mouth. The money raised from these diamonds would make a huge difference to the children's' lives.'

'And what part might Salvador Rodriguez play in all this?'

'As a trustee, he has promised that the money raised from the jewels will be put to good use.'

'Bel, you know that they should be handed over to the Colombian government.'

'And what do you think will happen to them? Some opportunistic politicians will most likely use them to line their own pockets.'

Tolo clicked his teeth and shook his head. 'And tell me, how did Salvador Rodriguez take the news about his aunt's crime?'

'Julian had told him the whole story, but he was still shocked and full of disbelief when we spoke. He assured me that although he considered her actions to be wrong, he believed her motives were born out of love and loyalty. He said that he would always be there for her.'

Tolo examined his shoes for a few moments and clapped his hands together. 'We haven't had this conversation. As far as we're both concerned, the diamonds were a fiction.'

'*Gràcies.*'

He gave a sigh. 'I have to tell you that Cruz Ramírez passed away a few hours ago. In the circumstances, it's maybe for the best. He never regained consciousness and so any remaining secrets died with him.'

Isabel looked glum. 'After all those years of incarceration, he gained his freedom only to wind up dead.'

'He chose his own path, Bel.'

They walked for a while in silence until Tolo suddenly turned to her. 'I feel that there's something still troubling you. Both cases are resolved, so I am guessing that it's about your Uncle Hugo?'

She nodded. 'I had a call from Emilio Navarro last Tuesday. He's a private detective I've hired to investigate Hugo's disappearance.'

Tolo frowned. 'Is that wise?'

'I believe so. He's discreet and has an excellent track record.'

'Why didn't you tell me about this?'

Isabel looked up at him. 'Why would I? It's a private family affair.'

'I thought I was someone you could trust.'

'I didn't want to bother you. You have so much on your plate.'

Tolo touched her shoulder. 'I always have time for you. Tell me everything.'

Isabel calmly talked him through the telephone conversation she'd had with Emilio Navarro, concluding with the death of the only eyewitness, the prostitute, Daniela Sanchez.

'So if your uncle was investigating one of Colombia's leading drug barons at the time of his abduction, it seems pretty likely, based on Sanchez's testimony, that he fell into Colombian hands, and that ETA had nothing to do with it. Have you had any further updates from Emilio since your conversation last week?'

'I left him a message today and he called back just a few hours ago. In the light of our conversation he has decided to go to Colombia as soon as possible for an initial recce.'

'So why the rush?'

'That's just what I was about to tell you. Yesterday Camila Cortez told me that shortly before she arrived in Mallorca, she had seen my Uncle Hugo at Mas's house in Bogotá. He was apparently held captive there for a fortnight.'

'Can that be true?' He stared at her intently. 'Do you honestly believe her?'

'Yes, I do. She couldn't tell me much more, but she has given me hope that he is still alive.'

He nodded slowly.

She continued. 'If Emilio comes across any hot leads once he's there, I'll go over to Colombia too.'

'You're not going without me.'

She looked up at him. 'I wouldn't expect you to do that. You have your work.'

He tutted. 'There are far more important things in my life than work, Bel.'

She hesitated. 'Yes, indeed. I suppose you and Lola Rubio will want to keep in touch, having worked so closely together during the Miranda case?'

Tolo stopped in his tracks, his brow furrowed. 'Lola Rubio? Are you mad, Bel? The woman was an absolute nightmare! A smart and ruthlessly driven young woman, maybe, but neurotic and so damned boring. You know when we had dinner one night, she would only eat raw vegetables and drank not a drop of wine.'

Isabel looked at him in some amazement. 'But you seemed to admire her so much.'

He laughed. 'Admittedly, she was exemplary at her job but the sort of woman I run a mile from socially. I'm sure we may liaise on work matters in the future, but thankfully I'm free of her for now.'

Together they walked along the silent street. In the distance they could hear the stutter of fireworks and marvelled at the illuminated sky, streaked with indigo and gold.

Tolo stopped and impetuously grasped Isabel with both arms. 'Thank God you're safe. In truth, we could never have solved these cases without you. You're as razor sharp as ever and your instincts never betray you.'

Taken by surprise, Isabel felt lost for words. She smiled while he struggled to compose himself.

'Now where is your car?'

She looked about her. 'It's in the next street. There aren't many Guardia officers about so we should be safe. Let's go up to Fornalutx. What about Ca N'Antuna for supper and later I can drive you back to your car. Or if you prefer,' she said coyly, 'you're welcome to stay over at Ca'n Moix.'

'I'd like that.'

She suddenly drew to a halt. 'Listen, I just wanted to let you know that I never invited Josep Casanovas to the Sant Martí event last night. He means nothing to me, and my interfering mother...'

He squeezed her arm. 'It doesn't matter. Pep told me when I phoned earlier that you were fed up with the attentions of Casanovas. It was, of course, none of my business. All the same, I was relieved and happy because I've been meaning to talk to you about something. Actually, about us.'

'Oh?'

He hesitated, a smile on his face. 'Let's wait until we have dinner. Otherwise we'll both starve.'

As they turned into Calle Morales, Isabel groaned. Three Guardia officers were buzzing about Pequeñito. One had already slapped an order under the windscreen wipers and another was peering into the interior. Isabel stepped forward.

'Come on, guys, it's only a little car. It's not causing any hold-ups.'

One of them narrowed his eyes. 'Bel! Is that you? Do you remember me? Paco? I used to be on the Palma patch two years ago.'

'Of course.' She shook his hand. 'Can't you let me off this time, Paco?'

He sighed. 'Not that easy. We've already issued a fine. Rules are rules. This is the one event where you can't pull these parking stunts, Bel.'

Isabel listlessly picked up the order and began studying it by the light of the lamppost. 'Well, I suppose I'll just have to bite the bullet this time.'

A hand suddenly snapped at the notice and whisked it into the air. Isabel turned round and found herself gazing into the reptilian eyes of Capitán Gómez. He smiled thinly and turned to Tolo and shook his hand.

'How charming to see you two lovebirds sharing the joys of the fiesta together. All the same, Isabel, you must know that parking in this central zone is strictly forbidden.'

'I know, I know...'

'Still, it is opportunistic that we have met. I have just been sent an e-mail from the Ministry of the Interior in Madrid praising the highly successful joint operation carried out between the Guardia Civil and Policía Nacional. All three of us are to be given commendations by the Minister of Interior. And Isabel, you will apparently be receiving a letter from the Minister himself thanking you for your input. And as for this...'

He held the fine before their eyes and in perfunctory manner tore it into shreds and watched as the pieces spiralled down onto the cobbles. He smiled cheerlessly at them.

'As we are in celebratory mood, let us ignore this little indiscretion.'

Tolo stepped into the front passenger seat as Isabel gave the captain a peck on the cheek.

'That's most kind of you, Álvaro.'

She had just started the engine when Capitán Gómez peered in at the open window with a slightly menacing smile on his face. 'May I wish you both an enjoyable evening during this temporary period of glasnost. Having said that, bear in mind that the peace accord between our two forces is unlikely to hold.'

As Pequeñito tore off along the narrow cobbled street, Isabel stole a glance in the rear-view mirror, but all she saw was a solitary lamppost emitting an ambient glow. Capitán Gómez, it seemed, had slithered off into the night with the stealth of a cobra.

Acknowledgements

As always, a virtual posy of sunflowers to my ever-patient husband Alan, son, Ollie, and Cecilia and Alex for their continued faith and encouragement. I would also like to thank my talented illustrator and friend, Chris Corr, who has accompanied and supported me on my literary journey from the outset, as well as editor, Lucy York. Grateful thanks too must go to designers, Chris Jones and Ben Ottridge, for their invaluable pearls.

Finally an appreciative hug for my friend, hotelier Vanessa Cabau, for generously correcting my accents and Spanish grammar along the way.

burrobooks

www.burrobooks.co.uk